Wickford Point

Wickford Point
John P. Marquand

*with an introduction
by Edward Weeks*

Time Reading Program Special Edition
Time-Life Books Inc., Alexandria, Virginia

Time-Life Books Inc.
is a wholly owned subsidiary of
TIME INCORPORATED

TIME Reading Program: *Editor*, Max Gissen

For information about any Time-Life book, please write:
Reader Information, Time-Life Books,
541 North Fairbanks Court, Chicago, Illinois 60611.

EDITORS' PREFACE

A more indolent woman than Bella Brill never lolled through the pages of a novel. When we first see her, she is engaged in polishing her fingernails. This turns out to be a level of physical activity and mental concentration well above Bella's norm. At our second meeting Bella is more herself. She is yawning. She has "not bothered to brush her short black hair or put on lipstick." On one occasion she seems to have borrowed somebody else's husband; but this dereliction is not as typical of Bella as her practice of borrowing money, clothes and cigarettes. With the possible exception of her mother, Clothilde, Bella is the champion cigarette moocher of all time. Where clothes are concerned, she reaches a high level of cunning, as when she influences her sister, Mary, to buy a dress that Bella herself plans to wear. On Mary, the dress is too tight; on Bella, it looks great.

Not much effort is needed to outwit Mary, who is even more torpid than Bella. The girls are the lively members of their generation of Brills. Brother Sid, the inventive one, can spend hours working out a new way to twiddle his thumbs. Brother Harry's life centers around his anxiety to preserve and possibly to exploit the Brill family connections.

The Brills sound like a communique from the War on Poverty, but they are afterblooms of the literary flowering of New England. Though they read few books, the Brills live off the reputation of

JOHN P. MARQUAND

their ancestor, the poet John Brill. He was almost as dull as his descendants, but He Knew Thoreau. Somehow John Brill became a legend, and the later Brills live in its aura. They are, by a kind of convention, "interesting people"—a phrase much used in the 1930s.

Could a book about the Brills and their rundown home near Boston possibly be interesting? *Wickford Point* is, in fact, one of the great American satirical novels, and hundreds of thousands of readers have been fascinated to learn what Bella and her siblings would do—or not do—next. This fascination is achieved by John P. Marquand's very special magic, and his secret is to some extent impenetrable. But some approaches to *Wickford Point* offer clues.

The reader is never directly exposed to the Brills. He sees them through the eyes of their second cousin, Jim Calder, who has been immersed in the Brill legend since his childhood but who, emphatically, is not a Brill. We are dealing, then, not with the Brills but with the relation between myth and life as exemplified by the contrast between the Brills as they are and the myth of New England literary tradition as it still lived when *Wickford Point* was written.

Even before we are introduced to the Brills (they are late risers) we meet Allen Southby—Dr. Southby, that is, master of Martin House at Harvard and author of *The Transcendent Curve*, which pursues the New England literary tradition through footnote after footnote. Perhaps the main point to be grasped about Dr. Southby is that he was born and reared in the Midwest, where the symbols of 19th Century New England continued to be taken a great deal more seriously than they were around Boston. Southby is the vestal (the word is not too inappropriate) who tends the altar flame. Clothilde, Bella, Mary, Sid and Harry are the all-too-human descendants of the gods Southby worships. Jim, poor soul, knows enough to laugh at Southby and even at the memory of John Brill —but he is to the end half-enslaved by the cult.

All writers—including, of course, historians—deal in myth. Some create myths and some explode myths. The satirist's way with them is more delicate. His function is to purify the myths through which a society sees itself, filtering out the residue of once-vivid beliefs.

The set of myths about Boston had more durability than those of other regions. Long after everyone had seen the South as it was, behind the screen of magnolias, people were still dazzled by images of Brahmin Boston. These images, never wholly false, had become overdue for correction. The region was ripe for satire and Marquand in his first successful serious book, *The Late George Apley,* began the work. As Edward Weeks, the distinguished former editor of *The Atlantic,* points out in a new introduction to this special edition of *Wickford Point,* Marquand in *Apley* not only satirized the life of a previous Boston generation, he also parodied its style. Since the style (Weeks calls it "lilac-scented") was a part of the myth, Marquand was calling attention to the contrast between Boston's reality and its rather overblown image of itself.

Wickford Point is in one sense a more direct attack than *Apley* and in another sense a subtler one. The tone of *Wickford Point* is informal and naturalistic, and Marquand's gifts of parody are confined to a passage from Allen Southby's novel and a snatch of John Brill's poetry. The subtlety, the essential magic of *Wickford Point,* lies in the way we are drawn into Jim Calder's ambivalent attitude toward the Brills. We feel his attraction for Bella, an attraction that he does not quite admit to himself. And consequently Bella— even Bella—becomes the object of our sympathetic interest.

Thus, Marquand succeeds at two levels: the people of *Wickford Point* come alive and the satiric social message, begun in *Apley,* is driven home. To all who savor the book the Brills become unforgettable and, simultaneously, a certain aspect of the Boston myth begins to fade from public belief.

John Phillips Marquand knew Boston and its environs as few writers did, but a certain detachment necessary to the satirist may be traceable to the fact that he was not wholly a New Englander. Born in Wilmington, Delaware, in 1893, he lived with relatives in Newburyport, Massachusetts, after the age of 14.

After Harvard, he drifted into writing—news reporting, advertising, commercial fiction. When in 1938 he won the Pulitzer Prize for *The Late George Apley,* he took a place near the forefront of

American social novelists. By the time of his death in 1960, his 30 books had sold more than five million copies.

Like Sinclair Lewis and James Gould Cozzens, Marquand put into his novels a great deal of factual observation. Whether he wrote about a banker *(Point of No Return)* or a businessman *(Sincerely Willis Wade)* or a professional soldier *(Melville Goodwin, U.S.A.)*, it was always clear that Marquand understood the milieu as well as the psychology of his characters. Environment cannot be sensed; it has to be reported. Most of Marquand's novels can be summed up as the relation between the childhood and adult environments of the central character. His work reflects the belief that early experience determines the man. Yet, because the American scene was changing so rapidly, his characters seem to be in rapid and suspenseful motion. "The road one takes," he once said, "no matter how far it goes . . . always turns toward home."

At his death, TIME appraised Marquand in words particularly appropriate to this book: "A satirist who more than half loved the subjects of his satire, an observer with a fond but unforgiving eye for detail, he left a record of American life that criticized without insisting on condemnation and entertained without stooping to farce."

—THE EDITORS

RTP INTRODUCTION

Edward Weeks was editor-in-chief of *The Atlantic Monthly* magazine from 1938 to 1966. A frequent lecturer and contributor to periodicals, he is also the author of *This Trade Writing* (1935); *The Open Heart* (1955); an autobiography, *In Friendly Candor* (1959); *Breaking into Print* (1962) and *My Green Age* (1974). He has lived in Boston since 1924, when he joined the staff of *The Atlantic*, and is a senior editor and a consultant for that magazine.

In the early 1920s when I was working my way through Harvard, I spent one summer as a companion tutor in York Harbor, Maine, and early in my stay I remember having pointed out to me a small, wooden shack off by itself on a rocky promontory. "That's where John Marquand lives," I was told. "He is trying to write a novel." It seemed that he had worked as a reporter, written copy for a New York advertising agency and published a few short stories before he felt ready to take the summer gamble of being a free lance. But you could tell from the looks of that little shack that whatever he was writing wasn't paying much yet. In the 16 years that intervened between that July and the publication of *The Late George Apley,* John scored his greatest success with a series of stories about a Japanese detective named Mr. Moto; they found increasing popularity in the *Saturday Evening Post,* and in time he rose to be one of the highest paid of its contributors, in company with Alice Duer Miller, Clarence Budington Kelland and Mary Roberts Rinehart. His in-laws, the Alexander Sedgwicks of Stockbridge, were not altogether happy about his magazine writing: despite the large fees this was not literature with a capital L. They wanted him to write books and his early books had been failures. All of this galled John, as it would have any young writer who is supporting his family and gradually acquiring a professional competence, and it stirred in him an angry determination to break away from the short story when the time was right for something more ambitious.

The break came in 1935. As Japan stepped up its assaults on China, he realized that Mr. Moto's days of popularity were numbered. John's marriage had gone on the rocks, and he was troubled and restive, which is a provocative mood for any novelist to be in.

To the dismay of his literary agent, he ceased writing suspense fiction and began to experiment in satire. He wrote to accentuate the changes which had overtaken American society in his home state, Massachusetts, and in its capital, Boston. He wanted to catch the unique blend of family pride and Puritan discipline which characterized certain Boston clans in the Back Bay. For months he worked at this experiment, and when he had finished 40,000 words, needing encouragement, he sent the manuscript in its half-completed state to his agent, Brandt & Brandt in New York. The report he got back was wholly in the negative: no magazine would think of serializing such stuff; no publisher would touch it. Deeply troubled, John appealed to his friend and publisher, Alfred McIntyre of Little Brown:

The last two months I have been working on a thing which I have often played with in the back of my mind, a satire on the life and letters of a Bostonian. I have now done some thirty or forty thousand words on it, and the other day showed it to a friend whose literary judgment I greatly respect, who feels it is a great pity for me to waste my time in going ahead with it. I suppose the most damning thing that can be said about the whole business is that I, personally, have enjoyed writing it, and think it is amusing, and think that it is a fairly accurate satire on Boston life. I certainly don't want to go ahead with the thing, however, if you don't think it holds any promise, and is not any good. Besides this, I do not, for purely artistic reasons, feel that the thing can be helped by any great changes such as injecting more plot, or by making the satire more marked. In other words, if it is not any good as it stands, I think I had better ditch it and turn my attention to something else. As this is the first time in a good many years that I have been in a position to write something which I really wanted to write, I naturally feel bad about it. I know you will tell me frankly just how it strikes you, and its fate rests largely in your hands. Tell me quickly.

McIntyre did tell him quickly. He said, "John, I personally think it is swell. I can't tell you whether it will sell more than 2,000 copies —it may be too highly specialized. But by all means, go ahead with it!"

McIntyre's judgment was amply vindicated in 1938 when *The Late George Apley* was awarded the Pulitzer Prize for fiction and soared to a sale which has not yet ended. *Apley* is not only a probing satire of Bostonians—of the bird-watching in Milton, of the iron discipline in the summer cottage in Maine, of the fastidious economy of Beacon Street; it is also a beautifully sustained parody of a way of writing about Boston once widely practiced and, at the time of the book's appearance, still held locally in high regard. There were some in the Back Bay who accepted it quite literally as a biography and who appeared at the Boston Museum of Fine Arts on Sunday afternoons asking to be shown the "Apley bronzes." Coming, as it did, after the gentility of Robert Grant's novels and the sugary romances with which Joseph C. Lincoln celebrated Cape Cod, *The Late George Apley* arrived with the shock of self-discovery.

In later years it came to be fashionable to say that *Apley* was the best novel Marquand had ever written, and this, of course, was infuriating to him, for as an ambitious satirist he was constantly seeking new directions and new targets in the works that followed. John himself used to tell the story of sitting beside Mr. Rantoul during lunch at the Somerset Club. Mr. Rantoul, who was deaf and only turned on his hearing aid when he wanted to be heard, said: "John, I have just read your new book, and I don't like it. It isn't nearly up to your *Sorrell & Son*."

"Thank you, Mr. Rantoul," said John in that high quaver of his which hid laughter, "but I didn't write *Sorrell & Son.* Warwick Deeping did."

Mr. Rantoul turned off his hearing aid.

This, of course, was Boston's way of saying that they wished he would take his satire elsewhere, that his shafts came uncomfortably close to home.

In *The Late George Apley* John Marquand was writing about the older generation, the generation ahead of his, and it is always easier to satirize one's grandparents and parents than it is to satirize one's contemporaries. In *Wickford Point,* which some regard as the most autobiographical of his novels, he is still devoted to the idiosyncrasies of the old, but the story is centered in and told through the eyes of Jim Calder, whose experiences at college, in World War I and as a professional writer make him seem like John's alter ego.

One advantage which *Wickford Point* holds over *The Late George Apley* is that Marquand plays it straight, telling the story in his own words, much as he might have spoken it to a friend, instead of writing in the stylized, lilac-scented prose of that early period which he had been parodying in *Apley.* Young Jim Calder, the hero-narrator of *Wickford Point,* comes much closer to us than does George Apley. He is swift in his understanding, he has a delightfully tough-grained sense of humor, and because of his strange and lonely boyhood, he appeals to our sympathy more deeply than any other male character Marquand was to portray.

The line which divides the autobiographical material in a novel from that which is clearly fictitious is usually a subtle one, but it is tempting to try to show to what extent Jim Calder's career parallels that of his creator, and this we can do thanks to a poignant profile by Josephine P. Driver, who graduated from the Newburyport High School the year after John Marquand. When John was 14 or 15 his parents, who were then living in Rye, New York, suffered a financial reverse and as a result of this John was sent north to live with his aunts in New England. He had been entered for St. Mark's School in Southboro, Massachusetts, but now the money was not available and instead John had to enter the class of 1910 in the

Newburyport High School. Boarding schools in those days had more glamor than they will ever have again: John had set his heart on St. Mark's and it was a bitter pill not to be part of it.

In her article, "The Young John Marquand," which appeared in *The Atlantic* in August 1965, Mrs. Driver stresses his feeling of isolation and of "Don't care." "If he had gone to St. Mark's," she writes, "or Middlesex, or Andover, he would more nearly have resembled his later well-groomed, well-polished appearance. He would not have been allowed to wait until his shaggy, unkempt hair reached his collar before having it cut; he would have been urged or commanded 'Stand up; don't slouch' as he walked. Some attention might have been paid to his fingernails and his grimy wrists, which emerged unhappily from too-short coat sleeves. His hesitant speech might even have been corrected to the point where, willy-nilly, he had to improve it."

She tells us that he took no part in the school activities, not even in athletics or in writing for the school paper; that he was not a wit; that his timid approaches to the prettier girls in the class were rebuffed; that he recoiled from his aunts' suggestion that he invite his classmates to supper "in the lamp-lit dining room at Curzon's Mill, with its gently decaying furniture and its grim portraits frowning down from the walls. . . . Not only was the house queer enough, in his opinion, but he could not imagine what the boys and girls would have thought of plump, wheezy Aunt Molly, whose dusty black clothes and preposterous hats were made to a style long out of date, or of Aunt Bessie, who, though she was conventional enough in dress, was an unheard-of phenomenon, an ordained Unitarian minister. There was Great-aunt Mary, too, a link with a time long past, who still wore a paisley shawl on her infrequent trips to Newburyport to call on friends or to go to church. She lived in a world of her own, which John was only occasionally permitted to enter."

The picture Mrs. Driver gives us of the shy and lonely boy standing at the edge of the senior prom looking on but without friends or a partner is both pathetic and telling, for out of this frustration and bitterness the satirist in John Marquand was to emerge. When in his novels to come Marquand found much to ridicule in the tradition and exclusive spirit of the fashionable boarding school, may this not be a pay-back still smoldering from his own disappointment?

The mortification which as a young man he felt for his aunts and especially for Great-aunt Mary had completely evaporated by the time he came to write *Wickford Point*. Aunt Mary, the prototype of Aunt Sarah in *Wickford Point*, was the spinster sister of his grandfather Curzon and a person of shining quality and independence. William Ellery Channing had proposed to her, and John Greenleaf Whittier, the Quaker poet, used to row across the Merrimack to call at Curzon's Mill. John intended to celebrate Aunt Mary, her attractiveness, her wit and the eccentricity which became more pronounced in age. She prided herself on coming from a family of shipowners, not ship captains; she served no liquor in her house, since it had once had a disastrous effect on an earlier Marquand; and until her death at the age of 87 she maintained a regime, candlelit, handwritten, do-it-yourself, faithful to the disciplines she had been taught as a girl in the Federalist period. For John she epitomized the virtue and durability of a New England he loved and hated to see changed.

The eccentricity in the novel is not confined to Aunt Sarah or Cousin Clothilde with her offbeat comments ("Clocks only make you later. They're not happy things."); it is endemic in the house, and in finest flower in that ingenious sponger, Sidney Brill. Marquand may have had plenty of family foibles to draw on but in matters like this he gave his imagination free rein. One of my happy memories of *Wickford Point*—and there are many—is the matter of the front door, which was supposed to be irretrievably closed and which had been left that way for months because nobody had bothered to deal with it, and how it was finally opened in a few moments of bored puttering by young Jim, who found that the trouble was nothing more complicated than an old love letter that had gotten wedged in at a crucial spot. There is loneliness and hurt and love in *Wickford Point*, and somehow, in the fast, crisp prose of that book, I have the feeling that the author is speaking to me more intimately than in any other.

The temptation to which every satirist is exposed is to go to extremes and instead of creating character to settle for caricature. John Marquand was always more interested in men than in women and the women in *The Late George Apley* are one-dimensional caricatures. But the women in *Wickford* live and breathe and complain, and they attract and provoke our interest much as they did Jim Calder's—the ineffable Aunt Sarah, the candid, ever-curious Clothilde, the prickly Bella, and the laughing, tempting Pat Leighton. They catch the eye and invite the imagination.

A country is fortunate to have a writer of Marquand's magnetism to hold up the mirror to its extravagance and hypocrisy. He wrote as he felt, and in his prose as in his conversation he laid about him in a vein of exasperation that those who enjoyed it will long remember. It was fun to watch him as he approached the verge of the preposterous: his pupils would enlarge, his lips seemed to curl in despair, his voice would rise until, with a sudden sniff and an outthrust of both hands, he pushed the folly away from him and over the cliff. His soliloquies on the TV Westerns, which he could reproduce with sound effects and even the commercials; his account of how his novels were emasculated when they were cut down to a third of their size for serialization; his description, point by point, of an abstract mural in one of the Harvard Houses were convulsively funny and could have come only from a man who loved life and who relished the American way of doing things, even when it was at its zaniest.

—EDWARD WEEKS

Wickford Point

I | Sid Sucks the Gasoline

At the top of Allen Southby's letter was engraved MARTIN HOUSE STUDY, and to the left in smaller type DR. SOUTHBY. This reminded everyone who had known him long enough that Allen had assumed this title as soon as he achieved his Ph.D. degree for studies in English and American literature. He first used it tentatively, among groups of undergraduates; later the women's clubs where he lectured had employed the prefix also; and finally, when the University Press published his volume *The Transcendent Curve*, his place in the scholastic world was irrevocably established.

That this work should have had a sale which pushed it in less than a year to well over a hundred thousand copies is a commentary on the priggishness of the book-buying public. The mass of information which Southby had gathered concerning early American literary figures was admittedly enormous, but not much of it was calculated to interest a layman. The style was difficult and turgid; even after considerable cutting the final draft ran over seven hundred and fifty pages in good solid type. Publishers have said that the bulk was what gave it its final success. When one saw it upon the parlor table in its heavy maroon binding, one could feel that here was a house of leisure and refinement, whose owner and whose family partook of The Finer Things of Life. There was, authorities explained, a "snob value" to the book, such as was once an attribute of Will Durant's *Story of Philosophy* and of Mr. Wells's *Outline of History*.

It possessed the same "plus quality," gave forth the mystic promise of doing good and of conveying—simply, it would seem, through its appearance—the belief that you too might hold your employer, the girl of your choice, and a dinner table spellbound, provided you took a few pleasant moments off each day to dip into the pages. You, too, might achieve that rare distinction of being the man who is just a little different, which comes from reading a thoroughly good book.

The reviewers took it up with an enthusiasm symptomatic of group hysteria, but I should like to wager that not one of them read all the way through it. Southby sometimes would quote their best remarks with a deprecating sort of humor designed to show that he knew very well that the critics had been too kind.

A glamorous panorama of the history of American thought, moving in a scintillating progress. . . . We defy the reader to put down Dr. Southby's book once he has picked it up.

There is a magic in the style which defies analysis; it flows in a trenchant stream; it is a Thames of style, moving with a deceptive tranquility past the spires of a modern Oxford.

It costs five dollars, but it's worth five hundred. This means that you and I can read it. [This came from one of the lower, less literary journals, which reached the great half-tapped reservoir of the partially enlightened.]

It would be interesting, I repeat, to know just how many actually did read it. I know I never finished it, and consequently have no real right to discuss it, except in so far as *The Transcendent Curve* influenced the Doctor as an individual. It was an achievement such as that which Dr. Lowes very nearly brought off in *The Road to Xanadu*: it was a book for scholars, read by laymen. There could be no doubt about its scholarship, since it very nearly got its author the presidency of one of the larger Western universities—very nearly, but not quite.

"My life is at Harvard," Allen told us once. "I am a Harvard man."

The Transcendent Curve did, however, get him nearly everywhere else he wanted to go, because he knew how to use that book, and its immense success in no wise turned his head from what he wanted: he wanted to be a man of letters, a figure more austere and just a trifle more formal than Professor Phelps of Yale. Yes, it got him where he wanted to go. He became a figure almost by saying nothing, but by developing instead what might be termed "an accessive inaccessibility." He never said much in public, which was just as well, but he had a way of phrasing what little he did say. He had a timing to his speech, as effective as the timing of an athlete. No idea of his was lost through haste or carelessness, nothing became pedantic through deliberation. In time his words began to possess an indefinable, adhesive, jamlike quality which gave them an importance not wholly susceptible of analysis. Allen Southby had known what he wanted, had always known what he wanted; he had that patient deliberateness of purpose which can make indifferent material travel far. Perhaps in the end the material ceases to be indifferent, but that is a debatable matter.

In time Allen even generated a sort of charm; and besides he was an eligible bachelor, the sort you think of as a bright young man, even when he has reached the age of forty. There was once a piece of gossip, for there are always those who hate success, that he practised before a mirror. At any rate he achieved his charm. He developed a way of holding a book and of marking the place with his long forefinger, carelessly but lovingly, at the same time resting his elbow upon the table and gesticulating gently with that book. It was a pose suitable for a portrait, which may have been Southby's intention originally. He also took pains with his dress. When he came to Harvard from Minnesota he brought his trunk with him, but Allen was quick to see that the garments within it were not correct; right from the beginning he had an unfailing instinct for doing what was suitable. He ended by wearing Harris tweeds and flannel trousers and by smoking an English pipe with a special mixture—although he did not like tobacco.

He also took to drinking beer out of a pewter mug. By the time he was taken into the Berkley Club he had developed a way of banging the mug softly upon the table, informally, and without ostentation. He used to say that there was nothing like good pewter; in fact he had a fair collection of it in a Colonial pine dresser— but he never did like beer. Nevertheless he sometimes had beer nights for the undergraduates. It was something of an accolade for an adolescent to be asked to Southby's to drink beer. It was more of an honor for one of his contemporaries, and one which I regret to say I never attained, to be asked up to his rooms to give the "lads" a talk on this or that, just anything. By aloofness rather than by assiduity he cultivated excellent social contacts. He attended only small dinners where there might be general conversation, but he knew when to listen. When an interest developed in wine-tasting, after the repeal of prohibition, Allen Southby was in the pioneering group, although he always said that his old love was ale or beer. He had a pretty turn at rhyme and you could always get him to dash off the right poem for any occasion, although he published only one slender volume of verse. He had the gift of knowing when to stop. What was more, he still kept young in appearance and in enthusiasm. He was amusing when he joined the ladies after dinner, and he was the sort of bachelor who never made himself troublesome with liquor or in taxis.

There is no particular reason to set this down unless it illustrates a reaction of my own narrow and embittered mind toward a very able man, toward a contemporary who was turning, through his own efforts, into a personage. Certainly it was all to his credit, and it can only put me in an unfavorable light to mention it—but, frankly, there were those of us who, because of our own inadequacies and sloth, jested coarsely about Allen. However, such was my own inconsistency that I was flattered when I received his letter. In fact I came close to forgetting that I actively resented the attitude he took toward me and toward my own efforts in the field of fiction.

4

"Just for a handful of silver he left us," Allen said the last time I saw him, "just for a riband to stick in his coat."

He was referring gracefully to my occupation as a writer for money. A week before he had made a pronouncement on the subject in the pages of a literary magazine. It concerned the danger of the first large check, of the giving-away of something fine, of the striving after commercial position, of superficial brilliance and brittleness. In spite of it all, I was pleased to hear from Allen.

"Dear Jim," he wrote. "What have you been doing with yourself? If you happen to be in the vicinity of Cambridge any night next week, how about coming to Martin House and having a chat about books over a mug of beer? I still read *Collier's* and *Liberty* and the *Saturday Evening Post*. I must, you know."

My Cousin Clothilde was in the dining room just then, and I was finishing breakfast, a meal which lasted almost indefinitely at Wickford Point.

"I've had a letter from Allen Southby," I said.

"Have you?" she answered. "Who is Allen Southby?"

"A critic," I answered. "He wrote *The Transcendent Curve*."

"What is *The Transcendent Curve*?" she asked. "Is it a book on sex?"

"No," I told her, "not exactly."

She sighed and handed me a paper. "I wish you'd read this," she said. "I don't understand it. It's a letter from the bank."

"It says you've overdrawn your account again," I told her, "for the second time this month."

"Give me a match, please," she said. "Not that box, it only has burnt matches in it. The other box, just there." She reached for a package of cigarettes beside her plate and shook it. "We never have any cigarettes in the house," she said. "Someone always takes them." I gave her one of mine and she lighted it. "The bank is wrong," she said. "I sent them a hundred dollars last week. It's stupid of them to be so annoying, but it doesn't make much difference, they always let me overdraw."

I folded Allen Southby's letter and put it in my pocket.

"Well, I'm going down to see him tonight," I said.

Cousin Clothilde sighed again. "You're always going somewhere, aren't you?" she said. "If you aren't going somewhere, you're always reading something. Why can't you stay here, now you're here? I'll send somebody downtown to get some cigarettes."

There was another letter beside me on the table, and now I reached for it with the idea of putting it unobtrusively into my pocket. It was in a heavy square Bermuda blue envelope, addressed to me in a handwriting which was boldly and carelessly feminine. It was a letter which I particularly wanted to read alone. For someone as vague as she was, Cousin Clothilde sometimes displayed an amazingly acute observation. She could nearly always see something which you did not wish her to see.

"Jim dear," she said, "whom's that other letter from? It looks so interesting. She writes the same way I do. I always did have such trouble with my writing until I just stopped trying."

I felt a momentary awkwardness for no good reason. It was as though she had surprised me in some furtive and discreditable action.

"It isn't from anyone in particular," I said, but I knew she would not believe me from the moment that I answered.

"Why, dear," she said, "it must be—from the way you put it in your pocket."

"Well," I said, "it's from a girl I know in New York. Her name's Patricia Leighton. I don't think you know her."

"Why, darling," said Cousin Clothilde, "I've never even heard you mention her."

"No," I answered, "I don't believe you have."

Her forehead wrinkled as she watched me.

"I don't think it's kind of you not to talk to me about things," she said. "I love to know whom you know and what you're doing. Sometimes you're so secretive, dear, just as though you were shy, or afraid of me."

"Well," I said, "perhaps I am."

"That's so silly, isn't it," she said, "when I always tell you everything?"

6

"I suppose it is, but then you don't really care much, except about what happens here."

"No," she said, "that isn't true. I always care about the children. I think about them all the time; and you're one of the children, dear."

I still do not know why it embarrassed me that she had seen Pat Leighton's letter. She would be writing me as she often did, asking me what I was doing and when I would be coming to New York. It would probably be nothing that I could not leave around, and everyone left letters everywhere at Wickford Point.

"Do you know her well, dear?" Cousin Clothilde asked.

"Pretty well," I answered.

"Well," said Cousin Clothilde, "she writes the same way I do." And then she dropped the subject.

Tranquil, soul-satisfying apathy settled over the dining room. The sound of droning insects came through the window like the soft breath of sleep; an oriole sang a few throaty, liquid notes and stopped exhausted; the leafy shadows of elm branches scarcely moved upon the lawn. A house fly buzzed and beat its head against the window screen. The collision made a metallic sound which was followed by silence. The fly rubbed its wings with its hind legs, but did not try again. As Cousin Clothilde gazed at the smoke from her cigarette I noticed a lack of customary sound. The tall clock in the corner had stopped.

"I stopped it last night," Cousin Clothilde said. "You can hear it upstairs right through the ceiling. It sounds something like an insect. Besides I'd rather not know what time it is. Everything goes on just as well. Clocks only make you later. They're not happy things."

Inertia held me for a while. I tried to think of what to do, but there was nothing much to do down there. It became an effort to do anything, but I struggled against surrender out of habit.

"I might as well go and see Southby," I said. "I may as well go now. There are some things I want to do in Boston."

"Why don't you ask him down here?" Cousin Clothilde said. "It's easier. He can spend the week end."

"The house is always full over the week end," I said. "There won't be any room for him."

"There must be somewhere. It's a big house," said Cousin Clothilde. "The girls can sleep together, and we can send someone downtown before then to get some gin."

"No," I said. "You wouldn't like him."

"Don't be ridiculous," said Cousin Clothilde. "I like nearly everyone except queer foreigners." She paused and flipped her cigarette ashes into her empty coffee cup. "And after all," she added, "I like a great many foreigners. I've always loved Mirabel Steiner. She'll be dropping in before long, just for a day or two."

"When she does," I said, "you'd better send me my food upstairs on a tray."

"You shouldn't be so intolerant," she said. "You know that Mirabel has always been devoted to you. She admires you. Just last winter she wanted to borrow one of your books. There weren't any in the apartment. Has Mr. Northby got something queer about him?"

"Southby," I said. "No, he hasn't."

"Then why don't we have him come Saturday night?"

"No," I said. "He wouldn't understand it here."

"Nonsense," she said. "Everybody always likes it here."

There is a phrase used by certain fiction writers which had always puzzled me. Mr. E. Phillips Oppenheim, for example, ends an interview by the curt sentence: 'He rose to his feet.' It had seemed difficult to understand what else a character could rise to, but in the dining room, while Cousin Clothilde watched me, that expression acquired a definite meaning. Halfway out of my chair, I had a desire to relapse again; it was an effort to rise to my feet, and when I was on them, they moved dreamily. I leaned over and kissed her. She was my father's cousin, but she looked amazingly young.

"I wish you wouldn't go away and leave me," she said. "I won't have anyone to talk to until someone else wakes up. If you're going upstairs, wake someone up. I can't sit here all alone. You're not really going away now, are you?"

"Yes," I said, "I may as well."

"I wish that people would look after me," she said. "No one ever seems to take care of me, and I take care of everyone, and I get tired of it sometimes."

My car was in a shed beside the barn. A heat wave shimmered from the twisted shingles of the barn roof and the building needed a coat of paint. A pair of swallows darted from the shed with low, resentful squeaks. They must have felt that the car would be there all day, presumably for their personal use. When I pressed the starter the engine turned, but nothing happened. A glance at the gasoline gauge told me why.

Out on the lawn near the garden a faint breeze, which passed through the trees, did not dispel the sultriness. Everything was very green—monotonously, luxuriantly green; everything stood in a gentle, reminiscent silence that rebuked me when I raised my voice and I called for the boy who worked around the house in summer.

"Earle," I shouted, "Earle!"

The gangling form of Earle Caraway appeared. Earle was using part of his high school vacation to mow the lawns. The rest of his time was spent in studying dramatics from a correspondence course.

"What's happened to the gas in my car?" I asked. "It was half-full last night."

"Mr. Brill borrowed it," Earle said. "Say, Mr. Calder—"

"What?" I said. "The gas?"

"If you're going uptown, could you get me a copy of *True Romances*, Mr. Calder, and a chocolate nut bar?"

"How the hell can I get you a nut bar," I said, "when there isn't any gas?"

"Ain't there *any* gas?" said Earle. "Ain't there any gas at all? Mr. Sidney said he was leaving a little. He had a rubber tube in his car. He sucked it out. He got up early. He said he was going to lay on the beach."

"Oh, was he?" I said. "Well, how am I going to get out of here?"

"I guess you got to wait till Mr. Sidney gets back," said Earle. "I can't think of any way unless you want to walk two miles up to Kennedy's stand. Say, Mr. Calder—"

"What?" I said.

"Nobody's paid me yet."

"You ask Mrs. Wright about it," I said. Sometimes I almost forgot that Cousin Clothilde's second husband was Archie Wright, and that she was not still Mrs. Brill. Although she had married Archie Wright twenty years before, three years after Hugh Brill's death, it still did not seem like a definite marriage.

"I asked her," Earle said. "She just says to wait."

Josie was in the kitchen peeling potatoes. Josie and her daughter were our domestic staff. A large tortoise-shell cat, that looked as though a squash pie had splashed upon her, was nursing six kittens under the stove. An old setter was searching himself for fleas under the kitchen table.

"That poor boy, Mr. Calder!" Josie said. "He's been asking and asking for his money. He wants to go with Frieda to the beach. He asked Frieda last night to go to the beach. I know he's been wanting to for weeks and weeks, Mr. Calder—and the Caraways are the nicest people. Earle's mother is a lovely lady. She's a member of the Woman's Club. Now I know dear Mrs. Wright has so many troubles, what with all the children here and everything, that she just doesn't think. I told Earle that he shouldn't pester dear Mrs. Wright. I'd be glad to give Earle something myself, but I spent it at the grocer's when we went downtown yesterday. Miss Brill—that is, Miss Bella—forgot her pocketbook."

Cousin Clothilde had moved to the back parlor. She was seated looking at a bunch of laurel leaves in the empty fireplace.

"So you're back," she said.

"Sid sucked all the gas out of my car," I said. "Why can't anybody buy gas except me?"

"He must have meant to leave *some*," Cousin Clothilde said. "Don't worry about it, dear. Sidney will be back with lots of gas. He asked me for my pocketbook before he went."

"Earle wants some money," I said. "He says he hasn't been paid for two weeks."

"I wish Earle wouldn't be a nuisance," Cousin Clothilde said. "Besides he doesn't do anything to deserve his wages. He just stands around looking at Josie's daughter, and he isn't very attractive. Do you think so?"

"I hadn't thought," I said.

"Darling," Cousin Clothilde said, "I'm so glad you don't have to go for a little while. Sit down and let me have a cigarette. Sidney will be back for lunch unless someone asks him to stay, and I depend on you so much. You're so much more reliable than all the others. Everybody seems to think that I have nothing to do but look after them. You're the only one who's ever looked after me. Have you a cigarette?"

"All right," I said, "I'll wait awhile, but I'm going to see Southby."

II | "Fair Harvard, Thy Sons . . ."

The family had always gone to Harvard. Once when Sidney's older brother Harry was on the verge of being fired on account of his low marks, he wrote a letter to the Dean which began: "As one of the fifth generation of my family to have attended Harvard . . ." It was his conviction, shared by his mother, my Cousin Clothilde, that this reminder was all that had been necessary to permit him to remain. There was a definite belief in the Brill family that this accumulation of generations at Harvard had an automatic scholastic merit. It was as though the conscience-ridden shades of their ancestors could prod them onward without their own added effort, and this engendered a comfortable feeling that some ancestor would always do something around midyears to provide a flash of intuition in the purgatory of the examination room. That accumulation of scholastic forebears had been useful in later life, in that it gave them a sense of intellectual competence. With their attitude, and the help of conversation, they developed an atmosphere of erudition and of inherited intellectual gift.

There was our great-aunt Georgianna, who learned Greek at eighty and milked cows in the socialistic experiment at Brook Farm. The Brills' own great-grandfather had written a volume of reflections on his travels through Europe, which no one had ever read. And then of course there was their grandfather, the poet known as "the Wickford Sage." Other members of the family also had been friends of intellectual figures in their different generations. In the suspicious environs of a town like Boston, where everyone is anxious to check on antecedents, it was commonly said that the Brills were interesting, that it was no wonder that they were brilliant. It made matters sensibly easier, even for me, although I was not a Brill. At any rate the family had gone to Harvard for five generations, and some of my own ancestors were in that company.

In spite of common sense, I leaned upon this thought, while I motored toward the residence of the Head of Martin House. Five generations of Southbys had not gone to Harvard and I am certain that Allen was aware of it.

When I was at Harvard it had been the fashion to live in ugly frame houses which lined the streets off Massachusetts Avenue, unless one had the money to live in a dormitory like Claverly. Some of us in our freshman year ate at Memorial Hall. We used to bang our glasses when visitors came to look at us from the balcony, and sometimes we had bread fights. Others preferred to eat in small cubbyholes in cellars that stayed open until all hours, like Butler's, and Jimmy's, and John's under the Lampoon building. It had not been healthy or desirable, but now that the entire academic scene had changed I did not feel at home. In the heat of the early summer evening the new buildings along the Charles were neither familiar nor sentimental objects. I had never understood why they were jammed so closely together, or why they had so many chimneys. The entries were like passages to a rabbit warren, but except for them everything was on a large scale. There was an effort to give the dignity of age to the woodwork. By a skillful treatment of the floors and walls clever decorators had simulated the imprint of centuries, but the illusion was incomplete. Somehow nothing is quite right when one suddenly spends ten million dollars.

The hallway of the Master's house looked to me so like something on the stage that I should not have been surprised if a maid in a mobcap had let me in. In the study, where I saw Allen Southby, everything was pine, fine old pine which had come from all

13

sorts of walls and attics, fixed with hand-wrought nails. The trestle table had a top of fine old pine, but the legs were palpable fakes. The mantelpiece was fine old pine from Maine, scraped and oiled—"from the fine old Custer house at Wiscasset," Southby said.

The walls of that perfectly proportioned study were lined with books, old leather volumes, carefully oiled. In a corner was the dresser containing Allen's pewter. It displayed nearly all the implements of an antique household, except those of a more intimate nature. There was even a pewter candle-mold by the fireplace. I wondered how many times some caller had asked what it might be for, and I could hear Southby begging him to guess.

Allen Southby was in slacks and a silk shirt. He had discarded a greenish Harris tweed coat, because the weather was hot, but that informal attire gave an added impression of industry. His graying hair was just sufficiently rumpled; his tanned face had just the proper lines of frowning concentration. It was a fine face that went exactly with the room.

"You haven't seen it, have you, Jim?" Southby asked.

"Seen what?" I inquired.

"The room," Allen Southby said. "I think it's amusing, don't you? It's given me a lot of fun." He added that the superintendent of buildings and his sister Martha, who had come from Minnesota to keep house for him, had let him fix it up exactly as he wanted.

"You ought to have a spinning wheel," I said, "just over by the fire, so the flickering from the backlog would strike its spokes on a long winter evening."

"You really mean," said Allen, "that I ought to have a spinning wheel? Or are you simply trying to be funny?"

"What do you think?" I asked.

"Oh," said Allen, "you're trying to be funny. But honestly don't you like it?"

"There's one thing else you might have," I said. "You haven't got a pair of ox-bows."

"Jim," he asked, "don't you really like it?"

"Do you care whether I do or not?" I asked.

"Well," said Allen Southby, "you haven't changed much, Jim."

14

"Haven't I?" I said. "It's kind of you to remember what I used to be." Then when he looked hurt, I added: "Not that you had any reason to, not the slightest reason."

"Now don't say that," said Allen, "please. You have no idea the number of times I've wanted to get you in here. But it's like old times, isn't it?"

"Yes," I said, "just like old times."

"How about some beer?" Allen asked.

"Have you any whisky?" I said.

He said that he had, and left the bottle near me on the table. "Thanks," I said. "You give me an inferiority complex. That's why I said what I did, in case you don't know it."

"That's plain rot," said Allen kindly, "just plain rot, or else you're laughing at me."

I took a swallow of my whisky. I wished I knew whether I was laughing at him or not. It is so hard to judge whether a man one has known for a long while is really first-rate or not. It is so hard to get away from personal pique and from one's own peculiar disappointments. I certainly had never made the reputation which Allen Southby had, and certainly I never would, although I had been industrious and did possess a broader background of experience.

Allen lighted a straight-grain pipe and exhaled the sweet smooth smoke of an expensive mixture. He began talking charmingly about his meeting with Joyce in Paris. He had always maintained that *Ulysses* was the one great work of an era. Portions of it had to be chanted, he said, for Joyce drew his inspiration directly from the medieval choirs. When one heard Joyce himself read, from *Work in Progress*, the dialogue of the old washerwomen, thumping wearily at their soiled Gaelic linen, then one understood his mystic word-music. Everything that Allen said made sense; everything he said awakened an intellectual curiosity. He was speaking of a world of ideas, of that lonely, rather grotesque world where anyone who writes must live. Yet I still wondered if something inside me were not laughing in a polite sardonic undertone.

He was a better man than I, one who had made the most of

his gifts. He was a scholar and he may have been the only adequate apology for leisure and social injustice, but he had shut himself into an ivory tower. He had no first-hand knowledge of what the rest of us might think, for he was removed from contemporary care by a comfortable income and by a succession of easy, uneventful years, until his ideas were as unconnected with reality as the furnishings of his study. In spite of all his research I could not help suspecting that he was incapable of understanding the spirit of his own or any historical epoch, because he had not lived in his own generation.

"Now you and I," he said, "you and I who write . . ."

He meant it in the kindliest way, pointedly including me with himself in a high brotherhood, but I found myself resenting it. He had been permitted by good fortune, or by faulty economics, to have the leisure in which to accumulate a number of facts. He had collated his notes on those facts and put them into a book. He was like one of those experts, whom any amateur could have knocked flat in twenty seconds, busy criticizing a fighter's technique from a safe seat at the press bench. He was speaking of creative writing, intimating that he, too, was a creative writer.

"Now you and I who write," he said, and he had no reason to bracket himself with me except that we both used pen and ink.

There was certainly nothing in my own professional career that should have made me scorn his company. I had followed the usual path of one who makes a living by writing fiction. First I had been a correspondent on a newspaper; then I had contributed stories full of action and of local color to that type of magazine known in the trade as the "pulps." I had graduated with others from the "pulps" into that more desirable field of periodicals the "smooths," called so, presumably, because their pages had a glossy finish that could hold photographs and half-tone illustrations. The "smooths" required an added ability in that they demanded less plot and greater skill in character delineation. I had also written several novels, none of which had been successful, although the critics called them "competent." I had always wanted to do something better, but never had, and probably never would. All

16

I could say for myself at best was that I could keep my place in my field as a technical craftsman if not as an artist, and, as a craftsman, that I could meet its competition.

I finished my whisky and soda and poured out another. Allen was on his favorite subject, the great past age of New England. He was speaking of Hawthorne and of the literary background. I imagine that he had forgotten himself in his discourse, if such a feat were possible. His voice with its perfectly timed emphasis was as vital and tireless as an actor's at rehearsal.

"The brittle, mechanized short fiction, the perfunctory, meaningless novel of today," he said—"we should do something about it. We all should try."

I resented that remark, because he was speaking of the art of fiction when he had never attempted to write a story, or certainly had never ventured to exhibit the result. He had never attempted to make something out of nothing, because he was too cautious, like most critics. It may have been that the rest of us had the blissfulness of ignorance, but at least we were able to manufacture character and incident, however bad, out of nothing but our thoughts and observations. We had a sense, poor perhaps, of detail and of dramatic unity. At any rate my kind had been bold enough to try.

"You see where I am leading?" Allen Southby said, and then I knew that I had been woolgathering again as I had at other Harvard lectures.

"What are you driving at?" I asked.

"At just that," he said, "at just that very thing. I am making a confession. All my preparation has led just to that."

"Just to what?" I asked.

Allen Southby smiled pensively, and then turned to me defiantly.

"I am going to come out in the open," he said. "I am going to write a novel."

"So that's why you got me here," I said.

"Well, not exactly," said Allen, "but in one way, yes. Of course, the thing I'd write wouldn't be like yours."

17

"No," I said, "it would be real, it wouldn't be perfunctory."

"Don't be bitter, Jim," said Allen. "I know the difficulties of commercial writing. I know them very well. You wouldn't mind looking at the first two chapters, would you, old man? You always have a lot of ideas. You see everybody has a good novel under his belt when he gets to be about forty. I've had rather an interesting life. You wouldn't mind glancing through the first two chapters? It's an autobiographical novel in a sense."

"Hand them over," I said, "I'll read them now."

It was amusing to observe that Allen became hesitant, now that he reached the point, and I knew the way he felt. He was no longer Dr. Southby, but a tyro who desired a favorable judgment or none at all. He was like a young writer in an editor's office, explaining the inner meaning of what he had written so that one could understand it before one read it.

"If it isn't good enough to show me without talking, don't show it," I said. "I've got to be getting home, I can't sit here all night."

"I want you to understand that it's a very rough draft," Allen explained, "not the finished thing, but just the bare skeleton of the idea. I don't want you to think it's the finished thing."

"All right," I said, and reached for the papers, but Allen did not let them go.

"Perhaps you'd better not read the first page," he said. "That's a little turgid. I didn't really get started until page two, and perhaps the first page isn't actually necessary. It's simply setting the scene."

"That's necessary," I said. "You have to set the scene."

Allen's fingers still gripped one edge of the manuscript.

"Jim," he said, "wouldn't you rather wait until some other time? You've drunk half a bottle of whisky."

"Whisky helps," I said. "I can read it quicker, and perhaps it will make me cry."

Allen's body squirmed in his barrel armchair.

"Now wait a minute," he said, "just a minute. I want you to

18

give this your serious attention, Jim. You mustn't look at it as though it were going into a popular magazine, because it isn't popular."

"As far as I'm concerned it's the first draft of *Vanity Fair*," I said. "You're William Makepeace Thackeray, and I'm Ticknor and Fields."

"Now wait a minute," said Allen, "please go about it in the right way. Please don't say some damned devastating thing without thinking. This is real to me, Jim, horribly real. It isn't one of these things that one dashes off for money. I don't want you to look at it as though it were. Of course I want your honest opinion. God knows that I'm not afraid of adverse criticism as long as it's constructive. I just don't want you to rip it up the back for no good reason, but I do really want your honest, considered opinion."

In other words that was exactly what he did not want, but I refrained from pointing it out to him.

"Hand it over," I said, "and don't be coy. If it's good, it's good; if it's lousy, it's lousy."

"But you will remember what I said, won't you?" Allen asked.

"I haven't forgotten a word," I told him, "and that's the truth. Go out and get me a little ice while I read it. I'll need another drink."

"Haven't you had enough?" said Allen.

"Are you afraid to leave me alone in the room with this thing?" I asked him, and I picked up the first page.

"Go on out and get some ice," I said.

Its appearance showed that it was not a first draft, but a manuscript which had been through the hands of a commercial typist, and I knew that I was on the threshold of what has always been a delightful experience—I was reading one of those novels written by the English Department at Harvard. Allen Southby had overreached himself at last.

I had finished the first paragraph by the time Allen returned

19

with a pewter bowl of ice cubes, and the first paragraph had interested me, though not for the reasons its author had intended.

The silence and peace [I read] which always come over the Wickford Valley at sundown settled benignly upon the farm of Jacob Sears. The heady smell of dung from the new-plowed fields mingled with the milky odors of the dairy. The incoming tide of the Wickford River lapped gently against the gray shale of the point. Ripple, ripple, ripple. Would the sound never cease? Ripple, ripple, ripple. It gave Jacob Sears an odd feeling in his belly.
"Jacob!" It was a voice from the house calling.
Jacob Sears belched.

Allen put the ice bowl gently on the table beside me.
"How's it going so far?" he asked.
"It's going fine," I said. "What was the matter with Jacob Sears's belly?"
Allen Southby winced. "I really didn't mean you to read that first page," he said. "The first page is simply the groping for a simple style."
"That's all right," I said. "It arouses my curiosity."
"Look here," said Allen, "are you sure you feel up to reading this tonight, Jim? I don't want you to play horse with it. I've read a lot worse paragraphs of yours."
"The first thing for you to learn," I said, "is not to be thin-skinned. I thought you were writing about yourself. I ought to be writing this story. My family has lived in the Wickford Valley always. My father's cousin was married to a descendant of the Wickford Sage."
"Good God," said Allen Southby, "you never told me that."
"But I thought you were going to write about yourself," I said again.
"I have put myself into the scene," he explained. "I have translated a good many of my experiences into that scene. As a matter of fact I know everything about every character in the Wickford Farm group from the Brill papers in the library."

"Did you ever know my great-aunt Sarah?" I asked.

Allen shook his head.

"Then you don't know anything about the Wickford group," I told him.

"Then why don't you write about it yourself," said Allen tartly, "if you know so much? I'd like to see the first two chapters of your novel."

"I might write about it if I had time," I said, "but no one would belch in my novel. No one at Wickford ever belched."

There was a faint pink flush under Allen's healthy tan. We were both being infantile, but the fiction which one writes is so essentially a part of one's ego that disparagement of it is worse than physical pain. Even after years of training one sometimes loses one's self-control.

"I'd like to see you try to write a novel about Wickford," Allen repeated. "Everything you write is based upon formula. You couldn't write anything else now. You couldn't write anything that wasn't commercial."

"Oh, I couldn't, couldn't I?" I said. "If I did, I wouldn't act like a prima donna when you read it."

Allen sat down stiffly and jammed some tobacco into his pipe.

"If you mean I can't stand honest criticism," he said, "you're very much mistaken. I gave you credit for a real sense of appreciation. I hope I'm not wrong."

The atmosphere was icy in spite of the summer evening.

"If you can sit still, I'd like to read the rest of it," I said. "I'm really interested."

"I don't mind what anyone says about my work," said Allen, "as long as it's intelligent."

"It can't always be what you want to hear," I said, "or it wouldn't be intelligent."

Allen lighted his pipe and began weaving his way about the room, now fingering a book, now looking out the window where the lights of the cars moved along Memorial Drive in endless progress, now picking up a piece of pewter and examining the marks. Occasionally I saw him from the corner of my eye, and

21

I knew he was cursing the impulse which had made him put his pride into my keeping. While I turned the pages, Allen's self-confidence was leaving him; he was suffering the tortures of the damned.

"How's it going?" he said again.

"It's going fine," I said. In a sense that manuscript showed care, but from a practical aspect it was an egregious exhibition.

Not so many years ago a teacher of the art of writing began the advertisement of his services with the announcement that millions of people can write fiction without knowing it. He would have been safer had he said that millions of people are certain that they can write fiction a great deal better than those engaged in the profession. Even so, it is my belief that the consistent craftsman of fiction is very rare. His talent, which is in no sense admirable, is intuitive. In spite of the dictum of Stevenson on playing the sedulous ape to the great masters, it has never been my observation that education helps this talent. On the contrary, undue familiarity with other writers is too apt to sap the courage and to destroy essential self-belief, through the realization of personal inadequacy. It encourages a care and a style that confuse the subject, and the net result is nothing.

Instead, a writer of fiction is usually the happier for his ignorance, and better for having played ducks and drakes with his cultural opportunities. All that he really requires is a dramatic sense and a peculiar eye for detail which he can distort convincingly. He must be an untrustworthy mendacious fellow who can tell a good falsehood and make it stick. It is safer for him to be a self-centered egotist than to have a broad interest in life. He must take in more than he gives out. He must never be complacent, he must never be at peace; in other words, he is a difficult individual and the divorce rate among contemporary literati tells as much.

It was patent that Allen Southby did not possess these attributes. Or if they had been his once, scholarship had made them sterile. The trouble was that he had set out to write a masterpiece. He

had tensed his intellectual muscles and had sweated in his earnest-
ness in order to make each word a jewel, each sentence a concise
gem of thought, and the whole a symphony of words; and what
was worse, you could tell that he had been thinking of what the
critics would say.

A veritable galaxy of beauty. . . . Here at least is a novel of America
with the mysticism of *A Blithedale Romance* and the rustic humor
of a Hardy.

Utterly breath-taking. . . . One need look no further for this year's
best seller.

"How's it going?" Allen asked. "Do you like it? Do you like
it really?"

Then I knew that the time had come to be kind, that everyone has some quality of mercy. The time had come to say something that would not wound him.

"You've given everything you have," I said.

Allen stood up very straight.

"Thanks, Jim," he said. "You really see that do you? You
really feel that? You're not laughing?"

"No," I said, "I'm not laughing."

"Then I guess everything's all right," Allen said. "Jim, I can't
begin to thank you. But go ahead and finish it."

It would have been unkind to laugh. He was trying like other
outlanders to write a novel of New England, and unfortunately
he had come from Minnesota. He was trying to be a fearless
modern Hawthorne, bringing to his work the physical aspects
of existence which he had gathered from the modern school.
His theme dealt with that transient intellectual blooming in the
Wickford Valley, which had once boasted a tenuous connection
with the life of transcendental Concord. Even in its unnaturalness
it was a scene with which I was partially familiar, because our
whole family was a product of the blooming, although I had not
thought of it just that way. It was the narration of a scholar,
decorated and redecorated by stray sprigs of knowledge, gleaned
from his research into the lives of the Thoreaus, Alcotts, and

23

the rest of the New England intelligentsia. When he left fact behind to rely upon his imagination, the result was very bad. The attempts at humor were elephantine; the attempts at naturalness genuinely embarrassing. Yet in spite of clumsiness the pages had the arresting quality which sometimes makes bad work more provocative than good. I might have told him a number of ways to fix up those pages, but he would not have listened. What piqued me was my previous discovery, which grew the more bizarre when I thought of it, that I was a part of what he was trying to say, and that I could say it better.

"Allen," I said to him again, "you've given it everything you have."

III | After All, It's Just Putting Words on Paper

I drove slowly out of Harvard Square and very carefully along the turnpike, anxious to make no mistake which might lead me into controversy with the state police. Though I assumed that I was not under the influence of liquor, the authorities might have given themselves the benefit of a reasonable doubt. At any rate there was not much necessity for caution, for the road, stretching uncompromisingly in its straight line over the low hills, was very nearly deserted. Now and then I passed a heavy truck moving on some nameless errand, but that was all which occurred to interrupt my thoughts. Allen Southby, though not in the way he had intended, had given me a stimulating evening. I had not thought before that anything about me or about the family might be interesting, and now I realized that my generation had lived through a span of change. Everything was fascinating and very vivid, like all ideas before you set them down on paper.

It was a cloudy night. When I drove down the hill, under the elm trees, everything at Wickford Point was foggy and as black as pitch where the headlights did not strike. In an exaggerated effort to be careful I ran into the rear wall of the shed before I shut off the engine and the lights.

Cousin Clothilde was sitting in the long parlor and Sid was sitting with her, looking at his thumbs as he revolved one about the other, and Sid's sister, my second cousin, Bella Brill, was putting red polish on her nails.

"For God's sake," I said to Sid, "don't do that."

"It's more than you can do," said Sid. "I can move one thumb clockwise and the other counterclockwise, both at the same time. I've been working at it all evening."

"Well, don't do it now," I said.

"I bet you five dollars you can't do it," said Sid.

"As soon as I get to this place," I remarked, "everyone says I can't do anything, and what's more no one does anything. It doesn't stand to reason, it isn't true, that you've been practising with your thumbs all night."

"Darling," said Cousin Clothilde, "you should be careful not to drink too much. It always makes you cross. Please let's not have everybody cross. Everybody keeps quarreling. Sid and Bella have been quarreling."

"Sid's just been talking," Bella said. "He's been giving us a lecture." She was looking at me, frowning. "What's the matter with you tonight?"

"There's nothing the matter with me," I answered.

Bella looked at me mysteriously from the corners of her eyes.

"Darling," she said, "that friend of yours, Patricia Leighton, telephoned you from New York tonight."

Cousin Clothilde was listening and Sid had stopped rotating his thumbs.

"All right," I said. "Did she say why?"

"I'm sure I don't know what she wanted," Bella said, "and she wouldn't tell me. I think it was rather fresh of her."

"It must be that she didn't want you to know, honey bee," I said.

"Oh, shut up," said Bella.

"Shut up yourself," I said.

"Darling," said Cousin Clothilde, "that isn't being kind to Bella. She went way into the other part of the house to answer your telephone call."

Bella looked at me again and everything about her became sweetly but innocently seductive.

26

"He isn't cross," Bella said. "I know when he's cross and when he isn't. He's just thinking about something. There's something on his mind and he doesn't want us or Pat Leighton to interrupt him."

"I wish you wouldn't think about something, darling," said Cousin Clothilde. "It always makes me nervous when you think. Your mind keeps jumping around and you can't sit still."

"Let him think if he wants to," said Bella.

"Where are you going?" said Cousin Clothilde. "Why don't you sit down?"

"I'm going out for a walk," I said.

"Why do you want to go for a walk, darling?" she said. "Sid, do you think he should go for a walk?"

"How should I know?" said Sid.

"Bella," said Cousin Clothilde, "you go out with him."

"All right," said Bella, "I'll go with you."

"I don't want anybody," I said. "I want to be alone."

Bella took my arm and walked beside me on the lawn. Everything was a different degree of blackness, beginning with the sky and river and ending with the house and trees. The bullfrogs were croaking in the pond in a strange, mournful chorus.

"I wish those frogs would shut up," I said. "I want to think."

Bella gave my arm a shake.

"You can't think here," she said, "any more than you can be alone. There's always something else."

She was right: there was always something else.

"Has it ever occurred to you," I asked her, "that we are all very interesting people?"

"Yes," said Bella, "it occurs to somebody nearly every day."

"And you take it for granted, don't you?"

"Yes," she said. "Everybody takes it for granted."

"I wonder why," I said. "There isn't any reason. Somebody must have been fascinating once. It may have been our great-aunt Sarah. She used to hook rugs and pick up pine cones. I wonder if our great-grandfather was fascinating. Somebody must have been."

"What's the matter with you?" Bella asked.

"I'm trying to get things into some sort of order," I said. "I'm trying to find out what the matter is with all of us."

Bella gave my arm another shake.

"Somehow we don't work right," I said; "no one except Clothilde. She's the only one who seems to go."

Bella's voice grew sharp. I could see her intent white face turn toward me in a startled profile.

"What have you been doing with yourself?" she said. "What are you thinking about?"

"Thinking I won't be able to sleep," I said. But I did not tell her why. She would not have understood the preoccupation which comes of balancing this against that before you set it down on paper.

If you try to get back to the beginning of your existence, you find that all subsequent action has been built upon the shifting sands of unsupported fact. You start with a lot of erroneous impressions supplied by your own untrained observation or foisted upon you by your elders. Then years later you discover that you never knew those elders at all, no matter how long you were thrown with them during the formative years of childhood; and finally the day comes when it is too late even to try to know them, when the blank façade of the generations stands before you to demonstrate the tragic impossibility of passing on experience. All that is left for me at present is to guess about the shady forms I used to see at Wickford Point, whose portraits and daguerreotypes are now in the little parlor, and whose carpet bags and boots and parasols used to be up in the attic until my Cousin Sue in one of her spells of economy sold them to an itinerant antique dealer.

When I was a child it took a long while to get anywhere, if you started from Wickford Point. When Charles, the black mustachioed French Canadian coachman, used to hitch my grandfather's bay pair to the light phaeton, it took an hour and a half of good smart trotting to get to town. That innovation, the trolley car, was just appearing, and occasionally as a treat we were taken on it for a ride. To reach the carline, it was necessary to take a walk of nearly half an hour, first through the east orchard, then through the lower pasture, then through the white pine grove, then through the swamp wood lot, and thence across Bowles's field, where the bull was, and through the Teach farm. You waited by the Teach stone wall for the trolley car, because it would stop at a white post across the main road. It was generally necessary to wait for quite a while. You could hear the car a mile away on the hill by the Newell farm; then the sound would die away as it stopped at Hoskins turnout; then there would be a hissing of the wires, and it would finally appear, reeling drunkenly on its uneven rails. That memory now is almost archaeological, for those country trolley lines, which were once considered such a prime investment, are now as extinct as the bustle. Yet Professor Edward Channing once said in a school history of the United States that the trolley car was the most useful of all inventions, since it brought so much pleasure and freedom to so many people. What is the use in trying, if the history books are wrong?

In those days at Wickford Point we were living on the comfortable tail-end of the Victorian era; but Wickford Point was so far removed from contemporary contacts that much of it was still early Victorian. Life still proceeded in the grooves worn by things which had happened before my parents were born, and those grooves are what I am trying to remember. My great-aunt Sarah never allowed the two huge brass kettles, used formerly for making soap, to be taken out of the kitchen closet. There was a tinder box on the table in the small parlor with which Aunt Sarah sometimes started the fire, because, she said, the sulphur matches smelled badly and the noise they made was startling. One was always sparing of the matches because they had once been novelties, and when the fires were going we always used paper spills to light the candles. One of the branches of the great elm by the front door was twisted because Aunt Sarah's mother used to have a pig hung from it in the winter. In the winter, as long as she was able, Aunt Sarah always put a few embers in the warming pan before she went to bed, and made tea from a kettle hung from a crane in the fireplace in the back parlor. She also had a collection of herbs in the long parlor cupboard.

At the age of eighty Aunt Sarah was a good hand with an ax. As a little boy I have watched her go into the woodshed, take off her shawl and poke bonnet and mittens, and cut short sticks for the parlor fireplace. At such times she used to regale me with an anecdote. Years ago when she was there in the woodshed splitting logs, the ax slipped and cut a deep gash just above her knee. She walked to the house, got out her oval sewing basket, threaded a needle with her best white silk thread, and sewed up the wound herself.

"Yes, yes," said Aunt Sarah, "it was the only thing to do. Who else was there to do it?"

A great many adults seem to forget how easily they accepted things when they were young, when, from the distance of their maturer years, they pity small children who must face a series of adjustments. Usually they are entirely wrong, at least according to my experience, for childhood seems capable of adapting itself to nearly any situation that does not entail fear or physical suffering. Thus when my parents died and when I was sent to Wickford Point to live with my great-aunt Sarah and her niece, my cousin Sue, it all seemed natural by the time a year was over.

I must have accepted Wickford Point in the same way that philosophers accept the universe, and I adjusted myself without a thought to the local peculiarities, including those of my great-aunt Sarah. My cousin Sue informed me later that Aunt Sarah was not what she used to be even before I was born; and it may have been, when Aunt Sarah and I became acquainted, that her mind was failing, but I was in no position to judge.

When it came to more practical matters I was obviously incapable of understanding them, nor should I have cared to analyze such ties as family relationships. Those are facts which dawn upon one gradually, and I suppose a great many of us never get them straight. For instance it was a long while before I came to realize that a gentleman named Samuel Seabrooke, who was my great-aunt Sarah's father, and whom I looked upon as her special property, was my own great-grandfather. It was later still before I got it clearly in my mind that my own grandmother was Samuel Seabrooke's daughter and just as much Aunt Sarah's sister as my great-aunt Georgianna, who died before I was born. Later still I discovered almost by accident that Aunt Sarah was a spinster, and that Cousin Clothilde and Cousin Sue were my Aunt Georgianna's surviving daughters and my father's first cousins. I never really understood how the Brills entered into our common picture until I was fourteen. Then I knew, only by fitting facts together, that John Brill, who in later years became the poet and the Wickford Sage, used to row frequently across the river to pay his respects to Samuel Seabrooke's three daughters, but that nothing had ever happened until John Brill's son Hugh, following his example, rowed across the same river a generation later and met my cousin Clothilde; and that was the beginning of all the Brills. When Hugh Brill died, Cousin Clothilde married Archie Wright and naturally she took his name, but as I said before, it always seemed to me that she was still a Brill.

It all appears simple enough now, once it is in black and white, but when I was a boy I accepted these people, living and dead, as inevitable figures in a legend of creation that was not unlike the Grecian myths. Sometimes it seemed to me that I knew as much about the dead as the living, for I heard about them all from Aunt Sarah when I came to Wickford Point. Her mind may have been failing, but I still am not sure. It was not dotage which had assailed her so much as a natural alteration of her mental processes. When she was an old lady she had simply developed an ingrowing preoccupation with affairs that were not contemporary, and also an increasing predilection not to look at the present. She may have been a difficult liaison with the past, but she was the only one I had. A stray word of hers, a dreamily acid allusion, are now all the means I have for explaining the ancient vigor of Wickford Valley, and for explaining the actions of those who descended from it. Nevertheless five minutes with Aunt Sarah were worth a hundred pages of Allen Southby's novel; and what was more, even if Allen Southby had seen her, he would not have understood her, for she was not words but the past itself, and all of Wickford Point had meaning when Aunt Sarah was alive.

When Aunt Sarah was seventeen she was a liberal with dangerous radical tendencies, and, like most of the liberals in her day, she exercised her trouble-making qualities in the abolitionist movement. The town, being made up principally of merchants, many of whom were interested in cotton, was on the whole pro-slavery, but the cultural environment of Wickford Valley had become different from the town. Wickford Valley inveighed against mercantile crassness, purely out of self-defense perhaps, and resorted to self-righteousness. Thus Aunt Sarah in her lifetime never would allow liquor or cards in the house, although her brother, Horace, used them both. Incidentally, her brother Horace came to an unpleasant end in an altercation with a gambler in the San Francisco Gold Rush. It is odd how easily one gets off the subject, speaking of the family.

During those days of the early 1850's, when the Fugitive Slave Act was enforced, it seems, from what Aunt Sarah told me, that Wickford Point was a station of the Underground Railroad, and that fugitive Negroes had a way of appearing there suddenly at night in boats or in the back of covered wagons. They were customarily kept down cellar for a day or so in what had once been a wine closet under the brick arch which supported the front parlor chimney. At the proper time Aunt Sarah or her sister Georgianna or my grandmother, aided often by some sympathetic house guest, placed these visitors in a boat and rowed them across the river to the cow stable of the Brill farm. After this they continued their way north by way of Exeter, and sometimes wrote back bread-and-butter notes telling of their safe arrival in the province of Quebec. Aunt Sarah used to keep a package of these letters in the Moorish cabinet which her father had brought from Spain when he was an agent for the Bosworth firm in Boston. Until her last years, she never threw anything away.

It seems that one evening when Aunt Sarah and my cousin

Clothilde's mother, Georgianna, were alone at Wickford Point, the Kennedys' hay wagon came down with a packing case that had been left on the main road by a carter from Boston. Mr. Moses Kennedy, who was a Quaker with correct sympathies, helped the girls unload the box in the south hay barn. Aunt Sarah went to the shop for tools and Aunt Georgianna hurried to the kitchen to boil some cracked cocoa. When Aunt Sarah and Moses Kennedy opened up the packing case they found a Negro man inside, just as they had expected, but the case had come from Boston wrong-side-up; the Negro was quite dead.

Under the circumstances there was only one thing to do. The body must be buried at once without publicity. They discussed the idea of getting Mr. Wade, the Congregational clergyman, but decided against it because Mr. Wade might talk. Instead Aunt Sarah called to Georgianna to bring from shelves in the back parlor library their father's copy of *The Ship Master's Assistant*, which contained a service for burials at sea. Moses got a shovel and a mattock out of the tool shed and dug a deep grave in the new orchard. There was some dispute about reading the burial service, which had the popish taint of the Church of England, but all three of them agreed upon it eventually. It was dark by then. Aunt Sarah got a ship's lantern and held it while Moses read the words. Then they laid the sods back carefully. Of course it was important not to mark the grave.

A long time later the incident became transiently famous when an account of it appeared in the collected verses of John Brill, the Wickford Sage. I remember two lines of the poem, not very good ones either.

> They laid him away with a prayer and a tear.
> The valley earth was his only bier.

Aunt Sarah always said it was a very beautiful poem, but then in her opinion the Wickford Sage took his rank with the greater Victorians. Years later there was some talk of putting a stone at the head of the grave.

"But can you imagine," Aunt Sarah said, "when they asked me where he was, I couldn't remember? The exact location had completely skipped my mind. Well, well, it probably doesn't signify."

It probably did not matter to her, but it did to me when she told me about it. I gained the distinct impression that there was a ghost in the new orchard, not a hostile ghost but a definite presence which was near me when I went to cut sticks for throwing green apples.

It is curious to reflect that most of the dogs that died on the place had their tombstones, but not Aunt Sarah's fugitive. Aunt Sarah's father was the one who started the dog cemetery near the south rock by the river. When a water spaniel, which a business acquaintance had sent him from London, died in 1822, he had a stone cut with an appropriate Greek quotation:—

To Perseus, gallant but gun shy.

Following Perseus were the dogs of that lost generation, somehow more real to me than many of the human beings they had followed. Their names reflected the romantic, scholarly instinct of the period—Lycidas, Byron, Portia, Werther, Giovanni, Unity and Keats. Some of the rougher stones had been cut by hand in the toolshed when there was no money at Wickford Point.

Once I told Cousin Clothilde that we should do something about the only human being buried on the place.

"I really don't see what there is to do," Cousin Clothilde said. "You don't know what his name was or when he died. After all he was an absolute stranger; besides I doubt very much if the story is true. Aunt Sarah was a little queer in the head when you knew her. Besides I never did get on well with her. She was always moving about, always doing something."

No one with the exception of myself ever seemed to be interested in what Aunt Sarah must have been once. It was only taken for granted that everything about her was peculiar.

for an hour to the point, around the south orchard and through the pine woods, and then in the open months worked for another hour in her garden. She took particular pains with her tomato plants, which she always placed in the same bed with her flowers. Her reason was that tomatoes were front lawn ornaments when she was a girl—"love apples," she used to call them, "each one like a valentine." She was back in the house by the time the postman came, in order to read her mail, which was generally from distant connections of the family. Then she did cross-stitch embroidery for an hour. After lunch she rested for fifteen minutes exactly, and then sewed her gingham ironing-holders or worked upon a hooked rug. After this she walked up the hill to see the view, and was back in time to read Homer in the original and to write in her diary before supper. After the evening meal she was in a relaxed and social mood. The lamp was lighted on the round table in the front parlor; every window was closed and the wooden shutters were drawn tight. The only thing of which I knew her to be afraid was the idea that some unseen face or some unseen thing might be staring at her from the dark. By eight or nine in the evening the air in that hermetically closed room was difficult to breathe, particularly in cold weather when an anthracite fire was burning in the grate. Cousin Clothilde's sister Sue would always be there with her after supper, and Aunt Sarah would read aloud tirelessly for hours to her or anyone who might care to listen. Her favorite book was Pepys' *Diary*, which she finished at least once a year, but when I was sent to Wickford Point as a boy, she went to considerable pains to read what she thought might amuse or interest me. She read me all the Waverley novels, and once she told me that she had first been obliged to peruse *Ivanhoe* behind the lid of her desk at the Northville Female Academy because it was considered a trashy novel. She also read me the complete works of Dickens, although in her opinion Dickens was not a gentleman. Sometimes she would take up Thoreau—"Dear Henry" she used to call him—and sometimes she would read the essays that "Waldo" had written—she was referring to Ralph Waldo Emerson. She had known all the intellectuals of that period and spoke of some affectionately and of some acidly, giving details that I wish I might remember. By half-past ten o'clock it was Aunt Sarah's opinion that the day's work was over.

"Get the backgammon board," she said then, and she would usually add: "My father brought it home from Lisbon the third time he sailed back from Canton, and I wish he were here to play on it now, so I wouldn't have to play with Sue."

I have often wondered how Cousin Sue stood it with the air in that small parlor growing closer all the while, but unflinchingly she rattled the dice and shifted the counters evening after evening. Toward the end she played Aunt Sarah's board and her own too, very quickly for an hour. At half-past eleven Aunt Sarah drank a half-pint of milk from her great-grandfather's silver ale can, and afterwards went to the side entry and took down her presentation copy of one of the works of John Brill, the Wickford Sage.

"It is time for a treat now," she used to say. "We can't go to bed without hearing from dear John." She always called him "dear John," and when she closed the book she always said:—

"I don't know what ever induced him to marry that woman. I told him he was a fool."

To my Wickford Nymph, was written in rusty ink on the fly-leaf, *from her Shepherd across the Valley.*

"Of course," Cousin Clothilde told me once, "Aunt Sarah must have had some sort of affair with John Brill. It wouldn't have been natural if she hadn't. People were dreadfully queer about those things in those days, and they made such a tremendous point of them. He was a dreadful old man with tobacco stain on his beard, and what's more I don't think he ever washed."

When the tall clock in the dining room struck midnight, Aunt Sarah would rise.

"I shall get my candle now," she always said, "the one that has a fish on it. My father brought it from Peru, the time he was nearly arrested by the Inquisition." Once she said to me, and I remember it because it was almost the only thing Aunt Sarah ever said to me that was not impersonal, "I wish you might have seen my father. He was red-haired and very handsome, vastly handsomer than you will ever be. You would have admired to see him."

Such small details as that sometimes possess a poignant sort of significance. Once, for instance, I knew a man whose grandfather at an early age had seen the elderly General Washington when he had made a triumphal tour through our neighborhood. The little boy distinctly recalled that the general had asked for a tumbler of water, had taken a paper of powders from his pocket and poured the contents into the tumbler. I have always understood General Washington a good deal better since hearing that account, although I do not know just why, except that it showed the presence of human frailty.

Aunt Sarah's father, Samuel Seabrooke, seems to have possessed no weakness whatsoever except a desire to stray away from home. He had impressed her completely with his perfection, until her recollection of him was as coolly symmetrical and as stilted as the copperplate calligraphy in the diary which he kept of his travels, and as impersonal as many of his statements in it concerning the wind velocity and the weather. Considering the chances he had of seeing interesting places, his observations have recently seemed to me surprisingly obvious.

"It is difficult and not infrequently painful," he wrote once, "to make headway against the westerly gales in the vicinity of Cape Horn."

"The yellow fever," he observed again, "carries off many in Havana every year."

"The native population of the city of Canton," he also recorded, "is very dense."

Aunt Sarah never explained, and certainly no one else can, what induced her father to take over Wickford Point in the early eighteen hundreds and to settle his son, his wife and his three daughters on the farm, unless he may have enjoyed contemplating the peace of Wickford Point when he was away from it. Like some of his descendants, he was away from it a great deal. Aunt

Sarah often intimated that he was a "great gentleman," and various legal papers such as title deeds confirm her estimate.

"An agreement," they read, "between Mark Kennedy, yeoman, and Samuel Seabrooke, gentleman."

His picture in the small parlor also answered this description. Our great-grandfather was always young and endowed with the spare Federalist beauty which is somehow reminiscent of the architecture of his time. His reddish weather-beaten face with its high cheeks, its complacent mouth, and its chin stiffened by a white cravat, did not show the slightest sign of self-indulgence or the enervating effect of humor. It was the countenance of a determined, active man with an adequate supply of physical courage. Aunt Sarah once told me that he defended a French plantation against the Negro revolutionists in Haiti, leading a charge himself, and he may very well have done so. When he was at home, Aunt Sarah said, he was at great pains to drink the water sparingly which came from the red pump under the elm tree across the road. His reason was that his travels often took him to dry countries where it was important to do with as little water as possible. This strict regimen perhaps resulted in the physical disabilities which were a prelude to his premature decease.

Besides Aunt Sarah's stray remarks he left other mementoes of his stay at Wickford Point. He used to teach Sarah and Georgianna the classics every morning before breakfast, and his collection of books remained behind him in the back parlor now that he was permanently away. These small leather-bound volumes of his gave the room an intellectual beauty. They stood beside the set of Molière from which his wife, when she was conducting a female seminary, had snipped the naughty words with a pair of scissors, giving no consideration to the context on the back of the page.

"Well, well," Aunt Sarah used to say, "Mother was always sweet and charming and quite the most broad-minded woman I have ever known. She smoked a pipe when she was eighty, a most unpleasant habit, but times were hard after my father's death."

It is easy to touch upon trivial details such as these that come upon one out of nowhere in the middle of a wakeful night. All I know of my great-grandmother is that she smoked. She had acquired the taste from an old Negress who came as a fugitive slave in the Underground Railroad. The old slave's name, Aunt Sarah told me once, was Granny Cadwalader, and she stayed in the house for six whole weeks and helped on the hooked rug which is in the north chamber. My great-uncle Joel, who married Aunt Georgianna after the Brook Farm experiment in West Roxbury, was another ancestral smoker. He said it helped the misery in his joints, although Aunt Sarah always maintained that no one ever suffered from rheumatism who drank from the red pump, because there was iron in the water. My own grandfather, I remembered, often suffered from severe indigestion when he came to Wickford Point from New York City, and once I heard him say: "It's that God-damned water from the red pump."

The library of Samuel Seabrooke, as I have said, stood beside the set of Molière. It contained the works of Fielding and of Smollett and of Sterne, and several volumes of Defoe, a good deal of Voltaire, of Racine; Dryden, Calderón, Petrarch and Boccaccio; Pope's *Essay on Man*; *Paradise Lost*; Dr. Johnson's *Shakespeare*, and also the Doctor's *Dictionary*, the Portuguese poets, Cervantes, and *Gil Blas*, all mixed together in exactly the same order that he left them. Probably he had always meant, as most of us do, to read them and arrange them once he had the time. On the shelf below were the *Iliad* and the *Odyssey*, Xenophon and Thucydides. "He always admired to read Greek at sea," Aunt Sarah said. Then there was his Latin—Horace, Tacitus, Suetonius and Plautus, and two volumes of Plutarch's *Lives*. Beneath the classics was the shelf of books that I believe he read more frequently, a Bowditch, a *Coast Pilot*, a set of charts, *The Ship Master's Assistant,* Cook's *Voyages*, and some guidebooks of Mexico, Peru and Brazil, in Spanish and Portuguese.

There were other books in the house left by older and more completely forgotten individuals, such as local books of sermons and Cotton Mather's *Magnalia*. But my great-grandfather had left something more poignant than his books. He was evidently the type of person who always brings things back and who enjoys being surrounded by objects from distant places because of their reminiscent value. There used to stand upon the mantelpiece in the little parlor an unobtrusive piece of black rock, which Aunt Sarah said had been chipped from the topmost peak of the Andes. Beside it was an Inca tobacco-pestle made in the shape of a llama. Until Cousin Sue lost them in some unaccountable way, there were also two pearls which it was said had been given him by a chief of the Sandwich Islands. Cousin Sue was convinced that one of the Irish maids had taken them in later years from the little drawer beneath the shaving mirror on her bureau, but in a house always full of possessions, where nothing was ever thrown away, things were apt to be mislaid. Once Cousin Sue looked for three weeks for her great-grandmother's silver ring box, only to find it in the cracker jar in the closet off the dining room. On another occasion she kindled the fire in the long parlor by mistake with a packet of her grandmother's letters containing some stray locks of Samuel Seabrooke's reddish hair. It was too late when she tried to reach them.

He also had brought back a number of pictures on religious subjects, which used to hang in the narrow hall upstairs, and downstairs were two pictures painted on copper, which he had found somewhere near Granada. Aunt Sarah was always careful to explain that all his more priceless possessions had been lost or sold. As it was, we used to eat off his Canton china every night until the cat chased a mouse around the second shelf of the china closet, and even after that stray eggcups and saucers would appear mingled with the Wedgwood that my grandfather had sent from New York.

For the rest, everything about him is silence, although I seem to know more than most people know of their great-grandfathers. He died leaving the shades of the Federalist period in the house and a young wife and family to make their way as best they could

V | He Wouldn't Know the Old Place Now

Samuel Seabrooke had received the farm at Wickford Point in part payment of a debt, and when he moved there with his family the general outlines of the place and most of the buildings must have been established. The main farmhouse was close to the Wickford River. It had been built in the late seventeen hundreds by one of the Macey family in Boston as a hunting lodge. The front of the house was square and handsome, painted an even white. Toward the rear a subsequent owner had added to the summer kitchen ell on different levels, so that in moving from one room to another you walked up and down steps through narrow passageways. A later owner had built a cattle barn not far from the house, and also two hay barns nearer the river. These were used to store salt hay, which once was brought from the marshes near the coast on flat scows. Beyond the buildings was a strip of pine and birch wood, and there was a cattle lane just behind the trees, which led past the south hay barn through the south orchard to the upper pastures. The entire holding was not more than a hundred acres and the farm was never, in its best days, first-rate land either for grazing or for tillage, but the situation on the point where the tidal river flowed, the formal garden, which had been planned at the same time as the house, and the old elms and oaks upon the lawn, made it picturesque. A number of visitors have commented upon the trees and the garden, including Bronson

43

Alcott, Thoreau, and Hawthorne, at the time when he was working in the Salem Customs, and, of course, John Brill. Their references to the place may be found among the pages of various brown cloth-bound books published by Ticknor and Fields in the sixties. Even Cousin Clothilde could quote a number of them, entirely from hearsay because she seldom read a book.

"Bowery, wind-embracéd Wickford Point."

"The lilac-bedecked Elysium, where the Seabrooke nymphs weave garlands."

"The white-walled Acropolis of Wickford Point, where there is good tea and better talk."

"When the sunset gilds the roses of Wickford Point."

"Wickford Point has always been, and may it always be, the home of noble thoughts and gentle laughter."

The place had a way of growing on one. Even when I was a small child my thoughts dwelt a great deal on Wickford Point, although we did not live there much. It was a definite solace to me even then to feel that I was somehow connected with an estate that was a little finer than anyone else's, more beautiful, less vulgar.

When I was eight years old this interest in Wickford Point caused me to learn something about it from my grandfather. We were living, that summer, outside of New York on a beach near Sandy Hook, and my grandfather customarily took the morning boat, a white boat with paddle wheels and a walking beam, to his office on Pine Street in New York. One morning very early my mother got out my blue sailor suit which buttoned sideways like a real sailor's.

"What do you think?" she said. "Your grandfather wants you to go with him to his office in New York to spend the day."

I did not say what I actually thought, which was that the prospect seemed formidable, because I knew that it would not have helped. After breakfast my grandfather led me down to the wharf. In spite of the warm weather he was dressed for business in a silk hat and a Prince Albert coat. We sat in his stateroom and drank lemonade, and looked out the window at the tugs and at the sails of the pilot boats. When other men in tall hats and Prince Alberts came in to see my grandfather he told them that I was his grandson and they made complimentary remarks.

I accepted the city as one accepts everything at the age of eight. I still remember the clatter of the carts on the cobblestones; I still remember the men working in cages at the office, and I remember the stir occasioned when my grandfather walked past. He took me into his own room and sat down at his roll-top desk.

"Would you like to cut some coupons?" he asked me. "George will help you."

George must have been a clerk. He brought some bonds and a pair of scissors and did most of the work himself.

"So you're going to be a banker too, Jimmy?" he inquired.

"No," I told him. "I'm going to be a farmer and live on Wickford Point." My grandfather heard me and turned his swivel chair.

"That's enough of that nonsense," he said. "Wickford Point isn't a farm—it's a white elephant. It eats up money faster than I can make it. You get those ideas out of your head, Jim. They were all going barefoot when I came to Wickford Point. You like to wear shoes, don't you? And don't tell me you want to be a poet. Do you want to be a poet and grow a beard and look for huckleberries? You're going to learn something about money if I can arrange it. Somebody's got to know about money besides me, and I'm not going to leave you much either. I can't support the whole damn family."

It was not a new idea to me that my grandfather supported the family. Frequently in the evening when the market had gone sour, he remarked that he was supporting the whole damn family, all his nieces and nephews, all his cousins, everybody. There was not one of them, he stated on such evenings, that was capable of raising a finger. I don't know why he should have thought that I was capable, but I believe he did. I had heard all this before, but I had never realized that there was anyone in the world who did not approve highly of Wickford Point.

"You can go to college," he said, "but you've got to do something afterward. I support the whole damn family, and they don't even know I'm supporting them. By God, they take it for granted that I should support them. Your grandmother was a beauty. I remember the first day I came to Wickford Point."

"What were they doing?" I asked.

"They were sitting under an apple tree," my grandfather said, "playing 'Quotations.' Clethra was painting a picture and they asked me to stay to supper and then they found there wasn't any supper. I took Clethra downtown in the carryall and bought some. That was forty years ago. I've been buying everybody's supper ever since, the whole damn family's supper. I'd be worth two million dollars now if I hadn't stopped that day at Wickford Point. When I die I'll still be paying for that supper, if there's any money left."

My grandfather smiled suddenly and I realized that he was not being unkind.

"They were amazing," he said. "Common sense was just left out of them. Clethra never understood where money came from, but she was worth it. She was the most beautiful woman I've ever seen." He paused because a clerk had come in from the outer office.

"Mrs. Brill is here, sir," he said.

It was my cousin Clothilde with billowing white sleeves and long white gloves. She kissed my grandfather and she kissed me too.

"Uncle Jim," she said, "I've just been to the bank. There must be some mistake somewhere. They say I've overdrawn my account."

"What the devil, Clothilde?" my grandfather said. "You had your check the first of the month."

"I know," said Cousin Clothilde. "There must be some mistake somewhere. I wish you'd speak to them at the bank, Uncle Jim. They shouldn't be careless."

"Where's Hugh?" my grandfather said. "Why can't Hugh look out for you?"

"Hugh is down at the boat races in New London," Cousin Clothilde said. "He wanted me to go, but I never know what they do at those Harvard races except drink with each other. I came down here instead to do some shopping, and when I stepped over to the bank to draw enough money for my ticket back to Boston, they told me that there was no money. Uncle Jim, I really wish you'd go to the bank and speak to them."

My grandfather opened his office door. "George," he said, "make out a check of three hundred dollars for Mrs. Brill."

Cousin Clothilde sighed.

"You're always so sweet," she said. "You're the only one who looks out for me. I have to have someone to look out for me. Jim will look out for me when he grows up, won't you, Jimmy?"

"Yes," I said, and Cousin Clothilde smiled.

"There's a pony and a new carriage at Wickford Point," she said. "Your cousin Hugh bought them, and I'm going to have you come up to play with Sidney and Harry next week. You'll be up soon, won't you, Uncle Jim? You're the only one who can manage Aunt Sarah."

"Now run along," said my grandfather, "and buy yourself some dresses, and don't let me see Hugh if you can help it. God knows why you married him when you had a dozen other chances. Is old Brill still around?"

"Yes," said Cousin Clothilde. "He's such a darling. He's so beautiful with his long, white beard. He was asking for you last week. He wants to see you, Uncle Jim."

"Does he?" said my grandfather. "Well, I know why. It's near the end of the month."

"He's a darling," Cousin Clothilde said again. "He rowed across the river last week. He brought me some white gentians. He's written a new poem about the river."

"Did he have on shoes?" my grandfather asked.

"Yes," said Cousin Clothilde, "of course he did. He's a darling."

"He's a humbug," my grandfather said, "and he isn't reliable."

47

Although the word "humbug" was new to me, it was obviously a term of derision. An inherited sense of fitness told me that it was an improper description of a great man. I remembered how old John Brill had placed his hand upon my head when I had been led to meet him. There had been a malodorous aura about his clothes, of apples, wood smoke, pine shavings and chewing tobacco.

"Another little pilgrim," he had said. "Intimations of immortality—you can see it in his eyes. Yes, Sarah my dear, I could manage with another cup of tea and two more buns."

My grandfather smiled again, and again I realized that he was not being unkind.

It was always hard to think of my forebears as people with thoughts and desires like my own. Even the pictures in the family albums—and there were a number of those albums, fastened with heavy brass catches, placed upon the third shelf of the whatnot in the small parlor at Wickford Point—even those pictures were unreal. The subjects sat in constricted positions, staring at nothing with cold grimaces that did not indicate either ease or pleasure. Some of the likenesses were tintypes and others were the faded brown of my father's well-colored meerschaum pipe.

My father and my cousin Hugh used to smoke those pipes very carefully in the harness room in the barn; Aunt Sarah, who had been sensitive about her mother's smoking, disliked the odor of tobacco in the house. My grandfather was the only one who was allowed to smoke without protest. He smoked three cigars a day from a private stock which had been given him by Mr. Vanderbilt in New York, and after each cigar Aunt Sarah opened all the windows and dusted off the curtains.

"He smokes," Aunt Sarah told me once, "because he went to sea."

To her mind allowances had to be made for anyone who went to sea, and she seemed familiar with the human weaknesses which were developed in that profession. The sea seems far enough away in these days, but to Aunt Sarah the ships were still coming in. She was living as she had as a young girl, through the days of the Gold Rush and the China trade. Every vice was understandable to her if a man had been to sea,—gambling, foul language, liquor and tobacco,—yet she was broad-minded enough to admit that the sea was necessary to a proper and self-respecting life.

She made this remark about my grandfather on a number of occasions and it always surprised me because he was in no sense a seafaring man, although he had sailed for China as a cabin boy at the age of fourteen. On his return he must have realized that the great days of shipping were over, for he never took another voyage; instead he became an errand boy in downtown New York.

My grandfather appeared there in the years before the Civil War at just the time that Horatio Alger's characters began to make their way. He was a Yankee who must have rubbed shoulders with Tom the bootblack and Jerry the street boy. He was a figure of the wicked days—one of the ogres who now darken the pages of liberal economic primers—but he was the one who kept Wickford Point from vanishing, and he was the one who enabled all its archaic complications to live into the present. I have sometimes wondered whether, if he could return to it, he might not repent having left a trust fund for the upkeep of the place. Curiously enough Mr. Caldicott, our trustee, whom I had always considered unimaginative, said the same thing once when I saw him in Boston.

"Well, Mr. Caldicott," I told him, "if he could come back, he wouldn't know the old place now."

Sometimes, however, I am not so sure that he did not come back, and that all the people who have ever lived at Wickford Point are not somewhere near it.

These matters are of no importance except for the light which they may throw upon strange vanished days which no one living can understand. Nevertheless those days were at the root of all our difficulties. All those stiff-necked figures in the picture album, with their heads supported by invisible brackets—all their likes and dislikes—all the endless anecdotes about them which have died into a strange hushed silence—have given Wickford Point its quality. As one tries to piece them all together, the responsibility becomes enormous, for one is speculating about history and toying rudely with the springs of change. We can interpret, but we can never know. All that is certain—and this is as sure as fate—is that these vanished people made things what they are.

VI | The
Front Door
Sticks

I always enjoyed the informality of a summer morning at Wickford Point. What I enjoyed most was a unique lack of stimulus combined with the absence of a personal responsibility. Every summer morning at Wickford Point was like every other morning, bringing the consoling message that it would be wise to attempt nothing all day long. There was no tang to the morning air; but instead, the heavy lassitude of too many trees and of too much summer combined with a drowsy sound of enervated birds and a muddy murky odor from the river.

I had occupied the same room in the house at odd moments for most of my life. It was one of the least desirable rooms, but I had never cared to move out of it. When I awoke, a good many days after that evening when I had read the beginning of Allen Southby's novel, I could see the grooves which a tame squirrel of mine had once gnawed on the post of my bed. Looking at the ceiling I could see the same cracks, the directions of which I had learned by heart when I had lain there sick with scarlet fever. It had been predicted for the last twenty years that the ceiling was due to fall, but the cracks seemed no larger and no different. The ceiling was like the balance of power in Europe or like the tottering economic fabric of the nation and all of Wickford Point, ready to fall but never falling. In the meanwhile the cracks meandered toward the wall in the irrational outlines of rivers and continents, giving a good imitation of a slightly demented page in a geography. The whitewash had flaked off into deserts and mountain ranges. The corpses of occasional mosquitoes were like other geographic symbols. While lying in bed it was possible to embark on a voyage across that cracked ceiling. It got you nowhere, but the same might be said of other journeys.

I could see the mark where I had spilled acid on the claw-and-ball foot mahogany table. I could see the broken knobs of the empire bureau, and the rack where I kept my shotgun, and the hole in the Oriental carpet which my Irish water spaniel puppy had chewed twenty years before. I could see my perfunctory and undistinguished Harvard diploma, and a photograph, which was growing yellow, of the officers and men of Battery C of the Three Hundred and Something Artillery, Bay State Division, taken at Camp de Souge in France. There had been a time when I could name every one of those hundred-odd men from left to right without hesitation. Once it would have seemed impossible that I could ever forget those faces, but now I was not sure which figure among the officers was my own. I could see the hole in the wall made by a revolver bullet from a boyhood weapon which I had not known was loaded—the putty still there, put in by Mr. Morrissey, who was the hired man then, so that Cousin Sue might not find out about it. I had been pretending that I was a cowboy or Daniel Boone or someone, and it was lucky that I had not shot off a finger. I had pretended that I was a lot of things in that room—a soldier, a fireman, a philosopher, a trapper, a poet and a great lover. No doubt I was still pretending.

When Aunt Sarah died it was suggested that I move to the front of the house, but I had grown used to my room by then. I liked the view from my window of the lawn and the hay barn and the green of the oak trees by the river. The back stairs were near it, making it possible to enter and leave in privacy, and I liked the sounds and smells of the kitchen.

It was a quarter before ten o'clock. I knew the hour, not only from the watch on the candle-stand by the bed but from the

52

angle of the sunlight through the window. It was time to get up. I could never sleep as long as the others at Wickford Point.

Josie was in the kitchen and the flies were buzzing about some unwashed dishes in the soapstone sink. She was feeding something out of a tin cup to Herman, her youngest child. The contents of the cup dribbled down Herman's chin and onto his rompers. The old setter got up and hit his head on the kitchen table and sat down again.

"I don't know how it is, Mr. Calder," said Josie, "Herman just doesn't seem to eat right. I've told him again and again not to slobber, but the poor little thing, it doesn't seem to go down the right way."

"I'll have my breakfast in here," I said. "I'd like some coffee and a boiled egg."

"Yes, Mr. Calder," Josie said. "I've got some water boiling right now. Don't rub against Mr. Calder, Herman darling. I was just saying to Frieda last night that I did hope you wouldn't be starting away somewhere and leaving us. Frieda thought you might be going somewhere, the way you do. There are only two eggs, Mr. Calder. They forgot to get any groceries yesterday, and I have been asking and asking for some more soap. Dear Mrs. Wright is so forgetful. She was going to send downtown yesterday, but Miss Bella went off somewhere and then Mr. Sidney got her pocketbook."

"What did he do with her pocketbook?" I asked.

"He took it with him to the beach," Josie said, "and then dear Mrs. Wright was going to cash a check, but no one could find her checkbook, and so she said it could wait until today. And Mr. Calder, Earle has been so worried, that poor boy was crying when he was cutting the grass this morning."

"What was he crying for?" I asked.

"That poor boy," Josie said, and wiped her hands on her dress and took the coffeepot off the stove, "that poor boy was just crying because he hasn't got any money. Earle is such a sensitive boy, and Frieda has so much attention. The nicest boys have always like Frieda, even if she hasn't got the clothes that some of the girls have. Of course I sew and sew and do everything I can, and then Miss Bella gave her that dress, the one with the pink dots on it that she spilt the rum punch on last week. The dear girl is so proud of that dress, Mr. Calder, and she wanted to wear it but Earle has never been paid, so he just can't take her anywheres. That dear girl is just as pretty as a picture. Why, when she was waiting on people at the church supper, there was a man staying with the Fewkses up the road who said that she ought to go to Hollywood. He said she would have a great future in the movies. I said to Frieda that Mr. Calder might know someone in Hollywood. I said that Mr. Calder knows folks everywhere, and Mr. Sidney said you knew some folks in Hollywood."

"What happened about Earle?" I said.

"That poor boy!" Josie said. "He was so happy when Frieda said she would go to the beach with him. First he tried to borrow a dollar from Miss Bella and Miss Bella hadn't any, and Mr. Sidney was gone with the pocketbook, and dear Mrs. Wright couldn't find any money, and all I had was fifteen cents, because the man came for the sewing machine money, and dear Mrs. Wright still owes me for two weeks. He just can't get the money to take Frieda to the beach."

"Tell him to come in," I said.

Earle came into the kitchen, chewing gum. The rhythmic motion of his jaws concealed all emotion. There were pimples on his adolescent face. His figure showed nothing that might connect him with high romance.

"You want to go down to the beach tonight?" I asked.

"Yup," said Earle. "Mrs. Wright, she hasn't paid me. She owes me fourteen dollars."

"Well, here's a dollar," I said.

"Thanks a lot," said Earle, and left us.

"Earle is a nice boy," said Josie, "really a nice clean boy. His father's on the WPA. It makes Earle so sensitive. His teacher says Earle has a great future. The Caraways are such lovely people, and he's so fond of you, Mr. Calder. He says you're a lovely man. It does seem, doesn't it, that everybody has his troubles?"

"That's right," I said, "everybody has troubles."

"They just expect Frieda and me to do everything," Josie said. "Miss Bella wants Frieda to wash all her underthings. They just expect to be waited on all the time, no matter how many people they have coming, and all the drinking and all the glasses, and they all put cigarette butts in their coffee cups, Mr. Calder. They're so careless that they don't seem to think of anything. If it wasn't for dear Mrs. Wright—if it wasn't for all these dear children of mine—"

"Never mind," I said, "Frieda will get married and be off your hands."

"It was so different when I came here first," said Josie, "when Miss Sarah was alive."

"Not much different," I said.

I leaned back in the kitchen chair and watched the flies buzzing about the sink. The kettle on the stove simmered. Life was going on at Wickford Point, moving slowly in the summer heat, a strange, unworldly life. It seemed to have no end and no beginning. Nothing was ever right and nothing was ever wrong. I did not consider speaking to Cousin Clothilde, because it would have done no good. I had made a definite financial arrangement and had paid her my expenses.

"Mrs. Wright will have some money on the first of the month," I said.

"Dear Mrs. Wright has so many worries," Josie said. "She's worried about Miss Bella. That Mr. Stackton who was down here, and then that Mr. Berg."

"Well, they've gone," I said.

"Dear Mrs. Wright," said Josie, "she keeps fretting about Miss Bella. It does seem too bad what with all her chances. They've all had so many chances."

"Yes," I said, "we've all had a lot of chances."

"Now it does seem to me," said Josie, "that if any of them

would do any work—there's lots of things folks could do around here, Mr. Calder. When the armchair in the front room began r get shaky, they could have glued it. I told Mr. Sidney myself that he ought to have got some glue, but they just waited until it broke to pieces, Mr. Calder. And then there's the front door. If someone was handy here, they could have fixed it, and now it's jammed so it won't open, and they just use the side door, Mr. Calder."

"It's the hinge on the front door, isn't it?" I asked. "Where is there a hammer and a screw driver? I'll fix it."

As I spoke, I knew that I was not going to fix it. I was comfortably sure that there would be some reason to prevent it.

"Earle was looking for the screw driver all day yesterday," Josie said, "and the hammer broke last winter, and those dear children scattered all the tools in the chest around the barn the summer before last. There ought to be a handy man on the place, Mr. Calder. It isn't for you to do such things. It's for a handy man." Josie rubbed her hands on her apron and sat down.

"Now I was telling dear Mrs. Wright," she said, "that they're laying off people in the shoe shop. I have a cousin who's a plumber."

"He couldn't fix the door," I said.

"He could try," said Josie. "He's the nicest man when he isn't drinking, Mr. Calder. He has lots of tools in his automobile. Now I think if you gave him a dollar he could come down and fix the door, and the toilet too—but dear Mrs. Wright, she says it isn't necessary."

I pushed back my chair from the kitchen table and walked to the window over the sink.

"Earle," I called. The gentle sound of the lawn mower ceased.

"Look in the back of my car," I said, "and get me a screw driver and a hammer and meet me by the front door."

"But you might make it worse, Mr. Calder," Josie said.

I did not answer. I already had a premonition that I would make it worse.

Outside, the heat from a blue summer sky had been partially

56

absorbed by the elms and the shrubbery, but the shade did not alleviate this heat; it simply changed its quality into a heavy greenish warmth of vegetable exhalation. The robins were chirping drowsily in the trees and the echo of the lawn mower still seemed to linger in that warm vacancy.

Earle appeared with the hammer and the screw driver, and it came over me that none of us had been taught to use our hands at Wickford Point. None of us were good at driving nails and we were rather proud of it.

"It's hot, ain't it?" Earle said.

"Yes," I said, "it is hot. Now, what's the matter with this door?"

"It just don't open," Earle said. "It seems like it's sort of sagged down."

The paint was peeling from the panels of the heavy front door. Trumpet vines were twined over it, and bees were buzzing dully. I lifted the latch and pushed against it, but it did not move. I examined the heavy hand-beaten hinges which were deeply encrusted with paint. It seemed necessary to get the door off the hinges, but there seemed no proper way to do it, and no way to begin.

"Something must have give somewhere, don't you think?" Earle said.

I jammed the screw driver tentatively at the paint above the hinges.

"Those ain't screwed on," Earle said. "It looks like they're riveted. A screw driver won't do any good, Mr. Calder."

I threw my weight against the door and it gave.

"There isn't anything wrong with it," I said. "Something's stuck in it." And I was right. I walked through the side door and into the front entry. There was a mass of paper wedged into the jamb near the threshold. By working the door back and forth, Earle and I scraped the paper out, and then the door opened and shut easily enough.

"Funny someone shouldn't have noticed that," said Earle. "Looks like a letter, don't it? Someone must have dropped it."

"You can put the tools back in my car now," I said.

When Earle went away I stood in the entry smoothing the paper in my hand. It had been crushed so that it was almost indecipherable. Judging from the few words I could read, it had belonged to Bella, and Bella appeared just as I was reading it. She was dressed in slacks, a striped jersey, and sandals, and she was yawning. She had not bothered to brush her short black hair or to put on lipstick, and she looked pale and sleepy.

"What are you doing, darling?" Bella said.

"I've been fixing the door," I said. "One of your letters got jammed in it."

"What letter?" Bella asked.

"It looks like a letter from your friend Berg," I said.

"You can give it to me," said Bella, and she snatched it out of my hand.

"Every time you walk across the room you drop something," I said. "If it isn't a letter it's a compact, and if it isn't a compact it's a dollar bill, and if it isn't a dollar bill it's a ring."

"I'm looking for a cigarette," said Bella. "Haven't you a cigarette?"

"No," I said, "I gave them to your mother."

"She's finished them all," said Bella. "I was in her room this morning, and then I went into Sid's."

"He's not smoking," I said. "His stomach's troubling him."

"I know," said Bella. "It goes in cycles. First it's his feet, and then it's his stomach. I didn't go there to get cigarettes. I looked through his pockets. He's used up all the money. I'd have looked through yours, but you always get up too early. Somebody's got to go down to the bank. Are you going downtown?"

"I don't know what I'm going to do," I said, "but anyway I fixed the door."

"I suppose you're going to do something," said Bella. "You always do something. I suppose you're going to read. I've got to get away from this, darling. It's getting on my nerves. Are you going away anywhere?"

I had never liked to discuss my plans with any of my relatives. It always provoked argument when any of us announced too definitely what we were going to do. It was easier to move quietly and suddenly.

"What makes you think I'm going anywhere?" I asked.

"Your bag was out in your room," Bella said. "The door was open and I saw it when I came downstairs."

"Well," I said, "I'm going to New York tonight."

"Why, darling," said Bella, "why should you be going to New York?"

"Business," I said. "George Stanhope wants to see me about that story I'm finishing. They want some changes."

"Oh," said Bella, "is that all?"

"Yes," I said, "of course that's all."

Bella put her head to one side in a shrewd and pretty way.

"It couldn't be that Pat Leighton has been calling you again?" she said. "I wouldn't like to have to pay her telephone bill."

"Listen, honey bee—" I began, but I did not have a chance to finish.

The telephone in the small parlor rang. Bella's face brightened. That sound from an outer world seemed to go through her like a healing electric shock. Small bright lights appeared in her violet eyes. The lazy droop left her lips. The ring of the telephone made her alert and charming. She was Bella Brill again, that amusing gay girl who was different, one of those remarkable talented Brills. She was the Bella Brill who could be the life of the party. Her sandals clattered as she darted out into the entry.

"I'll answer it," she said.

I myself could feel the stimulating effect of that ugly tinkling bell. It was not ringing with the mechanical pulse beats of a city telephone but with the long vicious rings translated by the frustrated finger of some girl at the local switchboard. It was a summons from the saner, outer world that was too busy to permit the overdevelopment of personal eccentricity. Over the lines the world was calling Wickford Point—the world which had exploited me in the journalistic trade, the world which had pushed me into France and had blown me out of the front-line trenches and had rubbed my nose in London, Paris and Berlin, and in Beirut and Peking. The same world was calling which had nearly cleaned me out in the crash of '29 and which was now taxing my earnings to give me a more abundant life. Everything you learned in it turned out to be wrong. It was as baffling and as fascinating as when I had seen it first.

Bella, skipping to the telephone, was arranging her exterior to meet it. She was now the intellectual, epigrammatic Bella Brill, the granddaughter of old John Brill, the homespun sage and poet of transcendentalist New England. I myself was changing, because the call might be for me. I was casting aside the minutiae of Wickford Point; I was becoming Jim Calder, who knew his way around. . . . It was an out-of-town call, judging from the insistence of the bell. It might be my agent in New York to converse about that story. It might be someone else asking me somewhere.

The wooden shutters of the small parlor were still drawn, making the small square room brown and dusky. I had an impression of the whatnot in the corner with the sea shells on it, of the braided rug on the green pine floor, of my great-grandfather's portrait, and of my great-grandmother's portrait over the coal grate, and of the Hogarth print which someone had found in the attic, and of the water color of the river which Cousin Clothilde's mother had done after she came back from Brook Farm, and of the broken Chippendale chair, and of the whole one. I was aware of all these things without really seeing them, just as I was sometimes aware of their presence in the dark. Bella was picking the telephone off the little table and was slouching down into the nearest Windsor chair.

"Hello," Bella was saying, "hello."

Her voice was no longer careless—it had a modulated allure; it gave a gay and provocative invitation; it told of a girl who was expecting something nice and was ready to try anything once. It was the voice which had taken away at least two of her sister Mary's boy friends.

"Hello," Bella said, and then something made her tone grow hard and her thin shoulders stiffen beneath her striped jersey. "What are you doing? What do you want? Excuse *me*." She was being elaborately polite. "But I do sometimes answer the telephone. It's my house as much as his. Yes, he's right here in the room. For heaven's sake stop being formal!"

Bella set down the receiver and got out of the Windsor chair. Her lips were drawn into a thin grimace which was more of a grin than a smile. Those bony shoulders of hers, her whole delicate body, were stiff and taut.

"It's Joe," she said. "He wants to speak to you."

"All right," I said. "That's what you get for running to the telephone."

The grimace about Bella's lips changed to a Mona Lisa smile, an expression with which I was familiar. It was a look of hauteur. She was no longer a play girl, but an aristocrat.

"You might tell Joe that he needn't call up here," she said. "There's such a thing as a sense of decency, when people are divorced."

"He didn't want you," I said, "he wanted me."

"Oh," said Bella, "you think so, do you? You might at least be loyal to your own family."

"Go out and get your coffee," I said. "He can call me up any time he wants."

"It's what I might expect from you," said Bella, "and you're not such a saint either. I know plenty about you. How would you like it if Pat—"

"Shut up," I said.

Bella laughed, a thin, provoking laugh.

"Everybody knows," she began, and stopped. I turned away toward the telephone and I could hear her running out of the room. I could hear her footsteps on the stairs in cautious haste. Bella would be going to the extension in the upper hall.

"Hello," I said, "hello, Joe."

Joe's voice was loud and amused.

"Hello, Jim," said Joe. "What the hell are you doing in that lunatic asylum? Are you in the psychopathic ward?"

I was pleased with his question because Bella was undoubtedly listening by that time. In fact I had already heard the receiver being gently lifted off the hook.

"I'm taking a rest," I said.

"Oh," said Joe. "Just sitting on your fanny, thinking? Is Sid there? Is he thinking too? You haven't any right to think. You're not a Brill."

Joe was bitter. I wished that he would not be so bitter, but I did not blame him much.

"Where are you, Joe?" I asked. I hoped he wasn't far away. It did me good, as it always did, to hear his voice. He said he was in Boston on his way to Vermont. He was going to speak at the Hilsop Literary Conference. He didn't know why he was going but his publishers had fixed it. Sam Maxwell had asked him as a personal favor. Sam was in charge of part of the program. Everything was going fine. They had sold a hundred and fifty thousand copies of his new novel, not counting the Book-of-the-Month Club. He couldn't very well go back on Sam. It was hot as hell in Boston and he was stopping at the Crofton. Sam was paying the expenses. They had given him a room full of fake Italian furniture with a Renaissance fireplace that looked like a funnel. He had been on the wagon for two months and he was going to stop right now. Why didn't I come down and we could have dinner? I told him that I would. Then he asked how Bella was, and I told her she was fine and something made him laugh.

When I set down the telephone I had a feeling that I had been away, although I could not define where I had been, but at any rate it was a long way from Wickford Point. Joe had never understood the place, or if he had he was not tied up with it. He was as sensitive as I was, probably more sensitive, but there were no cobwebs of the past about him.

By the time I had walked from the parlor to the dining room,

Sid had come down to breakfast. He was sitting hunched over the table in his shirt sleeves, stirring his coffee very carefully, watching the eddies that followed his spoon. Occasionally he would lift it up and allow drops to fall from it very gradually, one by one, back into the cup. I knew what he was doing; it was an exercise which he had contrived to test the steadiness of his hand. He had prided himself on his manual dexterity from the time he had decided to be a chemist, some years before, and now he was in the land of make-believe, thinking of someone like Alexis Carrel. He had not yet tied his necktie and the two ends dangled dreamily over the front of his white shirt.

"Good morning, Jim," said Sid. His voice was resonant, almost pontifical, a mannerism which he had developed lately. "Have you ever noticed the varying surface tension of coffee?" It made an erudite and interesting remark. Sid was always interesting.

"Did you ever think," said Sid, "that it would be quite possible to tell whether coffee is properly boiled or not simply by watching it drip from a spoon? It would not be necessary to taste it. I think this coffee has been boiled too long."

"It's been on the back of the stove for four hours," I said.

"I can tell it," agreed Sid, "by watching it drop from the spoon."

I sat down. That Confucian contemplation of Sid's was a part of Wickford Point, where almost any motion became significant.

"How's your stomach?" I asked.

Sid's face brightened.

"I lay in the sun on the beach all day yesterday," he said. "As long as I am perfectly still in the sun there doesn't seem to be any gas. It's only when I try to do some work."

"What are you working on?" I asked.

"I'm trying to gauge weights by touch," Sid said. "I've been trying for the last two weeks, picking up small objects and then checking my guess. I borrowed some of your socks this morning. Josie hasn't got around to the washing. Where's Bella?"

"Upstairs," I said. "Joe called up."

"He didn't call her up, did he?"

"No," I said. "He wanted me to have dinner with him at the

Crofton. Bella went upstairs to listen on the extension." Sid bent over his coffee spoon and uttered a single monosyllable.

"Bitch," he said, and then the dining-room door opened. Bella was with us again.

"What's that you said?" asked Bella.

"Never mind," said Sid. Bella sat down and put her elbows on the table and cupped her chin in the palms of her nervous hands.

"You called me a bitch," she said. "Jim's the only one on this place who can call me that." As she turned toward me there was an almost affectionate look in her narrow, violet eyes.

"And now," said Bella, "I'm about through with this. I've sat around long enough seeing you dribble coffee, Sid, and hearing about your bellyaches. You think you're a genius, don't you? Well, all it is is you're just too damned lazy to move. What did you do with that ten dollars you borrowed from Mary?" Sid shrugged his shoulders slightly and looked up from his coffee cup.

"Oh hell," said Bella, "what's the use? I'm going to get out of here. I'm going to spend the night at the Jaeckels'. Jim's driving into Boston. You'll drop me off, won't you, darling?"

"Yes," I said, "I'll drop you off."

"In the ocean," said Sid, "with a stone around your neck."

Bella looked at Sid and looked away.

"Darling," she said to me, "Clothilde wants to see you upstairs." She patted my hand gently. I knew why she called me "darling," because she wanted a ride halfway to town, and then there was probably something about Joe. She would want to ask me all about him.

A hard intentness altered Bella's glance from affection to efficiency, and I followed the direction of those violet eyes, which could change as rapidly as the surface of a hurrying brook. Bella was looking back toward her brother. Sid was holding a folded ten-dollar bill between his first and second fingers.

"So you've still got Mary's ten dollars," Bella said. "It wasn't in your trousers this morning."

"You have a small mind," said Sid. "If you're going to the

64

Jaeckels' you'll need to tip the servants. Take it." Bella's face softened.

"Thanks," she said, "ever so much, Sid darling. Don't you want me to get you some toast? Don't you want anything besides coffee?"

Then the telephone rang again.

"I'll go," said Bella, and she skipped away like a dancer—and she was a pretty dancer.

"Waiting for someone to call her up, isn't she?" said Sid. When she called me I knew she must have been, because I was not her darling any longer.

"That's for you," Bella said. "Why can't you take your own telephone calls? I have to spend all my time here doing things for everybody."

"Who is it?" I asked her.

"For God's sake," said Bella, "do you think I'm your private secretary? I don't know who he is. He's got a pansy voice." At first I could not imagine who it was, and then I knew that it was Allen Southby calling. His voice was crisp and businesslike, indicating that he was having a busy morning.

"Jim," he said, "I want to see you."

"That's fine," I said. "I'd like to see you, Allen."

"I mean right away," said Allen, "I mean tonight. I'm in a sort of jam."

His gay laugh, when I asked what sort, indicated that he was not really in a jam, that he was simply playfully using the vernacular.

"I mean," said Allen, "a purely literary jam."

"Oh," I said, "you couldn't be, Allen."

"It's about that novel, Jim," he said. "It's just that I've come to a point in it where I need someone who can listen. How does it happen that you've been holding out on me?"

"What are you talking about?" I asked.

Allen's answer was playful and very, very friendly, just the gentle chiding of a dear old friend who knows that his own dear old friend is sometimes up to games.

"You never told me," Allen said, "that you had any important New England connection until the other evening. Can you come down tonight?" There was an annoying, breezy implication in his question. He was saying that he knew that I would be flattered to come. He had that egotistical conviction common to some people in the throes of composition, that what he was doing was a matter of such vital importance that anybody would drop anything to be present at the birth of his ideas.

"I can't very well," I said. "I'm seeing Joe Stowe tonight."

"Joe Stowe!" Allen called back. "Why didn't he let me know he was here, I wonder. He always lets me know. Why, I could have put him up for the night. Where's he stopping? You just leave it to me, I'll get in touch with Joe."

Of all the arts I suppose that writing is the one which develops the lowest attributes, in that its very pursuit magnifies all the human failings. It encourages introversion, neurasthenia, insomnia, irritability and all forms of self-indulgence. It encourages a sensitiveness which makes one open to any sort of slight. It begets a type of personal inflation, for it is nearly impossible to continue without the consciousness of a definite gift of genius. It may be that one is misunderstood by editors, perhaps because one is too far advanced to be comprehended by the simple moron mind. It may be that this hidden gift still lies fallow, but there must be an inner conviction of its presence. It is what enables an author to walk airily among his colleagues and to dispense and to receive the bitter little condescensions of the trade. There is a jealousy in the writing profession which is peculiarly its own. Although I knew that I was jealous, I did not like to think that Allen Southby could get under my skin, because, of course, I knew in my own mind that he was my intellectual inferior. I wished to view him with detachment and the fact that he always succeeded in shaking that detachment was peculiarly unsettling.

"Who was it?" Bella asked.

"Allen Southby," I said. "You don't know him."

"He wrote a book, didn't he?"

"Yes," I said, "he wrote a book."

66

"I remember," said Bella, "it was recommended in the *Junior League Magazine*. Is he attractive?"

"Just as nice as he can be," I said. "He's living in Cambridge with his sister."

"Oh," said Bella. "Has he got some sort of a complex?"

"What good does it do to try to find out something about everybody?" I asked her. "It only gets you into mischief. Never mind about Southby."

Bella smiled. A dimple deepened in her left cheek and her eyes grew innocently wide.

"You just don't want me to meet him, because you know I'd like him," she said, "and he must have written a really good book because you're jealous. I'm going to read it. Clothilde wants to see you. I'll get Frieda to wash some stockings for me and press some things. Let me know when you're starting out."

VII | Age Cannot Wither Her, nor Custom Stale . . .

Cousin Clothilde slept in the long room which overlooked the river. From her window you could see where the channel curved past the point with its white pines, and you could see the white houses far across on the opposite bank. The river had a deep rich hue under the clear sky, and the spar buoys were bent upstream by the incoming tide. Cousin Clothilde was sitting up in a maple field-bed decorated by ancient, moth-eaten curtains. The room had been swept out and all the little odds and ends had been removed from the bureau and mantel, so that it looked white and bare and cool. It was almost like one of those rooms with a cord across the doorway which you might see in an old house opened to the public. It was like the room where Lafayette had slept or Washington's mother had died, and the furniture might have been contributed later by the Colonial Dames of America—not very good furniture, just odds and ends so that the room would not look entirely empty. Cousin Clothilde's brush and comb were on a low table before a blackened pier glass. There were a number of cigarette butts in the fireplace, three ginger ale bottles and some glasses on the hearth, and Cousin Clothilde was in a purple kimono which Bella's friend, Mr. Berg, had given her—it was not in good taste, as a gift or as a kimono.

"Darling," said Cousin Clothilde, "have you a cigarette?"

"I gave you all mine last night," I said.

Cousin Clothilde sighed.

"Everybody always takes my cigarettes," she said. "I don't know why none of my children can take the responsibility of having some in the house. Look in my upper bureau drawer, there may be some in there."

Cousin Clothilde's upper bureau drawer was mostly filled with stockings which did not match. There were also two broken Navajo brooches, one of my great-aunt Sarah's knitting needles, a yellow piece of Chinese ivory, a half-empty bottle of nail polish and a depilatory preparation, but there were no cigarettes.

"There used to be some there," said Cousin Clothilde. "I wonder if that girl of Josie's steals things. She might have stolen them."

This was the simplest explanation when articles were mislaid at Wickford Point, from the days of Aunt Sarah onward. Wickford Point always seemed to be surrounded by marauders and petty pilferers, obsessed by a particular desire to abscond with tooth paste, bits of soap and other toilet articles, or thimbles, needles and thread. Aunt Sarah also used to blame disappearances on the crows, for she had known a tame crow once that was always taking spoons out of the kitchen and hiding them under the shingles of the woodshed roof.

"Frieda is getting above herself," Cousin Clothilde said. "Bella lets her get too familiar. They're in the laundry too much together pressing clothes."

I sat down on the foot of the bed and looked out of the window toward the river. Cousin Clothilde liked to go over the general situation bit by bit without too much interruption. She sat quietly propped up in the four-post bed and gathered news of Wickford Point from all its diverging radii, like a general sifting information about the enemy.

"That child of Josie's—" Cousin Clothilde said. "There always seems to be one more. I don't think it's fair to any of the rest of us if Josie has any more children. That little Herman came

naked into the parlor yesterday. It was all right because it amused
Sid, and yesterday the cat had kittens in the china cupboard. I
suppose we shall have to drown them, but I want to keep them
long enough so we can see them frisk about. Sid loves kittens.
The front door is stuck. I think it's because the house has begun
to settle."

"I fixed it," I said. "A letter of Bella's got mixed up in it, one
from Mr. Berg."

"I wish Bella wouldn't drop everything everywhere," said
Cousin Clothilde. "Do you know I think her hair is beginning
to fall out? Everywhere I go I seem to see Bella's hair, and I
stepped on her lipstick yesterday. I thought Mr. Berg was delightful, didn't you?"

"No, I didn't," I said.

"Darling," said Cousin Clothilde, "you're always so hard on
people. You'd be so much happier if you saw the nice sides of
them and not the horrid sides. I thought Mr. Berg was charming.
He's in business, you know." Cousin Clothilde sighed. "It's nice
that Bella is getting interested in a business man for a change.
What we need is some money in the family and a little peasant
blood."

"How can he be hanging around here for a week," I asked,
"if he has any business?"

"Darling," said Cousin Clothilde, "it doesn't do any good to be
so suspicious. You're able to hang around, aren't you? Then
why shouldn't Mr. Berg? And probably Mr. Roosevelt is doing
something to his business. You can't tell about those things."

"I can tell about Berg," I said. "He's just one of those people
who appear, and Bella attracts them. All she has to do is to go
out on the street and whistle and along comes a Berg." Cousin
Clothilde had partially lost interest. She glanced out the window
toward the river.

"Once I made a water-color sketch of the river from here,"
she said. "What are you getting up for? Do sit down and don't
fidget. There are so many things I want to talk to you about,

70

darling. Bella doesn't whistle to people. It isn't fair to say that about Bella."

"Then she shakes herself," I said. "She does something."

"Well, it's nice she can attract men," said Cousin Clothilde. "It's always much nicer when there are men around. Everyone is much happier, much less nervous. I wish Mary could attract men. It would make things so much easier. I wish you wouldn't be so hard on President Roosevelt, dear."

"President Roosevelt?" I said. "I haven't been hard on President Roosevelt."

"Perhaps you haven't yet," said Cousin Clothilde, "but you were going to be. I should have voted for him if I had remembered to register. I never can remember to go to that place where you have to read something out loud. I know he will look out for me. I can see it from his face."

"He'll look out for you," I said.

"Well," said Cousin Clothilde, "someone has to. I'm just about tired of looking out for everybody. First it's Sidney and then it's Bella and then it's Mary—they all keep getting into my pocket-book—and then Josie is always after me for things."

"What sort of things?" I asked.

"All sorts of things," said Cousin Clothilde. She sat in her bed, looking very young with her two heavy black braids, only faintly gray, falling over her purple kimono. "Josie doesn't seem to keep anything in her head. First we're out of soap and then we're out of toilet paper, and there isn't anything to eat except a few things that Earle pulls out of the garden, and there isn't any gin. I wonder if Frieda steals the gin, or it might be Earle who takes it. I really thought he was quite unsteady the other day. Or it might be that man who comes selling cakes and cookies. I saw him in the kitchen talking to Frieda. He didn't even have the manners to get up when I came in."

"I knew of a plumber once," I said, "who stole a quart of whisky."

Cousin Clothilde sighed.

"The point is," she said, "I simply cannot go on looking after everyone. I'm not as young as I used to be. It isn't decent to have an old lady looking after a lot of grown-up children who ought to be looking after her. Now I don't mind Sid. Sid is always so restful. Do you know what Sid is doing? He's thinking of a system of playing the stock market, and do you know what Sid said? He said that if I had only let him have three hundred dollars to buy some shares in a stock called Ginsberg Chemical—"

"Ginsberg Chemical?" I said. "There isn't any such thing as Ginsberg Chemical."

"You probably haven't seen it," said Cousin Clothilde, "and the name really doesn't make any difference anyway. It was just some company that made something. I think Sid said that they made it out of sawdust, but it doesn't make a bit of difference. Sid said if I had only put three hundred dollars into this company, it would be worth twenty thousand dollars now or even more. Sid knows all about it, and I wish that Archie had the sense that Sid has."

I found myself growing mildly interested. In fact it was always interesting listening to Cousin Clothilde. Nearly every day she could weave a pattern with words, much as the less gifted Penelope had woven her fabrics by day to destroy them again by night.

"Where's Archie?" I asked. Cousin Clothilde reached under a pillow and drew out two letters.

"He's in Detroit," she said. "He's motoring with the Willoughbys. The Willoughbys know someone who knows Edsel Ford, and they think that Edsel Ford may want a mural."

"How do they know he wants a mural?" I asked.

"People like that," said Cousin Clothilde, "always want murals. You only have to make them feel they want them. Archie thinks that if he can only meet Edsel Ford, he can make Edsel Ford feel that he wants a mural."

"What sort of mural?" I asked.

"Any sort of a mural that Mr. Ford wants," said Cousin

72

Clothilde. "How should I know what sort of a mural he wants? But he must have a great many factory buildings. Archie can think of something."

"But Archie doesn't like machines," I said, "and the last time I saw him he said he was a Communist. He was going out to picket somewhere."

Cousin Clothilde folded the letter and put it back in the envelope.

"It doesn't make any difference whether you're a Communist or not," she said. "A Communist could do a perfectly good mural for Mr. Ford. Besides there was a Mexican Communist who did a mural for Radio City—that man who does things about soldiers stepping on nude people. What is his name? He was really charming."

"Well, they took his mural down," I said.

"Well," said Cousin Clothilde, "suppose they did. Mr. Ford can take Archie's mural down, can't he? Just as long as Archie does the mural."

"That's true," I said, "I hadn't thought of that." Cousin Clothilde opened her second letter.

"Sometime," she said, "I'll have to go back to the oculist. I keep having to squint my eyes to read, and my circulation isn't right. My hands are cold in the morning. I never could read Harry's writing." I was interested again. Harry Brill was my second cousin and her eldest son.

"What does Harry say?" I asked.

"He's coming up at the end of the week," she said. "He's motoring up from New York with Mirabel Steiner."

"What is he doing that for?" I asked. "Harry doesn't like Steiner."

"He's coming in her car," said Cousin Clothilde. "It probably is saving him a good deal, because he hasn't asked me for any money, and Mirabel Steiner loves it here, and she is so interested in everything. She's dreadfully interested in you. She said she would like to analyze you."

"Now look here," I said, "I told you—"

"Darling," said Cousin Clothilde, "she won't be here long. Harry will have to get back. He's very busy about something. And besides he's going to Easthampton next week end. You won't really have to talk to Mirabel. You can just sort of keep going away." Cousin Clothilde held the letter at arm's length and squinted at it.

"I hadn't seen this part," she added. "His bridgework has broken down."

"What bridgework?" I asked.

"Harry's bridgework," said Cousin Clothilde. "Don't you remember when he did that dance on the Yacht Club float at the Mayhews' costume party? He was dressed as a Greek in one of those ballet dresses. He slipped and loosened three front teeth, and now his bridgework has broken down. He went to that dentist, you know, that good-for-nothing one that I used to like so much. Dr. Jess had to take every bit of his inlay out of my mouth. I don't see why you don't go to Dr. Jess, darling. His specialty is massaging gums."

A bit of summer breeze came through the open window, hot and moist and redolent with the smell of fresh cut grass. It was like a breath of sanity, for I was being involved in the intricacies of Wickford Point again, where every small thing was of importance and where the mind wandered languidly to this and that with a strange midsummer's madness. We had touched on nearly all the family and now we had come to the dentists. The Brills all had trouble with their teeth. They were rather proud of it because it was a family trait.

"I shouldn't worry about Dr. Jess," I said. Cousin Clothilde folded her letter.

"The only point is that Harry's bridgework will have to be fixed. It's going to cost over two hundred dollars. I suppose Harry and Mirabel will bring up some other people too. I hope they do—the girls will like it."

"Well," I said, "I'd better be going."

"Why do you have to be going?" said Cousin Clothilde. "I

haven't even begun to talk to you. You're always running away somewhere. Didn't I hear the telephone ringing this morning? I suppose it was for Bella."

"That was for me," I said. "Joe Stowe rang me up—from Boston."

The delicate arch of Cousin Clothilde's eyebrows moved.

"Does Bella know it?" she asked. I nodded and the room was still for a minute, so still that I could hear a church bell ringing across the river. "She's going over to the Jaeckels'," I said. "I'm going to see Joe. He's in Boston at the Crofton."

Cousin Clothilde was motionless. She was looking at me hard. In spite of the wrinkles at the corners, her eyes were beautiful, the same violet as Bella's but lighter, softer. I knew what Hugh Brill had seen in them when he first rowed over from the Brill place, now a national shrine, across the river. I knew what Archie Wright had seen in them. He had tried to paint them often enough. I knew what Manet had seen in them at the time she had known him in Paris.

"Give Joe my love," she said.

"It might have worked," I told her, "if you hadn't—" I paused because there was no use going into details which she had never understood.

"Darling," said Cousin Clothilde, "I didn't do anything. I know you loved him, but it was all a mistake. It was the war and this and that. Give Joe my love. I wonder why it is I have so many white spots on my fingernails. There must be something wrong with my circulation. I wish you'd look at them, Jim."

She put her hand on mine so that I could see her fingers, and then again her thoughts drifted away and she began to laugh.

"What's the matter?" I asked.

"I was thinking about their wedding," she said. "Darling, do you remember how Archie got tangled up with the cat and fell down the entry stairs, right into that strange Negro who came from the bootlegger, the one who was carrying the tray of champagne?"

"Yes," I said, and I laughed too. I nearly always laughed when

75

she did. "And I remember how the tailor burned the back of Harry's trousers when he took them off to have them pressed. He was having it done in the shop right near the church downtown. Do you remember that?"

"Yes," said Cousin Clothilde, "so he couldn't go at all. He had to borrow a raincoat. I wonder if he ever returned it."

There was another silence and I could hear the church bell again, ringing across the river. The sound made me think that nothing which had ever happened at Wickford Point ever entirely left it, and that parts of everything which had happened were always waiting—ready to move forward out of nowhere when they were least expected. I was sitting on the edge of Cousin Clothilde's bed but the bell had brought my thoughts away to the abstractions of marriage and divorce. I was thinking that one could never tell in advance, no matter with what experience, whether any two individuals would achieve a successful or an unsuccessful marriage. There was too much hidden in every character, too many doubts, too many hesitations.

Then, while I was still thinking, Bella Brill's voice came to me out of the air around me, full of all those hesitations and those doubts. I was back for just a moment to the morning of that wedding day, suffering from the ghost of an old headache. I remembered how Bella had come into my room. She must have come while I was still asleep, for the first sounds that I had heard were thumping noises in the rooms below me, made by Mr. Morrissey arranging furniture for the wedding breakfast. When I opened my eyes my head began to ache and I saw Bella standing looking at me, wrapped in the Chinese robe which I had given her. It had been a good many years ago, but I could remember exactly how she looked then—dark-eyed and pale, half-frightened and half-elated.

"Jim," she said, "you've got to get up. Where were you last night?"

"Downtown at the hotel with Joe," I said. "I've got a headache, but don't worry about Joe. He'll be all right."

76

"I don't see why Joe should drink so much," Bella said, "just the night before he's getting married."

"It's just a custom," I told her. "The whole thing is custom."

"Well, you needn't have all got yourselves drunk," Bella said. "You have to get dressed right away, darling, and do something."

"Do what?" I asked.

"Everything," said Bella, "and I can't stand it if you ask me questions. They've all begun to come."

"Who?" I asked.

"Cousin Harriet's just come in a taxi from the station," Bella said, "and that bootlegger that Harry found is downstairs waiting for a check. And Archie won't get off the sofa."

My head ached worse when I sat up.

"What sofa?" I asked.

"Down in the parlor," Bella said. "He went to sleep there last night. He won't get up and Cousin Harriet doesn't understand it, and Sid is still asleep and Josie hasn't finished with my dress."

I reached for my dressing gown.

"What time is it?" I asked.

"Darling," said Bella, "it's eleven o'clock, and funnily enough I'm going to be married downtown at twelve, and do you know what they're asking? They're asking if I'm sure I want to marry him."

"Well, why aren't you dressed?" I asked.

Bella raised her clenched hands in a hopeless gesture.

"How can I get dressed if they haven't got my dress ready?" she cried. "And how can I tell if Joe's ready? How can I tell anything?"

"It's all right," I said. "You've got plenty of time. You do want to marry him, don't you?"

Bella raised her hands again.

"How many times," she asked, "do I have to say I do? Of course I want to marry him. I want to do anything to get out of here. Jim darling, everyone is downstairs."

"All right," I said, "all right."

"Jim!" Her voice was louder.

77

"Yes," I said.

"I've come to say good-by."

"Now don't be silly, Belle," I said. "You're not saying good-by to me at all."

"Well," said Bella, "it just seems that way. Everybody's making such a damn fuss."

"Don't worry, Belle," I said. "It's going to be all right. You couldn't find anyone better than Joe."

"Miss Bella," Josie was calling from the hall, "your dress is all ironed now, and it's just the dearest dress, and it's all taken in on the hips. Have you got something borrowed and something blue?"

I put my hand on her shoulder.

"Don't worry, Belle," I said again. "It's going to be all right."

My mind moved over the scene, slowly and a little sadly, because I had been sure it would be all right once she went away with Joe.

There was one good thing about the family: at the last moment we all could pull ourselves together and behave quite well. We all got through the wedding and everyone made that trite remark that Bella was such a pretty bride. I could have gone on thinking about it further because Cousin Clothilde must have been thinking about it too, while her hand still rested on mine.

"Weddings are such queer things," she said. "It would be much better if people didn't make such a fuss about them."

"It would have been all right," I said, "if you had left them alone. No one would leave them alone."

Cousin Clothilde drew her hand away and Bella's wedding seemed to move away with it. The wedding had become one of those incidents again to be put away carefully and forgotten like old clothes which are not worn out enough to give away and yet which are too old to continue wearing.

"No," said Cousin Clothilde, "nothing could have helped it, dear. He was really perfectly impossible."

I began to speak but she stopped me.

"Impossible for Bella, I mean. Don't be hard on Bella when you think of it. I do wish she would marry someone else."

We were interrupted before I could answer. There were always sudden interruptions at Wickford Point which confused logical trains of thought.

The door of Cousin Clothilde's room opened. It was her daughter Mary. Mary Brill was in a gingham dress; she had a towel around her head, and she was holding three silk stockings and a brassière.

"What will I do with these?" Mary asked. Cousin Clothilde sat up straighter.

"How should I know what to do with them, dear?" she said. "Do I have to tell everyone what to do with everything? Can't I rest here quietly in the morning without having everyone in the house come up and ask me questions? Whose are they?"

"I don't know whose they are," Mary said. "I found them in the laundry."

"Well, why didn't you leave them in the laundry?" said Cousin Clothilde. "What did you bring them in here for? Get them out of here, dear. I don't want to look at them."

"No one ever wants to look at me," said Mary.

This was a remark which Mary often made in the bosom of the family, but she must have known it was not true. A great many people enjoyed looking at her.

"It isn't you, dear," said Cousin Clothilde patiently, "it's just that I don't like to see a brassière in the morning, particularly if I don't know whose it is."

"No one ever helps me about anything," said Mary. Her face seemed to break into triangles and circles. She began to cry and left the room.

"Now there," said Cousin Clothilde, "now what did I say that should have made her cry? I was perfectly sweet with her, wasn't I? I don't see that I said a single thing to disturb her. Of course I know why she's crying—it's because she doesn't attract men. Can't you show her how to attract men? I should think that you or Sid or Harry could show her. Can't you do anything about it?"

"No, I can't," I said, "and besides you're not really correct. Just don't keep turning her into a problem. When she's happy she attracts men enough—and better ones than Bella. You make her feel inadequate."

"Well, go out and talk to her," said Cousin Clothilde. "She'll only cry more if I do."

"It won't do any good," I said. "She only wants attention."

"Of course she wants attention," said Cousin Clothilde, "but she doesn't want it from me. Please go out and talk to her."

VIII | Mary, Mary

From the head of the stairs I could see Mary running down the side entry past the row of wooden pegs where our coats used to be hung and past the table where they used to keep the candles ready for bedtime. Before I could call after her she had slammed the door and was streaking across the lawn with the stockings and brassière billowing behind her. She ran through the old garden, past the asparagus bed and past the ice house. I was afraid that she was going to step into what had once been a row of cold frames, but she avoided them and ran into the empty hay barn.

The pastureland at Wickford Point had been sold thirty years before to Mr. Casey on the main road, who kept a milk route and sold manure. There had been no cattle at Wickford Point since that time, but it still smelt of cattle around the barns. There was an odor of stale hayseed, which was combined with all those other musty odors, the sort which a realistic writer who deals with nature and the soil loves to describe in unpicturesque detail. The shingles were rotting badly, allowing ribbons of dusty sunlight to come through the roof, so that the long wooden building was not dark. Mary was standing in the center of the floor between the empty lofts where the hay wagons had once stood and the shafts of sunlight fell upon her thick yellow hair. She whirled about when she heard my step.

"I wish you'd go away," she said. "Why can't anybody leave me alone?"

It was my observation, based upon a certain amount of experience, that most women were attractive when they wept; at least there was a sense of helplessness and an appeal to the protective instinct that made one want to do something about it. Mary, on the contrary, was not attractive, for when she cried, she cried without repression and without regard to the artistic decencies. The floodgates of her soul poured from her patient eyes and caused her cheeks to swell and redden until she looked more like a hay fever sufferer than a damsel in distress. I hesitated to come too near her in case she might weep upon my shoulder and infect me with some of her sodden hopelessness, and there was not much use in saying anything to her, although I could understand a good deal of what was passing in her mind.

I thought of how she looked when she laughed. At such times I liked her better than all the others. She had more of her mother's kindness than the rest of them.

"You ought not to do that," I said. "You look like hell when you cry, Mary."

Her answer had an irrefutable sort of logic. "Nobody cares how I look," she said.

She always reacted that way when she was with the family.

"Well, it doesn't do any good to pity yourself," I told her. "If you haven't a handkerchief, wipe your face on one of those stockings. Your mother didn't mean to hurt your feelings. You know you shouldn't jump at her with a lot of practical questions."

Mary rubbed a stocking across her broad, blunt nose.

"It doesn't do any good not to pity myself," she said.

"What do you mean by that?" I asked.

She did not know what she meant very clearly, but she stuck to the point. "I'm sick and tired of waiting on everybody," she said and wiped her nose. "Somebody's got to wash Clothilde's stockings sometime. Somebody's got to do something. Josie can't do everything."

82

We were repeating an age-old conversation which would lead nowhere.

"But nobody asks you to do anything," I said, as I tried to express a logical but useless fact. "Don't you see that everyone had much rather that you didn't *try* to do anything? It makes people nervous and then they get cross, and it makes you tired and then you cry. Nobody wants anything done around here. You ought to try to adjust yourself to it."

"I can't," said Mary, "when everything's all so mixed up." She broke into a fresh spasm of sobs. "Sid wouldn't even let me pick up his room. Do you know what Sid does?"

"No," I said. It was better when her mind was off herself. She rubbed another stocking, a flesh-colored one with a run in it, over her eyes.

"He doesn't use his bureau drawers," she said.

The remark was confusing and I asked her what she meant.

"He doesn't bother to put his clothes in them," she said. "He just leaves them all over the floor, all his clean ones and all his dirty ones, and most of his suits, all on the floor. He says it's easier to find them. When he wants a shirt or a pair of socks, he takes one of those old canes that were in the hall closet and he just pokes around until he finds it. He doesn't even bother to stoop down. He just hooks it up with the cane and puts it on. It isn't funny either."

"I didn't say it was," I said. "But why does it matter to you? You can't do anything about it."

Mary looked at the hayseed on the old barn floor. She kicked at it with the toe of a high-heeled slipper.

"You don't understand," she said. "Nobody understands. I just want to be happy."

"Oh, is that all you want?" I asked.

Mary looked sullen and she looked puzzled too.

"That isn't asking much, is it?" she inquired. "I have a right to be happy, haven't I? Hasn't everyone a right to be happy?"

There was no telling where she had gathered the idea, whether from some boy friend or from some loose snatches of an evening's talk, but it reminded me of a Fourth of July phrase—"the pursuit of happiness." Everyone had a right to the pursuit of happiness, and how hard we chased it now! My thoughts didn't make much sense.

"You can't be happy if you're thinking about it," I said. "You're only happy when your mind is on something else, Mary. Then occasionally happiness comes over you when you don't notice it. Even so, it only lasts for a few moments. I shouldn't let it worry me if I were you."

"That's the way you always talk," said Mary. "If you'd ever been happy you wouldn't talk that way."

"Well," I said, "don't let it worry you."

"But I've been trying to think of something else," Mary said. "I've been trying to do something for other people. That's what I was doing this morning."

"Well," I said, "it doesn't always work. I guess I'd better be going back now."

Mary stared up at the holes in the roof.

"Sid wouldn't let me fix his room," she said, "and he borrowed ten dollars, and now Bella's got it. Bella gets everything, and now she's going to the Jaeckels', and you're going to New York."

"Well," I said, "you're not missing much." Mary sniffed but she was feeling better.

"That's the way you always talk," she said. "Isn't there something I can do about myself? Can't you ever tell me something?"

I reached in my trousers pocket and drew out a ten-dollar bill.

"There," I said, "don't worry about yourself any more, and don't let anybody get this away from you."

As I watched her holding the currency, the effect was amazing. The sunlight in the barn was suddenly bright. The barnswallows darting through the open door made joyful hurrying sounds.

The sun fell on Mary's yellow hair. The tears on her cheeks had vanished. Her lips moved into a delicately happy curve, and she looked the way she did when all the boys in the room wanted to dance with her. She looked the way she did on the rare times when she made Bella jealous.

84

"Don't let anyone else know you have it," I said, "until you've spent it. And that means you'd better spend it quick." It was just as though she had never cried.

"I wonder if there's any gas in the car," she said. "There ought to be enough in it to get downtown. Did you hear that Harry is coming up from New York, and Mirabel Steiner? Maybe they'll bring some boys with them. Do you think so? Mirabel's wonderful. Don't you think she is? How long is Bella staying with the Jaeckels? They'll probably ask her to stay for the week end, don't you think?"

"Yes," I said, "probably."

"But you'll be back, won't you?" Mary called. "Be sure to be back. You mustn't stay away."

I had already made up my mind not to be back if I could possibly help it. I wanted to return to some other environment where the strange trivialities of living did not magnify themselves into matters of vital significance; where cigarettes and gin and groceries had a way of appearing without undue effort; where there was something to discuss besides peculiar personalities. In other words, the family and the place were getting, as they always did after a brief sojourn with them, distinctly on my nerves. I wanted to convince myself that what the family did and thought amounted to very little.

By the time I had reached the asparagus bed, Mary caught up with me. I was thinking that the asparagus bed had been planted a hundred and twenty-five years ago, which was too long for a bed to bear asparagus fit to eat. The whole thing should have been turned over and replanted, but then nothing was ever renewed at Wickford Point—paint or shingles or trees or flowers. The whole place was like a clock which was running down, an amazing sort of clock, now devoid of weights or springs or hands yet ticking on through some ancient impetus on its own momentum. Always when you thought it was going to stop, it would continue ticking.

"You're going to see Joe, aren't you?" Mary said. "I don't think you ought to."

"Don't you?" I asked. "Why not?"

Mary had assumed a virtuous expression and a bright sort of superiority that was a good deal worse than tears.

"Of course I don't believe in taking sides," Mary said, "and I don't really feel angry with Joe, but it's just a matter of the family. Of course he's entirely lost his position now."

"What?" I said.

"His position," said Mary, "with everyone who matters. Of course everyone understands it was all his fault. He had his chance and he lost it. He won't get any help from the Brill name any more—and he would come back any minute if Bella would let him. She has only to crook her finger."

She was entirely serious about it. She was simply stating an accepted fact.

"Do you really mean," I asked, "that you think the Brill name means anything? Do you think that anybody remembers—"

Her laugh stopped me. It was an airy, collected laugh.

"Of course you're not a Brill," she said, "but lots of people think you are a Brill. That's why you go everywhere; that's why you know everyone, just the way we do. Harry says so, so does Sid. It doesn't matter whether we have any money or anything, because we're important."

I did not continue the subject with her, because I did not want to make her cry.

"You had better go and wash your face," I said. "Even the Brills wash their faces sometimes."

Mary laughed again, that same light, airy laugh which implied a favorable difference from less privileged human beings. Mary was no longer suffering from melancholia; she was now Miss Brill, the eldest daughter of that interesting family steeped in the best literary tradition, the granddaughter of John Brill, whose works were now out of print, but who in some odd manner had succeeded in elbowing himself into a place among the gods and half-gods of the Emersonian tradition. Mary had never seen him —but now she was Miss Brill. Mary had not read his works, but they were the keystone in her arch, and perhaps it was better to let it go at that.

I walked over toward the riverbank, and I realized that I had nearly lost my temper. It did not seem possible that I should have been disturbed by a harmless old man with a long white beard slightly stained by tobacco juice. That beard had been so dense and luxuriant that he had never needed a necktie, if he had ever worn one. I was angry at an old man a long time dead, who had done nothing more hostile to me than to pat my head when I was eight years old—as angry as though he were still living. Actually his demise had never been wholly accepted at Wickford Point. He was always being dished up at convenient moments; being wheeled out at teatime; cropping up in conversation. People kept asking if I were not in some way or other related to old Brill. It did no good to explain very carefully that I was not, nor to explain further that his verses were atrocious and that he was nothing but an overrated fraud who had battened on his acquaintance with the great figures of his time. No one in the present day had ever read or wished to read anything he had written, and yet he was a good deal more of a figure now than he had been while alive, when he was only an ungifted Boswell with a death grip on the coattails of his betters.

From where I stood by the riverbank I could see on the opposite shore the white house in which John Brill had lived. The literary shrine was now frequented by motorists from the Middle West who paid fifty cents to enter. A motor travel association had even published a page in their "Tours through Old New England" entitled "A Glimpse into the Brill Country." When you paid your fifty cents, a hostess would show you around the house. You could see the study, furnished with very bad Victorian furniture, exactly as Mr. Brill had left it, except that they had removed his plug of tobacco and his cuspidor. There were a number of framed autographed letters upon the wall from personal friends of Mr. Brill, which had not been there in his lifetime. The old gentleman had always kept them in an album to show to callers. Even the hostess didn't know exactly who Mr. Brill was, nor was this entirely the point. The point was the Spartan simplicity of those surroundings. Mr. Brill had loved to roam the hills. He had been on many walks with Thoreau. There was a dusty case in the hall containing birds that he had stuffed himself. Up in the ʰ droom you could see his walking boots, out in the woodshed was his ax. He had loved the dignity of manual toil, and even when he was eight-five years old he could be found in the wood lot up the hill—if he knew in advance that friends were coming. He also loved to whittle. There was a maple bowl in the dining room which he had made himself, and out of which he ate his porridge—when there were guests at dinner. Perhaps I might have liked him if I had been his contemporary, but now that he was dead he was not likable. From my point of view he had even done a good deal to spoil the river, for things which he had written about it lingered poisonously in my memory. Even now I could not get some lines of his out of my mind:—

> O river, mighty river,
> How often have I rowed on thee,
> Seen the wild duck thy waters shiver,
> In thy course pellucid to the sea.
> May our souls move on as tranquil
> As thy waters past the bank,
> Like the birds of Wickford, thankful
> To the Maker they must thank.

Surely I was right in allowing these lines to fill me with a definite and abiding horror. Certainly he had done better than that, but it was the worst I always remembered. Sometimes at night I would lie awake, conjuring up lines old Brill had written, and yet when I quoted them no one would believe they were his.

The river must have been wonderful when he was young. The shad would run up it in the spring and there was a run of salmon also. Now it had an oily odor from the cotton mills upstream. Down by the old landing where they used to tie the salt hay barges, the tide was going out leaving an expanse of thick black mud. The shore was covered with unsightly bits of driftwood. In spite of the farms along its edge the Wickford River gave the appearance of having been entirely forgotten. Its shores had a neglected look and our bank was no exception. Every afternoon, in the old days, my grandmother and her sisters had walked along a little path beneath the birches and the oaks to a grove of white pines on our point. There they would sit and read and sew with all the ordered industry of their generation. When my great-aunt Sarah was still alive, she would put on her bonnet and her shawl at least once a day to walk out there. I had used the path a good deal myself when I was young enough to wander about the place playing games of imagination, but that was all quite a while ago, and since then no one went there very often. Cousin Clothilde was never much at walking. She once said the point was a wonderful place to go when you were in love, yet as far as I could gather neither Bella nor Mary felt that way. I don't think Bella had gone as far as that even with Mr. Berg, and now the path was nearly grown over and no one had bothered to clear it out. Earle started to do it once, but it took him all morning to find something to clear it with; and then, when he did find the ax where it had been buried in the coalbin, the handle came off and he bruised his finger.

As far as I could tell, I was the only one now who went to the point. The jungle was creeping over it, laying a blanket of unkempt wildness beneath the straight trunks of the tall white pines. All the strange growth of unused places was rising among fallen branches, which snapped beneath one's steps, but once you were among the pines there was a solemn, restful silence. Even the noises in their tops were discreet and careful like repressed rustlings in church. I used to think when I was a boy that the pines were whispering of Wickford Point, and they were at their old game of gossip when I stood among them that morning. First there would be a whisper and then the breeze would blow them into a staid and melancholy sort of laughter.

"My dear," they were saying, "don't tell me you've never heard . . . the most amazing thing, I hardly venture to repeat it . . . as long as you understand that it's to be kept inside the family . . . it is so reminiscent of the others . . . and will you only look who's out here now—Jim Calder! He thinks he's changed, but

IX | It Won't Take a Minute to Pack

Bella was out on the lawn when I got back. She must have been working hard on herself, because she was nearly ready to leave. She always knew how to dress, although I had never seen her take any care of her clothes. When her clothes were not on her back, they were usually in a ball in her bureau drawer or somewhere in the bottom of a suitcase, except the ones which belonged to her mother or to Mary. Still they always had an air when she wore them, for she had the slender insolent figure of a clothing model, and a model's careless poise. Now she was no longer a sleepy girl in slacks, but Bella Brill, ready for the races, ready for anything. If she got all mussed up at a cocktail party she could give herself a shake and a pat and out would come every wrinkle so that you could not tell whether anybody had made a pass at her or not. Everything was very simple, but every line was right.

She had a blue silk dress and short cape and a felt hat of the halo type jammed tight over her short black curls. She was carrying a small bag that matched nothing in particular, which she had picked up at one of Willie Hewitt's parties in New York, after everybody else had gone. Everything about her was impeccable, but she created her usual illusion of not having much of anything on underneath. She had not got around to her footgear yet. Her delicately tanned legs were bare and she was wearing a pair of red mules.

91

"Where have you been, darling?" Bella asked.

"Out to the point," I answered.

"Now look here," she said. She was eager, brisk and business-like. "Suppose you snap into it, darling, and get on some other pants, and if they're not pressed, get Josie to press 'em. She's been whining in the kitchen all morning. Everybody's whining here and bellyaching. It's like that wall where the Jews wail in Jerusalem. Clothilde's grousing and so is Mary. That's why I'm waiting out here, because I can't stand it. Now go upstairs and get on some other clothes and let me see what sort of a tie you've got. And brush your hair in back, darling. You wouldn't have to look the way you do if you didn't want to. Why is it that I have to do everything for everybody?"

"Because everybody here," I said, "does everything for everybody."

Bella looked at me out of the corners of her eyes. "Don't get off any cracks, darling," she said. "I *do* do everything for everybody. How do you like the ensemble?" She pivoted almost professionally.

"It's nice," I said.

"It's Mary's," Bella said. "It isn't too tight over the tail, is it? Mary always has them too tight there, but she dresses so badly that nobody cares when she looks immodest. It doesn't look bad on me, does it? When I picked it out for Mary, I thought it might work in."

"What are you going to use for shoes?" I asked.

"I don't know why it is," said Bella, "that nobody can get anything around here done. Mary's darning my stockings. You might have thought that she was going to snap my head off when I suggested it. And Frieda's whitening my shoes."

"Don't get so excited," I said. "You might rip something."

"Don't be so damn sour," said Bella; but she was excited. "There's some cold lamb and potatoes for lunch. There won't be anything more until Mary goes downtown. Come on, let's get out of here before we both go nuts. Here's Frieda now."

92

Frieda came walking across the lawn, carrying two white slippers, each in a thumb and forefinger. She swayed gracefully at the hips. Her thick brown hair was woolly from a brand-new permanent for which Josie had borrowed the money from me two days before, saying that she could pay me back fifteen cents each week. Frieda was not being herself; she was being a glamour girl, a Cinderella from Hollywood, and she was not bad-looking. I did not blame Earle for crying when he did not have a dollar to take her to the beach. No doubt Frieda was going to make a lot of other boys cry before she was through.

"Hello, Frieda," I said. Frieda looked at me out of the corners of her eyes, a trick she had learned from Bella. She was wearing the dress with pink dots which she had inherited after Bella spilled rum punch down the front of it. A ribbon tied in a bow over the bosom, a bit off-center, concealed most of the damage. The stain might have come out altogether if there had not been strawberry in the mixture. Frieda smiled, the languid easy smile of a woman of the world.

"Hi," she said. She was not trying to be fresh or rude. She just wanted to show—and I could sympathize with her, since she wasn't being paid for it—that she wasn't a servant but just an old friend of the family out here to do Bella a kindly favor.

"Thanks, Frieda," said Bella. "That's darling of you."

"That's okay," said Frieda.

"Take these slippers back, will you, Frieda?" said Bella.

"Okay," Frieda said. "So long."

The house was built upon a peculiar plan, resulting largely from my great-grandfather's additions and improvements. The main building, which could be placed by its construction in the early post-Revolutionary period, had consisted of four rooms, two lower and two upper, with a low ell in back, containing the stairs to the upper chambers, and an open fireplace for summer cooking. This ell my great-grandfather had extensively enlarged in the early eighteen hundreds after a successful voyage. What had been the summer kitchen now became the back parlor, and there were rooms beyond it and a kitchen to one side and bedchambers above it. The first stairs had been closed up and now access to the upper floor was gained by the back stairs off the new kitchen, and by a narrow flight in the side entry. If one entered the back parlor from the lawn, it was necessary to cross the front parlor and the dining room to reach the stairs, and consequently there was never much privacy. Someone was nearly always crossing through the rooms, or bursting in through the narrow little passages leading through the wood closet to the kitchen, either on the way upstairs or to the bathroom out in back; and by coincidence the intruder was nearly always the one about whom the rest were talking. The best place for confidences was in somebody's bedroom upstairs provided no one else came in to borrow something.

When I came in from the lawn, however, the back parlor and the front parlor were both empty and, as Earle had not yet been able to find where the outside blinds had been stored and as there were no shades or curtains, the sunlight was coming through the lilacs and syringas that were growing up before the windows. Although the paper and the woodwork were a drab smoky sort of brown, the sun and the foliage by the small paned windows gave an effect of gold and green.

This dim cool light made the perpetual disorder of the room less noticeable, and gave it an appearance of agelessness. The furniture still remained almost exactly as my great-aunt Sarah had arranged it. There were even the same ornaments upon the mantelpiece and on top of her desk, except for a few delicate ones, like the small blue china dog that had held lamplighters in its mouth. It was difficult to perceive that the place was dusty and that the upholstery was torn and that Josie had neglected to remove last night's cigarette butts from the fireplace. It was possible to avoid the immediate sight of white rings by gin and water glasses, and the burns of cigarettes upon the console table and candle-stands. That gold sunlight which darted between the lilac and syringa leaves made a constantly shifting pattern on the dusty leather books that stood against the opposite wall. The sun might have been looking over my great-grandfather's library, vacillating between some favorite titles, now hitting upon the thick back of the *Guide to Peru*, now shifting erratically to the poems of Addison.

I observed the presence of these books and objects only in the half-conscious way in which one notices the friendly and the utterly familiar. The books always seemed to me closer to humanity than the furniture. They were more sensitive than the Chippendale end-chair with its broken back, or the Windsors or the Boston rocker, or the Queen Anne chair with its legs sawed off to fit Aunt Sarah's mother. I walked past more books into the entry of the small parlor.

The family photograph album was in its place upon the second shelf of the whatnot, between the two large snail-shells which my great-grandfather had brought back from Pago Pago. There was no reason for picking up the album except that Bella had told me to hurry. I was anxious to hurry in one way and in another way I resented it, for the small parlor was peaceful and full of nostalgic slumber. If it could only have remained so, I should have liked to stay there always. I seemed to have come upon it unawares, when the portraits on the wall had not expected any living intruder. I sat down in the small upholstered chair beside the coal grate with the album on my knees. It was the same chair in which old Mr. Beardsley, the Unitarian minister, once sat without noticing that Aunt Sarah's cat Prissy was there before him. I remembered what Aunt Sarah had said to Mr. Beardsley, a scrap of conversation which she often repeated.

"Did she claw you in the leg?" Aunt Sarah had inquired.

"No, Miss Sarah," Mr. Beardsley answered, "higher up."

They were delicate in those days, as careful in their manners as they were in their poses when they sat for those pictures in the album. I turned to one that I liked to look at best, a large group of the family and friends seated upon the lawn with the old oak tree just behind them. It had been a fine summer day in the eighties and you could almost feel the still, moist heat. It looked as if everybody must have laughed and worked hard over it. Old Mr. Mason, the photographer, whose son now ran the business and did undertaking on the side and still took all the high school class groups, must have driven all the way out from town in a hired hack. They had dragged some chairs from the back parlor out onto the lawn and also a lot of cushions, for it was just the beginning of the sofa-cushion era. The older generation were in the middle and the young people on the right and left wings, like the archers and slingers of a Roman legion, or else they were lying in recumbent positions in the foreground—the boys, of course, not the girls. A lot of the people in that picture I had never seen, except at family funerals; and, indeed, most of them by now had acted the definitive and principal rôle on one of those occasions. I could see Aunt Sarah and then my grandfather and my grandmother seated in armchairs with children and nephews and nieces all about them. My grandfather had an impatient look that I remembered, as though he were about to swear, and I knew why. He was having the same indigestion that he always had at Wickford Point when he drank that Goddamned well water. I could see my father with a handlebar mustache, and my mother with some sort of bustle. My uncle Percy and Hugh Brill were in striped blazers, with caps now seen only upon a baseball diamond. The young people carried strange pear-shaped tennis racquets and one of them had a mandolin. The girls were really very pretty although they all looked queer.

Now, just a few minutes before, my cousin Bella had been worried about her dress being tight over her posterior. Back in those days of bustles they didn't have to worry. The girls' dresses flowed down to their ankles, they had on tight little short-sleeved coats and some of them wore small felt hats. The one I liked best of all was Cousin Clothilde near the right-hand corner.

She was sitting sideways on a kitchen table, with her slender ankles dangling, and, forgetful of herself, she was looking at all the rest of them. She had that friendly, tolerant look of hers, combined with gentle amusement. She was more beautiful then, more beautiful than Bella, sitting surrounded by that tranquil sense of sureness which had never left her. It was the sureness that had made her say, upstairs just an hour ago, that Mr. Roosevelt would help her. Nothing had broken her inner tranquillity and nothing would ever break it. I liked her in that picture, for she was just the way I used to remember her, back in the days when our nurses would take Harry and me to the riverbank where we used to throw pine cones at Sid. She was just as I remembered her the day when she had stopped Aunt Sarah from striking me with her cane because I had picked a cardinal flower beneath the elm tree where they once had hung a pig.

I did not realize that anyone was behind me until I heard Bella's voice.

"For God's sake," said Bella, "haven't you done anything? Haven't you changed your clothes?"

"No," I said, "I was looking at the picture."

"Well, put it up," said Bella. "You all sit around here as if you had hookworm or something. There's no use trying to get anyone to move. We may as well stay and eat that lamb and potatoes now, and start off at four o'clock; but I'm going to see you into your pants first, so you'll be ready to go. Now come on, really, darling."

"All right," I said. "It won't take a minute to pack."

"I'm coming up with you," Bella said, "or else you won't put on a decent shirt or tie, and besides you may have a cigarette somewhere. Do you know I have been all morning without a cigarette?"

I noticed again what had struck me outside on the lawn, that Bella was excited. Bella could not deceive me, for I had seen her run through all her moods ever since she was a little girl, and an adult seldom develops a different set of reactions. In Bella's eyes and at the corners of her lips—she had been at work with her mother's lipstick, which was of a slightly different color tone from hers—was the bright anticipatory look of one of our Wickford Point barn cats waiting for the wire mouse-trap to be opened.

Perhaps the simile was not quite fair, but Bella's violet eyes had the same soft luminous qualities and her body swayed gently as though she were going to purr.

Her eyes and lips had an expression which I had observed when she used to be ushered upstairs in New York, scrubbed and tied up in a blue sash, to wait for the Christmas tree. There was no doubt that something new had appeared in Bella's life which had not been visible the day before. She was looking forward to that ride with me, and I knew it was not on my account; nor was it entirely because she was glad to get away from the family. There was something waiting for her at the Jaeckels', something that she knew about already, something which she could snatch at, some cosmic sort of Christmas tree. I thought I could guess what it was. It would be a man, and the most likely man would be Berg, the one who did so well in business that he could always get away from New York. It was not the first time that I had observed that Bella's taste in males was catholic and unpredictable. There had probably been some who were worse than Berg, but the time was coming when I should have to talk to her about this, although talking never did much good.

Something had happened to the cushion in the rumble seat of my car. It was my idea that Earle had dragged it out under some tree where he could sit with Frieda, but Earle had either forgotten about it or was afraid to remember. At any rate it made no difference. It simply meant that there was a lot more room for bags and things. Earle was standing near the car wiping some places on the hood where the barnswallows had misbehaved. Josie was at the kitchen door holding her youngest child by the back of its rompers so that it would not crawl under the wheels. Cousin Clothilde was at the side door in her silk wrapper, and Sid had propped himself up against the side of the house near the bed of white myrtle. Mary was looking out of the bathroom window. I had put my own bag in the back. Bella appeared carrying a round black patent-leather hatbox, which she had borrowed from one of the Clifton girls the time they had asked her up to

Seal Harbor two years ago, and which she had forgotten so far to return. The hatbox was bulging but it was adequate. If necessary Bella could go away from home for six months with just that hatbox, and she would have everything in it too, from slacks to a formal ball-dress.

Bella slid into the seat of the car with a swift nymphlike motion which caused her light blue skirt to fly upward disclosing her sheer silk stockings, her sister Mary's round garters in which Josie had taken a reef, and also a generous section of brown thigh. At this sight Cousin Clothilde, who generally seemed ageless, showed her age.

"Dear, your dress," she said.

"There's no use flying in the face of nature," Bella said. "Hasn't everyone got legs?"

Cousin Clothilde glanced meaningly at Earle and back at Bella, an obvious signal which Bella disregarded.

"But Bella," said Cousin Clothilde, "you haven't got any—"

"Pants?" said Bella. "Nobody wears 'em nowadays. And who would wash 'em if I wore 'em?"

Mary spoke from the upper bathroom window.

"Well, I wear them," she said. "You don't look decent."

"I know you do," said Bella, "and that's one of your troubles, sweetness."

Cousin Clothilde lapsed into the tolerant silence of one who accepts the universe. Josie took a firmer grip on her infant's rompers. Sid leaned more appreciatively against the wall of the house, and Earle returned to his work on the car's hood. Bella coiled herself comfortably on the small of her back. She conveyed the indefinable impression of one who is used to any situation which may arise in any automobile, whether in motion or stationary.

"For heaven's sake," she said, "why does everybody stand around? Can't you get into the car, Jim? There's no use doing any more rubbing, Earle. There are sea gulls where we're going."

Earle blushed and gave a high, shocked giggle. As Josie always said, Earle had been brought up in a lovely home among lovely people. Cousin Clothilde looked at me and frowned and smiled at the same time. That bewildered amusement was something I loved best about her, for it showed both her age and her perennial youth. She was asking me wordlessly if I did not think that Bella was perfectly charming, so beautiful, so gay. She was asking me if I did not think it was strange that some of those people whom Bella played about with in New York, some of those important people who are always looking for new talent in the motion picture business, had not snapped up Bella. She knew about a thing called a "screen test." Cousin Clothilde had been asking about screen tests often recently.

They were all standing there—as people had always stood at Wickford Point when someone was leaving, half-listlessly and half-wistfully, like dwellers on an island watching a ship sail—making their last requests now that we were going into the outer world.

"Darling," Cousin Clothilde said to me, "don't forget to bring some gin back with you and some cartons of cigarettes, and pick up as many papers of matches as you possibly can—we're almost out of matches."

"Jim," Sid said, "will you get me some bicarbonate of soda and some boric acid and an eye cup?"

"Mr. Calder," Earle said, "you haven't got me that copy of *True Romances* yet, and will you bring a chocolate nut bar, Mr. Calder?"

Frieda moved coyly toward the car and looked at me hard with wide brown eyes in a way she had learned after reading about charm on the woman's page.

"Could you," she said, "do just one little errand at some drugstore?"

"You'd better ask me, hadn't you?" Bella said.

"Bella!" said Cousin Clothilde.

Frieda's shoulders writhed and she forgot about charm.

"Just a lipstick, Mr. Calder," Frieda said. "They call it Orange Kiss. Can you remember, Orange Kiss?"

"Oh!" said Bella. "Watch yourself, Earle."

"Aw say, Miss Brill," Earle stammered, "nuts!"

I stepped on the self-starter. The trouble at Wickford Point was that everybody developed a personality. In a patriarchal system, if you didn't pay the help enough, they always turned into characters. I gave the engine a little gas to warm it up, but now Josie was speaking.

"Mr. Calder," Josie called, "if you was to see some bobby pins, Mr. Calder—"

"What?" I said.

"Bobby pins," called Josie, "those little things that hold the hair."

Bella nudged me impatiently. A roar came from Josie's youngest child.

"All right," said Josie, "all right, Herman dear. Herman wants to give you a kiss, Mr. Calder." Bella laughed softly and collapsed against me so that I could feel her shaking all over. Josie held Herman's face close to mine. Herman smelled of hard-boiled eggs, sour milk and other things.

"Pretend you're running for Congress, darling," Bella said.

Mary did not ask for anything, but then Mary had ten dollars.

X | Speak to Me of Love

We turned out of the yard and went up the hill beneath an arch of elm trees. At the summit there was a glimpse of the river on the left. Then came the shrubbery and the walls of dressed stone and the white buildings of the Jeffries farm, which a New York man named Mr. Henry Whitaker had bought five years before as a summer place. He had built a tennis court, and there were some tables with colored umbrellas beside it. The Whitakers had been there for five years but we had never spoken to them. They might be there for twenty and still they would be dwellers on another planet, for we resented their intrusion. We only gathered gossip about the Whitakers, and we still called it the Jeffries farm. We were passing the last hayfield of the Jeffries farm when Bella realized that she had forgotten something.

"Oh Jim," she said, "I've forgotten my purse. I thought it was in this bag. We don't want to go back, do we? Lend me ten dollars, will you?"

"All right," I said.

"Thanks," said Bella. "You're awfully sweet, darling." And she leaned against me comfortably and contentedly. "It's nice to get out of there, isn't it?" she said.

"Yes," I answered, because I was thinking and I did not want to talk.

"Everybody gets so damned screwy down there," Bella said. "They just sit and sit."

"Yes," I said.

I did not want to talk to her about the family. I understood about Wickford Point a good deal better than she did, because I had been there more often.

Bella lapsed into silence and, as she stared straight ahead, I had a glimpse of her profile. Her face was beautiful at any angle —but now I saw something new in it. There was just the slightest indication, so small that it was only a suspicion, that Bella might lose her looks some day. In spite of her beauty and her comparative youth—she was much younger than I was—Bella, like the rest of us, was getting on. Someday she would realize—perhaps she had a premonition of it now—that you can't be young forever. There would come the time, which often arrives quite suddenly, when the face matures, when the curves about the cheek and chin are not quite so youthful or so naïve as they were once. A time was approaching when little faults and greater ones would write their records distinctly upon her face, and now that time was almost there. Her features had always been sensitive, aristocratic, intelligent, and illuminated by what the experts call "charm" or "personality." Admittedly these attributes had not as yet departed. She was still the girl whom any man would select in a large room, the girl whom for some reason other women instinctively hated, except those few who were near enough her type to cope with her in the great free-for-all arena where no holds or bites or scratchings or tongue-lashings were barred. Nevertheless it seemed to me now that her face was a little sharper and a trifle thinner than I had ever remembered it. There was a new definition to the curve of her delicate nostrils which almost harsh. Perhaps it was there because she did not think that I was looking. There was a new straightness to the lips that so many men had wished to kiss, or had kissed, and the lines of her jaw were not so completely graceful as they had once been. Yes, Bella, like the rest of us, was getting on.

Her hand dropped on my knee for a moment in a careless caressing gesture.

"Darling," Bella said. Her voice was comforting and sweet. It was a comment, a soft, contented ejaculation, which needed no reply. When she touched me and when she spoke it was not difficult to understand why so many men had loved her.

I found myself thinking about love, but not on her account. I was thinking of it because we had passed the Jeffries farm. I was recalling that strange diseaselike quality which is love's peculiar attribute and which runs its course through the patient like the depredations of some particularly vicious virus of an infiltrable nature. You got it and there you were. It was worse when you were young, for after the first attack there was a hope of developing a degree of unreliable immunity.

Luella Jeffries used to live at the Jeffries farm. Her father ran a milk route and drank hard cider. Mrs. Jeffries was short and stout and used to take charge of the suppers at the Grange. Aunt Sarah and my cousin Sue looked upon them as uneducated farmers. I looked upon them as very noble people once. I would have died gladly for old man Jeffries, though I hope he never knew it. He certainly never knew that I used to lie awake imagining ways in which I could die for him. This greatest of all sacrifices was generally connected with Mr. Jeffries' bull, for the neighborhood knew that the animal was fierce and had chased Mr. Jeffries once. Frequently I imagined myself leaping over the barbed wire of Mr. Jeffries' pasture as the maddened animal thundered after the retreating form of that splendid man, who was courageous but slowed down by his years. I would tell Mr. Jeffries to run while I turned the bull from his course upon myself—to run, because Jeffries was Luella's father. Later I would be carried on a shutter into the Jeffries' kitchen, a beautiful place where the vinegar and grease had a heady ambrosial scent, and Luella would weep and kiss me then. I could tell her that I loved her, now that it was all too late.

This was only a single sample of my delirium. I never told Luella that I loved her. I was never able to say anything to her except infrequent monosyllables, for she was so infinitely far above me. She wore a shirtwaist with a high collar and had a big butterfly bow at the back of her hair. We used to meet on the trolley car going to high school. She sat beside me twice in all the time we went to school, but I never had the courage to take advantage of these accidents. Later she married Louis Bedard, who ran the Sea Food Lunch downtown. I sometimes saw her even now, behind the cashier's desk in the restaurant. Heaven alone knows why I ever loved her.

After all, love was a biological phenomenon marked by certain well-defined characteristics which repeated themselves almost exactly in nearly every normal human being. I sometimes wondered why people did not accept it as a definite and incontrovertible fact, instead of continually harping on the subject in music and in literature without ever getting anywhere. Even Dr. Freud's contributions, though interesting, seemed inconclusive. They had merely called an open season upon certain aspects of the malady not heretofore considered fit discussion for mixed society. Now, almost anywhere, an intelligent and liberated individual could dominate a dinner table with a thoughtful discussion of sexual perversions or of various intimate activities. All the really good writers of my time had explored this field at length and with conspicuous success, but had they gone any further than Tolstoy? Had they even said as much as Jane Austen, who said exactly nothing? I was wondering whether it was better to love afar and in vain, as I had loved Luella Jeffries, or to have one's love requited and then, when the disease had run its course, to find that one had not loved at all and to marvel at the things which one had said and done and written. Surely love made marriage dangerous, since neither contracting party was in a normal state.

First there had been Luella, and then there had been a little blonde out front in a musical comedy. She also had been above me, too ethereal, too beautiful. Then there had been the French girl whom I had picked up in the Botanical Gardens at Bordeaux. She had not been above me, but when my mind got to Michelle I decided it was time to stop. At any rate I was still good at idiomatic French, although scholars had told me that I spoke it with a provincial patois. I owed a good deal to Michelle, and, by odd coincidence, she too had married a restaurant proprietor. I had seen her at their little place three years before, just off the Rue du Bac, where D'Artagnan had once walked. She, too, was sitting behind the *caisse*, and I recognized her at once, although she weighed a good two hundred pounds. Michelle embraced me and she had been eating garlic. Her husband, M. Lubin, took me to the back parlor, where we drank some *fines*. Michelle, however, did not object when I paid for the dinner. In fact, I observed that she had jacked up the price on the table d'hôte ten francs. And then there was Madame, on the Rue du Bray—but that was another matter, when love and death were all in the same bed together. Perhaps the French understood about love; at any rate they treated it as a delightful malady.

Bella's violet eyes were half-closed, but her lips were just a trifle grim. Her expression made me wonder if she had ever loved at all. She had certainly talked enough about it. I wondered if she had been secretly in love with her father, her brothers or her mother. Certainly she had never given any visible sign of such undeveloped weakness. I wondered if she was what the Freudians—or was it the Jung school?—called ambivalent, a state which made her so unintegrated that love was very nearly impossible. It did not seem to me that she was unintegrated, but, after all, did it make much difference?

I drove the car almost without noticing as we came toward the main road. I had often put myself to sleep by traveling in my mind along it. Beyond the Jeffries farm was the lane which led to the cemetery and beyond that were the pine woods, warm and sweet. Next at a bend was a small white house, occupied by people whose name I had never known, and who, as far as I could tell, were unknown to everybody else. Then there was a tumbledown house with a great many brown hens in the front yard, occupied by Lithuanians. The next place belonged to Jimmy Casey, an Irishman who sometimes cut our hay and plowed our garden, when we had one. Then we were on the main road where the trolley had run once, near the abandoned brick schoolhouse, where a friend of mine, Pete Sickles, had tended the hot-air stoves. On the opposite side was Sam Kennedy's garage.

I stopped by the least expensive of his three gasoline pumps. I had known Sam when we were boys—it seemed a million years ago. Sam used to "go with" Luella once, and I had hated him, and since then we had never had a thing in common, and, when I came to think of it accurately, we had never had Luella in common either. Sam was pot-bellied now, dressed in a one-piece suit of overalls, not unlike little Herman's rompers, with the name of a popular brand of gasoline embroidered on his back.

"Hello, Jim," he said. "How do you do, Mrs. Stowe? Want me to fill her up?"

I told him to fill her up. There was an interesting aspect to his salutation; he called me by my first name, but he would not have done so to any of the Brills. I was almost a forgotten member of an ancient fellowship, but I was still part of the town. The Brills were from the city, but I was still a local boy. I gave Sam a bill, and after he had reached into his rompers for the change, he put his foot on the running board.

"Say, Jim," he said, "there was a party down from your place who had his valves ground and a new distributor and fifteen gallons of gas, eleven seventy-five—a black-haired, thin young fellow. He told me to send him the bill to New York, but he's never paid it. His name is Berg, Howard Berg."

Bella sat up straighter, but she made no comment.

"He must have overlooked it, Sam," I said. "If he doesn't pay, you let me know. But after this you might just as well settle for cash."

Bella sat up still straighter, but she did not speak.

"Thanks, Jim," said Sam. "How's everything? Writing lots of articles these days?"

Bella did not speak until we were out on the road again. I saw that I had made her angry, but I was angry too.

"That was a dirty crack," Bella said. "You can keep your mouth

107

shut and not talk that way—as though we don't always pay our bills."

"Well, I'm not going to stand behind any more Bergs," I said, "or any other poor whites who come down here visiting you when they haven't got enough money in their pockets to get home."

"Don't worry, darling," Bella said, "about your damned eleven dollars and seventy-five cents. I know what you think of my friends, so you don't have to say, but just in case you'd like to know—just in case it would interest you—Howard Berg isn't any two-cent pot-boiling writer. The money you have in the bank would be like a quarter to Howard Berg. Don't worry, your eleven dollars and seventy-five cents will be all right."

"That's fine," I said. "What do you know about Berg? Where did you pick him up?"

"Just in case you want to know," Bella said, "Howard Berg is one of the most important men in Wall Street. You could hardly be expected to know, but I hope that satisfies you, darling."

"Who told you so?" I asked. "Berg and who else?"

"Lots of other people you don't know, darling," Bella said. "Lots of other people you couldn't possibly know, who wouldn't care to meet you."

"Important people?" I asked.

"Yes, darling," said Bella, "important people. It might be a help to you, darling, if you were nicer to my friends. It's obvious you don't like Howard Berg, do you? He spoke of it himself. You were as rude as hell to him. If he hadn't been a gentleman, he would have beaten your ears off. It just happens that Howard Berg moves in certain social groups where you have never been invited, odd as it may seem, darling. He knows a great many writers who would cut you on the street, and playwrights and producers. Howard Berg is a very intimate friend of Sinclair Lewis, Ernest Hemingway, Booth Tarkington, and James Branch Cabell. How do you like that, darling?"

"Is he an intimate friend of John Galsworthy?" I asked.

"It just happens," said Bella, "that he had lunch with Mr. Galsworthy last week, when Mr. Galsworthy was over from England.

108

Mr. Galsworthy always calls Howard up. Now butter that one on your dry toast, darling."

I had her there. I paused to savor the beauty of it.

"Did you happen to know, honey bee," I said, "that John Galsworthy died five years ago?"

Bella smiled provokingly.

"It doesn't do any good to lie like that, Jim, just because no really fine novelist, no really worth-while writer, no really worthwhile anything, has ever honored you by his acquaintance."

"All right," I said. "Let's let it go at that."

"Yes, darling," said Bella. "I think we'd better let it go at that. Perhaps it will teach you to be civil when you see Mr. Berg again."

"What good does it do him to know writers?" I asked.

"It just happens," Bella answered, "that Howard Berg is a very intelligent, very cultivated person, who enjoys the relaxation of associating with his intellectual equals, darling. Some people, even writers, realize that they are helped by a gracious, civilized society."

"You mean," I asked, "that he keeps in touch with the finer things of life?"

"Oh, for God's sake, shut up," said Bella suddenly. "Don't start getting sour and pouring bile over everybody just because you can't be as successful as Howard Berg."

"Hooey!" I said.

"And you needn't start using foul language either," Bella answered. "If you can't behave yourself, shut up."

We did not speak for quite a while after that, although I began to feel warm and kindly toward Bella for the pleasure she had given me. We passed by the fountain where horses had once slaked their thirst and went more slowly down the broad street which marked the beginning of town. I remembered that Cousin Sue had once said that when she went downtown her self-confidence was greatly buoyed up by remembering she was related to the Brills. Even without this reassurance I felt no great inadequacy. We passed the First Congregational and the Baptist Churches and the All Saints' Episcopal Church and the Unitarian Church, and the Acme Furniture Company with a swinging hammock in the window, and Rolfe's

Drug Store where there was a sale of hot-water bottles, an odd sight for a summer's day, but everybody at the post office was saying that Mr. Rolfe was getting senile. Next was the Men's Toggery, where they were displaying tropical suits, and then Mason's Photographic Studio and Undertaking Parlor.

"Darling," said Bella.

"What?" I said.

"Let's stop and get some cigarettes."

I parked the car down by the news store and left Bella powdering her nose and staring disinterestedly at the sights on the brick sidewalk. The traffic policeman craned his neck out of the oversize collar of his baggy uniform and looked at me and looked away. He had been the town truant officer when I was a boy. Mr. Chipping came out of the Sailors' National Bank and walked across the street, and he didn't recognize me either. Inside the news store was the old cool smell of papers, candy, ice cream sodas and cigars, an aura which was kept in constant flux by two electric fans with pink paper streamers in front of them. Some men in straw hats and alpaca coats were at the fountain drinking soda. Two girls who dressed like Frieda were eating sundaes in a booth. The men rotated on their stools and looked at me. One of them slid down to a standing position. He was fat and might have been in the American Legion.

"Haven't seen you for a long while," he said.

I could not remember who he was. So much water had flowed under the bridge that I often found it difficult to recall names and faces.

"How's everything, Jim?" he asked.

"Fine," I said. "How's everything with you?"

"Fine," he said. "Glad to have seen you, Jim."

Out on the sidewalk we shook hands. Bella had finished powdering her nose.

"For heaven's sake," she said, "don't act as though you were in homespun and try to pull the old home town stuff when you really spend all your time snooting everybody."

I backed out the car and we started up the street past the traffic lights and on to the open road.

"Is Berg going to be at the Jaeckels'?" I asked.

"And why should it affect you, darling," asked Bella, "if Howard Berg is going to be at the Jaeckels' or not?"

"Well, is he or isn't he?" I asked.

"Suppose you ask when you get there, darling," Bella said.

"Thanks," I said, "I will."

Bella's voice was soft with a breathless hint of apprehension.

"What are you going to do?" she asked.

"Collect that garage bill, honey bee," I said. "No damned gigolo who had a spiritual lunch with Mr. Galsworthy last week is going to take me to town for his garage bill."

Bella's hand closed tight on my arm.

"Jim," she said, "don't do that, please, *please.*"

"Why not?" I asked.

"Please," she said, "that's all. It—it isn't the kind of thing that people *do.* You don't understand Howard. Jim, darling, please be nice. Besides—"

"Besides what?" I asked.

"Nothing," said Bella. "But please—it means a lot."

"Does it?"

"Yes," she said, "it does."

"Bella," I said,—there were times when I could get her to tell the truth,—"come across with it now. Has Berg asked you to marry him or not?"

Bella bent down and lighted her cigarette. There was a tremor in her fingers as she held the match.

"Please don't, Jim," said Bella, "please."

It was not difficult to think of her in a detached way, as though she were something which in no sense belonged in my life. I could think dispassionately of the beauty of her face and body, of her intuitive quickness, and of the indolence and intellectual superficiality which went with it. It was not hard to recognize that she was consumed by egotism and desires. The trouble was that her desires changed so fast that she could never be wholly sure of what she wanted—except that she wanted everything.

XI | Ride, Ride Together, Forever Ride

"Jim," Bella said. She had been silent for quite a while, which was not such a bad idea, and now I hoped that she was not going to talk about herself. I did not want it now because I was escaping again from that life and returning to the life which I had made for myself. Nevertheless I suspected from her tone that it was coming. We still had a half an hour of fast driving before we reached the Jaeckels', and I wished I were there already.

"I can't go on like this," Bella said.

Yes, it was the old, old story. She couldn't go on like this, and Cousin Clothilde couldn't go on like this, and neither could Harry or Sid. Each of them had said it almost daily, and still they went on just like that.

"I don't suppose you can," I said.

"I can't," said Bella, "I just can't stand it. I can't, *I can't.*"

"Then don't," I said.

"Then don't be so disagreeable," Bella said. "You know what I have to put up with. I don't mind Clothilde. She can't help it, but the way Mary and Sid and Harry just sit around there and talk. . . . Nobody does anything about anything. I can't go on like this."

"Well, what are you going to do?" I asked.

"Well, I'll do something," said Bella. Her voice became hard. She could rise to a crisis at odd moments. "Maybe I'll get a job."

Then she looked at me sideways to study the effect of her statement. I had heard her make it before, and I did not answer. "You don't think I can get a job, do you?" Bella said. "That's where you're wrong as usual. If I want to, I can sign right up tomorrow night. All I have to do is to call New York."

"Sign up for what?" I asked. Bella examined her nose in the mirror of her washed-gold compact, the one that had been given her last year when she was a bridesmaid at Jeanette Stackton's wedding. She had thought it was all gold for nearly three months. Bella's speech became languid and casual.

"I don't suppose," she inquired, "that you know Dr. Wilbur Frothinghope?"

"No," I said. "Who's he, a fan dancer?"

"That's so funny," Bella said soothingly, "so very funny, darling, to take swipes at people that you never really could know. It just happens—you say you're intellectual, but this shows exactly how intellectual you are—it just happens, if you ever read anything about science, that you might know that Dr. Frothinghope is a very important archaeologist. Dr. Frothinghope is a very old friend of mine."

"How old?" I asked. "Sixty-two?"

Bella smiled at me sunnily.

"It just happens that Dr. Frothinghope is younger and a good deal better-looking than you, darling. He's leading an expedition down into the interior of Guatemala to uncover a lost Maya city and to reconstruct a snake goddess pyramid. Funnily enough, he asked me to join the expedition."

"In what capacity?" I asked.

"Someday, darling," said Bella, "someone is going to wash your mouth out with soap and water. It just happens that Dr. Frothinghope has been interested in my drawings."

"Etchings?" I inquired.

"Oh hell," said Bella, "there's no use my wasting my time trying to be serious with any of you. Dr. Frothinghope said I could learn the ropes very quickly. I'm strong, a good deal stronger than you, darling, and I guess I could stand Guatemala a good deal bet-

113

ter than you could. At any rate, it would get me away from all of this. I'd be *doing* something."

There was no use answering if she wanted to go on. By this time I was reasonably sure that Dr. Wilbur Frothinghope was either a figment of Bella's imagination or a big name which she had heard mentioned and which she was now adding to her collection of other important names. Bella was revelling verbally in her world of make-believe.

"Well, I'd go if I were you," I said. But Bella was no longer interested. She had probably tried out the idea to see how it would work at the Jaeckels' at dinner, and she had already given it up as unsuccessful.

"Darling," she said, "what are you going to say to Joe?"

Ever since the telephone had rung the subject was obviously bound to come up, and now I was only thankful that it had not come up sooner. It would take only fifteen minutes to get to the Jaeckels' if I stepped on the gas; then I would be rid of her for a little while at any rate. After that she could project her personality anywhere she liked. She could throw her line about Dr. Frothinghope and Guatemala, or she could shoot big game in Zambezi, or die of alcoholic poisoning, or get arrested.

"How do you mean," I asked, "what I'm going to say to Joe?"

"I mean about me," said Bella.

"There probably won't be anything about you," I answered. Bella smiled in complacent negation.

"Oh yes, there will," she said. "He'll ask about me, and you know it, not that I care, because I can see him myself. He always talks about me when he gets drunk at the club."

I felt a tingle of anger. There was nothing she would have liked better than to make me angry. She was just getting herself set for a good scene, in which we could shout at each other and tell each other plain home truths, and which might end by her endeavoring to slap my face.

"Who told you that?" I asked.

"Oh, lots of people," Bella said. "There is such a thing as being loyal, darling."

114

"Meaning me?" I asked.

Bella took her lipstick from her bag and opened her compact again.

"Yes, meaning you," she said. "You're almost bright sometimes, darling. After the way he treated me, how do you think it looks to have you, one of my own relatives, playing around with him, getting drunk with him, probably talking obscenities? I ask you—how do you think it looks?"

"Well," I said, "how did he treat you?"

"You're not being either scintillating or funny, darling," Bella said. "Everybody else knows how he treated me if you don't. How do you think it feels to be abandoned by a man who has taken the best years of your life? That's what he did, the best years, when I might have meant something to somebody. If he'd only treated me halfway decently, I might have been anything he wanted—I might have been—"

She paused and snapped her compact case shut.

"Yes," I said, "you might have."

I felt sad and angry almost at the same time, because what she said was partially true. There was sometimes truth in her most brazen prevarications. I believed that it had been more of a blow to her pride than anything else, and it still hurt her pride. The little sneer at the corner of her mouth showed it, and the extra sharpness of her overpowdered nose.

"Oh, I've been over the jumps," Bella said. "I'm not complaining, but there are ways of doing everything. There are ways of being a gentleman."

The Brills had always considered themselves experts on gentility, and judges of a court of honor. I could not sit there and take it, and certainly she knew I couldn't.

"He's the nearest you ever came to seeing one," I said.

"Oh, is he really, darling?" said Bella. "Well, he's not, and no one else thinks he is either. The least thing a gentleman can do is to see that his former wife isn't starving when he's making a hundred and fifty thousand a year."

"You've never missed a meal, honey bee," I said.

115

"It isn't his fault I haven't," Bella answered.

She was back on the subject of alimony; it was always a sore point with Bella. We had been over the subject before, but we went over it again.

"You said you didn't want any," I told her. "You kept saying it to the lawyers all the time."

"He wasn't earning anything then," said Bella, "but he would do something now if he were a gentleman. If you had any family loyalty you'd ask him. How could I guess that he'd be successful? And now I haven't the price of a dress. How do you think I like it to have people know that you see him after what he's done to me?"

I spoke slowly and carefully. We had almost reached the North Shore by then.

"Joe's been a friend of mine for quite a while," I said, "and he's going to keep on being one, and you're not going to stop it, honey bee. So just forget about Joe. He took a beating when he was with you, and he's well out of it, and he knows it."

Bella was no longer beautiful. Her mouth worked as though she were chewing on something.

"Excuse me, darling," she said. "I forgot that you understood men better than women. That's the trouble with you and Joe. You neither of you are very good with women, are you? Why not confess it? When you see Joe you tell him from me that I'm well out of it, too. Tell him he doesn't know what love is. Tell him—"

She told me what I was to tell Joe in a harsh, parched voice. It sounded a good deal like a page from a book which comes to you in the mail in a plain wrapper. She told me a good many things about Joe which she had told me before. I listened while I drove the car. The whole thing made me sick and she would be ashamed of herself when it was all over. Her voice went on against my silence and finally died away.

"Jim," she said at length.

"What?" I said.

"I'm sorry, Jim. I don't know what gets into me sometimes."

116

"That's all right," I said. "Skip it. We're getting to the Jaeckels' now."

"Jim," she said, and I asked her what she wanted.

"Do you think Joe still loves me?"

There was an innocent enormity to the question. She was look-ing at me hopefully, almost like a little girl who wishes to be re-assured of an obvious fact. All her venom had left her. She had found release in that burst of words.

"Skip it," I said, "honey bee. Here's the Jaeckels' driveway."

She put an arm around my shoulders.

"Darling," she said, "you're awfully sweet. There's no one as sweet as you."

The funny thing was that I believe she meant it. The fine blue gravel of the Jaeckels' driveway was crunching beneath the tires. The white house which the Jaeckels had rented from somebody in Boston was standing on the cliffs. There were people on the terrace which looked out on the little islands. There was a cool salt breath of rockweed and the sea. We had both awakened from an unpleasant dream. She was Bella Brill again, one of those de-lightful Brills who knew everybody, and I was Jim Calder, that amusing cousin of the Brills. She was Bella Brill, ready to spend a week end with the Jaeckels, ready for anything. She was waving to someone on the terrace.

"Susie," she was calling, "Susie darling!"

She was going to have such a lovely time. There would be maids, bathrooms, speedboats. A houseman was coming already to get her hatbox. Bella was still waving. She was like the girl in the ad-vertisements for high-powered automobiles, one of those automo-biles for which the young couple has waited for years, having put up with countless little privations to acquire it. My car was the only contradiction to the picture, but Bella was doing her best.

"Susie," she called, "Susie darling!"

Bella Brill was getting off at the Jaeckels' and thank God for it! I should be getting away from the Jaeckels' in just a minute, but it would take a good many hours to recover from that talk

117

with Bella. I was wondering if one loved more or quarreled more in automobiles. The statistics would be interesting.

It was just possible, it occurred to me, that the Jaeckels and their whole unimaginative layout were just what Bella had always wanted. She may have wanted all those people and the ease of it and the sense of escape, so like the life on the *Queen Mary* or at a resort hotel. There were so many things you could do at the Jaeckels' that you didn't have to worry your head for a single minute. There were boats, swimming, badminton, croquet, and a lot of inflated ducks and seahorses which you could try to ride upon in the swimming pool. If these didn't work there was America's new gift to the world, the downstairs game room, equipped with a real bar which had lots of comic signs behind it about the "Ladies' Entrance" and "Spitting on the floor . . ." and all those games where you pushed a little ball with a plunger and watched it go into little holes guarded by nails. A lot of people could spend their winters doing that, and Tom and Susie Jaeckel didn't know any better; or if Tom Jaeckel did, when he got down there he was too tired to try. Bella could have it all if she wanted. It was certainly a long, long jump from Wickford Point.

The Jaeckels had been working for a good many seasons to get into the Beach Club, and they hadn't made it yet, and now Susie Jaeckel said she liked it here because you didn't have to mix with the summer colony; you could just see your friends without having a lot of stuffed-shirt strangers butting in. She and Tom just lived quietly, she now explained, and had their own friends to visit.

Almost before the car had stopped Susie Jaeckel and Bella had collided in an attitude of extreme affection. Susie Jaeckel was in tennis shorts. She was a type that would have done better in something else because she was overweight. If I had been a doctor, I should have investigated her thyroid.

"Oh, sweetness," Susie said to Bella, "sweetness!"

Then she saw me and the expression in her rather protuberant blue eyes confirmed my suspicion that she had been after Bella to

118

get me down sometime. I was a feeble link, but I might conceivably lead to some of the right people at the Beach Club.

"Sweetness," Susie Jaeckel cooed, "did you bring Mr. Calder down?"

"It's just the other way around, Mrs. Jaeckel," I said. "I brought sweetness here on my way to Boston. I'm afraid I'll have to push right on. Have you got everything out of the car, sweetness?"

"He's always making fun because I drop things," Bella said.

"But you'll stay for a Martini, won't you?" Mrs. Jaeckel said. "Just something to keep you company on that long ride alone— Judson's bringing them out right now, and we just must have somebody to help us eat all that caviar."

I was succumbing against my will to the material charm of the place. Bella had clamped herself firmly on my arm. Her sharp fingers dug like savage little claws into my coat.

"Of course he will, darling," she said. "He isn't in any hurry at all." Then just as we reached the terrace and as the voices of the Jaeckels' other guests rose to meet us, she had time to whisper to me poisonously:—

"Don't be so God-damned snobbish. Don't try to snoot Sue Jaeckel. She can do a lot for you."

I wanted to ask what Sue could do, whether it was of a physical, a mental, or a moral nature, but there was no time; we were on the terrace and Bella had already left me. She was being very charming, exchanging greetings and osculations with all sorts of people, both male and female. I did not know them, but they all looked healthy and they were very, very carefully dressed.

Tom Jaeckel had on brown doeskin trousers and a double-breasted coat of an even richer autumnal shade, which was buttoned tight over his barrel-like torso. His wide eyes and rather heavy lips and flattish nose made one think of a prize fighter, and he had a quick springy walk, which indicated that he was fast on his feet. There was no funny business about Tom Jaeckel. He was the general manager of the eastern division of one of the biggest motor companies in the country. He was an executive who could

119

handle personnel. I was glad that I was not among the personnel he handled.

"Hello, Calder," he said. "Glad to see you aboard." The hearty phrase didn't go so badly with him either.

"Hello, Jaeckel," I said. I rather liked him. At any rate he worked for what he had, and he was paying for the party.

"Judson," Jaeckel called. "Gangway for Judson."

The butler in a cutaway came with a cold Martini on a silver tray. He was a dignified man past middle age, the sort with whom you might shake hands by mistake—and you wouldn't have minded doing it. Suddenly I remembered Judson. I had not seen him for twenty years.

"Are you Judson who used to be at the Standishes'?" I asked.

He knew me right away and he seemed both glad and surprised to see me.

"Yes, Mr. Calder," he said. "Mr. Standish was a very fine employer, sir."

I looked across the terrace and back at Judson. We offered each other a wordless explanation for being at the Jaeckels'.

The man's face was as impassive and distinguished as the face of an elder statesman. He was looking tolerantly upon the scene, untouched by it and not amused.

The caviar rested upon cakes of ice and beside the table I saw Mr. Howard Berg. He had finished his caviar and toast and was rubbing his fingers carefully on a napkin. I never had paid much attention to Mr. Berg until that moment, for it was always easier to avoid Bella's friends as much as possible, but now he rather puzzled me. Like everyone else he was just a little too much dressed to be quite right. He wore white shoes, white doeskins, and a double-breasted blue serge coat with a white handkerchief jutting out a trifle too far from his breast pocket. The lapels of the coat were a shade too sharply pointed. His face was dark, as I had remembered it, and his hair was as shiny as patent leather, but he did not look like a tango dancer or a gigolo, nor did he look like a playboy.

"Hello," I said.

120

His greeting showed that he was trying to be cordial and to indicate that any relative of Bella's was a friend of his.

"Swell to see you here," he said.

It occurred to me that my previous estimate of him had been wrong. He did not look like a man who would leave unpaid bills behind him, but after a few amenities I took the matter up.

"I just stopped at the garage on the main road," I said. "The man there says he made some repairs on your car. He thinks you may have forgotten it. You know how those people are, just two jumps ahead of the sheriff." Mr. Berg looked concerned and he looked at me carefully for a moment before he answered.

"That bill was paid on the first of the month," he said. "If you give me the name and address I'll send out another check tonight." He took out a small notebook and a gold pencil and I gave him the name and address.

"Thanks for telling me," Berg said. "I don't like things like that." He paused. His eyes, I noticed, were a yellow brown. His voice was modulated without being well-bred. It possessed an excess smoothness reminiscent of his pointed lapels, and of his exquisitely folded handkerchief. "Please get this," he went on. "I pay my bills. I pay them promptly always."

I got it—that and a good deal more. He was younger than I was. He belonged to a group about which I knew very little, but he was stating a definite fact, confident of my understanding and acceptance. He meant he was not the kind who could afford to let bills go, not even little bills.

"Then you haven't minded my bringing it up?" I said.

"No," said Berg. "I appreciate it, really."

It is hard to understand what a woman sees in a man, because she almost always sees something that a man doesn't. What Bella saw in most of her boy friends was even more mysterious, but I could guess what her interest was in this one. He must have appealed to her sense of recklessness; he must have appealed to her curiosity, for it was hard not to wonder what he had been, what he had seen, where he had come from. He still stood near me as if he were as interested in me as I was in him, or else he did not

121

want to give the impression of getting out of the way. He simply stood there, evidently preferring that I should do the talking.

"Bella says you work in New York," I said. I was sorry as soon as I had spoken. It sounded as if I took, in the capacity of Bella's relation, an interest in his prospects.

"That's right," he answered, and he gave a firm name which sounded like a brokerage house. He even added a further explanation:—

"Business is pretty slack in summer, that's why I'm here so much. I hope you're staying overnight."

"I'm not," I said. "I'm going on. Sorry, I'd like to see more of you." Mr. Berg smiled pleasantly. There wasn't really anything the matter with him except that everything was a little unfamiliar.

"Sorry too," he said. "We might have had some bridge."

"You'd be too good for me," I answered.

"Oh no," he said, "I wouldn't say just that. Swell to have seen you."

It wasn't swell to have seen him, but he was interesting, new.

When I found Bella her voice indicated that she was finishing her third cocktail and that she was having a wonderful time. I put my hand around her thin bare arm and drew her a step or two away from the group which she had been entertaining.

"I'm going now, sweetness," I said. "I've just been eating caviar with Berg."

"Jim," said Bella. "What did you say to him?" It really seemed as though she might be frightened.

"I was wrong about him," I said. "The Bergs always pay their debts, but I'd look out for that boy, sweetness. Watch yourself."

She wrenched her arm out of my hand, but when I was a step or two away she ran after me.

"Jim," she said, "if I want you tomorrow or the next day, where can I get you on the telephone?" Her voice was a little breathless; she really wanted to know.

"Oh," I said, "afraid you're going to get into a jam?"

"No," she said, "of course not."

The complete candor of her answer told me that she was not telling the whole truth, and it came over me that she had not been natural all day in a good many little ways.

"Listen," I said, "are you up to something, Belle?"

"Why, no," she answered. "What a silly question!" And then she added before I could speak: "What makes you ask?"

"Because you said," I answered, "that you couldn't go on like this."

She hesitated a moment, and then she laughed.

"But, darling," she told me, "I say that all the time."

"It wouldn't be possible that you're trying to get in touch with Joe Stowe?" I asked her.

"You have such a funny imagination when you have a drink," she said.

"You wouldn't want to know where you could get me, unless you thought you might want me," I said. "You'd better tell me, Belle."

"I don't see why it is," she answered, "that you keep trying to make something out of nothing. I don't ask you any questions. You can get away with anything."

"All right," I said. "I'll be at Stanhope's office tomorrow and the next day and perhaps the next. I'd be careful, honey bee."

"Oh, be careful yourself," she answered. "I know why you're going to New York."

I knew that there was no use talking to her. In her present mood it would only be a waste of time, and besides I was glad to see the last of Bella for a little while.

"So long," I said, "and take a little solid food before you have any more Martinis."

XII | Autograph, Mr. Stowe?

When I turned left onto Beacon Street it was six-thirty in the evening, the end of a hot and sultry day. The Common was crowded with people, mostly men in shirt sleeves stretched out prone on newspapers. The fountain in the Frog Pond was turned on strong, and its basin was full of children whose cries drowned out the noise of the traffic and rose into the air with a sound similar to the chatter of blackbirds over Wickford Point. The marble wings attached to the red brick of the State House presented the only incongruous note. The rest was the way it should have been, even to the planting of the Public Garden.

I left my car and ignition key with the perspiring, gold-braided doorman at the Crofton. I never knew what he did with cars, because there was never any place to park them. Although the Crofton had been built for a good many years, it still gave, for no good reason, the impression of being garishly new. It was possible to converse with the headwaiter in French, and dazed Continentals who found themselves in Boston made for it at once. So did everyone in show business, and in fact everyone of importance from anywhere. This gave the lobby a certain distinction, and probably for that reason Harvard boys and debutantes liked to use the bar, and you could almost always see something striking and unexpected in the dining room.

Joe Stowe had been given a bedroom and sitting room especially designed for celebrities. It looked very much like the setting for that play of Benelli's in which the Barrymore boys had once acted—"The Jest." There was a Renaissance fireplace, a refectory table along the wall, copies of del Sarto, and some brand-new Renaissance furniture. There were also some upholstered chairs and a sofa, so that you did not have to use the others. Joe Stowe was lying on the sofa in his underwear; he got up when I came in and squared his shoulders aggressively. Even on the hottest day he never appeared to lose his nervous energy. No matter how tired he was, his mind was always restlessly active, and no matter where one saw him he had a capacity for being the same.

"Take off your coat," Joe said. "What's been keeping you so long? I've been waiting for you in this goddam museum nearly three hours. A little squirt from the publisher's has been up here talking to me. They're sending him with me to Vermont tomorrow."

"Who was he?" I asked.

Joe ran his stubby fingers through his sandy hair. His face was shining with perspiration so that little highlights glanced off his forehead and his cheekbones. I remembered what Cousin Clothilde had said about it once—an undistinguished face. The mouth was too large and the nose was too small and the greenish-yellow eyes were deep-set, but all the features came together when he grinned. His expression gave no immediate indication that he was a sensitive person.

"Who was he?" he repeated. "How should I know who he was? He's just one of those boys that all the publishers send out—one of those parasites who batten on you and me. They all look alike and they all dress alike and they all feed you a free meal and introduce you to somebody else."

"Well, don't get sore at him," I said. "He has to earn his living."

Joe walked over to the refectory table, fished for an ice cube floating in a watery bowl, weighed it between his fingers and dropped it back again because there was not enough to it to cool a drink.

"There's one thing," said Joe. "I can tell them what I think of

125

them right now, and they all come back for more. By God, they ought all to be drowned!"

He had not been drinking; he was simply experimenting with his blood pressure. It seemed curious to me that he never lost his capacity for excitement. He was always angry about something or crazy about something. Sometimes he got himself so mixed up that he was both things at once, and now he was dealing with a subject which was particularly dear to him, because many people in the past had taken advantage of him, and he hated all the business details of his life. He gave his shoulders another shrug as though an unseen hand had pushed him in the face.

"If everybody would just get together and be like me," Joe said, "we might all get along. The trouble with this country is that the producers are being sucked dry by the nonproductive class. For everyone who does something there are twenty who live off it. They're like the boy in the men's room who runs a little water and gives you a towel and then wants a dime. I say to hell with the whole lot of them. To hell with the dramatic agents and the literary agents and the moving picture agents and the publishers' agents. What I want is peace. How do they expect you to do any work if they keep after you all the time?"

He didn't mean half of what he said. It was only that he liked to hear himself talk. It gave him some sort of release, and he knew it was perfectly safe to talk to me since I knew what he meant and what he didn't. Something else was going on in his mind. He had a way of working at two things at once.

"What did he do to you?" I asked. Joe was pacing barefooted up and down the carpet.

"I'll tell you what he did," Joe said, "he damn near got me to write a book. He got me talking and he caught me with my intellectual pants down."

"Is that why you haven't got any on?" I asked.

"You know what they do," Joe said. "They always have some idea for a book that they want somebody to write. It's always some piece of non-fiction that must be done by somebody with

126

a name. Before I knew it, I got interested, and the next thing—do you know what he wanted me to do?"

"No," I said.

"Well," Joe said, "those books are always about America. Their minds don't work any further than that. It's always something about feeling the pulse of America from another point of view. You know what I mean. You know what they do. They take some Englishman usually, who can't get along at home. If they can't get an Englishman, they sandbag somebody else, and they send him across the continent on roller skates or in a balloon or submarine, so that he will get a new and interesting perspective and find out what the farmers in the Dust Bowl are thinking about. How do they know that anybody thinks? This time it was about the sharecroppers."

"That's very, very timely," I said.

I was glad to be back with Joe, not that anything he was saying made much sense, but it was nice to talk to someone who thought the same way you did. Writers are a very lonely lot, who generally can't get on well with each other beyond a certain point.

"Do you know what he almost did?" said Joe. "He almost got me down there in a trailer. He had the papers right out on the table. You've got to be careful of those boys. Once when I woke up in the morning I found I had to write the life of Calhoun, and once I nearly had to do a life of Henry Clay Frick—remember?"

I told him I remembered. Then Joe thought of something else, and he began to scowl.

"What made you tell that big poop Allen Southby that I was here?" he asked. "Don't you know that I always try to go through town without seeing him?"

"I thought he was a friend of yours," I said. "Besides we have to hand it to Allen, don't we? He wrote *The Transcendent Curve*."

Joe made a coarse uncomplimentary sound.

"It doesn't pay to be jealous, Joe," I said. "He's written a great book, a fine book. Beneath his pen the glamorous panorama of American thought moves in a scintillating progress."

He made another vulgar sound before I had finished. A lot of people had begun to be afraid of Joe.

"Now that you've brought up that point," Joe said, "let's admit I have to spend a lot of time not being jealous of other people. I'm pretty sick of being big-hearted, but just let me tell you I'm really not jealous of Southby, so now I have to *prove* I'm not jealous of him. He's asked us both out there to dinner and we have to go. Actually I pity him. I hope you understand."

"I understand. I pity him too," I said.

We both knew what we meant, for we both had the feeling that we could have done a good deal better than Allen Southby, given his opportunities. Yet there was no real reason for Joe to have been exercised about Southby, for Joe had had the reviewers eating out of his hand ever since the success of his last two books.

As I sat there looking at him in his undershirt and plum-colored shorts, I recalled what one of our most valued critics had written of his recent work.

"It is doubtful," he had written, "whether any living writer in English can equal Mr. Stowe as a master of prose. One must turn back far, and perhaps in vain, to match the sensitiveness of his ear."

You might have thought that he was ashamed of that ability of his, for he had spent most of his life trying to hide it, except when he was writing, just as he tried to hide his gentleness and compassion. Any mention of his style made him mad. He said that he hated literary style and that he wasn't one of the art boys.

"Well," Joe said, "we have to spoil a perfectly good evening to show that we aren't jealous. You want to take a shower? I'm going to take a shower. Well, anyway come on in and talk to me."

I followed him into a Louis Seize bedroom, where he took off his shorts and shirt. He was puffy around the eyes, but his body was very thin, almost emaciated, as it always had been. I saw the white welt of a scar on his right shoulder and I remembered where

128

he got it. He was already in the tub behind the shower curtains before I spoke again. The cold water had just hit him.

"Jesus!" he exclaimed.

"It won't be so bad at Allen's," I said. "Maybe Allen didn't tell you. He's writing a novel."

Joe stepped out of the bathroom with a towel in his hand. He came into the bedroom dripping wet and he looked worried.

"He didn't tell me that," he said. "Are you sure he's writing a novel?"

"He let me read some of it," I said, "and he's certainly going to let us read some more of it tonight. Wait till you see it, Joe. It's terrible."

But Joe still looked worried.

"How do you know it's rotten, Jim?" he asked. "What's it about?" His forehead was wrinkled; his eyes were anxious.

"He let me read the first chapters," I said, "about two weeks ago. It's a New England novel, the strong, fearless kind, lusty and robust. The hero belches on the first page."

Joe's reaction was unexpected; he still was looking serious.

"And you say it's rotten?" he inquired.

"It's worse than that, Joe," I said. "Just try to imagine Allen Southby trying and you'll have the right idea."

Joe shook his head and began pulling clean linen out of his bag. As he did so, his hairbrushes and some tooth paste fell on the floor, but he did not pick them up.

"You can't tell about those things," he said. "It's just possible . . . it's just the sort of thing that might happen. It might be good."

I knew why he was serious then. I felt an actual twinge of something that was almost fear.

"Now listen," I said, "it can't be good." My voice was almost pleading.

"You can't tell, Jim," Joe answered. "If it were a short story, it would have to be bad because you can't make mistakes in a short story. But with a novel you can do the most awful things and still get somewhere, and this talk about lusty robust work frightens me. Right now, if something is lusty and robust enough, almost anything is excused. Does he use the word 'belly'?"

"Yes," I said. "The hero has a sensation in his belly." Joe was tying a washable, light-colored necktie.

"It might just be that it's good," he repeated. "Think of all the good novels that are written by people who have never written anything before. Think of all the new talent that wins the publishers' Prize Contests every year. Think of all the frustrated schoolteachers and the sand-hogs and the policemen who write good novels."

"Allen isn't frustrated," I said.

"I know," said Joe. "It's a good thing that he isn't frustrated— but still you can't be sure. He may be writing a good novel, and if he does I don't think I can stand it. He hasn't done anything to deserve it. He isn't even bright; but he's just the sort of person who might do it."

"You wait till you see it," I said. "Ask him to show it to you. It's about the Wickford Valley." Joe looked startled.

"Has he done that?" he said. "I was going to write about the Wickford Valley myself."

"As a matter of fact I was thinking about it too," I said.

It was the first time that he had alluded to Wickford Point, and even the allusion had done something to him. Of course the subject was bound to come up, but I did not like to talk to him about Wickford Point. It gave me a feeling of divided loyalty.

Joe straightened his coat and looked at himself in the mirror.

Both Sidney and Harry had always given a great deal of thought to clothes. When those two got together and there was no immediate family crisis, they could spend hours discussing tweeds and the cut of lapels or discoursing on overtailored coats. They sounded almost like the page in the theater program which you read between the acts when every effort at conversation has failed. I never could understand it, since they never cared much what they wore themselves. I gathered that they felt personally freed from these sartorial shackles, because they were the Brills

130

and because everybody knew that they were the Brills. Neverthe-less the fact remained that Sidney and Harry felt themselves authorities upon clothes, and they had always agreed that Joe's taste in dress was not good. More recently they enlarged on the subject and said that his taste in dress was just what you would expect considering what he was.

Personally I thought that Joe looked rather well that evening in his tropical suit and Panama. It was true that his ties and his socks did not fit into any particular color scheme, but he looked better than anyone I had seen at the Jaeckels'.

As we descended in the elevator, which always seemed to carry, along with its passengers, the faint perfume of a beauty parlor, Joe made a suggestion:—

"Perhaps we ought to have a drink before we start," he said. "Then Southby's cocktails won't taste so bad."

When Joe appeared there was a decorous stir in the neighbor-hood of the hotel desk. The house detective near the elevator nodded to him.

"Everything all right, Mr. Stowe?" he asked.

"Nobody's got in there yet, Ed," Joe answered. The house detective looked happy. A member of the managerial staff bowed and said: "Good evening, Mr. Stowe." A boy with a pimply face, who had been sitting under a potted palm, got up so quickly that he mingled with the palm leaves.

"Mr. Stowe," he said.

"Yes," said Joe.

"I've been waiting to speak to you, Mr. Stowe," he said. "I'm the literary editor of the *East Boston High School Magazine*. Could you give me an interview, just for a minute, Mr. Stowe?"

There was no necessity to be nice, but Joe was nice to him.

"All right," he said. "they told me you were here and I forgot about it. I'm sorry I kept you waiting. It never pays to offend the press. What do you want? I'll give you just three minutes." They walked away into a corner behind the palms while I stood and watched.

"What is your favorite hobby, sir?" the East Boston High School editor was asking and I heard Joe answering similar questions without any display of rancor.

"They told me I couldn't get an interview, sir," the boy said.

"Well, you did," said Joe, "an exclusive interview."

Behind me I heard someone else speaking.

"It's Mr. Stowe," someone was saying, and someone else said: "He looks just like Sinclair Lewis."

I told him about it when we got to the bar, because I thought it might amuse him, but it didn't.

"I don't look like Red Lewis at all," he said. "Do you think I look like Red?"

The radio was going in the corner and the bar boys in white mess jackets were passing drinks and potato chips and bowls of popcorn. I was thinking of other Boston barrooms which had existed before it was customary for women to frequent them— the outlets of another lustier age, when the barkeeper always asked us if we were sure we were twenty-one. It had been a long while since anyone had asked that question.

Joe remembered those times too, but his mind was on the present. He was interested in the bar attendants and their monkey jackets. They reminded him of a recipe that D. H. Lawrence had given for making the world better, in *Lady Chatterley's Lover*. Lawrence's hero had said that humanity would be much improved if all men would wear short jackets and tight breeches. Joe could not remember why this would make the world better, but he pointed out that here we were in a laboratory where this was being tried and that still the world seemed to be about the same.

"No," I said, "it's better than it used to be."

"No," he said, "it isn't. It's absolutely the same."

"Just ask yourself," I suggested. "Aren't you better off than you were three years ago?"

As soon as I had spoken I was sorry, for I was bringing up again something which I had not wanted to mention. Joe looked grim and he had forgotten about *Lady Chatterley's Lover*.

132

"You're damned well right I'm better off," he answered. "It's like being out of prison. It's like being alive again. I'm sorry, I didn't mean to say it quite that way, but you know what I mean."

I knew exactly what he meant, and he meant a good deal more than he said.

"All right," I said. "Go ahead and say it."

"All right," said Joe. "To hell with the Brills! I still feel that way."

Before I answered, he gave a partial explanation, not that any explanation was really needed.

"They tried to ruin me," he said. "They tried to take out my heart and lungs and liver and stuff me with sawdust."

"They didn't mean to do that," I said. "They couldn't help it, Joe."

It was not the place to develop the matter further, over gin cocktails and potato chips with the radio playing swing selections. You would have to go back to Wickford Point; you would have to go back to all sorts of checks and balances to explain it, and at any rate Joe's answer interrupted me.

"The hell they couldn't help it," he said.

There was no use going on with it.

"Cousin Clothilde told me to give you her love," I said.

Joe's expression changed and for the moment he did not look angry.

"Jim," he said, "I wish I didn't keep worrying about Bella every now and then."

XIII | Of All
Sad Words . . .

There was no longer doubt that the ride to Cambridge would not be agreeable, and I began to pity myself as I faced it. It seemed to me that I was always finding myself, through no fault of my own, the arbiter of other people's difficulties. First Bella had sat beside me in the car, and no sooner was the seat vacant than there was Joe Stowe. I had never intended my car to become the sanctum of a psychoanalyst, and neither Joe nor Bella paid me twenty-five dollars an hour to listen to their naïve confessions.

"So you say they couldn't have helped it?" Joe said. "You know damn well they could have helped it. I've heard you say so yourself. You said I had a rotten deal."

"But they couldn't have," I repeated. It was a matter of survival, Joe. It was either you or they. They had to make you one of them or they couldn't have existed."

"Hogwash," Joe said; but then he seemed to have regretted his outburst.

"When I think back," he said, "it seems to me that I leaned over backwards to be considerate. I'm able to get on with people. I have a certain amount of sense."

"Cousin Clothilde sent you her love," I said again.

"Did she?" said Joe. "She never means anything she says, unless it's about herself. There's no relying on what any of them say. They'll talk themselves out of anything and you know it."

"I don't agree with you," I said. "Let's skip it, Joe."

Joe's head moved toward me quickly and I knew he was looking at me to determine how I felt.

"All right," he said. "I'm sorry, Jim."

"Then don't go sounding off to me," I said. "They're relatives of mine."

"All right," said Joe. "I'm sorry, Jim."

The sky was growing red with the sunset, which meant another hot day tomorrow. It made me think of the old couplet: "Red sky at night, sailor's delight." Perhaps I did not like the look of it because I was not a sailor. For me the red sky simply reflected mugginess and mental discontent. The traffic was very heavy on Commonwealth Avenue, and they were doing something to the street near the offices of the National Casket Company. I wondered if the time would come when all the façades of Commonwealth Avenue would conceal schools and businesses and doctors' offices. Certainly everything was changing fast. Business might be on the rocks, but everyone had some sort of car, and everyone was trying to get out of town as anxiously as though beating a retreat before an invading army. We crawled along Bay State Road and neither Joe nor I spoke, until we reached the new drive by the river, where we could see some small boats sailing and Harvard summer students rowing single shells. We did not speak but we might as well have been speaking; we both were thinking the same disturbed thoughts. We were both back at Wickford Point.

"Do you remember old Beaver?" Joe asked.

"Yes," I said. "Don't bring him up." He was referring to old John Brill, of course.

"Well, I don't have to have him with my meals any more," Joe said. "Thank God, I don't have to go to bed with him either."

"But you can't stop talking about him," I said. "Now go ahead and stop."

"Well," said Joe, "you never liked him. Just don't be sanctimonious, that's all I ask."

"Don't be a goddam bore," I said. "You've done everything you could about old Brill."

"Poopsy-woopsy," Joe said, and then was silent for a while.

"Jim," he said at length.

"What?" I answered. We were stopping at a traffic light by one of the bridges.

"Not that I give a damn, but how's Bella?" It was needlessly elaborate. He gave more than a damn and we both knew it.

"Bella's fine," I said. "I just left her with some people by the name of Jaeckel. She's planning to go to Guatemala on a scientific expedition with a man named Dr. Frothinghope."

Joe grinned.

"You must have made her sore," he said. "When she's sore she always thinks up a scientific expedition. Once she was going with Byrd to the South Pole. That was the night I told her she was knock-kneed."

"Well," I said, "she isn't."

"No," said Joe, "that's true, she isn't. I hope she's got some new boy friends."

"There's one at the Jaeckels' now," I said. "His name is Berg."

"That's fine," said Joe. "I hope she's having a good time, but God help Mr. Berg. What's he like?"

"He always pays his debts," I said.

"Jim," he said, "have you ever thought—" He paused and looked across the river.

"Thought what?" I asked.

"Have you ever thought that Bella might kill herself?"

I jammed my foot on the accelerator by mistake, and began to laugh.

"It isn't anything to laugh at," Joe said. "What do you think's so funny about it?"

"Don't worry, she won't kill herself," I said.

It was funny because everyone at Wickford Point occasionally discussed doing away with himself or herself.

"She might, you know," Joe said. The remark was not worth answering. Joe cleared his throat again.

"Is she happy, Jim?" he asked.

"Yes," I said. "She's just as happy as she always was."

"Well, that doesn't mean anything," Joe said. "Has she enough money?"

I drove the car over to the curb and stopped it. We were right in front of the Harvard Business School with a fine view of the new Houses across the river. I turned around so that I could look at Joe.

"Say," said Joe, "what's the matter?"

"I'll tell you what's the matter," I said. "You've got away from Bella and you'd better keep away. Now don't start getting soft. You're not to write to Bella, you're not to telephone her or see her. You're not to get mixed up in that again. If you do, it will only mean that she'll get into you for something, and everything will start all over. Bella's all right. She isn't going to kill herself, and she never gave a damn about you really. Do you understand? Bella doesn't give a damn for anything; she isn't made that way. She can't take time out caring for anybody because she has too much trouble looking out for herself. You're out of it, do you understand? All you have to do is forget about her."

"You needn't be so rough on her," Joe said. "If you won't stand up for Bella, I will."

"Don't you worry," I told him. "There's always going to be someone who's going to stand up for Bella. You're out of it. If she ever calls you up, don't answer. If you ever see her, cross the street."

Joe looked at me for a while before he answered, and I was pleased to see that his face had lost its generous expression.

"All right," he said, "I'm out of it, but is there anything I can do? She never knew I'd make a lot of money."

"There's nothing you can do," I said. "If anybody has to look out for Bella, I will."

"Oh hell," said Joe, "all right."

"Now that we have that straight," I said, "we are going to cross the Larz Anderson bridge and have a nice dinner with our old friend, Dr. Allen Southby."

Joe looked brighter. He was coping with a new idea.

"Do you really think he'll show us that novel?" he said.

"He'll certainly show it to us," I said, "because that's what we're here for."

"I wouldn't mind if you wrote a good novel," Joe said. "You're probably too old and you may have done magazine stuff too long, but I honestly wouldn't mind. And I wouldn't say that to anyone else, Jim, either."

"Thanks," I said, "that's handsome of you."

Then Joe began to laugh.

"What's the matter now?" I asked.

"I was just thinking," Joe said, and he laughed again.

"Well, go ahead," I said, "if it's so funny."

"I was just thinking," Joe said, "Bella always goes for phony intellectuals. How would it be if she got hold of Southby?"

"Don't be too hard on Allen, Joe," I answered. "Make a wax image of him and stick needles in him, but don't be too hard."

Joe rubbed his hand over the back of his head.

"Jim," he said, "it might have been all right."

"What might have been?" I asked.

"Bella and me," he said. "If things had just been a little different here and there—if we'd both tried harder—it might have been all right."

I turned toward him quickly.

"Don't fool yourself," I said. "We all get exactly what's coming to us. You ought to know by this time that there is no such thing as 'might-have-been.' It would always be the same."

I had not intended to speak so frankly, but I knew Bella well enough to know that this was so. She did not get along with Joe. And what was more, they would never get along, certainly not now after everything that had happened. I had heard each of them talk about it often enough, and each of them was entirely right according to personal standards, just as so many others to whom I had listened had been absolutely right when they discussed their marital disagreements through a haze of liquor or through a mist of tears. There was a horrid similarity to all those fallings-out, and the most shocking thing was the final fact that people who

138

had been together could never wholly escape from each other. They both knew too much. Each had an understanding of the other's weaknesses which was uncanny in its accuracy.

I was thinking of breeds of dogs reared to fight, no matter at what odds. If you once let them off the leash, they would cheerfully face the prospect of inevitable destruction, and Joe and Bella were like that. They each knew how to appeal and how to hurt. They would start exactly where they had left off in the same grim struggle. It seemed incredible that Joe did not have the sense to realize it, because a good part of his life had been consumed in studying human values. He was like the psychiatrist who spends his days directing the lives of maladjusted patients, and then runs away with his office secretary and gets a divorce himself. Joe understood everybody except himself and Bella Brill. I knew it would be hours now before those two would leave my mind again. I was leaving them; I was going to New York to attend to my own affairs, and I might even endeavor to enjoy myself; but those two would keep coming into my consciousness, and they had no right to do it. Individuals who pour out their troubles should be locked in concentration camps where they cannot disturb the rest of organized society.

Joe seemed to have forgotten Bella again: he was examining all the new Houses along the river which formed the concrete basis of the Harvard House Plan.

"What do you bet the students still never speak to each other?" Joe said. "What do you bet they all go and eat at their clubs in spite of the House Plan? What's the matter with you, Jim? You're not sore at me, are you?"

"No," I said.

"Then don't be so sour," Joe said. "Dinner with Southby's bad enough without your getting sour."

XIV | Evening
and
the Arts

After many years of effort Joe had learned how to adjust his personality to circumstances. He had never liked Allen Southby much and recently had begun actively to dislike him, yet you would not have guessed it. He became almost charming when we reached the Master's House. Allen was out on the steps to greet us, in white flannels and a gabardine coat. His graying, curly hair had just the proper wind-blown look, and he was smoking his pipe, lighted, I suspected, just when he had seen us coming. Joe too had suddenly turned into a man of letters and they both were very, very gracious; they exhibited pleasing manners developed from constant contact with other literary figures and from experience on lecture platforms.

"It's fine to see you," Allen said, "absolutely swell. Come in. I've got some cocktails in the study."

"I wouldn't have missed coming here for anything," Joe said.

"My sister's away," said Allen. "She always says I have my best times when she's away."

"That means you're working on something," Joe said, and he smiled at Allen playfully. "I know you like to be alone when you're working."

"Did Jim tell you?" Allen asked. "He really shouldn't have told you."

"He didn't need to tell me," Joe said. "After *The Transcendent*

140

Curve everyone's been waiting. You know the way rumors get around. Everyone's been saying it's a novel. I hope you're going to let us read it, Allen."

Allen's expression became modest but delighted.

"You really wouldn't mind looking at it, Joe?" he asked. "Of course I wasn't going to ask you, but if you really wouldn't mind . . . It's the roughest sort of draft."

"I've just been saying to Jim that I hoped you'd let me see it," Joe said. "That is, if it won't disturb you."

"As long as you realize it's just a simple draft," said Allen. "I should love to know if you think I have the right feel for the thing, if you think I have my teeth in it. Jim thinks so. Jim was a great help. I've done quite a bit since then."

"It couldn't be as good as the beginning," I said, "it simply couldn't."

The glance that Allen gave me showed that he could swallow nearly anything. I almost felt ashamed of myself; for after all I was his guest.

"I'm not sure, Jim," he said. "I think perhaps that what I've done since may be just a little better. I'm in the swing of it now, going ahead full steam. I simply couldn't stop now if I tried. It's the first time I've ever realized the lure of fiction."

"That's right," I said. "Don't stop. You mustn't stop."

"You needn't tell him, Jim," Joe said. "He couldn't stop, not if he feels that way."

Allen had led us into the pine-paneled study, where a pewter cocktail shaker and some small pewter cups stood on a tavern table before the empty fireplace. The sight of them reminded Allen of his duties as the host who must say something gracious about each of his guests.

"Let's not talk about my struggles now," he said. "You both know that sort of thing so well. Joe, we ought to get Jim to write a novel, shouldn't we? I mean something really serious. He has it in him if he'd try."

Joe looked at me complacently and back at Allen Southby and nodded in bland assent.

"What's more," said Allen, "I have a bone to pick with Jim. Here I am writing about the Wickford Valley, and he never told me until the other night that he had any connection with it. I've never seemed to associate Jim with it, but I always associated you, Joe. Sorry, old man, I didn't mean to bring that up."

"They have a dogs' graveyard there," said Joe. "You ought to see that graveyard."

"A dogs' graveyard!" said Allen, and his luminous eyes assumed an added brightness. "You don't really mean it. That's just the sort of odd bit I'm looking for. Here I've been sitting in this study, trying to recapture the spirit of that valley, and you two know it. Jim, you must promise to show me that graveyard. I can come down anytime."

I did not answer, and in any case he would not have given me the opportunity, for he had turned back again to Joe.

"I don't suppose you've seen your mail for several days," Allen said. "I don't suppose you've heard the news, Joe."

"What news?" Joe asked.

Allen set down his pipe on the table beside the cocktail shaker.

"It's safe to tell you. It's all settled," Allen said. "Your election has been ratified. I wish to welcome you in my position as an older but not as a more valued member. Joe, you've made the Institute."

"What institute?" Joe asked.

"The Institute of Arts and Letters," Allen said.

Joe lost a part of his poise.

"Oh hell," he said, "am I in that?"

"You certainly are," said Allen, "and now as an older member, I want to drink your health."

"I didn't ask to be in it, did I?" Joe said.

Allen laughed agreeably.

"No one has ever asked," he explained. "It is an honor which is thrust upon one." He lifted up the cocktail shaker and shook his head indulgently at his own forgetfulness.

"I clean forgot about the ice," he said. "Excuse me for just a minute, will you?"

142

Joe and I stood alone in the study against the background of Allen Southby's books. The pewter in the old pine dresser shone vaguely in the waning light. We watched each other until we were sure that our host was out of earshot, and then Joe made a face.

"God-damned patronizing bastard," Joe said. "How long do we have to sit here and see him throw his weight around?"

"Wait till you see the novel," I said softly.

Joe unbuttoned his jacket. He was examining the paneling and the books.

"Don't let's speak about it," he whispered. "It's going to be good. I know it's going to be good."

The cocktails were a credit to Allen in that they proved conclusively that he seldom drank them. He must have been aware himself of their deficiencies, for he came back with a pewter mug when he brought the ice.

"As you both know, my old love has always been ale," he said. "I hope you'll excuse me. Ale and a pipe are about as far as I've ever gone."

"You wouldn't mind if I smoked a cigarette?" Joe asked.

Allen laughed. It was a mistake to think that he was stupid or that you could make fun of him indefinitely.

"Don't jape at me," Allen said. "You have the outside view of the academic life, but we're really almost human here."

In a way he had put Joe in his place, and Allen was just as capable as Joe was. I grew more alive to this when we sat down to dinner in the Master's dining room, which had been architecturally prepared for the reception of an occasional distinguished guest who might be visiting the university. The food was brought in by an old Negro in a white coat. He was old Sam, Allen explained to us, who was the steward at the Vindex Club during term time and who came to Allen in the summer. I had nearly forgotten the Vindex Club until Allen mentioned it. It was the undergraduate literary club, whose membership included all nice boys with literary pretensions. They went there to listen to the discussions of their betters, and to strain their minds with epigrams after dinner. Allen had been taken in when he was an undergraduate and he must have spent a lot of time there later, sitting at the head of the long table dispensing charm, or taking a staid part in the literary revels. He was a good host now, with a keen intuitive interest. For a while his talk went back, as it had the last time I had seen him, to Irish letters—the natural result of a previous vacation spent in the neighborhood of Dublin. There he had been received, apparently cordially, by all the figures of a literary world with which I was unfamiliar, but Joe knew them and Joe became interested. They talked for quite a while about the "Anglos" and about Glendalough, and about Yeats and the Abbey, and about the Gate. They also exchanged anecdotes concerning various characters whose names reminded one of controversies in American municipal politics. They talked through salmon and salad while I listened, half-admiring Allen Southby, and very nearly grateful for his hospitality; and I thought how peculiar it is that food and drink can change one's estimate of character. There was ample opportunity for a number of melancholy thoughts while I listened.

When you are young enough, I thought, all sorts of unrevealed possibilities make you a person, but afterwards when there are no more possibilities you become a type. Nearly every old man sitting about a club is a type that fits into a category as readily as a butterfly or a bee or a praying mantis. Allen Southby was turning into a type and so was Joe Stowe. I wondered if I also were not slowly ceasing to be myself.

Allen was really very nice—I gathered that Joe had begun to think so, too—until he got back to the subject of New England. Then there was something pretentious about him which definitely grated, for there he sat like a self-invited guest assuming that he was part of a family that was not his. He was pretending to be a native, dwelling on austerities and eccentricities. He was particularly bad when he got back to the dogs' graveyard, which he did when dessert came in—cold apple pie and cream. ("A real New England dish," Allen explained. "I thought of having doughnuts, but that would be painting the lily, wouldn't it?")

He had stored Joe's remark about the dogs' graveyard carefully in his mind and now he wanted to hear all about it. It was rather skillfully done, I thought, for he obviously wished to reach a point where we must ask again to see his novel. When I told him some of the names and quoted from the inscriptions upon the little stones he laughed and laughed. He had a musical half-infectious laugh, and he said it was all *so* typically New England. He was still talking of New England when he led us back to his study for coffee. His investigations had given him a fascinating store of reminiscence, and he had also acquired a lot of salty stories about small hamlets in Maine, the kind that deal with ship captains and with rustics sitting around the country store. He could even give a very tolerable imitation of the accepted hinterland accent. He stuffed some aromatic tobacco in his pipe and offered us cigars, but he still went on talking while Joe encouraged him with complimentary words.

After a while Allen's enthusiasm began to wane. He obviously wanted us to ask about the novel; and though Joe must have known it, he never brought the subject up until Allen began to fidget in his chair. Joe was deliberately waiting for him to begin, and in a certain way it was not good manners. Then when the clock struck nine, Allen gave up.

"Were you really serious," he asked, "when you said you wanted to see this thing I'm doing?"

"Why, see here," Joe said, "I've only been waiting for you to ask me again, and so has Jim. Haven't you, Jim?"

Allen Southby drew a deep breath and set down his pipe almost with relief.

"I really do want both of you to see it," he said, "really. I haven't shown it to another soul except Martha."

"What did Martha say?" I asked.

Allen drew another deep breath and walked over to the drawer of his desk.

"She felt the same way you did about it, Jim," he said.

"Well, that couldn't have been better," I told him, "and a woman's reaction is always more important than a man's."

145

Allen had produced the manuscript from the desk drawer. He held it with a studied carelessness in his hands.

"You're sure it isn't too much trouble?" he said.

When everything was said and done, Joe might talk a lot but he was never actively unkind.

"No trouble at all, Allen," he answered.

"You understand it's just a rough first draft," Allen said. "I know Jim understands already. You won't be too hard on it?"

"Of course not," said Joe. "We know what first drafts are."

Allen Southby sighed. He had divided the manuscript in two parts.

"Here's the beginning, Joe," he said, "up to where Jim left off. I'll give Jim the rest of it and you can ask him for it when you're ready."

"All right," said Joe, "let's have it." But Allen still held the manuscript, behaving just as he had when he had shown it to me before.

"The first page is a little jerky," he said. "I was trying to get the feel of the thing. Jim made the remark that some of the language was crude."

"Jim ought to know better," Joe said. "You have to let yourself go, Allen."

"You really think so?" Allen asked. "Well, I *have* let myself go. I've tried to be absolutely myself. Here it is, Joe. Just remember the first page is rather rough." By this time I began to wish that Allen would be quiet.

"Are you sure you're comfortable in that chair, Joe?" Allen asked. "Is the light all right? Are you comfortable, Jim? I've always liked that Windsor chair myself."

I wished for heaven's sake he would shut up. The room was refreshingly quiet when we began to read, but Allen was still fidgeting about, first looking at us, then looking at his books. The sound of the motors on Memorial Drive came through the windows. Allen took down a large leather folio from the shelves and retired to his desk. As I sat there reading I was reminded of an examination room in the old days. Allen was behind the desk to

146

see that Joe and I did not cheat. He pretended not to look at us, but I knew he was not reading. Once I stole a glance at Joe. He was going at his work deliberately, dropping each page abstractedly upon the floor when he had finished it. Joe was a fast and accurate reader and he had been reading ever since I'd first known him, whether he was drunk or sober. At the end of fifteen minutes Allen spoke.

"What do you think of it so far?" he asked.

Joe looked up as though his mind had been called back from a long distance.

"It's amazing," he said. "Don't interrupt me, Allen."

"How far have you read?" Allen asked.

"Where he gets back from watching the cows in the stable," Joe said, "and finds her in the kitchen after everyone has gone to bed."

"You think that's all right?" Allen asked. "I was a little afraid about that part."

"You needn't be," said Joe. "Now let me go ahead."

"And you're really interested?" said Allen.

"It's going fine so far," said Joe. "Have you got any whisky, Allen?"

"Oh," Allen said, "I'm awfully sorry. Yes, yes, of course. I'll go and fetch some."

We sat listening to his footsteps as he crossed the hall and the dining room. The pantry door swung to behind him, and we heard him giving Sam directions. Then Joe got up, tiptoed toward me and held out his hand.

"Boy," Joe whispered, "it's all right. You win. Everything's all right. It's just perfectly lousy and his publisher will have to print it. I'm almost sorry for him now."

Joe and I did not make a pretty picture. I was almost ashamed of my relief and at my sense of vindication, but not wholly.

"Get back there," I whispered, "he's coming with the whisky." And then I raised my voice.

"It's very full-bodied, Joe."

"Yes," said Joe, "full-bodied."

We could hear Allen Southby crossing the dining room on

tiptoe. He had wanted to hear what we were saying and he had heard that it was full-bodied. There was a clink of ice and glasses. "Give me what you've finished, Jim," Joe said. "Pour me out a drink, Allen. It's getting better all the time."

The part of Allen's manuscript which I was reading was worse than the beginning, and each page which I finished confirmed a number of my opinions about practical writing. Considering the shelves of volumes in the stacks of libraries dealing with the art, it is amazing how little this great mass has ever contributed to any sensible discussion—probably because nearly all those books have been written by hangers-on at the edges of the trade. My mind strayed away from Allen Southby's manuscript as I thought of this, for I had gone once, like so many others, to this very type of literature in search of expert guidance. And now no matter how I racked my brain I could scarcely recall a single serious book on the craftsmanship of fiction written by a successful fiction writer. It must have been that few who could write had ever wanted to discuss it.

No one could teach anyone else to write. You could be as industrious as you pleased; you could steep yourself in the technique of all the Flauberts and Maupassants and Dickenses who had gone before, and out of it would come exactly nothing. That was the trouble with Allen Southby.

There is something revealing about amateur fiction which is particularly ghastly, for in this type of effort you can see all the machinery behind the scene. I could tell exactly what Allen had been reading before he had set to work. He had made a study of Hardy—it must have been a dreary task—and then he had touched on Sherwood Anderson and Glenway Westcott and O'Neill. He had been reading a lot of those earth-earthy books, where the smell of dung and the scent of the virgin sod turned by the plow runs through long paragraphs of primitive though slightly perverted human passion; but those others could write, and Allen Southby never would if he lived as long as Moses. Nevertheless I was finding the thing stimulating again. I was thinking of ways in which I might have changed it.

Allen was back at his desk, fiddling with his folio volume. He saw me right away when I paused and reached for the whisky glass.

"There's nothing the matter with it, is there, Jim?" he asked.

"No," I said. "It's very provocative, Allen."

"That's wonderful," said Allen. "Thank you, Jim, but we mustn't disturb Joe."

The delicate feeling of liking that I was experiencing for him, born probably from a sense of remorse, vanished with this remark. He was an intellectual snob and an intellectual climber. He had intimated without much tact that any adulation of mine was inconsequential now that Joe was there. He would never know that my remark had been completely truthful. Southby had been provocative because he was writing about something which I could understand far better than he could ever understand it. It was not the plot, which was horrible, that arrested my attention so much as his manner of writing. His pages resembled the efforts of visiting writers, who had spent their summers in Maine and on Cape Cod, to depict the New England scene. The effect was the same as when some Northern writer attempted an epic of the South, and could see nothing but nigger mammies and old plantations and colonels drinking juleps. These others, when they faced New England, saw only white houses, church spires, lilacs and picket hedges, gingham hypocrisy and psychoses and intolerance. Not even Kipling, the keenest observer who had touched our coast, could do it. There was something which they did not see, an inexorable sort of gentleness, a vanity of effort, a sadness of predestined failure.

I handed the rest of the pages to Joe and poured myself another drink. There was no need for conversation since Allen Southby did not want Joe to be disturbed. It was a quarter after ten o'clock and it was not unpleasant sitting there, listening to the noise outside the windows. First I wondered what was wrong with that writing, and then I began thinking about myself in the hazy disorganized way one thinks when there is nothing else to do. I believed that I was under no illusion about my literary skill. I

149

was not fool enough to attempt such a thing as Southby was attempting. It was all well enough to think of it, but even as I thought I knew that I should never do it. I did not have the energy nor could I afford the gamble, and a serious novel is a very great gamble for one who must live by writing. A five hundred dollars' cash advance might be all that I could get for a year's work, because the thing would never serialize. I knew that I should never do it. Allen Southby's writing was filling my mind with all sorts of noncommercial ideas. I would be in New York in the morning, and I would be having a talk with my literary agent, but I could not talk with him of those ideas.

My mind kept going back, as it did when I was restless, to scenes at Wickford Point. I was thinking of them all standing by the doorway when we drove away after lunch. I had seen more of New England in this one day than Allen Southby had ever seen. I remembered how Herman had smelled when he had been held up for me to kiss. I had been aware of strange jealousies and of odd habits and of undercurrents of inheritance which had nothing much to do with lilacs or picket fences. Then half-instinctively, without really meaning to, I was thinking of situation and plot. There were so many engrossing details of which one might write which could not decently be set down on paper. There was Wickford Point, for instance, and Joe and Bella Brill, and all the times we had had together, all those strange unprintable scenes which were really worth preserving. Some of them were bizarre, some of them were ugly, and some of them were beautiful.

"Well," Allen Southby was saying, "so you've finished it, have you, Joe?"

Joe picked up the manuscript, straightened the pages expertly, and handed them back to Allen, and Allen waited almost diffidently for him to speak.

"We all understand writing," Joe said, "so we don't need to talk much, do we, Allen?"

"No," said Allen Southby, "no, of course not, Joe. I just want a reaction, but of course I am open to suggestions. I can stand criticism as well as the next man, as long as it's intelligent criticism."

Joe nodded very gravely. Without saying anything he gave the impression of being deeply moved. I had seen him do the same thing before, and I nearly believed that he was in earnest.

"Now, Allen," Joe said, "I'm not going to say anything, although my inclination is to talk to you all night. I haven't been so excited for a long while."

"Were you really excited?" Allen Southby asked.

"So excited," Joe said, "that I won't sleep all night. There are certain paragraphs and passages that keep running through my mind—that scene in the hayfield where she comes to help him find his shirt, and that part about the old lady hiding her money under the loose brick of the hearth. I won't forget those for a long while, Allen, but I'm not going to speak of them. It would be too dangerous."

"How do you mean, too dangerous?" Allen Southby asked.

Joe picked up his glass, looked at it critically and drank its contents before he answered.

"You have it going now," Joe said, "at such a pace that I wouldn't have the rudeness to interrupt you, Allen. I might say something inadvertent which would break the flow of everything. That's why I'm not going to say a word, and Jim isn't going to say a word either. We're standing on the threshold of something which we must not destroy."

"But you like it, don't you?" Allen said.

"Do you think I'd talk this way if I didn't like it?" Joe Stowe asked.

"But don't you think you could just give me some idea," Allen suggested, "of the way you feel?"

Joe shook his head firmly.

"No," he said, "it would be too dangerous. It would be an insolence, Allen. That's the way I feel. You mustn't talk about it to anyone, not even to Martha until you've finished it. You're just at the point where a word might spoil everything."

"You really think it's as good as all that?" Allen asked.

"I certainly do," said Joe.

It was not right for anyone to look as happy as Allen Southby did. That luminous glow in his eyes was almost too good to be true.

"Joe," he said, "I can't thank you enough, really I can't. Will you read the rest of it when it's finished?"

"I certainly will," said Joe.

"Would it be asking too much—" Allen asked—"I don't want to be too presuming, Joe—but would you consider writing a line or two to be put on the jacket?"

"I certainly will," said Joe, "if my agent will let me."

I thought that Allen was going to ignore me altogether, but he did not.

"Jim," he said, "I'm ever so glad you liked it. Your interest has meant a tremendous lot. I shouldn't have dared to show this to Joe if it hadn't been for your encouragement."

"That's all right, Allen," I said.

He looked at me with his most beguiling smile.

"And—oh yes," he said. "When can I come down to Wickford? It would mean a tremendous lot to have a glimpse of things down there right when I'm in the middle of this."

"I'm going to New York," I said.

"Do you have to go to New York?" Allen asked. "When will you be back?"

"This week end perhaps," I said.

"Then let's make it this week end," said Allen Southby. "It's awfully good of you, Jim."

Joe buttoned up his coat.

"Thank you for everything, Allen," he said. "We'll have to be going now."

We did not speak until we reached the car, and I was the one who spoke first.

"God damn him," I said. "I didn't ask him."

"Well," said Joe, "he's going." Then Joe began to laugh and put his hand on my shoulder before I could answer.

"Let's forget it, Jim," he said. "Wasn't that stuff terrible?"

The trouble was that I could not forget it.

152

XV | All Aboard

"I don't blame you for being mad," Joe said. "He's a caponized professor. Forget about it, Jim."

"All right," I said, "but I can't forget about it. I keep thinking about how I'd write that thing myself."

"You do?" said Joe, and his voice was louder. "Well, I've been thinking about how I'd write it too."

"Oh," I said, "you have, have you?"

"But I wouldn't steal one of your ideas," said Joe.

"They're not worth stealing," I said.

Joe put his hand on my shoulder.

"You're sorry for yourself tonight, aren't you?" he inquired. "What's the matter? Has Southby got you down?"

"No," I said, "I'm just thinking, Joe."

I was wondering how it ever happened that Joe and I had been thrown so much together. When one came to think of it, there was an ominous sort of destiny in friendship, about which one could do nothing.

"Listen," Joe said, "do you really have to go to New York?"

I could tell that he had observed the bland way in which I had been ignored and I had a momentary suspicion that he was feeling sorry for me, and nothing from my point of view could have been worse. Such an attitude on his part would inevitably mean that I would end by being jealous of him also and I was doing my best not to be jealous of Joe Stowe. I had been telling myself for a long while that I was glad of everything that had happened to him, that I took a personal sort of pride in his career.

"There are some things I've got to do about a serial story," I said, "and besides I want to get away from Wickford Point."

"That's funny, isn't it?" said Joe.

"What's funny?" I asked.

"About Wickford Point," Joe said. "You all go down there and say how lovely it is, and then none of you can stand it. Everyone starts fighting and then everyone goes to Europe."

"You used to like it once," I said.

The cars which passed us from the opposite direction made dashes of light against the windshield, like uneven splashes of phosphorescent water. Joe's voice was grim when he answered.

"Yes," he agreed, "I loved it. It's all right when you're not mixed up in it. If you're going to New York, what are you going to do with your car?"

"Leave it in a garage," I said. "Sid always monkeys with it if I leave it at Wickford Point."

"Oh, my God," said Joe. "Sid's there, is he? Is Harry there? Has he got some new ideas?"

I told him that Harry was coming up for the week end.

"There will be that same muddy smell from the river," said Joe. "And the trees will be greener than anywhere else, and the hummingbirds will keep buzzing in the trumpet vines, and the plumbing will get out of order. And the tortoise-shell cat will have kittens and everybody will be unhappy in the parlor, and Sid will have indigestion and nobody will be able to stand it any longer."

There was no use answering. Joe remembered everything.

"There will still be some delphiniums in the little garden," he said. "I don't suppose anyone's ever got around to weeding it. I don't suppose anyone's cleared out the path to the point."

He paused and I did not answer. We were almost back in town before he spoke again.

154

"Jim," he said, "let's get out of this. It isn't good for you to hang around that place. Maybe we could do some work if we went away. I'm sick to death of being bothered."

"Where do you want to go?" I asked. "You don't want to be quiet. You like to be bothered."

Joe moved uneasily.

"Well, I need a change," he said. "I can fix it so we go out to China. What do you say, Jim? Or if you don't like China, there's Spain. How about going to Barcelona? Or if you don't like that, there's—"

"There's what?" I asked.

"Oh, hell," said Joe, "there's anywhere."

I knew exactly what he meant. He was thinking about Wickford Point; he was still trying to put it behind him.

"I'll think about it, Joe," I said, but I was reasonably sure that he would forget it all by morning. We were stopping by the brightly lighted door of his hotel by then, and you could see the shadows of the elm trees on the Common and the lights of the advertising signs beyond, which had once caused so much civic disturbance.

"That's fine," Joe said. "I'll get hold of you as soon as I finish this lecture business. I mean it, Jim. Didn't we have a hell of an evening?"

"Yes," I said, "terrible. So long, Joe."

"So long," he said, and we shook hands. He was just turning away when I called him back.

"Joe," I said, "there's just one thing. You keep away from Bella, do you understand? It won't do any good."

The lights above the door were full on his face when he turned back to me, and I remembered again what Cousin Clothilde had said—that it was an undistinguished face. You could see all the freckles and the oversized mouth and the deep-set yellowish green eyes. I had not been sure until that last moment that he was having a rotten time. He could do anything he wanted. There were plenty of other women in the world, and I happened to know he knew it,—offhand I could name three of them in New York,—

155

but he was still not having a happy time. Divorce is like a major operation. You think you are all right and then you have a sinking spell. He was standing there under the lights, and there was nothing much that anyone could do about it. It was like the ending of a story which no editor would want to buy. A while ago he had nearly been sorry for me, and now I was sorry for him, and I was the one who had started it. I was the one who had first taken him to Wickford Point. . . .

". . . She ought to meet some older men," Cousin Clothilde had said. "I mean some interesting men. What ever happened to that nice friend of yours, Mr. Lowe? The one you brought to Wickford Point? He's just the sort of man I mean—someone to take her mind off that Avery Gifford. I don't see what she sees in Avery. Can't you call up Mr. Stowe and ask him to dinner? . . ."

Joe Stowe put his foot on the running-board for a moment. "You damned fool," he said, "I want to keep away from Bella. That's why I'm going somewhere."

"What about Elsie Cash?" I asked.

It was hardly the time or the place to bring that matter up. Joe held out his hand again.

"Oh," he said, "oh, that . . . Well, so long, Jim."

The South Station had changed. It was as new and shiny and as streamlined as modern diplomacy. It made you think of five-point programs, of candid cameras, of leftists and rightists and of the People's Front; in fact, of all those elements that had cropped up to change the life one used to know. Down the center of the station were all sorts of gaily-lighted booths displaying books and periodicals—I saw Joe Stowe's last book out in front—and toys for the kiddies, which could be purchased by a conscience-stricken parent before it was too late, and giant orange drinks and liquor and flowers and nationally advertised confectionery. Yes, the station was changed, but it had the old allure.

There were the same porters and the same whiffs of smoke bringing the same electrifying message. The message was that you were getting away from it and going to New York, and after that you might go anywhere. You were getting away from what

156

was static; you were off to have a good time beyond correction and reproof. All the other times when I had left from that station returned to me, and the memories of nearly all of them were merry. There was the time when Cousin Sue had given the porter a dollar to see that I got back safely to my parents, and when we were driven across the city in a four-wheel cab. Then there were the times when Harry and I used to leave college for our vacations in New York. Cousin Clothilde always put me up in those days, in one of the brownstone houses which she and Archie Wright had rented. You could never tell from year to year just where their house would be. Some years it was in the East Seventies, and once in the Murray Hill district,—one of their nicest houses was turned into a speakeasy later on,— or again it might be down in Washington Square. And once I remember that the whole front of the house they had rented was being torn off and everybody lived in back, and you got mixed up with carpenters and contractors on your way to breakfast. It made no difference though; it was always a lot of fun wherever Cousin Clothilde and Archie Wright were living.

Harry and I used to come down together, always in upper berths, and when we arrived in the morning Cousin Clothilde was always up and glad to see us, and usually Archie Wright came down in his pajamas. As one looks back on it, Archie was very forbearing. It must have been hard on him, being married to a whole houseful of Brills, with me frequently thrown in. We were always getting into his bureau drawers to borrow his shirts and neckties. Occasionally around dinnertime he would be depressed, and once he said he did not know that he had married an orphan asylum, but generally he was affable, and he made Harry and me feel that we were his contemporaries.

No matter where they were living the house always had a certain style, and there was always something funny happening. Once in the old days, when there was more money, they had a French manservant who used to hoist himself up from the kitchen in the dumbwaiter, and who ended at last by coming into the dining room brandishing a carving knife. There were usually some interesting people around, artistic contemporaries, or else callers who might conceivably buy murals. One man who used to come there was named Algernon Weir, and he always would hold his left arm in front of him and pretend that he had an imaginary bird sitting on his wrist. Sometimes it made Cousin Clothilde nervous when he caressed the imaginary bird, but finally he went away somewhere. Lots of the people who came there one season would vanish, but in their places were always new and fascinating faces. There was another man, named Theodore Rudy, who took a great liking to me and sent me a bunch of roses. One winter there was a faith healer and the next there was a theosophist and the next there was a Turk. As I have said, there was always something funny happening, and it was refreshingly different from Harvard. Back in those days Archie Wright had met a man at Jack's, who had commissioned him to do a mural for a municipal court building in Iowa, and it really seemed as though Archie might finally get started. All this was before he became interested in capital and labor and allowed ideology to interfere with work.

There was a good deal of distinction about Archie's and Cousin Clothilde's lives then, because they knew everybody. There was something about the Brill connection which gave them a peculiar cachet in New York. All the schools were anxious to have the little girls go to them, because they were Brills. Sidney was away at St. Swithin's, and Mary and Bella went to Miss Lacey's. They had a French governess too, and every afternoon they were put into white starched dresses and allowed to come down to tea. That was almost the only time Harry and I would see them. Of course everything was different at Wickford Point. Archie Wright only went there twice in his life. He said he couldn't stand it.

A porter carried my bag and we walked over to Track Fifteen, where the tickets were examined by the conductor behind the desk.

"Lower nine," the man said. "Car one seven eight. You wouldn't care to change it to a section, would you?"

158

"No, thanks," I said, and he gave me back the stub of my ticket.

"Lower nine," I said to the porter. "Car one seven eight." And we walked into the cool smoky dark of the train shed. I had that old happy feeling of going somewhere, and at the same time I was living over a good deal of my life in that strange manner which occurs now and then when one is performing the conventional acts of the present.

"Car one seven eight," the porter said. It was all very much as it had always been, the same hushed narrow aisle of green curtains, the Negro in his white coat asking in a whisper when I wished to be awakened. It was like some scene in the play called "Outward Bound." No one ever knew who lay behind those curtains and no one ever cared. The dimly lighted aisle was a timeless place, so that the thing that happened next was not surprising.

I heard a voice behind me, a careful voice which was rather flat. A youngish man was speaking to me and I did not know him from Adam.

"Hello, Jim," he said. "Aren't you Jim Calder?"

"Why, hello," I said, but I didn't recognize him and he saw that I didn't.

"I'm Avery Gifford," he said.

"Of course," I said. "Hello, Avery." And after that there did not seem to be much to say.

"Are you going to New York?" he asked.

"Yes," I said. "I suppose you're going to New York too. Let's go into the washroom and smoke a cigarette."

"I don't mind watching you," said Avery, "but I've given up cigarettes."

"Have you? Why?" I asked.

"It's bad for my wind," he said, "and maybe you've read the statistics. Heavy smokers die sooner."

"And you want to live?" I said. He looked a little puzzled, but I had remembered everything about Avery Gifford by this time.

"Yes," he said, "of course I want to live."

"That's fine," I said. "You didn't the last time I saw you."

"Oh," he said, and his tanned face grew redder. "Oh yes, that."

We sat together on the long seat in the washroom. A heavy man in his undershirt and trousers was brushing his teeth. We watched him without speaking until he finished. While we sat there silently Avery Gifford looked as though he distrusted the impulse which had made him speak to me, and that last remark of mine must have told him that I remembered a great many things which he would not care to discuss. We sat there mutely examining the metal wash-basins and the cuspidors.

"Well," I said, "how have you been?"

"Very well, thank you," said Avery. "How have you been?"

"About the same as you," I said. "Where are you this summer?"

"Where we've always been," said Avery, "at Nahant."

"Still at Nahant?" I asked.

"Yes," Avery answered. "We always spend the summers there." He shuffled his feet uneasily on the linoleum. "I'm married you know," he added.

"Yes," I said, "I know. You married one of the Bosworth girls, Betty Bosworth, didn't you? You sent me an announcement."

"Oh yes," said Avery. "We have three children now, a boy and two girls. I wish you'd stop in to see us sometime. I'd like you to meet Betty."

"Thanks," I said, "I'd like to, Avery."

We both must have known that I would not stop in, and I also knew that he did not really wish I would, but it was nice of him just the same. He sat with his forearms resting on his knees, clasping his hands together and unclasping them. He was dressed in gray flannels that were a good deal the worse for wear; there was nothing in his appearance to show that he had inherited ten million dollars, and I rather liked him for it. While he sat there, thinking of something else to say, not wishing to speak of what was on his mind, the thought came back to me again that love as viewed objectively is nothing but a disease and that Avery, when he fell in love with Bella Brill, had contracted that disease just as inadvertently as one contracts a head

160

cold from riding in the subway. Or had it been like that? It was possible that there might have been some wild and unfulfilled streak in Avery's nature and some latent revolt against the environment which now held him. If so, he had lived it down. Yet even now he wanted to speak of Bella.

"I read some of the things you write sometimes," Avery said. "I have half an hour to kill every evening on the train. Have you been out to see the tennis?"

"No," I said. "Have you?"

"Yes," Avery answered. "The tennis was very good this year."

I could not help but wonder about him and about his life. That life of Avery Gifford's was so far apart from anything I knew, so completely ordered in its security, so undeviating and so admirable; nor was it entirely sterile if he had produced three children.

"Why are you going to New York, Avery?" I asked.

"Well," he said, "someone had to go. It's about the income tax. I always try to keep away from New York as much as possible, but someone in the family had to go." He clasped his hands together and unclasped them again, observing his fingers intently, and then he cleared his throat. "I was sorry to hear about Bella," he added.

He had come to it at last, and no doubt he felt better now that it was over.

"What about Bella?" I inquired.

Avery lowered his voice and still looked at his hands. "The divorce," he said. "Perhaps I shouldn't have spoken of it."

"There's no reason why you shouldn't," I replied. "A lot of people have."

"I don't like gossip," Avery said. "It must have been hard on Bella. She's so highly strung, so delicate."

"It's just as well it's over with," I said.

It was the best reply to make, but his remark about her being delicate surprised me. It meant that he had never known what Bella was at all. He was one of those pedestal-putters, like many

161

of the rest of us. So there was Bella enshrined still in the mind of Avery Gifford, forever beyond him, forever virginal and pure. It was better to leave it just that way.

"How is Bella?" he asked.

"She's pretty well," I answered.

"She would have been fine about it all," Avery said. "I kept wishing there was something I could do about it."

"There was nothing you could do, Avery."

"I don't suppose there was," said Avery. "That's what Betty said, but I wish there had been. When you see Bella will you give her my—" He paused as if he had checked himself. "— my kindest regards?"

"Of course I will," I told him; "but Betty is absolutely right."

Avery got up and very nearly stumbled on a cuspidor.

"Yes," he said, "of course she is. Betty's wonderful." He seemed to have forgotten that I had never met Betty. "Betty always has just the right reaction. She's the one who made me go down to New York on this thing. Well, I suppose I'd better go to bed. I don't suppose we'll meet in the morning. I'm staying at the Cosgrave, but I'm afraid I'll be busy all the time. It's nice to have seen you again. Be sure to give Bella my regards."

"Good night, Avery," I said.

The green curtain closed behind him and I was left alone. It was an odd coincidence to have seen him there that night, for he fitted in with all my other thoughts and took his place among the imponderables. Suppose she had married Avery Gifford, she could not have stood it for more than a year or two. Once she had told me that herself, but even so she might have married him. There would never be another chance like that for Bella Brill, and I was the one who had spoiled it. Bella and even Cousin Clothilde had been careful to remind me that Joe Stowe was my friend.

"Aboard," someone was calling, "all aboard." She would have met Joe in any case, but I was the one who had brought him to Wickford Point.

162

XVI | You Dear Delightful Women

I had often wondered why Bella had not married Avery Gifford. Aside from love, if love had ever bothered her, it must have been a struggle for Bella to turn him down; for Bella always had her wits about her, even when she did not use them. She must have seen security staring her in the face, generous and unbounded, hers forever. And Avery Gifford had been a nice boy too. The Brills, who always studied social desirability, had conceded that the Gifford family connection had been quite as good as theirs, except that the Giffords might have too much money. It might have been a very brilliant match, though I happened to know that old Colebrook Gifford had been harassed by the prospect and that Mrs. Gifford—the one who had sent a young man from her house because she had seen him sweeten his ginger ale from a pocket flask—had been obliged to consult a psychiatrist. As I sat solitary in the train, I suddenly knew exactly why Bella had not gone through with it. The unexpected apparition of Avery Gifford had explained everything, for I had seen him as Bella must have seen him long ago. He had not represented security; instead he had represented the unknown. He had signified continuity, and Bella had been afraid. He would have taken her away from Wickford Point and Bella had been afraid. There was no security at Wickford Point, but there was something else—the ghost of a vanished

163

security, which had developed into something necessary—and all of Bella's seeming boldness must have been make-believe. It is difficult to realize that all sorts of irrational, indefinable fears are deep inside of all of us ready to spring up when we least expect them, and the worst of it is we do not know of what we are afraid.

I could remember when there had been security at Wickford Point, when the house had a clean, soapy smell, when there were plenty of people in the kitchen to do the work, and two outside men to tend the garden and the grounds. That was when my grandfather was alive and before my great-aunt Sarah's mind was failing. The subsequent change was gradual, like the decline of the Roman Empire, and children do not often notice such essentials, although they observe most of the things that grown-ups forget or take for granted.

When I came to live at Wickford Point Aunt Sarah had already grown very forgetful. She had given up fine embroidery and her work on hooked rugs was somewhat ragged. When she read aloud she would sometimes repeat a page because she forgot to turn it. There were no longer any pilot biscuits in the cracker jar in the closet off the dining room, and there was only one woman in the kitchen. There was also a succession of housekeeper companions who helped out with the work and with Aunt Sarah and who sat with us at table. I never minded any of this, because I was allowed to wear old clothes and to walk into the house with rubber boots if I had been shooting ducks or rails down the river.

Aunt Sarah often used to think that I was my father or someone else, but she was always very kind to me, for she always said that it was nice to have the boys around. She was not as kind to Cousin Sue. Sometimes at supper, which usually consisted of pale scrambled eggs and toast and cracked cocoa, Cousin Sue would be taken with a violent fit of sneezing. This always exasperated Aunt Sarah. After Cousin Sue had sneezed twice, Aunt Sarah would hit the table with the handle of her knife.

"Leave the room, Sue," she would say, "until you have stopped sneezing."

Both Aunt Sarah and Cousin Sue were interested in Unitarianism and homeopathic medicine, but their absorption in the Brills transcended these. Cousin Sue was enormously proud that the family was connected with the Brills. She was always looking for signs of genius in the Brill children, although she never deposited money for them in the savings bank until they were two years old, so that she could be sure they were not idiots. She got this from Aunt Sarah, who was always afraid that there might be an idiot in the family, but once this barrier was crossed, Cousin Sue was sure they were geniuses. Cousin Sue was always wishing that they could be with us more frequently. Harry was my contemporary, and Cousin Sue was particularly interested in him.

"If Harry were only here now," she would say, "he would so appreciate the beauty of it all."

From my acquaintance with Harry I did not think he had much eye for beauty. He was much more interested in electricity and in jigsaw puzzles. However, I agreed with Cousin Sue in that I always wished the Brills were there.

Cousin Clothilde used to bring the children up every summer quite early, and then a little later generally go abroad with Archie Wright.

Cousin Sue was delighted about Archie Wright. It was so nice, she said, for Clothilde to marry again, and natural that she should marry such a brilliant person. Cousin Sue was always anxious to see him and always hoped that he might come up to Wickford Point. She never could understand that Archie did not want to see her. She never knew that he had hidden in the pantry once when she came to New York, and then escaped through the back door and stayed at the club until Cousin Sue had returned to Wickford Point. She always wanted until the last day of her life to have a good long talk with Archie Wright.

When the Brills came down to Wickford Point the whole place changed. There would be Harry and Sid and the two girls and quite often two maids to look after them. These maids usually gave notice at the end of two weeks, but afterwards we always got along. Of course Bella was very young at that time, and Mary was not much older; nevertheless Cousin Sue could see what Bella would become eventually.

"Bella is turning into a very beautiful young woman," she used to say. "She is going to be just like her mother. I do wish the children wouldn't make such a noise. I cannot hear myself think."

I could understand what Cousin Sue meant. Of course Bella was too young for me, and I was secretly in love with Mr. Jeffries' daughter up the road, but when I could remove my mind from this amatory problem, I used to think that I was Henry Esmond and that Bella was Beatrix Castlewood. Bella was usually a little cold to me at first because she had been to Miss Lacey's School and she did not know exactly where I belonged, but she always got over it in a day or two. She was the one who always wanted to be doing things. Mary was like Sid and preferred to sit in the house. Bella used to wander around the place, and after a while her dresses would get so dirty that no one could do anything with them. She would keep teasing me to take her for walks or down-river in the canoe where we could go fishing off the jetty. If it wasn't that, she wanted me to read poetry to her. She had an astonishingly good memory for poetry.

"She is certainly going to be a poet like her grandfather," Cousin Sue said. I never agreed with Cousin Sue, that Bella was as pretty as her mother. In fact Cousin Clothilde seemed so beautiful that I was almost afraid of her. She used to stay in bed smoking cigarettes until just before luncheon, and as she smoked I knew it could not be immoral. She would send for various members of the family to come to see her while she lay there.

"You'll have to entertain me, Jim," she said. "I can't be expected to stay by myself all morning." It never occurred to me to wonder why she did not get up like the rest of us.

"Tell me what they are doing downstairs," Cousin Clothilde would say. "What's Aunt Sarah doing? She's vaguer this year than she's ever been before. I never did like Aunt Sarah. She is really a disagreeable old woman, and if Sue wants to see me, will you tell her I have a bad headache, please? She keeps talking and talking until it makes me dizzy. I don't see how you stand it, Jim dear. I've always said you shouldn't be left down here. I hope Bella isn't in the cow barn again. When you go down I want you to get Mary to sort out the stockings in the upper bureau drawer for me, and I wish you could get Sid to go for a walk with you and Bella. You're such a comfort, darling. I wish you'd tell me about Mr. Morrissey. I know he drinks and I do hope he isn't getting into trouble with any of the maids. You don't think he will, do you?"

"Who? Mr. Morrissey?" I said. "He's married and has two children."

"Darling," said Cousin Clothilde, "that doesn't make a bit of difference. I wish you could ask them to get me some safety matches and not these matches that scratch on anything. I really don't see how you stand it, dear."

"I like it," I said.

"It's all very well to like it," Cousin Clothilde said, "but that's different from living here all the time. It will be better when you get to college."

"I suppose so, but I don't mind it here," I said.

"But you mustn't get to like it too much, Jim dear," said Cousin Clothilde. "I like it too much myself, and it isn't good for anybody."

She treated me exactly as she might have treated someone who was her own age—which is a very difficult feat for an adult to achieve, for it has to be spontaneous.

Everyone, with the possible exception of my great-aunt Sarah, took it for granted that Cousin Clothilde needed a great deal of rest and personal attention. Consequently Cousin Clothilde arranged things with no effort on her part so that all the life of Wickford Point revolved around her whenever she was there. Whether she was in bed or sitting beneath the oak tree on the bank, she did not like it if anyone else was busy; yet Cousin Clothilde was not tyrannical like other women I have known who have dominated their environment. We were never afraid that she might fly into a temper or that her feelings might be hurt. She

167

never stooped to any such wiles either consciously or unconscious-
ly. We all waited upon Cousin Clothilde, and we all came when
she called us because we liked to do so. She had that useful power
of making everyone pleased and anxious to do things for her. Indeed the only person at Wickford Point who avoided her was my
great-aunt Sarah. Aunt Sarah was too old to say much, and moreover she always seemed to be busy. She kept working in her garden or walking to the point with her basket for chips, or up the
hill to the pigsty to feed the pigs, moving through a world in
which she could perceive only dimly the shapes of Cousin Clothilde
and the little Brills. Her mind was occupied with vanished personalities, and ghosts were always walking with her. I can recall
only one time when she sat and talked with Cousin Clothilde as
the rest of us did, and that occasion was rather unsettling.

I think she usually looked upon Cousin Clothilde with disapproval, because she never had liked people who were not industrious. One afternoon, however, she came upon Cousin Clothilde
sitting on the lawn under the big oak tree, looking at the river.
Cousin Clothilde was in a light lavender dress and she was looking
very pretty, and Aunt Sarah sat down on the bench beside her.

"Clethra," she said to Cousin Clothilde, "have you finished
already with the washing?" Cousin Clothilde must have been
startled, and not without justice, for Aunt Sarah had mistaken
her for my grandmother.

"I am not Aunt Clethra, Aunt Sarah," she said.

"Well, well," said Aunt Sarah, "if you're not Clethra, I'm sure
I don't know who you are. If you want to play a guessing game,
I'm sure you may do so, if you've a mind to, Clethra, but it would
be nice to know if you've done the washing first. Georgianna is
getting back this afternoon."

"But I'm not Aunt Clethra, Aunt Sarah," Cousin Clothilde said.
"I'm Clothilde, Aunt Sarah dear, Georgianna's daughter."

"Well, well," said Aunt Sarah, "it doesn't really signify. Georgianna is coming back from that farm this evening and it may be
that Mr. Hawthorne is coming too. I should admire it if you put
the spare-room bed in order."

"But my own children are sleeping in the spare room, Aunt Sarah dear," Aunt Clothilde said.

"Well," said Aunt Sarah, "I don't see how that signifies, Clethra, if Mr. Hawthorne is coming. I've watched you this afternoon. You're forever sitting still and letting me do all the work, and I will not have it. Do you hear, Clethra? Mr. Brill is rowing across the river this afternoon, and I shall be sitting here myself."

"Oh," said Cousin Clothilde, "my God! Sue! Where are you, Sue?"

Cousin Sue hurried as fast as she could across the lawn, stumbling occasionally because she had mislaid her spectacles.

"What is it, Clothilde?" Cousin Sue asked. "Oh goodness gracious, what is it?"

There were a good many things which Cousin Clothilde did not like, but there were not many of which she was afraid. In this instance she was probably more puzzled and exasperated than afraid. It could not have been mentally comfortable to have been wandering with Aunt Sarah in the land of shadows.

"She insists that I'm Aunt Clethra," Cousin Clothilde said.

"Oh good gracious," said Cousin Sue. "She isn't Clethra, Aunt Sarah. She's Clothilde. You remember Clothilde."

"Clothilde isn't grown-up," Aunt Sarah said. "I saw her in the garden only a few minutes ago."

"Aunt Sarah,"—Cousin Sue sounded as if she were about to cry,—"Clothilde's grown-up. She married Hugh Brill, don't you remember? You must have seen one of her children in the garden. It's time to come into the house now to get your medicine, Aunt Sarah."

"Well," said Aunt Sarah, "it doesn't signify if I get confused sometimes, does it? If you get to be my age, Sue, as I hope very much you won't for your sake, you may grow somewhat confused yourself. Well, well, I'm sure there's no use upsetting yourself either. It really does not signify at all, for everything that I have said remains absolutely true."

She may have been very nearly right that it did not signify at all, for there had been so many people at Wickford Point that

169

their personalities did become entangled. Cousin Sue was certainly growing more and more confused herself.

She was having a very difficult time paying the bills, for instance, and Cousin Clothilde could never be bothered with them. The children were always running through the house and Mary was generally having a crying spell just when it came time to pay the bills; and then Cousin Sue would keep spilling ink on her checkbook and the balance was never correct; and besides, the bills were always getting into the wrong cubbyhole in the block-front desk. Also, more than once Aunt Sarah burned them all up because she thought that they were some of her old love letters. Everything else was always being mixed up in Cousin Sue's desk too, because Bella kept getting into it and fingering all its appurtenances such as the petrified shark's tooth which our great-grandfather had brought back from the Galapagos Islands, and the delicate little balance for weighing letters, and Bella spoiled all the pens because she was busy writing a story about a girl who lived with a gnome in a castle. Everything possible was done, of course, to allow Bella to write it, since she was showing the literary instincts of the Brills, but it was no help to Cousin Sue.

"There isn't anyone to look after anything," Cousin Clothilde said to me once. "There ought to be a man to take care of things. Your cousin Hugh was never interested and Archie has so much else on his mind, and besides Archie doesn't like it here. There should be some man to do the bills. I wish that one of the family's old friends would adopt me. It would be such a beautiful thing to do, and so many of them have so much money. I'm tired of doing everything for everybody. It's high time that someone else did."

This idea of adoption was something which Cousin Clothilde brought up very often, and certainly it might have solved a great many problems. Her ideas were often logical—but though she wanted things done she did not want to see anyone do them.

I have a different impression of Wickford Point today from any I had then. Just now, I can see that Wickford Point was like a floating island that once had been solidly attached to the mainland. I can see it being severed from realities when I was still very young, and drifting off, a self-contained entity, into a misty sea. It was a land almost entirely sufficient unto itself, and governed by the untutored thoughts of women—although this does not mean that others did not assert themselves.

The right of self-determination was not even confined to human beings. When Aphrodite, the tortoise-shell cat, wanted to have her kittens in the lower bureau drawer in the bedroom above the back parlor, it was necessary to move a good many things, and as the time for the accouchement approached, chairs were placed in the upper hall in a sort of barricade so that Aphrodite would not be disturbed. When Clara, the old setter bitch given to Cousin Sue by a man whom she had met fishing for pickerel through the ice in the north pond—when Clara began to get ugly in about her twelfth year, she would take up a position on the landing of the front stairs and she was very much upset when anyone came near her. So we all had to use the back stairs until Clara finally died. Then there was the trouble with the two cows that were still kept at Wickford Point. They only gave enough milk to feed Aunt Sarah's two pigs, so they were not much use to us, and their main desire was to eat the white phlox in the small garden where the sundial stood. Cousin Sue told Mr. Morrissey that it would be kinder to let them in. Finally, the cows were allowed everywhere, until Mr. Morrissey's rheumatism got so bad that we gave up keeping them. When Hector, the last of the trotting horses, reached the age of twenty he began kicking out the side of his box stall, until Mr. Morrissey decided it was better to fix a place for him in the back shed. It was easier, Mr. Morrissey said, in the cold weather, to tend Hector there instead of tracking away out to the barn, and Hector liked it better too. I always remember him sticking his head out of the back shed by the kitchen door, and he had what was left of the deep apple pie after Sunday luncheon.

"And why," said Mr. Morrissey, "should not the poor beast have a little comfort in his old age who has wanted it all his life?

171

He was always after wishing to be a house dog and not a horse."

Something definite is conveyed by that idea of Wickford Point turning into a floating island and drifting imperceptibly away from the mainland of integrated values. It is the same thing that was happening in other families and social groups cut off from the humdrum discipline of life. There were no real breadwinners left on the place to convey a healthy impression of economic necessity, and the nearest thing to economics was the appearance of dividend checks from two small trust estates which arrived each month as regularly as the changing of the moon. Thus there was not much necessity for timekeeping. Mr. Morrissey, whose work with the two cows had demanded a certain punctuality, never owned a watch. He had instead a highly developed faculty for telling the hour, both summer and winter, by the slant of the sun; he was assisted by the whistle of the blanket mill across the river, which blew at seven o'clock each morning, and Mr. Morrissey always said that the management of the blanket mill would not permit the boys to sleep one minute overtime. However, he was not so sure about the closing whistle.

"Them limbs," Mr. Morrissey used to say,—he always referred to industrial employers by this uncomplimentary term,—"would be only too likely to keep the boys and girls inside for five to fifteen minutes extra."

At one period a man named Mr. Pennybacker came on the trolley car every Sunday morning, except in very snowy weather, and wound and regulated all our clocks. This I believe had been my grandfather's idea. These timepieces used to go reasonably well under Mr. Pennybacker's care until he had a shock one night in the poolroom over the barbershop downtown. He appeared at Wickford Point several times after that, but on each occasion he had forgotten to bring his own watch, so that his visits were of less and less use. He finally disappeared forever and then the morale of the clocks began to break. The French clock in the back parlor became filled with smoke from the fireplace, as Mr. Pennybacker had always said it would, and then the spring in the kitchen mantel clock broke; nobody ever could remember to wind the banjo clock upstairs; and finally the tall clock in the dining room, made on London Bridge in 1682, was the only one which went, but, like Aunt Sarah, its age had made it eccentric. Its striking mechanism grew disordered and then its hour and minute hands kept coming loose. Thus it might be nine o'clock in the morning and the chimes would ring for two and the hands would point to half-past six. We always kept this clock wound, however, because Aunt Sarah grew fidgety and nervous when it stopped.

Finally no one ever consulted a clock at all, since it was easier to ask Mr. Morrissey what time he guessed it was, and, as Cousin Clothilde said, it didn't really matter. Nothing had ever irked her so much as punctuality when she was young, and now there was no real reason to be punctual.

More and more we exercised that marvelous adaptability of the human race, now that Wickford Point was drifting. As time went on, what was left of useful frugalities and industries began to assume perverted forms. Cousin Sue inherited from Aunt Sarah a serious attitude about string, which grew gradually more pronounced. You never could tell, according to Cousin Sue, when a piece of string might be a very valuable necessity, and to illustrate this point she would read us a story from Maria Edgeworth's *Parents' Assistant* called "Waste Not, Want Not," in which the little hero met a dangerous crisis in his life successfully because he had a piece of string in his pocket. I was so impressed by this that I carried string in my pocket for several months without ever finding occasion to use it. There was an Indian jar, placed in a lamp bracket on the wall of the little parlor, where all string from bundles was customarily stored. When this became full, string was put in an Indian basket given to Cousin Sue by some relative unknown to me, who had been in New Mexico. When this was filled also, string was left everywhere, and once Cousin Sue dislocated her shoulder by becoming entangled with some that she had left on the back stairs.

This attitude toward saving things was an instinctive trait in

Cousin Sue. You never could tell, she said, when you might need wrapping paper or newspaper or copies of the *Atlantic Monthly*, and so all printed matter was bundled up and placed in the attic. Once a traveling junk-dealer, who had somehow lost his way from the main road, purchased an attic full of newsprint for fifty-three cents, and he would have paid more, too, if the rats and squirrels had not found their way into most of it. Cousin Sue never wearied of recalling this instance, for it went to show that there was really a profit in saving. Each year such small matters assumed an increasing importance at Wickford Point.

Of course, most of us thought that these aspects were intensely amusing, and they and the personalities at Wickford Point furnished endless hours of aimless conversation. When I sat in the little parlor and tried to read, Cousin Sue would often sit there with me and try to read too, but usually her mind would keep leaving the pages at a tangent. She was devoted to Aunt Sarah, whom she considered a very important figure, every one of whose ideas was logical and right, but didn't I think that Aunt Sarah was getting increasingly difficult? Then there was Maggie, who worked in the kitchen. Maggie, in Cousin Sue's opinion, was a thoroughly good woman, much better than that young Josie who had helped her, and who was always thinking about her husband and her children up the river. Maggie would be perfectly all right if Clothilde didn't keep asking her to do so many things that all the food on the stove kept burning up. Did I know that Maggie believed that the sun danced for joy on Easter morning, and that she had written to her father in the old country to send over a blackthorn stick? When did I think that there were going to be any more kittens, and did I notice that Mr. Morrissey was unsteady on his feet last Monday? Of course Clothilde had great responsibilities with all the children, but did I not think that Clothilde seemed worried about something?

Later in the day Cousin Clothilde would be in the long parlor.

"Thank heavens," she would say, "that Sue is upstairs resting. Close the door gently, so it won't disturb her. Isn't there some way that Sue could keep resting all afternoon? Have you seen Bella give the imitation of her looking for her glasses? I don't know why Sue puts up with Mr. Morrissey. He's growing lazier every year."

Mr. Morrissey admitted that he was growing lazier. Every dom'd thing, Mr. Morrissey said, was getting itself broken. Now the hoe was broken and Miss Sue said she couldn't afford the money to get him a new hoe, and how could you keep the weeds out of the driveway if you didn't have a hoe, or hoe the garden either? Nobody ever appreciated what he did with all the dom'd kids getting into the tool box and losing everything. And did I know the latest? Mrs. Wright had told him that after this he was to call us Master Jim and Master Harry and Master Sid. Would you believe that he could call me Master Jim in a free country after he had known me all my life? And when he had gone down-town to get the meat the butcher was worrying about the bill, as though Miss Sue did not have plenty of money. It was lucky for me that I was going to school and getting an education. He would not be working here, and that was the Lord's own truth, if he had an education. His son was learning how to play a trombone and his daughter was learning French. They were calling him "lace-curtain Irish" down the street, but this was a free country, was it not? Had I ever heard, he wanted to know, about the last troubles in Ireland, and would I like to sit down and hear of them?

It is hard to convey the charm of these random discourses, but they were of great importance at Wickford Point. The Brills were wonderful at describing this life. When they returned to the city after the summer was over, all that they had experienced assumed a social value. The Brills were always so delightful; such extraordinary things were always happening to the Brills, things which would never happen to other people.

I too have dined out on Wickford Point anecdotes quite often, but never just that way. Somehow I succeeded in leaving that island of make-believe as it drifted from the shore, and some-

175

how the Brills stayed with it. No doubt the psychologists have varied names for their condition, connected in the inartistic way of science with characters in the mythology of ancient Greece. Still I prefer to think of Wickford Point as I have started— breaking from the land most of us know, and floating off into miasmic haze. It was not a bad island either, as such places go, but dangerous for strangers if they chose to stay too long.

I reached the mainland just in time when I was going on eighteen. It happened, as the politicians are fond of saying now, because it was planned that way. I received a letter from Mr. Caldicott, who attended to the family affairs, saying that he wished to see me in Boston on a certain day at a certain hour. I had never laid eyes on our trustee, and Cousin Sue was very much excited. She said that Mr. Caldicott was a thoroughly nice man and an old friend of my grandfather's, and that Mr. Morrissey would drive me to the station to take the eight-ten train. Mr. Morrissey himself was quite excited because no one had been to Boston for several months. He hitched Hector to the buggy and I put on a suit of blue serge clothes and a green necktie.

It was necessary to allow a long time to get down to the station because Hector was growing stiff in the forelegs. I remember the drive especially because Mr. Morrissey was unusually silent.

"I'll be back tonight," I said. "I'll take the car and walk back through the woods."

I could see the white smoke of the train already, and when the engine appeared, moving gingerly up to the river bridge, Mr. Morrissey's manner struck me as somewhat strange. I have sometimes wondered what he had heard through that grapevine of intelligence that surrounded Wickford Point.

"I'm thinking you won't be back for some time, Jim," he said.

"You're crazy, Mr. Morrissey," I said. "Good-by." But Mr. Morrissey was not crazy. It was a long while before I came back again to Wickford Point, not perhaps in the space of measured time, but in the important measure of experience. It was the last time that I was to see Mr. Morrissey on the basis of the cordial

176

and homely familiarity which had developed between us. Mr. Morrissey and I would seldom again sit together drinking hard cider while he regaled me with bawdy stories, and with gossip about the local girls of easy virtue. I might see Wickford Point and I might love it still, but I would never be the part of it which I had been once. Wickford Point could work no magic for me out where I was going. It was no shield to my sense of inferiority, because I did not possess the imagination to romanticize it. I felt that I was different, but unlike the Brills this knowledge gave me no sense of careless ease, and I was never able to use it as an adequate excuse for failure.

XVII | Ante-Bellum Boys

It might be possible to write another *David Copperfield*, starting at the ending of that era just before the war, when there was a happy feeling of certainty about nearly everything. Mr. Caldicott, more than anyone I have ever known, possessed that sense of certainty. It was connected somehow with rather dingy marble-tiled office hallways, and with procrastinating elevators that climbed like spiders through a web of steel cables. His office was a part of it, with its green baize tables and black walnut book-cases. Begonias grew in sunny windows overlooking the gray stones of cemeteries that marked the resting place of Revolutionary soldiers. Four per cent meant safety and there was no income tax on money invested in the securities of Massachusetts corporations. There were Sunday dinners with roast beef and Yorkshire pudding, ending with vanilla ice cream and followed by a baseball game out on the lawn, or by some indoor game of intellect if it were rainy. I can't remember everything very clearly and I am glad of this, because I do not think the clumsy uncertainties of adolescent years and their hideous mistakes and embarrassments are happy recollections.

Mr. Caldicott once said that it was a pity the income from my grandfather's estate had not permitted me to go to a good preparatory school before going to Harvard, but that we should have to make the best of it under the circumstances, and later I found out what he meant. There was a sort of snobbishness back in those days which seems almost unbelievable, although perhaps youth is still conventional when it has turned eighteen. It was necessary then to attach oneself to something and to be a certain type of person. Harry Brill did not have any trouble because he came to Harvard from St. Swithin's, where he had learned a good many of the amenities. I could never have afforded to go, but the Brill name always seemed to take the place of money. He used to introduce me to his friends sometimes and he used to tell me what I should do, and I have always appreciated his generosity. I can understand now that it was necessary to see the right people and to wear the proper sort of clothes. It was not surprising under the circumstances that I barely nodded to Joe Stowe for quite a while, although we were in a good many courses together. They say that everything is much better now, beginning with the freshman dormitories and ending with the Houses, and that all the students know each other and exchange ideas in a perfect spirit of democracy—but personally I can hardly believe it.

I did not wish to be on familiar terms with Joe Stowe, because being seen in his company was not a social asset. During his first two years at Harvard he did not dress well, and he came from the Woburn High School. We both went out for the *Crimson* in our freshman year and we both were dropped. In the middle of our junior year we were both allowed to enter an advanced course in English composition, and this was the first time that we became friendly. It was necessary for us to speak to each other, because we had to criticize each other's work, and besides Joe Stowe had begun to learn a good deal about dress and deportment. Also he had been taken on the *Harvard Advocate*, not that this mattered very much, but it was something. First we began to talk to each other after class, and then we went in town to the theater. On one of these occasions Harry Brill saw us drinking beer in the Holland bar and he spoke to me the next day.

"You don't want to play around too much with that bird Stowe," he said. "It won't do you any good."

"I'll play around with anyone I want," I answered.

"All right," said Harry, "but it won't get you anywhere."

It is only necessary to refer to a picture of Joe Stowe taken at that time to realize what Harry meant. Even the kindly art of a portrait photographer could not conceal the freckled blotches on his cadaverous callow face. He was hollow-chested; one of those high stiff collars then in fashion accentuated the thinness of his neck and made his head with its reddish hair assume an appearance that was almost botanical. It was hard to think that Joe Stowe could have looked that way until I examined similar pictures of myself.

Harry was not referring entirely to Joe's looks either. The last elections for the Vindex Club were coming off, and as I had not been able to get into anything else, Harry was doing his best for me. He had arranged that I should see a good deal of people like Nat Frisbie and Arthur Wills and Allen Southby, and Harry was telling all his friends that here was their chance to do something. My attitude, which was purely defensive, was of no great help. Being reasonably sure that I was not going to get into the Vindex Club, I had taken a lofty position. I said to hell with it, that I would join it if they asked me, but I didn't mind if they didn't, and that I didn't think much of the people who were in it anyway. I said I didn't think much of Nat Frisbie when it came to that, but Harry understood me. He knew that I wanted to get into the Vindex Club; I only hope he never knew how much. It seemed like a matter of life and death in those days, as though I could not face the world if I did not make it. That was why I said that I did not give one solitary whoop in hell and that I probably wouldn't go around there much anyway.

This point of view alarmed Harry, because he really thought a good deal of me.

"It's just because they don't know you, Jim," he said, "and it doesn't do any good to talk like that. If you'll just try to be nice to them when I bring them around . . ."

There is no use going into my social failings; I only bring the matter up at all because it made me friendly with Joe Stowe. It had never occurred to me that Joe Stowe also wished to get into the Vindex Club, having some naïve idea that membership was based upon literary merit.

He told me all about it afterwards when he told me about everything. Joe Stowe used to say that he had had a bad time at Harvard. The Stowes were a perfectly good family in Woburn and Joe's father owned a small mill there and had six children. His mother was in the Daughters of the Revolution and president of the Woman's Alliance. Joe's father was hard-working, and later became president of the Rotary Club. Joe was never bitter about Harvard; he simply said he had had a rotten time because he had expected something different. This expectation was due largely to his having read too many of the works of Ralph Henry Barbour. He had thought that one made friends at Harvard by shaking hands with people, and he did not know that there was anything like a club system. He did find, though, that he never seemed to meet anybody whom he really wanted to know, until his junior year. I was surprised to learn from him that he had harbored an especial aversion to me. He did not like my accent and he thought I was a snob. He said that he had gone out of his way on several occasions to be markedly rude, and the worst of it was that I had never noticed. Later it seemed to him that when he was cordial and really wanted to be agreeable, his classmates became suspicious that he was trying to get something out of them. He never cared for anyone in his class very much. It used to make him particularly angry when the class secretary in later years wrote him letters which began "Dear Joe." He could not forget that Nat Frisbie, who was secretary, had never spoken to him.

If it had not been for the English course, he might never have known me either, and that course in itself would not have helped if it had not been for the Vindex Club. He told me once, a long time later, that when he heard I had not been taken into the Vindex Club he stayed awake a good part of the night wondering whether or not to speak to me about it. And he finally did one day. I remember the instance very well, because it ran completely counter to accepted convention. We were crossing the Yard over one of those boardwalks between banks of melting snow with our unbuckled overshoes rattling with every step.

"Say," Joe Stowe said, "I hear you didn't get into the Vindex Club."

It made me turn beet red to have my shame publicly commented on by a person like Stowe. Even Harry Brill had not ventured to speak of it, and no one with a proper sense of reticence would have mentioned it aloud.

"What's that to you?" I asked.

Joe Stowe stammered and looked so ashamed of himself that I understood he had not meant to be unduly familiar.

"I just wanted to tell you I'm sorry," he said, "and they'll be sorry someday. You and I are the only people anywhere round who can write, and they didn't take us in. Yes, they'll be sorry someday."

"Well, I don't give a damn," I said.

"That's fine," said Joe. "I was rather afraid you would. Well, that's all I wanted to tell you."

I felt much better after he had finished, and I was grateful to Joe Stowe. It seemed as though he were the only person who understood me and that he and I were apart, watching cynically a misguided mob. It was not a healthy attitude, but it had its compensations.

The odd thing is that I can still feel a twinge of that old bitterness; for the hardest thing to live down is some ancient affront to vanity. It did no good to realize that Joe Stowe and I were much less agreeable than some of our more precocious classmates, like Harry Brill for instance, who was able to cover his inadequacies with all sorts of noisy and eccentric tricks. Joe Stowe and I were slower in developing.

All this may show why Joe and I finally came to know each other so well and why I brought him to Wickford Point. Cousin Sue kept asking and asking if Harry and I did not want to bring down some of our friends, which was the last thing that Harry and I wished, for we were absolutely certain that no one would understand Aunt Sarah or Cousin Sue at all. It was not the usual sense of shame that one has for one's parents and relatives either. We simply knew that Wickford Point was unusually peculiar. I used to talk with Joe about it—I don't know what ever started me but I continued because he was interested—and finally he was always asking about Wickford Point, and he laughed in exactly the right way about the things I told him. We went down there once in the spring of our junior year.

"You mustn't mind if it's queer," I said, and Joe said he didn't mind.

It was the middle of April and the frost coming from the ground made everything wringing wet, giving the woods and fields that sodden, hopeless look so peculiar to New England in the early spring. While we waited for the trolley car near the railroad station I began wishing that I had not brought Joe along, for I was sure that he was not going to like it. It was already late afternoon and a clammy mist was beginning to rise over everything now that the sun was going down. The trolley car was so crowded that there was hardly room for our bags on the rear platform. It was just the time when the shoe-shop workers, who lived in the country by the upper bridge, were going home, and Mr. Riordan, the conductor, was very busy. He kept pushing himself back and forth sideways in the crowded aisle. When he was ringing up the change, his mouth was so full of stubs and transfers that he looked like a retriever, but he had time to get in a word with everyone.

"Spruce Street," Mr. Riordan would call, "Monroe, Buchanan, Elm." I knew all the names by heart, and Joe said that all the streets in every town had just about the same names.

Mr. Morrissey came to meet us in the two-seated wagon at Hoskins Turnout, and Hector, still shaggy in his winter's coat, was unusually stiff and slow. The road was so thick and muddy that several times we had to get out and walk in order to help Hector, but Joe did not mind. It was growing dusk when we started going downhill toward Wickford Point, and all the trees along the road had the distinguishing features of old friends, b cause they were our trees. Joe Stowe had not spoken for a while, and I began to be afraid again that he would not like it and that he was growing tired of Mr. Morrissey's retailing all the news. Josie had two of her children staying on the third floor, and Nauna was getting feeble in the hind legs. Henry Green, who lived up the road, had said that he would give me a new Llewellyn bitch, and he had been asking why I had not been out shooting last autumn. Miss Sarah was getting to be more of a handful than ever, and they had a new one of those practical nurses looking after her, named Miss Jellicoe. Then he asked me if I knew that Miss Bella was down there.

"Miss Bella?" I said. "Why isn't she in school?"

"It seems like there was a little trouble," Mr. Morrissey said, "but it wouldn't be for me to say at all."

"Who's Miss Bella?" Joe asked.

Hector was holding back against the breeching. The misty dampness by the river had made us turn up our coat collars. Over in the west by the hills across the river there was a pink glow in the sky, cold, but not the cold pink that was there in winter.

"She's a kid," I explained. "She's my second cousin—Harry Brill's sister. I don't know why she's here. All the Brills are in New York."

"Oh," said Joe, and he did not speak again. I was feeling the old sort of anticipation which came over me every time I went down that hill, although nothing had ever come of it. I was feeling that old choking sense of loyalty for the place and a pleasure so intense in the idea that I was coming back that any obtuse remark of Joe's would have set my nerves on edge. I was waiting, just as I always waited, for the first sight of the house around the turn, and I could see the roofs of the hay barns already. Then I saw the great elm with the bent limb, bare and plumelike against the pink of the sky, and then the house with lamplight in the dining room and parlor windows.

"You see," said Mr. Morrissey, "the crocuses are up."

184

The twilight silence was broken only by the soft slop of Hector's hoofs and the turning of the wheels, and there was that first faint scent of spring which came partly from the earth and partly from the snowdrops and the yellow and purple crocuses which had seeded themselves upon the lawn, and partly from the damp bark of the trees and shrubs. There was no longer the sharpness of winter in the air, and a whiff of wood smoke went with all of it, showing that someone had put fresh logs on the back parlor fireplace on hearing the sound of the carriage.

"It's just the way it ought to be," Joe Stowe said. "It's just the way everything ought to be when anyone comes home."

When we pulled up by the side door, Mr. Morrissey addressed me confidentially.

"I'll bring a pitcher of hard cider up to your bedchamber," he said, "after I've put away the horse. Only don't you tell Miss Sue."

The door was opened before we had time to climb down. Cousin Sue was standing on the threshold, leaning backward on her heels and fumbling nervously for her spectacles in the pocket of her skirt, and of course her spectacles were not there.

"How do you do," Cousin Sue was saying, "how do you do." And she nodded her head vigorously.

"This is Mr. Stowe, Cousin Sue," I said.

"How do you do," said Cousin Sue. "It's so nice of you to come with everything so soggy underfoot. You must be related to Harriet Beecher Stowe. I quite see the resemblance."

"Not Harriet Beecher Stowe," Joe answered, and he shook hands.

We were in the side-entry by then.

"Just hang your coat on any peg," said Cousin Sue, "any peg at all." She was very nervous, as she always was with strangers, and she was now talking animatedly to Joe.

"I always think of the Stowes as being related to the Hildreths," she said, "not the Lexington Hildreths, because, of course, he was the one who kept the two wives and the two families, one at each end of the town. Of course it isn't nice to refer to, but I suppose you know all about him. It isn't the Lexington Hildreths but the

Duxbury Hildreths, the ones who were so interested in molasses in the sixties."

That faraway, eerie quality was coming back with the comfortable, musty smell of the warm side-entry, and I could see all the bedroom candles safe on their shelf beside the stairs. First I felt the embarrassment which Cousin Sue always caused me, until I saw that Joe Stowe was not confused, and what was more he appeared to appreciate her.

"I don't know the Hildreths in Duxbury," he said, "but I wish I did."

Then Bella came running downstairs, jumping down the steps two at a time. She was all legs and black pigtails, and in the Miss Lacey plaid school uniform. She stood up on tiptoes and threw her arms around me.

"Jim," she said, "did you bring me any candy?"

"No," I said, "I didn't know you were here."

"Didn't you know?" Her voice was loud with rapture. "Didn't you know I got suspended, Jim? What do you think of that? It's really true. Isn't that just too wonderful? I got suspended."

"Bella," said Cousin Sue, "don't do so. Don't talk so. Don't make such a noise; it will disturb Aunt Sarah. Don't do so. I can't hear myself think. And this is Mr. Stowe, Bella."

"Oh," said Bella, and she made a curtsy the way her governess had taught her. "You're sleeping across the hall, Mr. Stowe, and I'm in the big room where Mother usually sleeps; and Jim, you're in your room in back, and we all of us use the back bathroom, and I'm coming to talk to you this evening, Jim, and you needn't try to lock me out, because the lock on the door doesn't work. So there."

"Bella," said Cousin Sue, "don't talk so. You shouldn't go into Jim's room, Bella."

"Oh fluff," said Bella. "I always go into Jim's room. If I haven't got enough on my bed, I'm going in to sleep with him."

"Bella," said Cousin Sue, "don't talk so. Please don't talk so."

Bella was young enough so that it was funny, and even Cousin Sue was mildly amused, although she was careful of the proprieties.

After we had left our bags upstairs, we came down to the front parlor where Aunt Sarah was seated in the upholstered chair near the coal grate, busy making lamplighters from strips of newspaper. When she saw us, she took off her glasses and blinked and smiled, and Miss Jellicoe made a series of gentle cooing sounds.

"We've been waiting for them, haven't we, Miss Sarah?" Miss Jellicoe said.

"Yes, indeed," said Aunt Sarah. "Come here and kiss me, Henry."

"It isn't Henry, Aunt Sarah," Cousin Sue said. "It's Henry's son. It's Jim. And he's brought a friend from college."

"It doesn't signify, Sue," said Aunt Sarah. "I know Henry when I see him, but I did not know he was bringing Robert with him. I had thought that Robert was in Canton."

"It isn't Robert, Aunt Sarah," said Cousin Sue. "It's a friend of Jim's. It's Mr. Stowe."

In the meanwhile I could hear Miss Jellicoe talking to Cousin Sue in a hasty undertone.

"I have tried," Miss Jellicoe said, "I have just tried and tried. I've been over it twice, Miss Sue, but Miss Sarah doesn't seem to understand, poor darling. It's just as though she didn't want to understand."

"Well, well," said Aunt Sarah, "I guess I know Robert when I see him without my being told. We must have a good talk later, Robert. How is the new comprador?"

"He's doing very well," Joe said.

"And I do hope Mr. Lawson Sturgis is not drinking too much."

"No," said Joe. "When I left him, Mr. Sturgis was very well."

"What is she talking about?" Cousin Sue was whispering. "I don't know what she's talking about." And for that matter neither did anyone else, but one could not help being interested. For a moment a veil was lifted from a mysterious past, and Joe was neither puzzled nor alarmed. He was perfectly polite as he wandered with Aunt Sarah in that past.

187

"I suppose the Merediths were there?" Aunt Sarah said. "How were matters on the islands?"

"Much the same as usual," Joe answered.

"You gave the packet to Mr. Thurston, I hope," Aunt Sarah said. "I do hope the queen is learning her alphabet."

"Yes," said Joe, "the queen can almost read by now."

"Dear me," said Aunt Sarah. "And I suppose you put in at the Ivory Coast?"

"Yes," Joe said, "we touched there."

"Well," said Aunt Sarah, "the owners must be very pleased."

"Aunt Sarah," said Cousin Sue, "it's just Jim's friend from college. It's time for you to go now with Miss Jellicoe."

"Well, well," said Aunt Sarah, "it does not signify. I should admire not to have you continually interrupt me, Sue. It does not signify. He's made the voyage."

My respect for Joe Stowe had grown enormously and Cousin Sue had also begun to like him very much. She confided in me that Mr. Stowe was able to appreciate the beauty of things.

When I poured him a glass of cider upstairs in my room before supper, I apologized for Aunt Sarah, but he stopped me.

"You mustn't talk like that," he said. "I wouldn't have missed it for the world."

"But how did you know what she was talking about?" I asked.

"I just guessed it," Joe said. "I had a grandfather who had been to sea and I used to hear him talk. You mustn't apologize. You ought to be proud of it."

Everybody liked him and he fitted into Wickford Point as though he belonged there. Later when we were in our pajamas talking in front of the fire in my room, he did not seem surprised when Bella appeared with a bedquilt wrapped around her nightgown.

Bella wanted to tell all about the family, about Cousin Clothilde and the picture which Archie Wright was painting, and the funny things which had happened, and about how she had been suspended from school. It seemed that she had smoked a cigarette at recess on a dare and that Miss Lacey had found her, and she gave an imitation of just what Miss Lacey had said. "It doesn't really amount to anything," Bella explained, "and Clothilde doesn't really mind. Of course she was annoyed when Archie began to laugh, but you know the way they all are. Mary cried about it, but Mary's always crying, and so now I'm down here. I don't like it so much down here without anyone, and Aunt Sue just talks and talks. You know how she is. And this new one, this Miss Jellicoe, is perfectly horrid, really, Jim. She keeps correcting me and doing mean things. Of course Miss Lacey will have to take me back. Clothilde says she can't afford not to, considering my name and family, and besides I'm doing awfully well in English. I'm going to be a writer. What do you think of that?"

It was amusing to hear her but I don't think either Joe or I felt quite at ease having Bella sitting cross-legged on my bed with her two black braids hanging in front of her and looking something like one of the Italian pictures in the Art Museum. We were more prudish in those days.

"Aren't you going to give me some cider?" Bella asked. "Mr. Morrissey always does. You needn't look that way, Jim."

"All right," I said, "here's some cider. Suppose you keep quiet now, we want to talk."

"All right," said Bella. "Tell him about Wickford Point. Let's sit up and talk all night. Nobody will know."

Joe and I had been talking about sex before Bella came in, and now the subject was barred. As I look back upon it, we talked a good deal about sex in those days, with very little personal experience. We never should have thought of carrying on with nice girls as one did in the postwar decades, although of course we all knew or had heard of girls who would co-operate in a certain amount of mild experimentation. It was a strait-laced age, when nearly everyone was amazingly pure. We sat there for a long time, while I told stories about Wickford Point and then Bella suggested more stories, and finally what with the cider and the smoke in the room her head began to nod.

"You'd better go to bed," I said.

"Oh fluff," said Bella, "I'm not sleepy. Please Jim, we're having such a good time."

"We're all going to bed," I said. "We're all sleepy."

"All right," said Bella. "Kiss me good night." And I kissed her. Then she did a surprising thing, and perhaps it may have been a fatal thing, although she was scarcely eleven years old, and it should have made no difference. She walked over to Joe and kissed him too.

"Good night, Joe," she said. "At first I thought you were perfectly horrid, but now I think you're awfully nice. You'll come down and stay here for a long while in the summer, won't you?"

"Well now," Joe said, "would you really like to have me?"

"Everybody would," said Bella. "Well, good night."

It was cloudy over the river, but the clouds were not thick enough to blot out a faint light of the moon, and so everything outside was either black or misty white. The lines of everything were like the work in a Chinese landscape. I had never seen Joe look so happy. You might have thought it was the first time he had ever fitted in anywhere, and his mind was all full of ideas. He did not want to go to sleep.

"We might go to Canton, you know," Joe said. "We might get a job in the Standard Oil."

"Yes, we might," I said. And then his mind returned to Bella. "She isn't like Harry," he remarked.

"No, she isn't," I said, "but all of them are pretty queer."

"Now don't talk like that," Joe answered, and he looked indignant. "That's a stuffy way of putting it. I don't believe they are."

I have often thought of that scene since, and I have often had the futile wish that everything might have remained as it had been in my warm smoky room that night, with Bella just a little girl with long black pigtails and violet eyes and red lips; and that was how Joe Stowe felt about it later. Already he was beginning to like Wickford Point and Cousin Sue and Aunt Sarah, and he was never able to forget the time that he had first seen them on that day when the frost was coming out and when the air was cool and damp with spring.

I was so nearly asleep that I was only conscious of the sound of the wind in the pines by the point, when another sound disturbed me.

"Who's that?" I asked. "What is it?" And Bella's voice answered from the dark.

"It's me, Jim," she said. "I'm just opening the door between our rooms. You don't mind, do you?"

"No," I answered. "What's the matter? Are you afraid of the dark?"

"It's lonely in there," she said. I could not see her, and her voice came out of nowhere, like a spirit's trying plaintively to make itself understood. "I'm lonely and I get to thinking that no one is just like me. Do you know what I mean?"

"Yes," I said, "I know, but you'd better not think that way." We forget so often that personality is almost completely developed around the age of four.

"I can't help it," Bella said. "I just keep thinking that I'm different from everybody else and it makes me lonely when I try to be like other people."

"Well, don't let it worry you," I said.

"I wish there were some people who were like us," Bella said. "I wish that Mr. Stowe was like us."

"How do you know he isn't?" I asked.

"I just know," she answered. "He isn't like us."

"Well, it's a fine thing that everybody isn't," I said.

There was a silence before she spoke again, as though she were thinking.

"I think I'll go to China, Jim," she said.

"Leave the door open and go back to sleep," I told her. "I'm tired."

There was one thing about her which was a comfort: she was still young enough to do what you told her. . . .

"You must come again, Mr. Stowe," Cousin Sue said. "Come again when it is not soggy underfoot."

But things moved so quickly then. He always talked of coming, but he did not come again until Aunt Sarah died.

XVIII | The Service Will Be Held

Students have a very tiresome way of analyzing fiction. When I was at Harvard all the types of narrative were labeled and classified like beetles in a case, and of them all there was one variety that I felt was peculiarly awkward. It was called the "peep-hole method," in which the story is told by someone who keeps seeing the main characters at odd moments. I still think it is dangerous, but I do not know any other way to tell about Bella and Joe Stowe.

The war started before Aunt Sarah died. Cousin Sue used to tell me that she had shown a real interest when they read to her about the German atrocities in Belgium, although I did not entirely believe it. Her death was not hard for anyone except Cousin Sue, who had been devoted to Aunt Sarah so long that she was suddenly entirely without occupation. Identical telegrams were sent to Harry and me at Cambridge in October, 1916, our last year there.

"Aunt Sarah passed away quietly and suddenly," they read. "Funeral the day after tomorrow."

I was talking to Joe Stowe when mine arrived, and Harry came in shortly afterward. Our paths had grown so divergent that I had not seen Harry for quite a long while. He was engaged in a great many activities that kept him out of his room most of the time—which was just as well, as he was having a great deal of trouble with his bills. He had owed a clothing bill for two years, and then there was a set of Balzac's *Human Comedy* and a special edition of the unabridged *Arabian Nights* and some other similar items purchased from a book agent, and a typewriter and a camera. The installments on all these were overdue, and the representatives who kept coming in to see him so disturbed his work that he was better off somewhere else.

"Well," Harry said, "that's that. I suppose everybody's got to go down there." He showed no great interest in the event; not that he was hard-hearted, he was simply very busy and absorbed in his own affairs.

"I wonder if Archie will come," he said. "I suppose someone will bring the girls. It's a nuisance, isn't it?"

"Well," I said, "we'd better go down on Friday morning."

Death was so far from us in those days as to be an impossible personal contingency. We could only consider the details and hope that everything would be done properly.

"It's really going to make things a whole lot easier," Harry said. "We ought to be able to bring some friends down now sometimes. I suppose we'd better take the nine o'clock train. I'll sleep on the couch here if you don't mind, and then those bill collectors won't get me."

He kept looking at Joe Stowe while he was speaking, obviously annoyed by his gaucheness in not leaving. I wondered myself why he kept on staying.

"Do you think it would be all right," Joe asked, "if I went down too?"

Harry raised his eyebrows, a trick he had learned recently and one that I knew annoyed Joe.

"I did not know that you'd ever seen her, Joe," he said.

"I took him down last spring," I answered.

"I liked her," Joe said. "I'd like to go, if you don't mind."

"Of course we don't mind," said Harry. "Come ahead. I

193

don't see why you liked her. I never did." But Harry was displeased, and he said so after Joe left.

"Now that goes to show you," Harry said.

"Show me what?" I asked him.

"It goes to show," Harry said, "what happens, Jim, when you play around with anyone like that. What made you take him down there? Now he's trying to suck up to everyone. He knows you can't refuse when he asks to go to a funeral."

"He never had any such idea," I said.

"Oh," said Harry, "didn't he?" And he raised his eyebrows again. "Now I've told you and I've told you that you have to be careful about the people you are seen with. You've been seen with Stowe so much that you've ruined yourself. A lot of people have told me that, Jim. A lot of people were beginning to like you before you started playing around with Stowe."

"You go to hell," I said. "He's a friend of mine."

"All right, all right," Harry said, "but it doesn't help you to play around with someone who hasn't your background, and it's bad for Stowe too, Jim. You ought to think of that. It's the sort of thing that gives a man like Stowe ideas. The next you know he'll be trying to marry Mary, and how would you like that? You've got to think of those things, Jim."

"Don't worry," I said. "He wouldn't look at Mary."

"Well, why wouldn't he look at Mary I want to know?" Harry said. "Mary's all right, isn't she? He's just the sort of person who might marry her on account of her name."

"What about her name?" I asked. Harry looked pleasant and raised his eyebrows again.

"It's time you faced facts, Jim," he said. "If your name's Brill you can meet all the right sort of people. Look at the people in New York. Look at the people in Boston who know the Brills. Personally I don't care, but Stowe's just the kind who would think of that. He could go anywhere he wanted if he were married to a Brill."

I began to laugh.

"You know damned well," said Harry, "that the only way

194

you've ever gotten anywhere is because you're connected with the Brills."

"But you were just telling me," I said, "that I haven't gotten anywhere."

"Well, it's your own fault if you haven't," Harry said. "I've done everything I could—every single thing. It isn't my fault if you haven't taken advantage of it. It isn't my fault if you don't see the right people."

"Well, never mind," I said.

"All right," said Harry, "I won't. I don't want to make you mad, Jim."

Harry was generally worried about seeing the Right People. It was his opinion that if you just met the Right People everything else would happen automatically. They would ask you to parties and for long visits in the summer. When you were through with college, the Right People would give you a job and the Right People would see that you met the Right Sort of Girl. Harry knew lots of the Right Sort of Girls, and he used to go to call on them every Sunday. Harry was always trying to reduce life to a simple formula. He never could get it out of his head that there was an easy way to learn everything and an easy way to do everything.

There is an irony in this philosophy which struck me as we grew older. Without trying to meet the Right People, I managed to get along as well as Harry. I do not mean that Harry was unpleasant in his efforts. He had that complete confidence of all the Brills that he was always wanted everywhere. Later, when we came back from the war, I have known him to go to a great many dances where he was not asked, and even once or twice to Long Island for the week end when he was not asked either, simply because he honestly believed that there had been some mistake about the invitation.

Aunt Sarah's was the first funeral in the family which I can remember clearly, but almost instinctively I knew what it would be like. Everyone was there whom one expected. Cousin Clothilde and Archie, and Sid, who was wearing one of his first pairs of long trousers, and Mary and Bella had arrived the night before. They were all at the door to meet us when Mr. Morrissey drove us from the turnout, and this time Wickford Point was beautiful, not gray as it had been in spring, but brilliant, clear and cool in the October sun, and as motionless as though it stood reflected in still water. The poplars on the hill had turned to a flashing gold. The elms were the yellow of imperial China and the ferns on the riverbank were orange, and the leaves of the great oaks along the bank had begun to turn into a dull garnet-red. Thus everything at Wickford Point, and all the distant bank across the river except for the stands of pine trees, was yellow-red or orange, or else dull brown, and above it all was the October sky, as benign as a sky in the tropics, and the river below made a path of deeper blue.

Archie Wright said that the whole color scheme arranged by nature was in excruciatingly bad taste, and that he never had liked railroad posters. I accepted this, because it was exactly what Archie Wright would say; one had to remember also that Archie Wright was having a disagreeable time. It had not occurred to him that he would be the eldest male in the family, and when he discovered it, he left the house for a long walk.

Cousin Clothilde did not look happy; she had always made it clear that anything to do with death disturbed her very much. First she kissed Harry and then she kissed me, and then, when I had kissed Mary and Bella, I introduced Joe Stowe.

"This is Mr. Stowe," I said. "He knew Aunt Sarah." Although Cousin Clothilde looked puzzled, she was very polite, because she always did like men.

"It's so nice of you to come, Mr. Lowe," she said. Then Cousin Sue was shaking hands with him and she began talking quickly while we were still there on the driveway.

"Mr. Stowe is so familiar with such things," she said, "you don't happen to remember when Aunt Sarah was born, do you, Mr. Stowe?"

"My dear," said Cousin Clothilde, "how should Mr. Lowe know when Aunt Sarah was born? I'm sure I've never heard."

196

"Well, there's no harm in asking, is there?" said Cousin Sue. "It was all in the family Bible, the large one, the Breeches Bible. It isn't my fault if I can't remember where it was put, Clothilde. It always used to be in the cupboard by the back parlor fireplace."

"Perhaps I can help you find it," Joe said. "I'd really like to help."

"How nice of you, Mr. Lowe," said Cousin Clothilde. "Mary, will you please go with Cousin Sue and Mr. Lowe, and Harry, will you walk to the point and see if you can find Archie? Jim darling, I want you to come upstairs with me. You're always such a help, darling; and Bella, I want you to see that no one knocks on the door, no one, I don't care who it is. Oh my God, there's that undertaker again. Will you speak to him, please, Jim?"

Mr. Mason, perspiring freely in a heavy Prince Albert coat, appeared around a corner of the house, carrying a heavy camera on a tripod.

"Hello, Jim," he said.

"Hello," I said. "What's the camera for, Mr. Mason?"

"I just brought it along in the hearse," Mr. Mason said, "in case someone wanted a picture. Lots of people like pictures."

"I'd put it back if I were you, Mr. Mason," I said. "I don't think anyone wants a picture."

"Well, you never can tell," said Mr. Mason. "I'm just trying to do everything I can. Listen, Jim. Now they say they don't want the hearse. They're taking her up there in a farm wagon. Now that's no way to carry Miss Sarah."

"You'd better do what they say," I said.

"Listen, Jim," said Mr. Mason, "do they want the coffin open, or do they want it closed?"

"How should I know?" I asked. "It isn't up to me."

"Well, its got to be up to somebody, Jim," said Mr. Mason. "Miss Sue wants it open and Mrs. Wright, she wants to arrange the flowers and she won't go into the room unless it's closed. Now which is it I'm going to do, Jim?"

"I don't know," I said. "I'll tell you later."

"I'm just trying to oblige, you understand," said Mr. Mason. "I've buried nearly everybody downtown and most of them like the coffin open."

"Jim," Cousin Clothilde called, "Jim. What are you talking to him for? Will you please send that man away?"

It suddenly occurred to me that I was the one who must do everything. Harry had gone to find Archie Wright and I knew he would not come back for as long a time as possible. I had to do something about which I knew nothing, and the only possible one who might be of assistance would be Joe Stowe.

"Jim," said Cousin Clothilde, "come upstairs and bring some cigarettes if you have any, and Bella, no one is to knock on the door."

Cousin Clothilde, once she was up in her room, seated herself upon an ancient chaise-longue which had been my grandmother's, and leaned back upon the faded upholstery and closed her eyes.

"Darling," she said, "give me a cigarette and see if you can find something to put over my feet. My feet have been as cold as ice ever since I came into this house last night. There always has been something wrong with my circulation when I'm nervous. I can't do everything, can I, Jim? I never *have* liked funerals. And what do you think happened last night? Just as soon as I got into the house, Josie and that Miss Jellicoe wanted me to come—wanted me to come to see how Aunt Sarah looked—when she was laid out."

"Laid out?" I repeated.

"It's something they do to dead people," Cousin Clothilde went on. "I'm not quite sure what it is, but I nearly got in there before I understood. And then Sue's feelings were hurt because I didn't want to see Aunt Sarah, and then her feelings were more hurt when I wouldn't let Bella and Mary see her. These things they do about dead people are so terrible. That frightful undertaker you were speaking to—he really seems to act as though he liked it, and I can't do everything, can I, Jim?"

"No," I said, "of course you can't."

198

"And no one has been here to help me at all," said Cousin Clothilde. "I don't know where Archie is. You might think he would have stayed in the house now that everyone will be coming in just a little while. Your cousin Harriet isn't here yet, and she's the one who always manages funerals. It isn't really as though you or I or Archie or someone had died, dear, and Sue is so unstrung. She's been up here talking to me and talking and you know what her voice is like when she's excited. It goes right through my ears as though I had an abscess. I don't know why Harry can't ever do anything. He has just gone away somewhere. I wish you'd hold my hand. No one has paid any attention to me all morning."

I held her hand and it was very cold. Her last words gave me a strange suspicion that she was jealous of Aunt Sarah.

"It really isn't as though it were you or I or Archie," she said again. "She was so dreadfully old."

"What do you want me to do?" I asked.

"I have to arrange the flowers," Cousin Clothilde said, "down there in the back parlor. She's in the back parlor now, and no one else can make the flowers look well. I certainly don't want Sue to try to do it, and I certainly don't want that man to touch them. The whole place is full of flowers and they keep coming and coming. I can't go in there, Jim, with the coffin open. I want you to go down there first and close it."

Cousin Clothilde got up from the chaise-longue.

"I don't suppose it would be right to bring the cigarettes down," she added.

"No," I said, "I don't suppose it would."

"I always can arrange flowers better if I stop and smoke a cigarette and look at them," Cousin Clothilde said. "I shouldn't mind, but someone might come in, that man or someone, and Aunt Sarah never did like to see me smoke. Do you think my dress is all right, dear? It's one that Archie's fond of."

Her dress was dark blue, very long, and it fell in folds like a Grecian drapery—not mourning, for the family did not believe in mourning. We walked downstairs together into the dining room first, where Josie, with two girls to help her, was arranging plates on the table. One of the girls was Luella Jeffries, whom I had loved once, but that was all as irrevocable now as what had happened to Aunt Sarah.

"Good morning, Luella," I said, and I didn't even feel a twinge when I said it. Josie came up to me and whispered, because it was a time to speak in whispers:—

"We have the nicest piece of ham, Mr. Calder. Cold ham and cold roast beef and hot potatoes. That was dear Miss Sue's idea and we wanted to do everything for dear Miss Sue. Mr. Calder —have you seen her yet?"

"Who?" I asked.

"Dear Miss Sarah," Josie whispered. "She's in the back parlor now in that black silk dress, the one that dear Miss Sarah was so fond of."

"I'm going in to see her now," I said.

Cousin Clothilde and I walked through the front entry and into the front parlor and there we found Cousin Sue sitting with Joe Stowe. Cousin Sue got up hastily when we entered and dropped her handkerchief and her spectacle case upon the floor.

"Oh good gracious," she whispered, and Joe picked them up.

"Jim," Cousin Sue whispered, "I wish to speak to you privately for a minute. No, I'd rather that you didn't hear, Clothilde. Will you come into the front entry?"

As she walked into the front entry I noticed that Cousin Sue kept fumbling in the pocket of her skirt.

"Are you going in to see her now?" Cousin Sue whispered.

"Yes," I said.

"She's very beautiful," Cousin Sue whispered. "Here's her knife."

"Her what?" I said.

"Her knife," whispered Cousin Sue. "You remember her knife, of course, that she always carried in her pocket when she went walking? You remember how she said she wished to be

200

buried with it? If I go in they would ask me what I was doing and then they would take the knife away from her. You know what I mean."

I took the heavy worn clasp knife, and for the first time I realized that all of Wickford Point was close to tears.

"All right," I said, "but I'd better close the lid of the coffin so that no one else will see it."

"Thank you," whispered Cousin Sue. "She will appreciate it so."

I put the knife in my side pocket and I heard the tall clock in the dining room striking nine, although the hour was eleven-thirty. I wanted to tell Cousin Sue that I was sorry, but instead I opened the door of the back parlor and closed it behind me carefully, so that the latch hardly clicked.

I could see the sun on the lawn outside, and the yellow leaves of some birch trees by the river, but they seemed a very long distance off now that I was alone. The coffin was at the far end of the room, beneath two pictures of Wampoa harbor that showed the Mandarin barges and foreign ships at anchor. The air was heavy and sickly sweet with the scent of flowers, and the chairs and sofas had been arranged—first the Chippendales and the Queen Annes, and then the banister-backs and the ladder-backs—ready for the family. Those empty chairs gave an air of hushed expectancy as they waited for the end of something which was already ended. I walked between them, trying not to hit them, and looked down at my great-aunt's face. The features were unfamiliar, hardly bearing the family resemblance, for she belonged already to the greater family of the dead. I laid the knife beside her and closed the lid of the coffin. Then I opened the door of the small parlor and told Cousin Clothilde to come in.

Mr. Beardsley, the Unitarian minister, arrived at twelve, while Cousin Clothilde was still busy with the flowers. Harry and Archie Wright were both in the parlor by then, and Archie seemed delighted to see me. He wanted me to go outside with him, but Mr. Beardsley wished to review the selections he was to read. He outlined them carefully, sitting in the very chair in which he had once sat upon Aunt Sarah's cat.

"But you have forgotten one thing," said Cousin Sue. "There is no poem of Mr. Brill's."

"That's true," said Harry. "People will be expecting a poem of Grandfather's."

"Why?" asked Archie Wright. "She wasn't married to a Brill." Cousin Sue's spectacle case slid from her lap and she stooped to pick it up.

"Aunt Sarah always read a poem of his," she said, "every evening, just before bedtime."

Mr. Beardsley looked at Harry.

"Can you suggest any particular poem?" he asked.

"Well, no," said Harry, "not at this instant."

There was a moment's silence. "Isn't there a poem called 'Wickford Elegy'?" Joe asked.

"That's just the one I was trying to remember," Harry said. "Do you think you can find it, Joe?"

Archie Wright put his hand on my shoulder.

"Jim," he whispered, "let's get out into the fresh air." I walked with him down the little path to the drive.

"There they go," he said, "bringing in the Brills. There's something about New England that's always terrible. Look at the faces, look at the house, look at the trees, look at the sky. No wonder Clothilde gets nervous when she's here. What's she doing now?"

"Arranging the flowers," I said.

"There wouldn't be anything to drink in the house, would there?"

"Mr. Morrissey keeps some hard cider up in the barn," I said.

"Well, let me be a hypocrite and drink some hard cider up in the barn," said Archie. "Please help me just as soon as possible to be a hypocrite."

"Why don't you like it here?" I asked him.

"Because there's nothing natural," said Archie, "not even the

202

trees. Not even the vegetation has ever obeyed a human impulse. Are you sure Clothilde is busy with the flowers?"

Archie Wright did not need to tell me he was agitated. It may have been that he was like Cousin Clothilde, used to receiving a certain amount of attention.

"I don't want any of this when I die," said he. "My God, here comes the minister."

It was true; Mr. Beardsley was walking up the drive to join us, a small stoutish man with beetling brows and iron-gray hair.

"A beautiful day," said Mr. Beardsley, "a perfect day."

"Yes," said Archie. "It is a perfect day."

"I hope," said Mr. Beardsley, "that the day is some consolation for the sadness that brings us all together. It is true justice that another artist should be here. This has been the gathering place of many writers and artists, Mr. Wright. I have heard Miss Sarah say that Hunt was here often in his youth."

"I hope you don't consider Hunt an artist," said Archie.

"Fashions change, I suppose," Mr. Beardsley said. "This is a day of change. It is so hard to keep up with the alterations of the world, although I always try. It seems only yesterday that Jim was a little boy. Jim, can you tell me what they have decided? Will the casket be open or will it be closed?"

Everyone was beginning to arrive—all the friends and all the family. A great many must have come up on the eleven o'clock train from Boston, and they were driven out by the new taxi service. Mr. Caldicott came in the first cab with Mr. and Mrs. Bissell, who had been friends of Mr. Hugh Brill and old friends of the family. Mr. Caldicott nodded to Archie Wright without bothering to shake hands, and asked me to take him into the house where he said he would sit and wait because he did not wish to meet anyone. Then came Cousin Harriet and Cousin Tom Wills and their son Roger. In three minutes Cousin Harriet had her husband and Roger and Mr. Mason working out the seating arrangements, placing the family in one room and all the neighbors in the small back parlor; and she had Archie Wright

203

collecting the cards that had come with flowers. She found time also to kiss Harry and me moistly.

"Darling boys," she said to us, "darling, darling boys. You are such a comfort to everyone, I know. And darling Sue and darling Clothilde. Where is Godfrey Caldicott? I must see Godfrey Caldicott."

We all knew she wanted to see Mr. Caldicott about the will, and of course the will was the only reason why Mr. Caldicott was there at all. Then all the neighbors began to arrive, most of them old people from the river farms who had known Aunt Sarah once. They came driving up in buggies, and Mr. Morrissey helped to tie the animals around the barn. They all came crowding into the house silently, and I took my place with the family in the back parlor.

"Where is Mr. Lowe?" Cousin Clothilde whispered.

I shook my head because I did not know where he was; and there was no time to find him, for Mr. Beardsley had risen with his book. He was beginning to speak in a thin solemn voice, and I wondered if anyone really listened to him or whether his words moved only half heeded through the thoughts of others as they did through mine. I could hear the cadence of his voice and that was all, nothing but the measured rise and fall of syllables.

I was not thinking that Aunt Sarah was dead, because that was an accepted fact; I was thinking rather of her absence. She had gone, and she had taken Wickford Point with her. The house, the parlor, and the books had their familiar appearance; but now everything about them that mattered was going, moving into space like the echoes of Mr. Beardsley's psalm.

It was a shocking sort of illusion, and I wondered if other people also had it. There was no way of telling from the polite attention of their faces, but everything about me felt as empty as Mr. Beardsley's words and as devoid of any definite meaning. . . .

"Easy, boys," said Mr. Mason. "Up a little higher in front. That's it. Take it easy. Norman, get the flowers now, and hurry."

We were out of the house again in the sunlight, and Aunt

Sarah was in the farm wagon, and we were following behind, up the hill to the cemetery. I did not notice who was walking beside me until I heard Joe Stowe speak.

"Jim," he said, "isn't Mrs. Wright wonderful?"

"Yes," I said, "she is."

It was not that I loved Aunt Sarah, because she was too old to love. I had not believed it possible that she could take everything away. When it was over, I saw that no one felt as I did, except possibly Cousin Sue.

There was relief in the sound of the clattering dishes and the voices when we all returned to the house for lunch.

"Jim darling," said Cousin Clothilde, "will you see if you can get me a glass of water? And then I wish you would find your friend, Mr. Lowe."

"Stowe," I said.

"Why didn't you tell me before, darling," said Cousin Clothilde, "that I wasn't calling him by his right name? I think your friend is charming. Why haven't you ever spoken of him? You're so queer about things, Jim. And Archie thinks he's charming too. He's the first Harvard man Archie's ever liked."

"I'll find him," I said. "Do you think it would be all right if I went out for a while after lunch?"

She looked up at me quickly.

"Why, of course, dear," she answered. "We feel the same way about things, don't we? Isn't the family dreadful? Everyone is always dreadful at a funeral. Harriet will be wanting Mr. Caldicott to read the will, but there's no reason for you to be there. Mr. Stowe can stay and play with the little girls. He's such a help."

Upstairs in my bedroom closet my clothes were in exactly the same disorder as when I had last left them. I put on rubber boots and a canvas shooting coat. My shotgun, a Purdy which had belonged to my grandfather, was in its case on the closet shelf with a box of shells beside it. I walked down the back stairs carefully and found Nauna, my setter bitch, under the tubs in the laundry. She was growing very slow and stiff, but when she saw the gun and coat, she scrambled out, whining and wagging her tail. The paddles were where I had left them in the old barn harness room, and the canoe was under scrub birch on the point. I shoved the canoe through the brown grass into water and lifted Nauna aboard. As I did so, I could hear the pine trees whispering above the scrape of the canvas against the grass, and for the first time that day I felt a sense of deep relief. The gun and the canoe and the ooze of the mud beneath my feet were things which Aunt Sarah had not taken.

My hand was on the stern and I was just about to get in, when I heard someone calling me and saw Bella standing on the bank.

"Where are you going?" she asked.

"Upriver," I answered, and I knew what she would be asking next.

"I don't care if I get dirty," she said. "I want to go."

"All right," I said. "Come here." I waded back, picked her up and set her beside Nauna in the canoe.

"You're going up the creek after woodcock," she said, "aren't you? I guessed you were as soon as I saw you going out of the barn. I was afraid you were going to take Mr. Stowe. I'm glad you didn't. He wouldn't understand as well as me."

"Sit in the middle and don't move around," I said.

We were out of the grass by then and just on the edge of the channel. A light breeze sprang up, heavy with the muddy smell of water and with the cool faint odor of withered pickerel weed and wild rice.

"You know what I mean," she said. "He wouldn't understand."

"Don't talk so much," I told her. I could hear the waves slap against the bow, not loud, but gentle and definite.

"All right," she answered, "I won't talk."

It took half an hour to reach the creek. It would have been easier to walk if Nauna had been up to it. I wanted to get her to the covert fresh, because she was still a good worker for short periods and not as flighty and wild as she had been once. I had bought her from Nathan Stoddard down at the old Stoddard farm near the river bend, and Nathan Stoddard had trained her himself. We passed his house just before we turned into the creek, and there he was, a heavy man with a drooping gray mustache, seated under an elm tree near the bridge. He said he wasn't feeling so well what with the rheumatism and the water in his leg, or else he would have been down to the funeral, except that maybe Miss Sue would not have wanted to see him. This was true, for it had always been Cousin Sue's and Aunt Sarah's conviction, fortified by general gossip in the neighborhood, that Nate Stoddard was immoral. When he saw Bella, he looked more cheerful, for he still had an eye for the girls.

"Ain't she grown?" he said. "My, my, ain't she pretty! Just like Clothilde. Are you going up to the Nason covert? There ought to be a bird in there." He groaned and pulled himself up from the log where he was sitting.

"I never thought it would git to this," he said. "Have you got the Purdy?"

I pointed to the gun where it lay against the thwart.

"Now shoot quick," he said. "If you can't see, shoot at the sound, and keep the bitch in. I wish I was going."

"Come ahead," I said, but I hoped he wouldn't. I wished that everyone were not growing so old. I wondered if he would take away something when he died.

"I guess I ain't up to it, Jim," he said. "The water keeps gitting into my leg. The doctor says it's a sight. When the water gits into it, it swells like a balloon. Mind you shoot quick . . ."

The tide was running out, but it was still high enough so that I had to duck my head when I pushed the canoe under the wooden bridge. Just as I did so, he called to me again.

"What?" I called back.

"Who did Miss Sarah leave her part at Wickford to?" he called, and I said I didn't know.

There was plenty of water in the creek, and there was a chill autumnal feeling above the water now that the afternoon sun

207

was getting low—just a touch of that congealing dampness which would turn into thick white ribbons of mist at sunset. The trees close to the bank cast shadows over the brown surface, and little puffs of breeze rattled through the marsh grasses, which were already sere and frostbitten.

"Are we almost there?" Bella asked. She never could sit still in a canoe for long. I told her we were nearly there.

"Harry wouldn't do this, would he?" she asked.

I landed the canoe by the stone wall at the place we called Nason's Landing, and pulled it up on shore. Then I helped Bella and Nauna out and tied a bell on Nauna's collar. I had to help them both over the wall and through the barbed-wire fence, where, just as I thought, Bella tore her dress; but she said she didn't mind. She walked behind me exactly as I told her, to the place where the maples grew above the alder thickets. It was beautiful covert, heavy over low damp ground, just the place where a woodcock flight would stop. There were birds. They must have dropped in, the night before. I could tell as soon as I sent Nauna in, and she knew her business too. While I stood at the edge I could hear the bell, and I could see her quartering back and forth through the alders and the grass. She was out of sight when the bell stopped tinkling.

"Stand still," I said to Bella, and then I spoke to Nauna. "Hold it, girl," I said, "hold still." I saw her motionless, half-crouching, her tail out straight, and I can remember every second of it— the smell of the dying leaves and the moist earth, and the way the sun glinted on the red and gold of the maple. I was glad that I was not dead. There are some things that stay with you always, more powerful than love or hate. I knew that nothing that had happened to me was worth a candle to a time like this.

"Go on," I said, "go on."

The bird came out, a flash of brown, as though someone had hurled it up from the bushes. For just a second it was outlined against the sky, more like an abstract problem in marksmanship than a living thing. I fired and the Purdy jarred against my

208

shoulder. At the same instant that ball of feathers paused suspended and then dropped down straight.

"Go get her," I called.

"Did you kill it?" Bella asked.

"Yes," I said, but I did not think of it that way. It had been a problem of ballistics. It was always just like that. Nauna came trotting up, wagging her tail.

"Drop it, girl," I said, and she dropped the woodcock at my feet and sat looking up at me while her tongue lolled from the corner of her mouth. I picked up the bird and smoothed the feathers and examined the awkward hammer-shaped head and the long bill.

"Let me see," said Bella, and I let her hold it before I slipped it into my pocket.

"I won't marry anyone," Bella said, "unless he's someone who goes gunning."

We were having a fine time. I don't remember when I had a better time, and I wish that Bella could have stayed like that. It might have been possible if everybody, as she said, had not always sat and talked. We were away from the talking then. Nothing anywhere around us was inconsequential, nothing confusing, and we were good companions without ulterior desires and ignorant of all those strange unknown complexities developing within us.

I remember what she said when I told her it was time to go. A child has a strange unclouded understanding. Her dress was torn and her hair was coming out of its braids where the alder twigs had pulled it. She had forgotten that she was Bella Brill, and I had forgotten a good many things about myself, such as Harry and the Vindex Club, and why I did not get on with people like Allen Southby, and that I was not a success at college. I had forgotten about the war and the *Lusitania* and the troubles on the Texas border, and about what was going to happen to me, and how I was going to earn my living.

"I wish we didn't have to go back," she said, "not ever."

209

And I often wish, not so much for myself as for Bella Brill, that we never had gone back.

We had the tide with us when we were out on the river again so that the current took us down, and the light was growing golden in the west.

"We can talk now, can't we?" Bella said. It was really the first time that we seemed to be on an equal footing. She told me a great deal, for example, of how Archie and Clothilde kept fighting. She said they would probably be fighting now. And she told me just why she hated Miss Lacey's School and how she never got on with the other girls, because it always seemed that she was jealous of them or they were jealous of her. Miss Lacey thought she had peeked over Nancy Bronson's shoulder during an examination, and of course she had never peeked, but you couldn't stop seeing things, could you, if a girl like Nancy Bronson was such a fool as to leave a paper right under your nose? There were all sorts of things that she wanted to do, and no one understood her except Archie—sometimes. She wanted to go out to the war and drive an ambulance, or perhaps to go on an exploring expedition. There must be all sorts of places where you could go. Archie wanted to take her to Italy, but now there was a war you couldn't do that exactly. Archie always wanted to go to war, and I told her I did, too.

We were back at Wickford Point before I realized that we should not have gone away. I was just pulling the canoe up and turning it over when Harry came out to meet us.

"Where have you been?" Harry asked. "This is a hell of a time to go away and leave me doing everything. It doesn't look right, Jim, with everybody here, and Caldicott's sore about it too. He wants to talk to you and he's missed two trains waiting."

"What does he want?" I asked.

"Don't you know what he wants?" Harry answered. "Aunt Sarah's left you her share of the place."

"She couldn't have," I said. "There must be something wrong."

"Well, she did," Harry said. "There isn't anything wrong about it. As a matter of fact, everybody's glad. But you should have been here, Jim. The only one who's mad is Cousin Harriet, and Archie and Clothilde have been having a fight. What did you get? Anything?"

"Six woodcock," I said.

"Did you?" said Harry. "We could get the steward at the Club to cook them, if you were only in the Club."

"Well, I'm not," I said.

Harry put his arm around my shoulders. "I wish you were," he said. "You know I did my best for you, don't you, Jim? If they only knew you the way I do."

"Never mind," I said, "I don't care." And I did not care at the moment. Nothing Harry had said was of any importance. I was only sorry, very sorry, I was back.

"How's Joe Stowe?" I asked.

"He's fine," said Harry. "I don't know what I'd have done without him. He's been talking to Aunt Sue, and Clothilde likes him, everybody likes him. He's going to spend the night. My God, look at Bella."

"Oh," said Bella, "for goodness' sake, shut up, you and your old clubs! Who cares about you and your old clubs? I've heard people talking about you. I know a lot of things about you, Harry Brill."

"Is that what they teach you at Miss Lacey's?" Harry asked.

"You never mind about Miss Lacey's," Bella said. "If I were just to tell you what the girls think about you at Miss Lacey's! You tried to kiss Nancy Bronson, didn't you, and she slapped your face. Did you know he tried to kiss Nancy Bronson, Jim? He tries to kiss everybody; he doesn't care how young they are. It's just kiss, kiss, kiss."

"Suppose you go up the back way, Bella," I told her, "and change your clothes before anybody sees you."

"All right, Jim," said Bella, "but just you ask Harry about Nancy Bronson. He tried to do it right behind the door at Christmas-time. It's just kiss, kiss, kiss."

211

"Don't be such a liar," Harry said. "No one's going to kiss you, Bella."

"Oh," said Bella, "aren't they? That shows how much you know about it."

"Go ahead," I said to Bella, "quick, and change your clothes."

"All right, Jim," she said. "Joe Stowe tried to kiss me. What do you think of that?"

Harry walked with me more slowly to the house.

"Little liar," Harry said. "She just says anything that comes into her mind."

It was something I had never imagined, and I did not believe it either.

"God help anyone who marries her," Harry said.

XIX | Little
Mr. Make-Believe

"All aboard," they were shouting, "all aboard." The train moved slowly and then it gave a jerk, the way the midnight always did, as if the train crew resented sleeping passengers. I was lying in my berth going through another of those nights that had nothing much to do with sleep. The memories of Joe Stowe and Wickford Point mingled with everything else so that there was no definite demarcation between sleep and consciousness. It was like one of those nights in France when you knew that you would be awakened in the darkness before dawn, and when you were not sure whether you would live through the next day. It was like those nights when we lay in blankets in the open air on hard uneven ground. It was like the times on shipboard in a storm, or like the blackness in a Chinese inn or Eastern caravanserai. Those were the times for dreams. You might be at the other end of the earth, but you were never far from home. Every minute that you had lived was with you.

Now and then the train would stop, only to jerk forward and start again, and every jolt would set my mind in a new direction, until I finally fell asleep. It was seven o'clock when the porter jerked at my bedclothes and told me that the cars would be moved out into the yard in half an hour. Although it was still early in the morning, the buildings on Forty-Second Street and the asphalt of the pavements seemed to have retained the heat of the day before. It was that sodden, treeless heat peculiar to New York. It was the beginning of another sweltering day, plus all that accumulated heat.

I recognized the landmarks within a short radius of my dwelling place. They had been washing down the streets, and there was the fishstore on the corner and the stationer's shop and the taxicab stand and the tailor's. They all were there, entirely unchanged, and this always gave me a sort of surprise. My apartment, up two flights of stairs, with its living room, bedroom, bath and kitchenette, showed signs of long disuse. Mrs. Flanagan, who lived in the basement, had not been any more careful about dusting it than ever. She had rolled up the carpet and put some cloth over the pictures, and newspapers over the books on the shelves, and some more cloth over the couch and chairs. I was glad to see that she had not moved the papers on my desk, although she had undoubtedly read them. The water in the bathroom ran rusty at first, as it always did when it had not been used for some time, but all the things in the medicine chest were just as I had left them. It all gave a sense of restfulness, but no impression of permanence. I could leave the place for a year or for good when the lease was up, and no one would care; this knowledge pleased me sometimes, but not that morning.

There is nothing more dangerous than a sense of loneliness in New York, because once the realization is strong enough you stop being lonely right away, and then all sorts of things begin to happen.

I told myself as I was bathing that I had come to New York entirely for business reasons, but when I was dressed again my mood changed. The place was too bare and there was too much of myself in it. I picked up the telephone on the desk and listened to the buzzing in the receiver. I had been away so long that I dialed the first three letters of the exchange according to Boston regulations. Then when I found what I had done, I re-dialed. I told myself that Patricia Leighton might not be in town, although it was a weekday. As I listened to the automatic ringing of the bell, I was afraid that she might be away, and then I heard her voice.

214

"Hello, Pat," I said. "Did I wake you up?"

"Yes, you did," she said. "When did you get in?"

"Just now, on the midnight."

"Oh," she answered, "well—"

"Nothing," I said, and I heard her laugh. "I just thought I'd call you up. That's all."

"Where are you now?"

"Up here," I said. "Flanagan hasn't dusted anything."

"Have you had breakfast?"

"Yes," I said.

"What did you have for breakfast?"

"Orange juice and a boiled egg."

"Have you been having a good time?"

"No," I said. "Have you?"

"Yes," she said. "I've done fine without you."

"Well, that's good," I said.

"Did you buy a new suit?"

"No," I said.

"Do you want to marry me?" she asked.

"No," I answered, "not particularly."

I heard her laugh again.

"What are you doing today?" she asked.

"I'm going to see Stanhope," I said. "What are you doing to-night?"

"I'm going out," she answered.

"Where are you going?"

"How should I know?" she said. "Just out. Do you want to come here for dinner? Marie will cook it for you. You'd better or else you'll get into trouble."

"I've got to see Stanhope," I said.

"You'll have enough of him by then," she said. "I'll be back early."

"How early?" I asked. "I don't want to sit around there alone."

"Early enough," she said. "You'll wait for me, won't you?"

"All right," I said, "I'll wait."

215

"Well," she said, "good-by, Jim."

She might as well have been with me in the room. Her tele-
r'.one was beside her bed and I knew exactly how she must look.
I told myself that it wouldn't do either of us any good. It was
one of those things that happen, like going outdoors and getting
more cold when you think you are over the cold you have.

The great thing about Pat Leighton was that she made me feel
that I amounted to something. She had been taught, presumably
by her mother, that it was wise to encourage men to talk about
themselves, but her encouragement was not perfunctory. I had
talked about myself to a good many people without any satisfactory results, for I could always see what they wanted. Pat, on
the other hand, never wanted anything. I had never thought
much of men who tell all their troubles to women. It had always
seemed to me a juvenile habit, and I had never told Pat my
troubles, but I could tell her a lot of other things. She would be
amused about Allen Southby and about Joe Stowe and Bella. I
felt better after hearing her voice, but that feeling vanished slowly
when I reached the Stanhope office.

Even in the small reception hall entirely furnished in American pine, where people no one wished to see customarily waited,
there was a sound of typewriters and of perspiring efficiency. It
was ten o'clock in the morning when I arrived, but already a
good many undesirable callers were seated on early Colonial set-
tles. Two of them were young men, one with a beard in a blue
shirt and one without a beard in a pink shirt. There were also
five or six women of various ages, and all of them thought that
they could write. They would probably go on thinking so for a
long long time, perhaps forever, just as I thought that I could
write. We glared at each other with a sort of hauteur peculiar to
our trade, until Miss Everest, a pretty girl who was addressing
envelopes behind the desk, looked up. For a moment I was afraid
that she would ask me to wait there with all the others, since we
were all equally sure that Mr. Stanhope was most anxious to see
us, but she did not.

"Oh, Mr. Calder," she said, "won't you please go right into Mr. Stanhope's office? Mr. Briggs is there."

I walked down a hall of partitioned offices where the typewriters were clicking, past the dramatic department and the motion picture department and the accounting department, to the corner office where George Stanhope worked.

He was behind a big table upon which were two telephones and a pile of manuscripts, a box of cigarettes and a picture of a police dog. I never knew what the police dog had to do with it, because Stanhope did not own one. He was talking to John Briggs, one of those contact editors who make the rounds of agents' offices once or twice a week.

"Hello, George," I said, "hello, John. How are you?"

"Hello, Jim," John Briggs answered. "Do you want to come out to lunch?"

"He can't," George Stanhope said, "not today."

"Do you know the difference between a New Deal Democrat and a toe dancer?" John Briggs asked.

"No," George said, "he hasn't heard it. Go ahead and tell him, John."

"Well, stop me if you've heard it," John said.

"That's all right," George Stanhope said, "he hasn't heard it."

"That's right, John," I said. "I haven't heard anything. I've been away."

"Well, it a good deal like the one about Roosevelt and Jim Farley," John Briggs said. "Stop me if you've heard it."

I didn't stop him. I listened and laughed, not altogether mechanically, but all the while I was thinking that I had been afraid of John Briggs once. When he had told me long ago that his magazine was buying a story of mine about a sing-song girl, I felt I had achieved the ultimate by being in contact with him; but now I knew that he had his troubles too.

He took a manuscript from his briefcase.

"Here's the Sylvia Lane," he said. "We couldn't keep it,

George. We don't any of us know what the matter with it is. It just somehow doesn't seem to go."

"Sylvia's going to feel badly," George said.

"Well," John Briggs answered, "it just doesn't seem to go. It's just another boy and girl in the moonlight who misunderstand each other."

"All right," said George. "They'll buy it up the street."

"All right," said John, "let them buy it up the street. We've got too much about young love. Have you got anything else for me today, George?"

"We've got one of Jerry's dog stories," George said.

"Oh," said John, "it's about time we had a dog story. The customers always go for dogs. Why don't you write a dog story, Jim?"

"About the dog being misunderstood?" I asked. We were old enough friends for John Briggs to indulge himself in out-of-hours humor.

"The dog is always misunderstood in a dog story," he said. "They think he wet the rug, and he didn't do it, and then he is beaten and the Master is going to have him chloroformed until the dog finds a Prowler in the cellar, but the Mistress understood him all the time."

"And here's a Stickney," George said. "It's called 'High Death.'"

"My God," said John, "another Stickney?"

"He's right back in his stride," George said. "He's over his nervous breakdown and he's in Provincetown."

"Aviation?" John asked. "We're rather short on aviation."

"That's it," George said. "I picked it up last night, and I couldn't put it down."

"Is there a hostess in it?" John asked. "We're low on aviation. The Chief was asking for one yesterday."

"Yes," George said, "there's a hostess. It's a good story. I couldn't put it down."

We both knew this was true. George Stanhope's enthusiasm was invincible, and everything he read was new.

218

"And the hostess misunderstands the pilot," I suggested.
"Of course the hostess misunderstands the pilot," John Briggs
said. "How else can you have an aviation story?"

"The pilot might misunderstand the hostess," I said. "That
would be new."

"Don't mind Jim," said George Stanhope. "You'll like it,
John."

"Well," said John, "I've got to be going. Tell Jim the verdict,
will you, George? That serial of yours, Jim, it's going fine, but
the Chief says there ought to be more boy and girl."

"More boy and girl?" I repeated. "Why, it's all boy and girl."

"It won't take any changing," John said, "just one or two inserts will do it. The boy and girl don't quite build up. You can
do it this afternoon; it won't take any time. I've told George the
idea for it, and George will tell you."

"You mean they don't misunderstand each other?" I asked.

"That's it," George said. "There isn't enough conflict between
the boy and girl. Jim will fix it, John. Tell the Old Man that Jim
will start working on it right away."

"I wish you'd come out to lunch," John said.

"He'd better stay here and fix it," George said. "Tell the Old
Man he'll fix it. When they meet for the first time at the houseparty, they'll hate each other."

John Briggs put his briefcase under his arm, waved his hat at
us, and closed the door.

"Jesus Christ," I said.

George Stanhope stood up, mopped his face with a handkerchief and lighted a cigarette. He was used to dealing with tem-
perament. He had the soothing quality of a physician, and though
I did not want to do what he suggested, I knew that I was going
to do it.

"It's as good as sold, Jim," he said. "I just took the responsibility of saying you would do it. Now we can block it out right
here." He picked up the telephone. "Muriel dear," he said,
"I'm talking to Jim Calder. I don't want to be disturbed unless
it's important—only an important call. Sit down, Jim. Take

219

off your coat. All you and I need is half an hour to fix it up.
I told the Old Man you would. You have a valuable personal
relationship with the Old Man. Personally, I think there's
enough conflict, but he wants a little more. It's just a matter of
mood. There has to be something, that intangible sort of something that you're so good at."

"Damn it," I said, "I'm sick of it." I sounded like a child
quarreling with its nurse. The telephone rang before he could
answer.

"Yes, Julie," he said. "Well, what did Robert say about it?
Well, what's Robert's idea of price? We wanted seven hundred
and fifty. It will hurt Mabel's feelings if we don't get it. All
right, this one stays at the old rate." He put down the telephone
and pressed a button.

"I'm awfully sorry, Jim," he said when his secretary came in.
"This won't take a minute. Just take this telegram, Kay. 'To Ma-
bel Winkler. The *Purple Book* has gone crazy about "The
Moon Is There." Isn't that swell? Congratulations. George.' "

"Ten per cent," I said.

"Yes," said George Stanhope. "Where was I? There has to be
something, a subconscious sort of dislike between them, and then
they come together. Now when Chloe meets Geoffrey at the
houseparty just before the pearls are stolen—and that's grand
about the pearls, there's music in it—all you have to do is to
show that unconscious antipathy. She doesn't understand him.
There is liking, of course there is liking, but beneath that liking
is distrust. That's all you have to do—inject the element of conflict. Just as she touches his hand, she wants to hold it but something makes her pull away, and he wonders why and she cannot
tell him and she says something nasty to him, some remark
that she is sorry for when she is thinking in the night."

"And then he tries to get into her room," I suggested.

"No," said George, "no, no, no. You know what I mean, Jim.
It's just something that has to be there, just that subtle something,
and no one can do it better than you can. She doesn't trust him

but she loves him. She wants to believe, but she can't believe. Of course he can't get into her room, not when there are a million readers." The telephone rang and he picked it up.

"Yes," he said; "yes, Cyril." And he picked up a pencil too, and began drawing circles and cubes upon a piece of paper. "It's just swell, Cyril. That new ending is simply swell. It's just what we wanted—where they forget everything and fall into each other's arms—but you've got to cut the beginning, boy, you really have to. I know it's a shame to let any of it go, but you can save it and use it in something else sometime. All right, I'll send the boy over with it this afternoon." He put the telephone down.

"Now, where was I, Jim? Yes, when Chloe meets Geoffrey, just at that first contact, she hates him, although she is physically drawn toward him from the very first—"

I sat there listening, looking now and then at the masses of office buildings outside his window, and watching occasional clouds of steam rise above the roofs, although only heaven knew why anyone needed steam on a day like that. I sat there wondering how he did it, how he could remember everything he had read, how he could always play so expertly with that land of make-believe, with all the futile, brittle thoughts of others. I knew what he wanted. I hardly had to listen to what he told me because I understood the trade. We were engaged in depicting life as someone else wished it, and there had to be conflict in that life. Perhaps it was truer than I thought, perhaps there was always conflict.

That enthusiasm of George Stanhope's was what kept us all going. It even filled the Early American room outside. Those of us whose spirits were faint were buoyed up by that perpetual optimism. He was in the business and he knew exactly what he wanted, but he had a sense of fitness and of creative understanding—admitted that the work he handled was very seldom art. This escapist literature for a hopeless but always hopeful people possessed a quality of artisanship that demanded high technique. We both took a pride in our product, not the wild free pride of an artist, but the solid pride of a craftsman. George Stanhope was

221

awakening my interest, as he always did, while he moved among the characters in that half-world of the imagination governed by editorial fact. Those rather bloodless people we created were all compelled to fall into a formulated pattern. Their manners and appetites were curbed by the prejudices of uneducated minds. They could not use bad language. It was very, very dangerous for them to practice adultery or seduction. After their moment of conflict, they must receive a definite and just reward, a reward to be ratified by the hopes of tired subway-and-commuting juries. When one was weary, one thought of this artisanship of popular fiction as slight, a somewhat ghastly parody on life. But then again, perhaps it was not, for was not all human intercourse governed by arbitrary laws of its own? All life was a story, uglier and less perfect than the ones we wrote, but with its own grim scheme.

George Stanhope was perspiring, laboring with excitement in that land of make-believe.

"Definitely she doesn't trust him," George Stanhope said. He always used the word which was fashionable at the moment. Just now everybody was using "definitely."

"Why?" I asked. "She's a nice girl. Why in hell shouldn't she trust him?"

"Because if she trusts him you haven't got any story," George Stanhope said. "Definitely, Jim, she *can't* trust him."

"But why can't she trust him?" I asked.

"It doesn't matter why," George said, "as long as she doesn't. Wait a minute, don't interrupt me. I'll tell you why. Here's a good one, Jim, and it fits into everything you've done. She doesn't trust him because she is afraid that he will destroy her."

"Oh," I said.

"That's it," said George. "We want to get this straight before our minds start going around too much. She definitely doesn't trust him because she's definitely afraid that he will destroy something that's inside her."

"What's inside her?" I asked.

222

"I've got it," said George. "Wait a minute, don't interrupt me, Jim. Her own beliefs inside her. Her beliefs may be cock-eyed, but she is destroyed if she loses her beliefs. The beliefs rise from her background. Her childhood has put the ideas inside her."

"My God," I said.

"What's the matter?" asked George Stanhope. "Don't you like it, Jim? Doesn't it hold water?"

"Yes," I said, "I guess so. I was thinking of something else."

"Well," he said, "we won't talk about it much longer or else our minds will start going around in circles. But now we have something definite, not complicated but definite."

Now when Joe Stowe met Bella Brill, I wondered, had they always mistrusted each other? I tried to get them out of my mind and to listen to what George was saying, but I could not. Bella had been afraid; I remembered that once she had confessed it to me. She told me that she always harbored a strange exotic fear that someone would destroy her individuality. This may have been why she spoke so often of Sympathetic People and of People who Understood.

"Are you listening to me, Jim?" George Stanhope asked. "Now get this. This is important, Jim."

There was that continual feeling of inadequacy in Bella Brill. You had to know her well before you guessed it, and perhaps I was the only one who guessed, for I had struggled with that same sense once. It is so easy to excuse oneself on the grounds that "no one understands" and on the basis that one is "different." Perhaps Clothilde and Harry and Sid and Bella and Mary were all afraid. They had lived in a world of their own so long that they could not face another world. Theirs was a land of fiction as delicate and artificial as the efforts of George Stanhope's clients. It was the land of Wickford Point and the land of a great belief that they were Brills, unlike other people, and very, very remarkable.

"You see what I mean?" George Stanhope asked.

"Yes," I said, "I see what you mean. More conflict."

223

"And you can do it, can't you?"

"Yes," I said, "I can do it. I hoped that they wouldn't have to misunderstand each other for once, but I can do it."

"Well," George said, "that's that. How've you been, Jim? Did you see Joe Stowe in Boston? I wish he could settle down and do some work. I think he's better, don't you?"

"Yes," I said, "he's better all the time."

"You aren't worried about what I told you?" he asked.

"No," I said, "of course not. I can fix it."

"Just a little more conflict," said George, "between the boy and girl."

"That's what Joe had," I said, "but it wasn't a happy ending."

George Stanhope leaned his elbows upon his writing table.

"Joe didn't say anything silly?" he asked. "He didn't say anything about your going away with him somewhere?"

"He suggested it," I said. "I'd rather like to go."

"Now listen!" said George. "You can't and he can't, Jim. You're saving some money now. You can't give that up. Where do you want to go?"

"East," I said.

"Now, Jim," said George, "we'll have to talk about this some more. Let's have some lunch. You'll feel better after lunch. What do you suppose Joe ever married her for, Jim?"

"He was in love with her," I said.

"No sooner I get one writer over a divorce," George Stanhope said, "than right off another gets into trouble or else someone falls in love. Let's go out and get some lunch."

That was the way it always was, lunch and talk about ideas, but things were changed now that Joe's name had been mentioned. Both of them were with us, Joe Stowe and Bella Brill.

XX | You Can't Get Away from It, Darling

Marie gave me my coffee on the terrace of Pat Leighton's apartment. Pat had taken a penthouse the winter before, after she had been put in charge of the advertising of one of the large department stores; and she could afford it, since her salary had been raised to twenty thousand a year. She had to work hard for that salary. She had to spend most of her time thinking of full pages in newspapers with smart lines about lingerie or furniture or whatever it was they were featuring, but she could afford a five-room penthouse.

"Does Monsieur desire some *fine*?" Marie inquired.

"Thank you, yes," I said.

It occurred to me that Marie knew a good deal, in fact too much, about me, but it may have been only fair since I knew a lot about Marie. She still spoke her native tongue with a Breton accent and she had been working for Pat for five years. She had been brought up on a farm near the ancient town of Dol, had been in service in New York City for twenty-five years, ever since she was a very young girl, and she weighed two hundred and fifty pounds. She had been married for most of that time to an unknown character named Pierre, who was the second salad chef at the Waldorf, and between them they were saving enough money to retire before long to France. Marie, in spite of her

225

long absence from home, had absorbed nothing from America except her wages. In fact, she often said frankly that she despised America as a place inhabited by barbarians and Indians and fit simply for the accumulation of a comfortable competence. Marie was agreeable to me because I was not as barbarous as other Americans, having taken part in a war in which she had lost two brothers. Also I had prevented her once from buying stock in a dry oil well.

"It is a very warm evening," said Marie. "Why does not Monsieur be informal and divest himself of his coat?"

"If you will permit," I said. "Thank you. You are most gracious."

Marie's strong white teeth glittered in the dusk.

"Monsieur loves to amuse himself," she said, "but there, that is more comfortable."

She stood beside my chair in the half-light, still holding the bottle of brandy. We were by ourselves in space, looking down upon a carpet of electric street lights. There were lights above the streets also, puncturing the black shadows of the buildings that stood out against the fading glow in the sky. It was cooler than on the ground, but it was very hot. Marie was waiting to ask me something. It was comforting to know that her question probably would not be personal, and certainly would not refer to any relationship between Mademoiselle and me, for Marie was always discreet.

"Might I ask Monsieur a question?" Marie inquired.

"But yes," I said. "Why should there be harm in asking a question?"

"Would Monsieur advise an investment in the General Motors Corporation?" Marie inquired. "Mademoiselle has suggested it for my savings."

"No," I answered, "keep it in the bank."

"Monsieur confirms my own judgment," said Marie. "Monsieur is very kind."

A sound inside the penthouse interrupted her.

"It is Mademoiselle," Marie said, and she moved away quickly and adroitly, in spite of her great bulk. "Good night, Monsieur, and many thanks."

It was true that she knew a good deal about me, but then she did not care. I could hear her speaking to Mademoiselle inside, something about plans for tomorrow, and then a minute or two later Patricia came out on the terrace.

"Hello, Pat," I said.

"Hello," she answered. "Aren't you going to kiss me, Jim?"

"Marie hasn't gone home yet," I said.

Patricia laughed. There was always something about me which amused her.

"She can stand it if I can," she said. "I'm awfully glad to see you." She drew away from me, but her hands were still on my shoulders.

"Pat," I said, "we ought to cut this out."

"Why?" she asked.

"Because you're a nice girl," I told her, "and it doesn't look well, Pat. I don't want you to be talked about."

"You're a nice boy too," she said. "That is, as nice as any boy can be when he gets to be your age. I can stand it if you can, Jim."

"I don't want you to stand it," I said.

"Darling," said Pat, "you can move in here any time. You need me to look after you."

"I don't want you to look after me," I said.

"Give me another kiss," she said, "and sit down and finish your brandy. I'm going to put on something loose."

"You're loose enough already," I said, and she laughed at me again. Everything was always all right when she was there. There was never any furtiveness or sin, and yet I could not understand why it was all right. She came back again in the green taffeta deacon's robe I had brought her from Moscow and asked me for a cigarette, and I asked her what she had been doing.

"Dining with business acquaintances," she said. "Never mind. Tell me about Wickford Point."

I told her a good deal about Wickford Point and it usually made her laugh, but now she did not laugh.

"That's why you're so queer about things," she said. "New England must be awfully queer. What did George Stanhope say?"

"There must be conflict," I said. "The hero and heroine must misunderstand each other. She must be afraid of him, afraid he will destroy her."

"That's rot of course," she said. "Look at you and me. We don't misunderstand each other. We understand each other very well, and I'm not afraid you're going to destroy me, because I know you couldn't, and we're both reasonably happy, and there isn't any conflict either."

"Some people are afraid," I said. "Now there's my cousin, Bella Brill."

"Oh," she said, "that little—Excuse me, Jim."

"That isn't fair," I said. "You don't know her well."

"I'm just speaking in generalities, darling," she answered. "Bitches are always afraid. You ought to be old enough to realize that every bitch is a coward."

"Perhaps that's why they're bitches," I said. "I'd never thought of that."

"Darling," she said, "it always feels so nice when I give you a new idea. Would you take me down to Wickford Point, or would you be embarrassed?"

"I'm going down on Friday night," I answered. "You'd better come along."

"It would be fun, wouldn't it?" she said. "I might, you know, just to see you squirm. Who's going to be there?"

I did not think it would be fun in the least, when I thought of her with all those other people.

"A man named Southby is coming," I said, "Allen Southby."

"The one who wrote *The Transcendent Curve?*" she asked.

"Yes," I said. "He's pretty terrible; he's writing a novel now."

She was looking at me through the dark, and even if she could barely see me, I knew she could judge my expression by the tone of my voice.

"That's more than you're doing, Jim," she said.

There was no need for her to tell me that, and it was not kind.

228

"I can't afford the time," I said.

"That's nonsense, isn't it?" she answered. "I don't like what I'm doing and you don't like what you're doing, but we don't both have to do it."

I was under no illusions about myself, and I told her so. "But I've never been kept yet," I said.

"That's because you're afraid, too," she said, and she put her hand over mine and held it tight before I could answer. "You're afraid, but you're not a coward, darling. I know what you're thinking about. You're thinking of packing up and going away somewhere."

"How did you guess that?" I asked.

"Because I've seen you do it before," she answered. "I'm going with you this time."

"Oh," I said, "are you?" She did not answer, and I did not speak for a long while either.

"Jim," she asked at length, "what are you thinking about?"

"All sorts of things," I said. "The war. All sorts of things."

"All right," she told me, "go ahead and think. But just remember you can't get away from anything by thinking."

She was right about that too. There were so many people who could never finish what they started. For example, Harry Brill could never finish anything, nor Sid nor Bella nor Mary. They were always starting something and then dropping it because they had eyestrain or neuritis or because there was something more attractive just around the corner. But war was something you had to finish once you started. I always remembered that.

XXI | . . . Parlez-vous

The nice thing about a war is that when one comes, you can drop everything and go to it, and everyone will say that you were exactly right. I suppose if there were another war, I should hurry to it right away, provided I could pass the doctors, and I should be just as anxious as before to slough off everything. We were all caught in an inescapable wave of mass hysteria, which suddenly swamped the country. Definitely, as George Stanhope would have said, it was something over which one had no control. If all your friends were going, it was only common sense to go along. The wave broke over us almost overnight, sending us in all directions, and when it receded we were never quite the same again; but it was common sense to go along, although it was difficult to know exactly why we were going, and oddly enough, this seemed unimportant. Even at the time, however, the reasons for going to France seemed peculiar. Most of them were based on a generally accepted fact that if we did not go over there, the Germans would certainly come over here. It was difficult to work out how the Germans would get here, and it might have been better to have waited until they came.

Harry Brill knew somebody who had an uncle somewhere who could get him into aviation, but I went to Plattsburg and Joe Stowe went too. We waited in the rain for three hours outside a Boston office to get our names down, so as to be sure to be among the first. It was unthinkable that we might be left behind when everyone was going. Even so, we lived in hourly fear that we might have applied too late.

As I look back, such fears were a continuous obsession. First we were afraid that we would not get there, and when we did, we were afraid of being dropped as of unfit caliber for officers and gentlemen. This was a thought that stalked behind us in the wooden barracks and outside the barracks too, where regular army officers appeared at odd moments with notebooks and pencils, putting down black marks. If you did not listen attentively to the lectures, if you were low in the weekly examinations, if you were found improperly buttoned or if you were caught in the latrine with a cigarette, you might not become an officer and gentleman. The training period at Plattsburg was a curious sort of nightmare.

After all, the details do not matter much, for most of them are lost in larger parts of a bad dream, of which most of us hated to speak for quite a long while afterwards. You lost sight of friends and enemies in the mazes of that dream. There were always new contacts and new faces that disappeared as soon as they became familiar—faces of enlisted men, and of bad officers, and of good officers; unrelated snatches of conversation in the sun and in the rain.

Captain H. L. Wyre commanded that officers' training company. I remember him largely because he was the first of his kind I had ever seen. The perfection of the flare of his breeches and the angle of his shoulders extended to the impassive lines of his deeply tanned face. He made it very clear to us that it was impossible to turn out a soldier in three months, and he often expressed a wonder that we wanted to be officers when the life of an enlisted man was considerably easier. I had no conversation with the Captain until a week before the whole thing ended, except for the times when he asked my name and put a black mark in his book. One evening however, after retreat, when the first sergeant, a Yale halfback named Stevens, told us to fall out.

"Calder," Captain Wyre called, "Calder."

The sound of my name was so unusual that he had to call again before I understood that I was wanted. Then, of course, I hurried toward him and saluted just as I had been taught, while I tried to think what it was that I had done wrong.

"Well," said Captain Wyre, "what's the matter, Calder?"

"Sir," I said.

"I asked you what the matter is," Captain Wyre said. "Why do you look surprised?"

There was something about the conversation that was wrong, for I had never considered Captain Wyre as a human being.

"I was surprised that the Captain knew me," I said.

The Captain took out his notebook, turned the pages deliberately and made a mark with his pencil.

"That's all," he said. I saluted and turned away.

"Come back," the Captain said, "and try that again, Calder. That 'about face' was very badly done."

In those curious days such a conversation had a nerve-shaking importance. When I walked down the aisle of double-deck bunks, a dozen people were gathered about mine already to discover at first hand just what the Captain had said, and to balance every word.

"He wanted to know why I looked surprised," I said.

Although everyone tried not to show it, I could read the general opinion that I was through. Joe Stowe was the only one who thought differently.

"He wanted to talk to you, that's all," he said. "It's just a funny way they have. He did the same thing to me yesterday. He probably was lonely."

"Why should he be lonely?" I asked.

"Why shouldn't he be?" said Joe. "I'd be lonely in his shoes. Or maybe he was full of fun." I did not agree with him about the last. When I saw him Captain Wyre was never full of fun, but I saw him only once again—for three minutes the next evening.

"Calder and Stowe," the first sergeant said, "will report to the orderly room after this formation."

232

Captain Wyre was seated at a bare pine table, examining some papers under an unshaded electric light.

"Candidate Stowe reporting, sir," Joe said.

"Candidate Calder reporting, sir," I said.

Captain Wyre set down his papers.

"At ease, gentlemen," he said.

I remember how my heart beat in my throat, and my feeling of suffocating dizziness, simply because a West Point captain had referred to us as "gentlemen."

"Headquarters has asked for two first lieutenants," Captain Wyre said, "to report at Hoboken at once, for duty overseas. You two gentlemen will leave on the train tonight. There will be no time for going home. You will have an opportunity to buy your equipment in New York. There will be time to get officers' braid and pins in town."

I cleared my throat, but even then I found it hard to speak.

"Does the Captain mean that we are first lieutenants?" I asked.

"Commissioned before the expiration of the training period," Captain Wyre replied. "Calder has seniority and will take the orders. Any other questions?"

"Jesus," said Joe Stowe, "I thought you were going to fire us, Captain."

Captain Wyre's lips twitched faintly. It was as near as I had ever seen him come to smiling. He pushed back his chair and his voice changed.

"You don't know what you're getting into. You ought to be trained for three years more, and then you mightn't amount to anything, judging by your language. Good night and good luck, gentlemen." We shook hands and saluted.

"Jesus," Joe said when we were outside. "General Pershing must be having trouble."

That was the way it always was; you either couldn't wait or else you were always waiting. You were always being moved without knowing exactly why. The suddenness of the change left a cold sensation in my spine. A minute before, France had seemed a long way off, and now that it was near, now that I was thinking

233

of the casualties, I had a sudden desire to see Wickford Point again, and no desire at all to go to France.

"How are you feeling?" Joe asked.

"All right," I said.

There were always new faces and new voices. We were assigned to a four-berth stateroom with two other lieutenants in what had been the second class of a former German liner and we were under orders not to come on deck until we were told. One of the boys was named Hofstadt, and he came from Kansas, and the name of the other was Yancey, and he came from Alabama. Joe and I had the upper berths and they the lower ones, because they had arrived first. Yancey did most of the talking. He hadn't had time even to find a girl because he didn't know his way around, but there would be lots of girls in France. He wanted to know where we all came from. He thought this was a hell of a room for officers and he wondered when we ate. It would be a hell of a place with all these stairs if the ship should sink. I can remember his words going on in a long tiresome drawl. Like Captain Wyre I never saw him again but once, and that was in the woods near Cuisy. He was not talking then because the side of his face had been blown off. He must have gone over with the first lot of the infantry from Hill 302.

It was late when we were finally allowed on deck. The lifeboats had been slung over the sides, and out in the bow some sailors were lounging around a six-inch gun. Down on the same deck near the forehatch, a Y.M.C.A. secretary was handing out postcards, and pamphlets on venereal diseases, to some enlisted men. It was hard to tell just why anyone should want a postcard at the moment. Ahead of us, upon a lead-colored sea, six other transports with their sides painted in stripes were being led toward the curve of the horizon by a gray battle cruiser, and we were all standing on the passenger deck listening to an address by a reserve lieutenant from the Navy. He was telling about the watches that must be kept aboard ship and how we must report anything we saw, anything at all, even a bird or a piece of driftwood.

"Now remember," he said, "you are sharing the responsibility with the Navy. When you are on watch, the safety of everyone on board may rest with you. That's all."

"Nigger-loving bastard," Mr. Yancey said.

"How do you know he loves niggers?" Joe asked.

"Well," said Mr. Yancey, "because he talks that way."

No one paid much attention to him, because you could tell that Mr. Yancey was endeavoring to show off, and talking to keep his spirits up. Astern of us the sun was going down, sinking through a murk of clouds, straight into the sea. There was nothing behind us except the sun and the water, absolutely nothing. It was as if everything we had left, the homes and the faces we had known, had never existed, or as if they had all been rubbed out as an eraser rubs the sentences and geometric figures off the board at school.

"Well," Joe said, "there's nothing left, is there?"

The war does not afford a very profitable subject for discussion, although the period explains what is the matter with a good many of us who were in it. Now when you hear it discussed at the war dinners and reunions, you wonder what it was all about. There are always the same songs about the caissons rolling and about the French they are a funny race, parley-vous, and about the peculiar sexual habits of Mademoiselle from Armentières, and about how General Pershing won the war back in Chaumont, the Y.M.C.A. and the M.P.s. Then along come the stories, all of which sound about the same: the one about the German prisoner, and about how someone got a medal for not doing anything, and about some conversation with a general. And after that you begin to argue about just where C Company of the 78th was at noon on the thirteenth, and you know it wasn't where someone said it was because you were there yourself at noon on the thirteenth, and C Company wasn't, and then somebody says that wasn't so at all. Then someone who has had a little more to drink bangs upon the table and tells how the military police raided a cat house in Bordeaux, and finally someone else tells how he won the war single-handed. It was all an accident, of course, and anyone else would have done the same thing in his place because it was the only thing to do. Those have never seemed to me very merry evenings, for there is always a sadness in the background. It is all so far away that you cannot believe that you were there at all. It is like a broken plate the pieces of which can never be put together.

There is no doubt, though, that all the noise and all the uniforms made it hard to settle down. When I met Joe Stowe in Paris after the Armistice, I had not seen him for six months, and we sat in the Café de la Paix drinking brandy and asking what had happened to people we had known.

"Do you want to go home?" Joe Stowe asked.

"No," I said, "not particularly."

He grinned at me across the table.

"That's fine," he said. "I'm going to get a job on a newspaper someday, but not just yet. There's a way of getting mustered out here, if you know how to do it."

"There's a way of doing everything," I said.

"There's a man I want you to meet," Joe Stowe said, "a Britisher. You'd better come along."

"Why?" I asked. "What for?"

"Because you don't want to go home," Joe said. "You'd better come along."

You were always going to strange places in Paris then, where somebody knew a girl, or somewhere else. The man Joe knew was a Major Mosby, who was living in an apartment on the Rue Jacob, three flights up. I can still remember the yellowness of the street lights and the smell of garlic in the kitchen of the concierge—a stout woman with a face not unlike Pat Leighton's Marie.

"Mademoiselle Annette has visitors," she said. "The officers are too late."

"It is not Mademoiselle we are seeking," Joe told her, and his French was much better than mine. "It is the British officer, Major Mosby."

236

"Oh," said Madame, "that is different. I had not understood that Messieurs the officers were serious."

It is strange to remember such trivial bits of conversation when you have forgotten so much that is important. Major Mosby was in a shabby dressing gown, drinking whisky by himself and smoking Macedonia cigarettes.

"Ah, Stowe," he said, "good evening."

"This is a friend of mine," Joe said, "Captain Calder."

The major nodded without shaking hands. His hair was growing grizzled, but his age was uncertain. His face was leathery and hard, as nearly everyone's face was then.

"Are you familiar with the use of the machine gun, Captain Calder?" he asked.

"Yes," I answered. "Why?"

"The Chinese," he said, "are looking for machine-gun officers. Three hundred dollars gold a month, and all expenses paid."

"You're going out to China?" I asked.

"Quite," said Major Mosby. "Commissioned by my old friend, General Feng, to pick up a few likely officers. No trouble about the money. Stowe's joining up and three or four others. Jolly if you should come along."

"Three hundred dollars a month," I repeated.

"And all found," Major Mosby said. "No trouble about the money. Not the slightest trouble."

I looked at Joe and he nodded at me.

"I know a way you can get your discharge here," he said. "It's all right. How about it, Jim?"

"All right," I said, "I'll go."

There are disadvantages in doing such a thing as that; but there are compensations later on, for later you have a good deal to think about. In the space of a split second you can look back on the sort of person you once were, with a cool objective wonder.

It surprised me that I was so quiet and careful now, trying

for some reason to save money. I was sitting there beside Patricia Leighton on the terrace of her penthouse and in the short silence that had fallen between us I had been to places which she had never seen. I might take her back with me sometime to every place I had known, but she could never see what I had, for all of it had vanished.

"Jim," she said, "what are you thinking about?"

"About the time I got back home," I said, "November 2, 1925."

"Why are you thinking of that?" she asked.

"I don't know," I said. "There isn't any explanation."

"Don't worry," she said. "I like to have you think. What happened when you got back home?"

"That's the funny thing," I answered, "the most curious thing about it. Nothing happened. Nobody really seemed to understand that I'd been away. It just seemed to everyone that I had been around the corner. They just asked what I was doing—that was all."

And that was true. Life means so very little, most of it— particularly someone else's life.

"There wasn't anybody to talk to," I said. "That was the funny part about it."

"November 2, 1925, " she said. "I was in college then. You might have talked to me. Where did you go on November 2, 1925?"

"To Cousin Clothilde's, of course, I said, "as soon as I got off the dock."

"I suppose you would," she said. "What happened when you got there? What did you think of them when you got back?"

"That's the funny thing about it," I said.

"You told me that before," Patricia said.

"Well," I repeated, "that's the funny thing about it. They hadn't changed at all. She had overdrawn her bank account. They hadn't changed at all."

I hesitated for a moment, considering whether or not it

would be better to thrust all those thoughts back where they had come from, since they had nothing to do with Patricia Leighton. I hesitated also because of my disapproval of men who pour out their souls to women, although a woman can stand physical pain and conversational boredom much better than a man.

"Of course," I said, "Sid and the little girls had grown up, but it didn't really make much difference because they were just what I had expected them to be. They had grown up, but they hadn't changed at all. Now that was funny, wasn't it?"

"No," she said, "not so very funny."

"Well," I replied, and I wanted her to understand what I meant, for I had never exactly expressed the idea to anyone, "it struck me as remarkable, when everything else was so different from the way I had expected it. There was Cousin Clothilde hardly any older, with her account overdrawn at the bank, and Archie was away somewhere to see someone important about a mural. There was someone who knew somebody who was doing something about something down in Washington, and it really did seem as though Archie would get a chance to paint the wall, and Sid was getting ready to be a biologist that year, and Harry was out of a job. He had been doing something with marine insurance but it hadn't given him an opportunity to develop, and he knew someone who was going to introduce him to the president of something else. You could always get along if you knew the right people."

I had expected her to laugh, but she did not, and her silence made me feel that there was something wrong with my narration. I wished that I had not told her any of it, now that she was not amused.

"It must have been curious," she said.

"It was a little," I answered, "because I wasn't used to it."

"Jim," she asked, "do you mind if I ask you a question? I know you're very loyal. You won't be angry, will you?"

"No," I said, "go ahead. Ask anything you like."

"I don't like the way you say it," she said. "But never mind. . . . Didn't it strike you as a little ugly?"

Something inside me gave me an odd, convulsive start, as though I had betrayed some secret that no one should have known except myself. It was something that had been in the back of my mind for a long while, although I would not have admitted it, certainly not to her.

"Exactly how do you mean 'ugly'?" I repeated.

"Ugly," she answered, "because they hadn't changed."

"That's true," I said. "I had never thought of it in quite that way."

"It always makes me so happy," she said, "when I give you a new idea. I love you because you're not afraid of a new idea. It was ugly because she wouldn't let them change."

"Who?" I asked. "Who wouldn't let them change?" But I knew exactly what she meant, although I would not have admitted it to anyone alive.

"Your Cousin Clothilde," she said. "It must have hurt you, Jim, because it hurts you now."

"That isn't fair," I said. "You've never even seen her."

"Don't you see," she said, "that's exactly how I know, because I've never seen her? And you wouldn't know because you love her so much. You're always so loyal. You'd be happier if you weren't so loyal—but then I wouldn't like you. There's no reason why you shouldn't love her. She couldn't help it. There are lots of things that I can't help either. I can't help you, for instance, or this. She didn't want them to change. It doesn't mean I blame her."

"How do you mean?" I asked. "She loves them all. Why shouldn't she want them to change?"

"You're so clever sometimes," she replied, "and it's so simple. Perhaps a man can't understand it, but any woman would. If they changed, don't you see, she'd lose them? She couldn't do things for them any more—nice, generous things, I mean. Any woman wants to do nice, generous things. She wants to man-

240

age someone. She'd like to manage everyone because it means that she's doing something. That's why I want to manage you."

She paused but I did not answer.

"That's why she put them all in a little house," she said, "not a real house, but an imaginary house."

"Don't you think you're growing rather complicated?" I asked.

"No, not at all," she said. "Part of every woman wants just that. It's somewhere in everyone. She put them in a little house, and then she made them afraid to get away, because it was different outside."

"Afraid?" I repeated.

"Yes," she said, "of course. It's so easy to make anyone afraid. I wish I could make you afraid to get away—but then I wouldn't like you. I'm glad you got away."

"Away from what?" I asked.

"From all that," she said. "From her, from all of them. Didn't she try to get you back?"

"That's hardly accurate," I said.

"Didn't she?" she asked.

"The way you set it down on a scientific chart, life's quite a mess," I said. She laughed at me, and it made me feel better, less uncertain, less uncomfortable. There are so many things that it is better not to think about.

"It isn't scientific," she said; "that's why it is such a mess; but just the same I rather like it. I'm glad we're both alive."

"You're quite a girl, aren't you?" I said. "You can take it all apart and put it back again."

"Well," she answered, "that's what we're here for, isn't it? Everybody has to do it. Everybody has to try."

"Not necessarily," I answered. "Why not let it go?"

"No," she said, "it's better if you try. That's what we're made for, darling. So on November 2, 1925, you went right there, of course."

"Of course I did," I said, "and you'd have done it too.

I came back there because they were a part of me, because I loved them. I still love them."

My words sounded hardly decent when I spoke them aloud, yet I felt that surge of old loyalty coming back from the past just as it had on November 2, 1925, though heaven knows why I should have been so accurate about the date.

"Suppose," I suggested, "that you stop taking me apart."

"I don't have to," she answered. "You're all apart already, darling. But just the same you seem to go, and I like the way you go. New England must be awfully queer."

"You're quite a girl," I said again. "You must have read a lot of useful books. But just the same you're not entirely right. Ugly is not the word for it, and I'll tell you why: because nothing is ever ugly when Cousin Clothilde's around."

"Well," she said, "perhaps that makes it worse, doesn't it? Tell me about it. I love to hear you talk."

XXII | November 2, 1925

I finished with the customs at three o'clock in the afternoon. The Brills were living on Twelfth Street then; they were always moving from one to another of those houses which were in partial repair and obtainable at a very low rental, if you took them from month to month until they were turned over to the wreckers to be finally torn down. I said good-by to all those people whom you meet on a ship, and whom you always think you will look up again sometime, but never do. I said good-by to Mrs. Frelinghaus from Chicago and to the German I played chess with and to a girl named Dorothy Padmore, who used to have cocktails in my cabin. She was really a nice girl and probably should have known better, and now that the bond salesman, whom she had said she really didn't want to marry at all, had come to meet her at the dock, she seemed relieved to see the last of me and rather surprised about everything.

"Good-by, Jim," she said. "I think I must have been crazy."

"Don't let it worry you at all," I said. "But it might be just as well not to tell Mr. Staunton. I wouldn't if I were you."

"Don't you think I ought to tell him?" she said.

"No," I said, "absolutely not. Just consider it as an interlude. Good-by, Dot."

I gave the porter fifty cents to have my steamer trunk and

pigskin kit bag carried out to a line of taxicabs that waited at the end of the pier. The driver was not cordial when he discovered that I was going only as far as West Twelfth Street. He was a red-headed, flat-faced Jew, and he began to behave like a child who has lost a toy, until I asked him what was the matter. It appeared that he had been down there waiting for the boat, in order to maintain his place in line, since ten o'clock that morning, and now he was going to receive a fare that amounted only to sixty cents and something more for the trunk.

"Never mind," I said, "you can take me up Fifth Avenue first, and through the Park. I haven't been here for quite a while."

He was cordial after that, and he was telling me of his domestic difficulties by the time we reached Fifth Avenue; moreover he revealed a store of useful information. He thought at first that I was jesting when I said that I had never seen a traffic light or any of the fleets of taxicabs painted in different colors. He was interested in a protective sort of way when he understood that I really did not know how to cope with prohibition.

"You must have been off somewhere, mister," he said.

"Yes," I said, "I've been away for quite a while."

I had thought that everything would be the way I had left it, as might be true in Paris or Berlin or Rome or London. I had forgotten how New York could burst out every year into a new rash of novelty. Everything was being torn down and built up again. The number of automobiles was un-believable. Of course I got used to it in a day or two, and I know now that what I saw was only the beginning of the boom days; but, on coming suddenly out of an older world, it was hard to adjust myself.

"Well," I said, "let's go back to Twelfth Street."

It was quieter there, although lower Fifth Avenue had been turned over to the garment trade. At Twelfth Street

244

there were a great many of the old brick and brownstone houses, with basement entrances under the front stoops, and with double doorways and vestibules. When the driver stopped at the number I gave him, I felt for the first time that I was really back, even before I rang the bell.

Sid was the one who opened the door and he was entirely grown-up, a frailer edition of Harry with the same distinguished Brill nose and the rather small Brill mouth. I recognized him at once by the limp way that his hands hung out of his sleeves. I remember the momentary blankness on his face, and the slight supercilious watchfulness that the Brills always assumed when they were confronting strangers. They did not know that I was coming or where in the world I was, but Sid recognized me almost at once. It was one of the few times I had ever known him to express deep and earnest enthusiasm.

"Jim," he shouted, "Jim!" And without bothering to look at me again, he actually ran across the black-and-white marble of the hall and opened the parlor door.

"It's Jim," he shouted, "Jim's come back!"

They were all there in the parlor, and it looked just the way parlors in the Brill houses in New York always had, for no matter where the Brills were the furniture went with them. I saw the piano, and the sofa that was bursting through its upholstery, and the tapestry of a man in armor ogling a shepherdess, which was intended to represent a Biblical scene. These all came from Archie Wright's studio, when he used to have a studio. Clothilde was lying upon the sofa and there was tea in front of the fireplace where cannel coal was burning.

There was just a moment in which I saw it all before Cousin Clothilde kissed me; Mary, who was all grown-up, tall and straight, with blue eyes and very bright red cheeks, and with her heavy yellow hair coiled in a loose knot, kissed me and began to cry, and then I saw Bella, and she was grown-up too. I had never realized that she would be so beautiful or that her beauty would give me a sense of shock.

She had been sitting on a low stool near the fire, talking to a man I did not know, and she got up with a quick impatient flourish of her hips and shoulders, so that her dress swung away from her slender legs as if it were hardly a dress at all. Her dark hair had not yet been cut short and her violet eyes were wider than I had ever seen them. I had that single glimpse of her before she threw herself at me, and for once she did not stop to think whether she was effective or not.

"Jim," she called, "darling, darling." And she began to cry too, just for a moment, with her head on my shoulder, saying: "Aren't you going to kiss me, Jim?"

I kissed her, longer than was necessary perhaps, and then I kissed Mary again and then I kissed Cousin Clothilde again, and then I shook hands with Harry. Harry had grown stoutish and his hair was getting thin. He had on a blue suit with pencil stripes.

"Jim," he said, "I'm awfully glad to see you. The Somerbys said they saw you in Berlin when you came down from Moscow."

"What Somerbys?" I asked.

"The Talcott Somerbys," Harry said.

"Oh," said Bella, "to hell with the Talcott Somerbys. Jim doesn't care about the Talcott Somerbys. Can't you get Jim a cup of tea? Or maybe he'd like some gin. Get him some gin, Harry. Oh, and Jim, I forgot—you'll excuse us, won't you, Avery? Jim's just got back."

I saw what she had forgotten. It was the man who had been sitting close to Bella by the fire. He was standing up now, evidently ready to go away, and he looked half-confused.

"This is Avery Gifford," Bella said, "a friend of mine."

It was the first time I had ever seen him, but there was no need for that added explanation. I knew from the way he shook hands with me and from his desire to please that he was in love with Bella. He would have been a fool if he hadn't been, I remember thinking. He was a nice boy, who looked as if he had

246

just come out of a shower bath, his yellow hair carefully brushed, his eyes conscientious and kindly.

"I'm awfully glad to meet you, sir," he said. "Bella has talked so much about you. My brother Tom said he met you in the war."

"Oh, yes," I said, but I couldn't remember him at all.

"It's awfully good to have seen you, sir," Avery Gifford said. "I must be going now. I guess I'm in the way. You'll come up for the game on Saturday, won't you, Bella?"

"Are you going to Harvard?" I asked.

He said, Yes sir, that he was a senior; and then Bella went out with him into the hall.

"Well," said Cousin Clothilde, "thank God, he's gone. He's awfully stupid, Harry, don't you think? I wish Bella wouldn't stay out in the hall with him. Mary, see what Bella's doing out in the hall. And Jim, you haven't brought your bags in, have you? Harry, go out and see about Jim's bags. Just call down the cellar stairs to Frank. Tell him to bring them up to the room next yours."

"Who's Frank?" I asked.

"He was in the house when we rented it," Cousin Clothilde said. "He was living down in the cellar. He just keeps on living there. He's very useful carrying things, and sometimes he brings in boxes and things for kindling. He's having trouble with his wife, and his teeth are very bad. I don't like to look at him because I always see his teeth."

Then I knew that nothing had changed and I began to laugh and Cousin Clothilde began to laugh.

"Oh Jim," she said, "I'm so glad you're back. You're the only one who understands everything. Bella, I wish you wouldn't slam the door—it goes right through my head." Bella was back again. She sat down on the sofa beside me and leaned against my shoulder.

"Jim," she said, "darling, why you're just the same!" It was true in a way.

"Where's Jim going to sleep?" she asked. "Isn't he going to have the room next mine?" And she got up and went out i⌐ o the hall again.

"Frank," I heard her calling, "take that trunk into the room next mine."

Cousin Clothilde looked at me and glanced meaningly toward the hall.

"Isn't she beautiful?" she said. "I always knew she would be. There are so many people who are mad about her, Jim, and just yesterday there was the nicest man here, a friend of Archie's who has something to do with placing people in Hollywood. He couldn't take his eyes off her. Everybody wants to paint her picture. You must help me, Jim dear. Harry just won't help at all. He knows everybody, but he just won't help."

"What do you want me to do?" I asked.

"Someone must bring some friends around," said Cousin Clothilde. "She ought to meet some older men."

"That Gifford boy looked all right," I said.

Cousin Clothilde sighed.

"I mean some interesting men. Whatever happened to that nice friend of yours, Mr. Lowe, the one you brought to Wickford Point?"

"Stowe?" I asked. "Do you mean Joe Stowe?"

"Oh yes," she said. "He was so interesting. Couldn't you call him up and have him over? He's just the sort of man I mean—someone to take her mind off that Avery Gifford. I don't see what she sees in Avery. Can't you call up Mr. Stowe and ask him to dinner?"

"He was in Rome the last I heard of him," I said. "He was doing some work for the News Alliance."

"In Rome?" said Cousin Clothilde. "Why, Archie's taking Bella to Rome next month."

"Why?" I asked.

"Will you fix that pillow in back of my head, dear?" Cousin Clothilde said. "I keep getting a pain in the back of my neck.

248

The osteopath doesn't understand it. Archie's always been talking about taking her over to Italy, and it may get her over Mr. Gifford. She doesn't really like him, Jim. I know she doesn't like him."

"Are you going too?" I asked.

"Darling," said Cousin Clothilde, "just sit down. It makes me feel so tired when everyone walks around. The children are so perfectly useless, darling. Someone has to do something for Mary, and Sid is taking a course in biology. I don't know how long he can stand it because it makes him sick cutting up frogs. I really don't see why they should cut up frogs. I always think of the noise they make at Wickford Point. And Harry is out of a job. I couldn't go away. I don't know why it is that no one can do anything. You must talk to Bella, darling."

"All right," I said.

"And you must tell me what you're going to do, and everything you've been doing."

"All right," I said. I knew that she was not really interested in what I had done, but somehow I did not mind, because I knew that she was glad to see me, as glad as I was to see her, and that nothing else mattered. I looked about the room. Sid had come in and was sitting near the fire. Mary was standing by the window and Bella was in the hall, quarreling with Harry.

"I know where you were last night," Bella was saying, "and that's why there isn't any money left. How did it help you get a job, taking her to Pierre's to dinner?"

"Nothing's changed at all," I said.

"No," said Cousin Clothilde. "Nothing's changed at all. They don't any of them do anything. Mary, will you go upstairs and get my purse and give Harry some money to go out and get something for us to eat, a steak or something? You and Bella can cook it if Sally doesn't come."

"Who's Sally?" I asked.

"The maid," said Cousin Clothilde. "She comes from

Harlem. She reads horoscopes in the afternoon, and sometimes she's late, but Mary and Bella can start with the dinner."

"Bella never helps," said Mary.

"Well," said Cousin Clothilde, "don't argue, dear. I'll help or someone will help. My purse is upstairs in the upper bureau drawer."

"There isn't any money in it," Mary said. "I looked."

I was right; it hadn't changed at all. Cousin Clothilde looked at me, and we began to laugh. I thought at first that I might take them out somewhere, but it was more fun staying there; it was the first time in a long while that I had felt at home.

"I'll go out with Mary," I said. "We'll go and get some dinner."

Mary put her arm through mine. "There's a rabbi on the corner," she said, "who sells sacrificial wine."

"She means sacramental wine," Sid said. Mary pulled at my arm.

"It doesn't make any difference," she answered. "Jim knows what I mean. Sacrificial wine or sacramental wine, what difference does it make?"

Mary held tight to my arm just as she had when she was a little girl. She wanted to talk about herself and about all the family, because I had been away so long, she said, that I ought to know about everything. She had finished with Miss Lacey's School and had been chosen the best-liked girl in the class, most resembling the Lacey School ideal, but Bella had been fired. Perhaps no one would tell me that Bella had been fired, and it really made no difference, since Bella went everywhere. Mary had thought a little of coming out, and Clothilde had given her a tea at the Caryatid Club. Bella had said there wasn't much sense in coming out when everyone knew you anyway. Besides Mary couldn't get on with boys unless she knew them very well. Avery Gifford had been her friend before he met Bella.

"But I can't do anything about it," she said. "Why should anyone look at me when Bella's here?"

I realized that this would always be Mary's problem as long as Bella stayed at home. It was her character—too mild, too sweet. She would always be Bella's foil. She would always feel conscious of her deficiencies when Bella was there. The sooner Mary Brill got away from home the better.

"If Bella would only get married, it would be all right," she said. "It must be funny coming back and finding everyone grown-up."

"Yes," I said, "it's funny."

"I might get along better," she said, "if I didn't have to do all the work. There just isn't time. I'm going to unpack your clothes as soon as I get back. I guess we're a queer family. Do you think we're crazy?"

"Well," I answered, "every family is. That's the trouble with a family."

"But other families do something," Mary said. "There's always someone doing something. Well, here's where we get the sacrificial wine. It's better in the summer when we're back at Wickford Point."

"Why?" I asked.

Mary Brill looked up at me and smiled.

"Because we belong there," she said. "No one is expected to do anything at Wickford Point."

You always had a good time in the evening at the Brills'. A friend of Cousin Clothilde's, a Mrs. Wetherbee who had just had a henna rinse, came in when dinner was nearly ready and talked about sex. Before dinner was on the table several other people came in also. A man named Oswald Fisher, who sometimes wrote something for the newspapers, helped Harry mix the gin. Cousin Clothilde hoped that Mr. Fisher would not get drunk, but Mr. Fisher did. There was also an artist named Jonas, who did work in gesso for an interior decorator, and a girl named Florentine Gaspard, whom Mary had met in a speakeasy once, who wanted me to go somewhere with her, anywhere, and when she said anywhere she meant anywhere. After a while she wanted me to go upstairs with her because Clothilde wouldn't mind at all.

Cousin Clothilde sat watching them all, while the steaks were broiling, and she was the best person in the room, entirely untouched by the company.

"I have the nicest friends," she said. "Wherever I go they always come around me. I knew that Florentine would like you. She's so distinguished. I hope you see a great deal of Florentine."

"There doesn't seem to be very much in the way of seeing all there is," I said.

Cousin Clothilde frowned.

"It's just a way she has," she said. "You mustn't be so hard on people, darling. I thought she was peculiar too until I found out what a dreadful time she'd had. It's so much happier to be tolerant. Here comes Mirabel Steiner. I want you particularly to know Mirabel Steiner."

"Does everyone drop in for dinner?" I asked.

"Yes," said Cousin Clothilde, "usually at dinnertime. That's the pleasant thing about having dinner, isn't it?"

Mirabel Steiner wore Navajo jewelry and she smelled of musk. She was studying psychology at Columbia and she had been analyzed by Dr. Freud.

"You," she said, "I've been waiting for you."

"That goes for me too," I answered. "I've been waiting for you all my life."

"That's true," Miss Steiner said. "You didn't know it, but you know it now."

"That's just the way she is, darling," Cousin Clothilde told me. "She's been such a help to me. She knows everything about everybody."

Harry was passing the cocktails and everyone was talking. By the time dinner was ready, everyone was talking louder. Everyone knew a good deal more about China and Russia than I did, so there was no need for me to speak. Harry knew about everything because he had seen so many people who knew.

"Don't be so hard on people, Jim," he said. "These are all

damned interesting people. I'm sorry Fisher's so drunk. You'd be crazy about him. You've got to be easy on people. You never know when they can help you."

"Does Florentine help you?" I asked.

"Well," said Harry, "she knows a lot of people. Sooner or later everybody comes here, Jim, and you ought to see it in summer at Wickford Point."

"I wouldn't miss it for the world," I said.

They were still talking downstairs when I went up to my room. I unlocked my trunk and took a few clothes out and laid them on a chair, and then there was a knock on my door. It was Bella.

"Jim," she said, "do you mind if I come in?" She had changed before dinner into a violet dress that matched her eyes, although its color was not so deep. I have never been able to understand much about women's clothes, but I remember that the lines of that dress were very simple, giving an air of innocence which was not innocent at all. I remember that it was a beautiful dress which looked incongruous in the dusty room with its single bed and broken bureau. The Brills never minded much where anybody slept. Bella was like her mother, entirely untouched by all the smoke and noise downstairs. Her lips were childishly solemn and her eyes were demurely steady.

"Jim," she said, "darling."

"Yes," I said.

"You're going to stay, aren't you? You're not going to leave us, are you?"

"No, not for a while," I said.

"I was afraid you might. You see how everything is, don't you?"

"Yes, I see how it is," I said.

"Well," said Bella, "God damn them all!"

For some reason I felt no sense of shock at the words, for they seemed as natural as though I had spoken, and I knew exactly what she meant because I felt that way myself.

"Jim," she said, "kiss me. I'll feel better if you kiss me, dear. Those bitches. . . ." Propriety told me that she was too young to use the word, and yet I did not mind it. It was not difficult to kiss her. She sat beside me on the bed and I held her in my arms.

"Jim," she said, "someone's got to help me. You're the only one."

"All right," I said, "I'll help you, Belle."

She was silent for a moment and then she put her arms around my neck. I could feel her close against me, as though she were wearing no dress at all.

"I'm so afraid," she said.

"Don't be afraid," I told her. "You're too damn beautiful to be afraid."

"Jim," she said, "I have to get out of this. I can't stand it, Jim! They. . .God damn them all—except Clothilde!"

"Yes," I said, because I knew exactly what she meant.

"Or else I'll go to hell," she said. "Please help me, won't you, Jim?"

Of course she was exaggerating, but exaggeration is useful if it illustrates a point of view. Everybody sometime or other revolts against environment, but she meant more than that.

"You'd better talk to me, Bella," I said, "and then we'll get this straight. How do you mean you're going to hell?"

It occurred to me that I was not such a bad person for her to talk to either, for I had seen a good deal—more than she would ever see.

"I mean I'll be getting like them," she answered. "I'm getting more like them all the time."

"How do you mean?" I asked. "You have to be like them in a way because you're one of them. You can't get away from that."

But she could not tell me what she meant. She could only deal with nonessentials in a torrent of words, and she pushed herself away from me, sitting up very straight.

"You know," she said. "What do you ask me for? It isn't kind to ask me. It's getting worse and worse—everybody sitting and complaining, everybody taking things from Clothilde. You don't know what it's like, Jim, you just don't know. Look at Harry, he's your age. Look at Sid. There isn't anybody. I don't want to be like that. They're so—" She stopped and beat her fist against

254

her knee. "I'll have to get out of it, that's all, Jim." And she began to cry.

She never had cried easily like Mary, and she was ashamed of herself for crying.

"You mean you want to be a part of the everyday world," I said. "I know, Belle. Don't cry."

"Yes," she said, "that's what I mean exactly."

"And you're worried about something?"

"Yes," she said, "I'm worried." And then I made a practical suggestion that sounded very flat when I made it.

"The best thing for you to do," I said, "would be to work. If you feel this way, go out and get a job."

Bella looked at me and stopped crying.

"They wouldn't let me, Jim," she said. "Can't you see them"— Bella wrinkled up her nose—"if I tried to get a job? Darling, that isn't what I meant. I want to get away."

"Well, Archie's taking you to Italy," I said.

Bella's voice grew sharp.

"Darling," she said, "please don't say that. You don't call that getting away, do you? Oh, don't. I'm so worried, Jim."

I knew her so well that it did not seem as if I had been away at all, and I realized that I had been almost dull.

"That boy who was here, the one who called me 'sir,' "I said, "is that it, Belle?" But she did not answer.

"Do you love him, Belle?" She looked at me out of the corners of her eyes and clasped her knees with her delicate white hands.

"I don't know," she said. "Sometimes I do; sometimes I don't. Jim, I wish I knew."

"If you did, you would," I said. "He looks like a nice boy. Does he want to marry you?"

She nodded without speaking, looking at her hands clasped tight about her knees. She did not love him, but she wanted to love him.

"He's everything I ought to want," she said. "Jim, I'm so afraid."

"Of him?" I asked. She shook her head.

"It's what he sees in me," she answered. "He wants me to marry him right away."

I tried to think that there were a good many other attributes to a marriage besides love, and I selected the most obvious one for the first.

"Has he any money?" I asked.

Her eyes were wide, almost incredulous, when she answered.

"He's one of the Giffords," she said, "*the* Giffords."

"What?" I said. "Those Giffords?" Bella nodded and I knew better why she wanted to love Avery Gifford then.

"I've been to see his family," Bella said. "I was there last summer lots of times."

"How does it feel when he kisses you?" I asked.

Bella looked at me sideways and smiled.

"It feels just fine," she said. "He's so gentle; he's so darling, Jim."

"Well," I said, "that's something."

Bella did not answer at once.

"Jim," she said, "I'm so mixed up. Sometimes I think I'm not fit for him, and then, when he's away, I miss him. And then I want to marry him, and then I don't. I don't want to marry him if I don't want to, Jim."

It seemed to me that I had heard the same speech before, but I could not tell where until I remembered that girl, Dorothy Padmore, on the boat.

"Lots of girls have a hard time making up their minds," I said.

"But if I don't what will happen to me?" Bella asked. "What *will* happen, Jim?"

"It doesn't matter," I said. "There'll be someone else. Just get that in your head, Belle, because I know. There's always someone else."

Bella shook her head.

"Don't be silly," she answered. "There won't be anyone else like Avery Gifford, Jim. If I go up to that football game, will you come up too? I want to take him up to Wickford Point."

"All right," I said.

"Except I don't want to exactly. I'd much rather go up to Wickford Point just alone with you. Do you remember when you took me shooting, Jim?"

I told her yes, that I remembered.

"Jim," she said, "if I don't want to marry him, will you take me away somewhere—not Italy, but some place where people have queer clothes? If I don't want to marry him, you'll help me get away?"

"Yes," I said, "I'll help you get away." When I was in my twenties and even in my thirties, it seemed so desirable and so simple to help people get away; and perhaps I might have helped her, if it hadn't been for Avery Gifford and Joe Stowe.

XXIII | Up and Out

Cousin Clothilde always had one great complaint, which was to be expected since everyone in the family had some individual grievance. Cousin Clothilde used to say—I had heard her say it often long ago, and now she was still repeating it—that nobody in the house ever got up and out, particularly the men. Archie, for example, always took a hot bath in the morning. He would lock himself in and then lie in the tub and read *Das Kapital* for such extended periods that often Cousin Clothilde was afraid that he had died in there, especially as Archie never answered when she knocked upon the door. In fact once Cousin Clothilde called the police, thinking that there was a burglar in the bathroom, because she was sure that Archie was up and out, but she was wrong. When the plain-clothes man broke the lock, Archie was in the tub.

When I got up the next morning, I already felt perfectly at home. The house was somewhat dingier than any of the Brill houses I remembered. There was no couple in the kitchen, but only the colored maid who read horoscopes. Nevertheless I was experiencing the customary sense of lassitude and the old lack of desire to see what was going on in the streets outside. It was already ten o'clock, but no one was up except Harry, who was still in his wrapper and pajamas sorting the morning mail, drinking his coffee with one hand and dividing the letters into piles with the other.

258

"I thought you might be up early," Harry said, "that's why I came down. There's no use getting out until lunchtime; that's about the first minute you can hope to see anyone."

He set down his cup and used both hands on the letters. "Look at those bills," he said, "look at them. They're going to worry Clothilde. She's always thinking about money. You haven't noticed that yet, have you?"

"Is there any trouble about money?" I asked.

Harry made a rotary gesture with his hand and wrist.

"Certainly not," he said, "absolutely not. It's only Clothilde. All she has to do is to go on a budget. There would be plenty of money, if she only started on a budget. If I could just handle it for her, why everything would be all right."

"What good would a budget do?" I asked.

Harry patted the top of his head where his hair was growing thin.

"It would take a certain amount of firmness to run the budget," he said. "It would have to be absolutely iron-clad. Now my idea is this—" Harry began counting off points on his fingers. "One: so much for light, heat, rent and service, computed from a monthly average which could easily be arrived at. Two: a contingency fund."

"What sort of contingencies?" I asked.

"All the usual contingencies," Harry said. "Two: a contingency fund—well, for dentistry and medicine. Three: an allotment for recreation. Four: a miscellaneous fund for unexpected incidentals, and Five: an iron-clad fixed allowance for every member of the family, over which they must not run under any circumstances. Now I could manage that. It's lucid, isn't it? Simple, plain common sense. What is more, it's business sense. Wouldn't you think that would be completely comprehensible? Now on the one hand there's efficiency and order. Let's try not to let our emotions run away with us. What is there on the other hand?"

"Go ahead," I said, "you're being lucid. Have you ever tried living on a budget?"

Harry moved his hand again in a rotary gesture and ended by pointing at me.

"The same question might apply to you," he said. "It might apply to anybody, and the answer is that your question is completely immaterial. Either you or I could live on a budget if we had to. We are not speaking about ourselves—we are speaking about Clothilde. We are trying unemotionally to straighten out a tangled situation. There is no need for personalities to enter in. The trouble with everyone"—Harry waved his hand in a spiral gesture, upward—"down here in the winter, or up there in the summer at Wickford Point, is that everyone deals in exhibitionist emotionalism and mutual recriminations whenever the subject of money is mentioned. Suppose we place ourselves above it. What is there on the other hand?"

"All right," I said, "what is there?" It was the Harry Brill I had always known.

"On the other hand"—Harry shrugged his shoulders elaborately—"there is inefficiency. Clothilde's check comes on the first of the month. She received it the day before yesterday, and then it's a question of who gets to her first. There is no idea of a budget. Personally, I got to her first this month for clothes, but I was just two minutes ahead of Bella. You may have noticed that Bella was a little out of sorts last evening, but I'm not dealing in personalities. We're dealing in facts and figures. If it isn't Bella it's Archie. Or if it isn't Archie, it's Sid. I'm not blaming anyone. It's simply because of inefficiency, and it's a damn humiliating situation. The logical result of it is that when the bills come in, they can't be paid. It's plain that something has to be done, isn't it?"

"Have you taken it up with Cousin Clothilde?" I asked.

Harry shrugged his shoulders again and sank back into his chair, a weary and defeated man.

"Again and again," he said, "again and again and again. She doesn't understand it at all; and when I try to explain it to the others, my perfectly logical suggestion is greeted with laughter. I have to go outside this house to have my ideas taken seriously.

260

Emotion keeps creeping in. It is impossible to talk here without emotion."

"What does Cousin Clothilde say?" I asked.

"What would she say?" Harry answered. "You know Clothilde. She simply doesn't understand. She seems to feel that I am trying to seize financial control, when I simply say that there's money enough for everyone. Her mind invariably goes back over a familiar trace. She only asks why the men in the family don't support her, and why she should support the men. Now that's a logical question, but she will not see that it has nothing to do with the present situation. Do you know what I think sometimes? I think that she likes to see everyone coming to her for money. It gives her a sense of power. Yet, on the other hand, she sympathizes with my point of view."

"What point of view?" I asked.

"That there's enough money for everybody," Harry said. "She understands this perfectly. Up to a certain point she is absolutely consistent, but she doesn't seem to be able to go beyond that point. She begins by saying that she wants someone to look after her. She wonders why we never do, and she wants someone to adopt her."

"Adopt her?" I repeated. "Has she been talking about that, again?"

"Naturally it's just a pose," Harry said. "She likes to talk about adoption in front of Archie and Sid and me, but when we try to do anything to try and help her, she won't have anything to do with it. It makes an unlovely situation."

It sounded outrageous to me at the moment, but only because I had been away for such a long while. In a day or two or in a week or two I should be used to all the Brills again. Just then, however, I regarded Harry Brill very curiously. He had grown older, but there was no change whatsoever in his mental processes. It seemed to have done him no good to live. I thought of Bella the night before, and I could understand her better when Harry began to talk.

"Why don't you get out and do something?" I asked. Harry leaned back in his chair and looked at me over the edge of his long thin nose.

"Now that's a boring thing to say," he said, "very, very boring. Do something? I'm trying to do something."

"That isn't what I meant," I said. "I'd rather be out digging ditches."

Harry's face reddened slightly.

"That's an obvious remark," he said, "and a very silly one. It just happens that none of us is obliged to dig ditches. And why in God's name does everybody use that simile about digging ditches? If you imply that I'm not willing to work, you are very much mistaken. It just happens that I am in a position to wait until I can strike upon something which is worth while. Even Clothilde sees that. She doesn't begrudge me that chance. Everything I've done leads to something. I've served an apprenticeship in a number of jobs, and now I know what I'm worth."

"All right," I said. I had not the slightest desire to quarrel with him. "You're old enough to do something—that's all."

"My God," Harry said, "why can't you drop that phrase about 'doing something'? What have you been doing except running around the world, amusing yourself? And now you come back here and talk to me about 'doing something.' I suppose you've been listening to the girls. You don't even know what I have been doing. I've been in banking and real estate and insurance. Accidentally you've found me when I'm out of work, and when I'm out of work the whole damn family jump on me. Why in hell should I do something when no one else does? And now they're after Sid to do something."

"All right," I said.

Harry's face had assumed a strange expression.

"Suppose you mind your own business," Harry said.

"All right," I said. I must have had some intuitive realization that they were beyond any useful criticism, as they moved according to some system entirely their own. That morning was the

262

nearest I ever came to criticizing, but Harry must have known how I felt. He dropped his cigarette into the bottom of his coffee cup and pushed back his chair.

"Don't get sore," he said.

"I'm not sore," I answered. "I don't give a damn."

"Well, don't get sore," Harry said. "I don't blame you. You don't understand it, Jim. I'd better go upstairs and get dressed. Clothilde's coming down now." He picked the bills up from the table and put them in his dressing-gown pocket. "Don't tell her about those bills, I'm going to burn them up. They'll only annoy her."

Cousin Clothilde had on a dark blue broadcloth dress. When she stood by the tall window and looked out over the back yard, her profile was much the same as Bella's, and she seemed almost as young.

"There isn't any letter from Archie," she said. "He's so careless about writing. You're not going out yet, are you? Sit with me while I have my coffee. Have you a cigarette, darling? You mustn't hurry to go out."

"All right," I said, "I won't hurry."

"I never have hurried," said Cousin Clothilde. "It never does any good. What's Harry been talking about?"

"About bills," I said. Cousin Clothilde sighed and flicked the ash from her cigarette.

"Harry's always talking about bills," she said. "I wish he'd help me with them, but he never helps at all. All of the men in the family just think I'm here to feed them. I have to sit and worry about them all the time. Nobody worries about me."

"Oh yes, they do," I said. "You don't notice it, that's all."

"No, they don't," said Cousin Clothilde. "I sit and worry about everybody. First I worry about whether Archie is happy, and then I worry about Mary's different attitudes, and then I worry because too many men like Bella. There's something strange about Bella. She doesn't seem happy, Jim. Then I worry about Sid. I think he works too hard. It isn't good to use your mind too much, and then I worry about Harry. He knows everyone; he has every opportunity to do something."

"He's lazy," I said. "He always was and he still is. You've made them all lazy, you're making me lazy now."

Cousin Clothilde laughed.

"Darling," she said, "I'm so glad you're back. Now they're all so big, so grown-up, that I need someone to help me, but it isn't true about being lazy. Harry isn't lazy. He's always up and out, trying to see someone. So many people say that he ought to do something. I think perhaps he's done too much."

"Done too much?" I repeated.

"Yes, that's what I really think," Cousin Clothilde said. "It seems to me that he may be overtired. If he didn't move about so much he might find something to do that interested him— but then why should he do anything?"

"I don't exactly follow you," I said.

"Well," said Cousin Clothilde, "why should anyone do anything if he doesn't have to? After all, I love to have them here. I don't like it when they're away, but I do wish there was a little more money. I don't see what that old Mr. Caldicott is doing, looking after the estate, and Mirabel Steiner and Mr. Fisher don't see what he's doing either. All the stocks are going up everywhere and yet he doesn't make any more money for us. I wish you'd go up to Boston and see Mr. Caldicott. Harry's been to see him, but it doesn't do any good."

"I'm going up this week end," I said. "Bella wants me to go with her to Wickford Point."

"But, darling," said Cousin Clothilde, "why do you have to go out this morning?"

"I have to see a literary agent," I said. "I thought I might try to do some writing."

"Harry always talks about it too," said Cousin Clothilde. "I think it would be very nice if he did some writing, but you don't have to go right now, do you? Be sure to be back for dinner, won't you? Archie may be here."

264

"All right," I answered. "I'll be back."

Outside in the street I was in a world I knew again, and it was as though I had been out of it for quite a while. I was back where there was an actual struggle; but then, I thought, the Brills were different from other people, and I was glad that they were different. Until I had seen them I had forgotten that most of life was dull.

The Stanhope offices were uptown in a new building on the fifteenth floor. The hall outside was done in early American furniture and the girl at the desk said that Mr. Stanhope would see me in just a minute. I waited for an hour and a half before I saw him. Finally I sat in an upholstered chair, looking at him across his table while I tried to explain to him why I had come. He was dressed in a russet brown suit with a russet brown tie, and even then he had that picture of the police dog in front of him, and I watched him, while I talked, draw squares upon a piece of yellow paper.

"You've been around quite a lot," Mr. Stanhope said. "Did you ever run into a man named Stowe, Joe Stowe?"

"Yes," I said. "We went out to China after the war. Joe's a friend of mine. He's in Rome now."

"He sent me some things," Mr. Stanhope said. "If he only had his feet on the ground he might be good. I wish I had him over here. I'd like to talk to Stowe. If I could talk to him, I think he would sell. What makes you think that you can write?"

"I've been a correspondent for four years," I said.

Mr. Stanhope looked out of the window.

"That doesn't mean a thing," he said. "Does Stowe think you can write?"

"Yes," I said. The telephone beside him rang and Mr. Stanhope picked it up.

"No, Mabel darling," he said, "it won't do any good for you to come in to see me. It's just a matter of the ending. The boy and girl have to come together in each other's arms—otherwise it's splendid. No darling, that isn't much of a change. It's just as logical for them to fall into each other's arms as not. That's

265

all they want down there—just an indication of love." Mr. Stanhope set down the telephone.

"It doesn't do any good to talk," he said. "Write me a piece of fiction and bring it in. Then we'll know where we are. If you write Stowe, tell him I spoke about him, will you?"

"I thought I might try to write a book," I said. "I was out with Feng for three years in China."

"No," said Mr. Stanhope, "no, no. Nobody's ever heard of these Chinamen. Do you know anything about sing-song girls?"

"Yes," I answered, "quite a lot." Mr. Stanhope drummed his fingers on the table.

"Now that's something," he said. "They were asking up the street for a story about a sing-song girl to go with their new four-color process. I've got it—Shanghai. Do you know Shanghai?"

"Yes," I said. Mr. Stanhope stopped drumming on the table.

"Now wait," he said, "just a minute. I want to get this straight. Of course, I can't write it for you . . . but something like this . . . the boy and girl are in Shanghai. She's come out there to marry him, and the sing-song girl gives him up. How about doing something like that?"

"I might," I said.

"All right," said Mr. Stanhope. "It's just an idea, you understand. Write it and I may be able to tell you whether you can get anywhere. What did you say your name was?"

"Calder," I said.

"Be sure to tell Joe Stowe I was speaking about him," Mr. Stanhope said.

I had been given a guest card to the Cosgrave Club, east of Fifth Avenue, and when I had finished with Mr. Stanhope I walked over to it, across Forty-Second Street, past all the new shops. It was nearly lunchtime and the Club was crowded. First there was a room decorated with the heads of African animals, bearing names which were beginning to be used in crossword puzzles, and off it was a bar, where the barkeeper mixed gin cocktails from private bottles and flasks supplied by the members; and beyond was a long, dark hall with writing tables. I was moving toward one of the tables when someone called me. At first I could not remember who he was, but finally I recollected that he was a man named Henry Follen in the class below me at Harvard.

"Hello, Jim," Henry said. "You haven't been around here much, have you?"

"No," I said, "not much. I've been abroad."

"Oh," said Henry. "Well, we must get together sometime. You wouldn't be interested in some life insurance, would you?"

"Not right now," I said.

"Well," said Henry, "we must get together sometime. A lot of people we know have passed out of the picture already. Funny, isn't it, how suddenly people pass out of the picture?"

"Well," I said, "it all depends on what the picture is. You can pass out of some pictures rather quickly, Henry."

"Well," said Henry, "I'll see you around here sometime. We must get together."

As I sat down at the writing table, my mind was still occupied by the phrase he had used. It was really more applicable to life than it was to death. In life one was always passing in and out of pictures, particularly when one was young—good pictures or bad pictures, it did not matter which. I had been in the Brill picture that morning and then in the Stanhope picture and now I was in the picture of all the Henry Follens I had known, who were engaged in selling bonds and life insurance and in trying, in the conventional ways permitted our class, to justify their existence. I selected a piece of notepaper and looked at it for a while before I began to write. Joe Stowe and I had been in and out of a good many pictures and it had been a long while since we had communicated with each other. Yet I knew that things would be just the same when we met again. There would be none of that barrier that stood between people like Henry Follen and me, making me feel lonely and out of place.

"Dear Joe," I wrote, "I have just been to see Stanhope. He was asking about you and he thinks you're good. He wants me to write a story about a sing-song girl. He doesn't know what one is but he has heard about them. You'd better come on back home just to keep me company, or else I'll be wanting to get moving again. It's pretty terrible because I don't believe there is anyone here to talk to who knows anything about anything, but I am not sure yet. I am going to Boston the day after to-morrow and then up to Wickford Point. It's queer getting back. It's consoling to know I've saved enough money to keep me for a while. By the way, Bella is going over to Rome very soon with Archie Wright. You remember Bella, don't you? Be sure to look her up, and give my best to the old crowd at the Russie if any of them are left. You'd better come on home or you'll forget just what it's like. . . ."

XXIV | They Say It Loves a Lover

The Giffords lived in one of those tall brick houses on the water side of Beacon Street, and I called there to take Bella and Avery Gifford to Wickford Point. I drove up from New York in a second-hand Dodge which I had just bought. The body was shabby, but it had one of those engines which never wear out, and it rattled and creaked through the November dusk. I climbed up a flight of heavy brownstone steps, and rang a bell which was answered by a white-haired maid who looked at me suspiciously. It was one of the houses built shortly after the Back Bay was filled in, and its interior was much the same as all the others—a dark hall finished in walnut with a small parlor on the left, a somber dining room in back, overlooking the river, and a broad, carpeted staircase leading to the second floor.

"Master Avery and the young lady are not back yet," the maid said, "but Mr. Gifford would like to see you upstairs in the library."

It was plain that Mr. Gifford wanted to see me but that he did not like to see me. He was standing by a window which looked across the Charles River Basin, in a room with portraits and a black marble mantel and heavy sets of books. I knew what he would be like because I had seen a good many people like him in my youth. He was a tall, thin-faced, stoop-shouldered man in a baggy gray suit with a heavy gold watch-chain. His hair was gray and his mustache was a reddish gray, and he was smoking a thin and very cheap cigar.

"Oh," said Mr. Gifford. "You're Miss Brill's cousin, aren't you? How do you do?"

We stood looking at each other for a moment and I saw that he was embarrassed. He did not know me and he did not know where to place me.

"Won't you sit down?" he said. Somehow I did not like being there much, because he was worried; he was not only wondering who I was, but what I was.

"I've heard Mr. Caldicott speak of you often, sir," I said.

"Oh," said Mr. Gifford, "Godfrey, you know Godfrey Caldicott?" His tone was slightly incredulous, but shaded at the same time with a note of hope.

"He looks after our family affairs," I said. "I haven't seen him for quite a while, because I've been abroad."

"Oh," said Mr. Gifford, "you're in business, are you?"

"Not exactly, sir," I said. "I came back. I thought I might write."

Mr. Gifford sat down heavily in an overstuffed brown velvet armchair.

"Then you must have an income," Mr. Gifford said more cheerfully. "No one can live from writing."

"Not enough to live on, sir," I said, "but I've saved a little money."

Mr. Gifford stared hard at the end of his cigar. I knew what he was driving at, and I knew the way he must have felt as he sat there coping with an unknown and dangerous quantity which had entered his life. He did not like me and I did not like him much, but at the same time I felt sorry for him.

"My wife has a very severe headache," Mr. Gifford said. "She has been ill in bed for the last two days. I'm sorry she can't see you, Mr.—"

"Calder," I said.

270

"Oh yes," he answered. "Excuse me. Mr. Calder—Calder—it seems to me when I was a young man there were some people in Nahant by the name of Calder. That couldn't be your family, could it?"

I told him it was not, and Mr. Gifford looked again at the end of his cigar.

"My wife wanted to talk to you," he said. "Let me see. The Brills wrote something, didn't they?"

"Bella's grandfather was the poet," I said, "the famous poet."

"Oh," said Mr. Gifford, "yes, I understand. I wish my wife were here. I suppose you know—" He paused and I did not answer, although it was clear what was coming. Mr. Gifford coughed.

"I suppose you know," Mr. Gifford said, "that Avery wants to marry Miss Brill. We never suspected such a thing. It's been a shock to both of us, a very great shock. I don't know if I can explain to you what I mean."

As I looked across the room at Mr. Gifford I knew that he intended no rudeness. He had not been aware of his own frankness, that was all, and I felt no resentment towards him.

"You mean that you want Avery to be happy," I said.

I think he liked me after that; at any rate his manner changed.

"It's kind of you to put it that way," Mr. Gifford said. "I mean he isn't her sort of person. I don't mean anything against her. I've no doubt she's very charming, but she isn't his kind of person."

"No," I said, "she isn't."

Mr. Gifford moved uneasily in his chair.

"Of course Avery will be very comfortably off," he said, "but I don't refer to material considerations. I mean that when people marry, they should marry the same sort of person. They should not be too excited about it, if you understand me, Mr. Calder. There should be a community of friends and interests. Marriage is a damnably serious thing."

"I suppose it is," I said.

"I know it is," said Mr. Gifford. "Now when Mrs. Gifford

271

and I were married we knew what we were doing. After all, we lived next door. The war's changed everything. By the way, would you care for a glass of whisky?"

"No thank you, sir," I said.

"Since the war," said Mr. Gifford, "everyone has been meeting too many different sorts of people. Avery has been meeting too many. All I'm saying is that I want Avery to be happy."

"I understand you," I said, "perfectly."

"It's good of you to say so," Mr. Gifford answered. "This has been very hard on us, particularly on my wife. There isn't anything you could do about it, is there, Mr. Calder?"

"How do you mean?" I asked.

Mr. Gifford spoke abruptly.

"You couldn't stop it, could you?" he inquired.

"No," I said, "of course I couldn't."

Mr. Gifford sighed and fumbled in his pocket for a match. "I didn't mean to ask you exactly that," he said. "Avery's so damnably excited. I can't do anything with Avery." He stopped and relighted his cigar. I wondered why I was not angry with him, for instead of being angry I was finding him sympathetic. He was only trying to say that he and his kind were different from ours, and he was too worried to say it properly.

"I don't think," I said, "that Bella is so anxious to marry Avery."

Mr. Gifford dropped his match upon the Oriental rug.

"Not anxious to marry Avery? Good gracious," he said, "why not?"

"She feels a little the same way about it that you do," I said.

"Good gracious," said Mr. Gifford, "I don't see why."

"Well, she does," I answered.

"Now come," said Mr. Gifford, "any girl would want to marry Avery. What's the matter with Avery?"

"I don't know," I said, "because I don't want to marry him."

"Well, you like him, don't you?" Mr. Gifford asked. "Everyone likes Avery."

"Yes," I said. "Bella likes him too."

272

"You're not offended with me, are you?" Mr. Gifford said. "I haven't meant to be blunt—but Avery's my son."

"I'm not offended at all," I said. Then Mr. Gifford sat up straighter. The front door had opened and we heard the voices of Avery and Bella in the hall downstairs.

"Avery," Bella was saying, "don't be silly. *Avery!*"

Mr. Gifford and I both must have felt the same sort of chill embarrassment.

"I don't suppose," said Mr. Gifford, "that there's a damn thing that anyone can do."

"Except let them alone," I said.

Mr. Gifford sighed.

"I hope Eleanor didn't hear," he said. "It will only make things worse."

They were running up the stairs and then they were in the library. Avery Gifford looked very nice and Bella looked very nice. The only trouble was that she looked a little too proper, a trifle too neat, and Avery was too full of conversation.

"Hello, Father," Avery said, and he shook hands with me. "I didn't see you at the game, sir," he said to me. "Where were you? We were near the cheering section. We'll be ready to go to Wickford in just a minute, sir, just as soon as Bella and I say good-by to Mother."

"How are you going to go?" Mr. Gifford asked.

"Jim, that is Mr. Calder, is going to drive us down," Avery said. "That's your Dodge outside, isn't it, sir? There's no engine like a Dodge engine."

"You and Bella can sit behind," I said.

"No, we won't," said Bella. "We'll all sit in the front seat." She turned toward me and held out her arms.

"Darling," she said. "How are you, darling? We won't be a minute. I'll just go and get my bag."

"We'll just say good-by to Mother," Avery said. "She'll be hurt if she doesn't see you, Bella."

Then Mr. Gifford and I were alone again. Mr. Gifford was staring at the door, but he collected himself.

273

"Mr. Calder," he said, "you must come to dine with us sometime. Would you care for a cigar to smoke on the way?"

His words meant nothing, but I understood them. They expressed a father's hopelessness, a weary sort of surrender. Mr. Gifford was realizing all over again that there was not a thing he could do.

"Avery!" We could hear Bella's voice from the floor above. "Not right here in the hall! Don't be silly, Avery!"

When Cousin Sue saw Avery Gifford, she said that he was just as nice as he knew how to be, which was nearer to the truth than she may have intended. On all that ride from Boston down to Wickford Point, Avery Gifford was just as nice as he knew how to be. Conceivably he had never been so happy in his life as when he sat in the front seat with Bella and me on the way to Wickford Point. Avery was a lover and in love and Bella seemed rather to enjoy it.

I don't remember what Avery said, but I do remember that he was trying to be pleasant to me; and I did not blame him, for I knew the way he felt. He knew at the moment that I was one of the finest fellows in the world and he wanted me to like him. I could understand that it was dreadfully important to him for me to like him and I tried. The trouble was that he kept calling me "sir," and I became tired of that deferential monosyllable which put me on a pedestal, away from struggle, away from appetite and passion. I was barely thirty at the time and I felt no physical incapacity.

As I drove the car and tried to like him, I felt toward him exactly the way the world feels when they say it loves a lover. Actually I don't believe that the world loves a lover at all; it only tolerates him as a person afflicted by a certain stage of a common biological disease. It tolerates him, because most of the world has had that disease at one time or another and will probably have it again. You love a lover because you want to be loved if you should ever again turn into a lover; there is no other reason. Actually all lovers are consummate bores, and almost the only good thing about them is that they are often generous, and may be easily fooled. I remember thinking that Avery Gifford would be amazed at some later day if he could see himself as he was then. He was talking too much, he was laughing too much, and he never should have tried to be so funny. Bella was laughing too, but I saw her glance at me out of the corner of her eye just once, and I guessed that she agreed with me.

Cousin Sue and I sat in the little parlor that evening. The lamp on the round table was lighted and the shutters were drawn and all the doors were closed. Cousin Sue was sitting in the small upholstered chair which my great-aunt Sarah had always used, and she held a handkerchief between her fingers, twisting it nervously back and forth, as she often did when she had difficulty keeping her mind on anything.

"Where do you suppose they are now?" Cousin Sue asked. "It's time they should come in, don't you think?"

"They're all right," I said. "It isn't cold outside."

Even with the shutters closed I could hear the wind from the river in the trees. The warm yellow glow of the table lamp only accentuated the outer darkness, that heavy autumn darkness that always made Wickford Point remote. I had not been there for eight years and now the room seemed smaller, and Cousin Sue seemed smaller and much older, but that sense of unworldly remoteness was unchanged and it was not unpleasant. Actually it brought me peace, a feeling for the first time that I was safe at home, and all the things that I had brought back in my mind fitted in with our solitude. I could hear the sound of the sea, and of railroad trains, and of voices speaking in strange tongues, all the while that Cousin Sue was talking. Although her mind kept darting here and there, without apparent reason, it required no great effort to follow her.

"You spoke to Josie, didn't you?" said Cousin Sue.

"Yes," I said. "Josie's looking fine."

"She's a thoroughly good woman," said Cousin Sue. "Did you see her child?"

"Yes," I answered.

"Her little girl is very charming," said Cousin Sue. "I deposited five dollars for her in the bank. Her name is Frieda. Do you think the bank is safe? Have you been to see Mr. Caldicott?"

"Yes," I said. "Everything's all right."

"Mr. Morrissey's rheumatism is very bad," she said. "Did you know the doctor gives him bitter, allopathic medicine? Did it seem to you that Mr. Morrissey had been drinking?"

"Just a little cider," I said.

"Jim," said Cousin Sue.

"Yes," I said.

"Did I tell you that Nauna had to be put out of the way?"

"Yes," I said, "you told me."

"Jim," said Cousin Sue, "did anyone in China remember your great-grandfather?"

"No," I said. "No one seemed to remember."

"I thought they might," said Cousin Sue. "He was so interested in Canton. Jim, that Chinese general, was he an interesting man?"

"Yes," I said, "General Feng was very interesting."

And she wanted to know more about him. Of all my friends and family Cousin Sue was the only one who really wanted to hear about the traits of General Feng.

"He used to do conjuring tricks," I said, "in the evening, after dinner. He enjoyed that best of all. You see he was sold to a conjurer when he was five years old, and he used to travel to all the fairs."

"Yes," said Cousin Sue, "yes, of course."

"He used to do tricks with mice," I said. "He was very fond of mice, and sometimes he would take a whole bowl of goldfish out from under his robe."

"Yes," said Cousin Sue, "yes, of course. What did he used to say when he took out the goldfish?"

"He used to say 'Dooey,' " I said, " 'Dooey, dooey dooey,' and then he would pull the goldfish out from under his robe."

"Yes," said Cousin Sue, "yes, of course. The Chinese are always such industrious people, don't you think? Jim, what do you think is coming out of Russia?"

276

"You asked me that," I said. "It's hard to tell."

"Mr. Morrissey doesn't know either," said Cousin Sue. "Jim, where do you think they are now?"

"Who?" I asked.

"Bella and Mr. Gifford," said Cousin Sue. "Jim, what do you think of Mr. Gifford?"

"He's all right," I said. "He's very nice."

Cousin Sue nodded and twisted her handkerchief quickly.

"Yes," she said, "he's just as nice as he knows how to be. Do you think he means to marry Bella?"

"Yes," I said, "I think he'd like to."

"I hope the Giffords are nice people," said Cousin Sue. "Bella is turning into such an interesting young woman, don't you think? Here they come now. I hear them in the entry."

When I listened I could hear them too, and then I could hear them walking through the dining room and banging against a chair, which meant that the dining room lamp had gone out. They both had that look of having been out where the wind was blowing. Bella had on an old cape which she must have picked up in the side entry, and she took it off and handed it to him, casually as though she had always been handing things to him. When she looked at me her eyes were bright.

"Jim," she said, "have you been sitting here all the time? Why didn't you come out on the point with us? It's beautiful out there. The moon's up on the river. Well, I'm going to bed."

I looked at them both, but I could gather nothing definite from their faces. I knew that she had taken him there to see what he would be like and I wondered what he had been like, but I could not tell. Nevertheless something had made Avery Gifford quietly happy.

"Bella's tired," he said. "We've had a long hard day."

"Well," said Cousin Sue, "I think I shall go to bed myself. Are you going, Jim?"

"Not yet," I said.

"I guess I'll stay and talk with Jim—that is, with Mr. Calder

277

—that is, if you don't mind, sir," Avery said.

"Of course I don't," I said, "and for goodness' sake call me Jim."

"Yes sir," Avery said, "that is, if you don't mind." Bella began to laugh.

"Oh fluff," she said, "of course he doesn't mind. I'll see you upstairs, Jim. I'll come in and kiss you good night."

"I thought you were going to sleep, Bella," Avery said.

"Well, I am," said Bella, "but I always kiss Jim good night. I've always done it and I always will."

"Good night, Mr. Gifford," Cousin Sue said. "Jim, will you give Mr. Gifford the candle in the entry with the fish on it. And don't forget to blow the lamps out. Good night."

Cousin Sue felt strongly about cards and liquor, but now that she had gone to bed I brought the bottle of whisky from my suitcase and glasses and water from the kitchen.

"Here's looking at you, Avery," I said. "I hope you come down often."

"Thank you, sir," said Avery, "thank you very much."

"Sit down," I said, "and for God's sake don't call me 'sir.' Call me 'Jim.' Now try it."

"Yes, Jim," Avery said.

"Well," I said, "now you're here, how do you like it? You have to come here, Avery, to know the family."

"I like it very much, Jim," Avery said. "I only hope you like me."

I filled up my glass again and pushed the bottle toward him.

"Yes," I said, "I like you fine. You're a nice boy, Avery."

I meant what I said. He was a nice boy, and he looked very pleased, so pleased that he stammered. Now that I had told him not to call me "sir," he kept calling me "Jim" just as often.

"Jim," he said, "I hope you like me well enough—I suppose you know I want to marry Bella, Jim."

"Well," I said, "what does Bella say? You'd better pour yourself another drink." He took a swallow from his glass without

278

answering and I spoke again. "I can't think of anything better," I said, "if Bella wants it, Avery."

Avery looked across the table and the lamplight fell on his thick blond hair. He had a good mouth; his face looked amazingly young, although I could not understand why his youth should impress me, unless because he was the sort of person who would always remain young.

"She wants to think it over, Jim," he said. "She says we can be engaged when she gets back from Italy. That means we're as good as engaged now, don't you think? She just doesn't want to tell anybody until she gets back."

"Well," I said, "that's fine."

Then, as Avery continued speaking, I realized that he was telling me everything he had been wanting to say. He was telling me so much that I felt half-ashamed to listen. He was explaining in detail just how he loved her and why he loved her. Of course, there had been other girls—after all he was twenty-one —and he had petted occasionally with other girls. He didn't suppose they used to do this, but now everybody did. He had thought that he had loved other girls, but this was different. This was real love. You could only love the way he did once in your life. Bella was so delicate, so spiritual, so different from other girls. There was something holy about her; it made him really believe in God, although of course he had already been confirmed. He didn't believe that many people could ever have felt as he did—that God had meant him to love her—but now he knew that this conviction was what real love meant. There she was and there he was, and God had meant it. He kept thinking of her all the time, whether she was there or not. No one understood her the way he understood her. Even when she did not speak, he understood, and now he was so happy that he could not think, so absolutely happy.

It was hardly proper to sit there and hear him. I had felt the same way two or three times myself, except that I had never been as nice as that boy was. Bella had told him that I also understood her, he said, so that I could sympathize with his belief that she was a rare person and that none of her family appreciated her, in spite of her always being so sweet and gentle to them all.

"They have made her afraid," he said, "and she's so gentle and so delicate. I want to make her happy. I want to take her away from it, Jim. I have never spoken to anyone like this in my life."

"That's all right, go ahead," I said.

"What I mean," said Avery, "I don't mean to be rude—but they don't understand her. She doesn't like it with her family, Jim. She's unhappy all the time. I know she is and I want to take her away."

I set down my glass and looked at the portrait above the writing desk of a middle-aged lady in a lace cap with a reddish nose, Bella's great-great-grandmother. No doubt someone had wanted to take her away too, though I could not see why.

"Away where?" I asked.

"Away from everything," Avery said, "where she can be happy, Jim, always happy. You see I understand her. I know that I can make her happy."

I was able to appreciate his mood. He was the only one who understood her. He wanted to take her away where she would be with him always, always, where he could bring out the best in her and make her always happy.

"You see what I mean, don't you?" Avery asked.

"Yes," I said, "I see what you mean. What about your family, Avery?"

He looked at me and his glance was less luminous.

"When they really know her, they can't help loving her," he said. "Everyone who knows her, loves her. You love her, don't you, Jim?"

I pushed my glass away from me. I understood what he meant, but I wondered exactly what it was that I felt, because while he was talking I had been thinking of taking Bella away from it all myself.

"Yes," I said, "with limitations."

280

Avery blushed.

"Yes," he said. "Of course I didn't mean you really loved her."

That reply of his made me feel very old, and burdened by the weight of my experience. The time had come for me to say something to him, and I could never again reach the heights where Avery was poised.

"Well, Avery," I said, "that's fine—" and I paused to pick up my glass, aware that I was speaking wearily. "It's a good idea to think these things over, Avery. She says she wants to get away. Perhaps she does, but it all depends where, doesn't it? There are things you don't notice that you get accustomed to, Avery, but you miss them when you lose them. Well, that's fine, but you'd better think it over."

"If I thought all my life, I'd think the same thing," Avery Gifford said. "I know what you mean, but I don't have to think this time. I know."

"Well," I said again, "that's fine. But don't do anything until Bella gets back from Italy. Then you'll be absolutely sure. Well, Avery, good night."

"Good night, sir," Avery said, and he shook hands.

Then when he went up to bed I opened the front door. The breeze from the river was growing cool and sharp and I was glad to feel it. That intensity of Avery Gifford's had made me very tired. It had the violence of inexperience, the awkwardness of youth, and yet there had been something in it which had been honest. I was wondering how a woman could do such a thing to a man. I was wondering if women really liked doing it. They did if they loved also. I was wondering if Bella really loved him. If she didn't, it would not be fair. I wondered if she knew that it would not be fair, and if she knew, I doubted if she cared.

My room upstairs was almost exactly as I had left it on the day I had packed to go to training camp eight years before. Josie told me that Cousin Sue had ordered the door closed as soon as I left, and that she had not allowed it to be opened until she

281

heard that I was back. Then Josie had come in and dusted it. Sometime, she said, she meant to give it a good cleaning. As long as I could remember someone had always been proposing to give my room a good cleaning and no one had ever done it. That gesture of Cousin Sue's touched me a great deal, and I have always been sorry that I never thanked her for it, at least as much as I should have. Everyone at Wickford Point took Cousin Sue so much for granted that she never got what she deserved.

The field-bed was right beside the wall, and the writing table with some of my old textbooks was over against the window. I set my candle down, lighted the kerosene lamp and opened the table drawer. The things inside it, all those useless things one throws into drawers, brought a good many memories back. It was as though my life had been snapped off suddenly, as though I had returned from the dead. It was curious to think that if I had been killed somewhere, all those odds and ends would still have been in the table, waiting there for nothing, and most of them had been waiting too long already. There were two spoon hooks for pickerel and a letter from a girl named Daisy Royce asking me to come to her house to dinner before a dance. I recalled that I had gone and that I had been stuck with Daisy at that dance for a good two hours, but there was the letter as though time had ended when it had first been written. There were half a dozen number eight shells, the brass ends of which were turning green. A mouse had made a nest out of some receipted bills. There were also some pencils and a lot of yellow scratch-paper and a broken dollar-watch and a shirt button and some collar studs. I took the paper and a pencil out and laid them on the table, then I took off my coat.

It was as good a time as any other to start writing that story about the sing-song girl. Until I actually faced it, I believed that it would not be difficult to write a short story, but now I recognized the complete loneliness of the trade as I stared at my blank paper. I was no longer dealing with facts. My mind was groping in the lamplight in an effort to draw the illusion of living people out of thin air. It had never occurred to me until that moment that the effort would be fatiguing or unpleasant; it had never occurred to me that it would be worse than manual labor. And when I sat down before the table on a creaking bedroom chair, I did not realize that I should be doing this sort of thing for years. I did not realize that writing would almost always be a disagreeable task, and that nothing which one sets down on paper ever wholly approximates the conception of the mind. As soon as I faced it, I did not want to write. Instead my intelligence presented a number of excuses for stopping before I started. The light was bad, the chair was uncomfortable; I felt tired; I wanted to read a book. I would always be seeking for excuses, ever after, not to write; and I have often wondered why I began at all.

"She lived," I wrote, "like a doll, near the edge of the French Concession. When she appeared upon the street, her *amah* followed her, carrying a square bundle wrapped in silk, and behind the *amah* came her strong man. When she sang, her high falsetto voice was shocking to occidental eardrums, but the Chinese said her voice was beautiful. Her name, when translated into English, was First Spring Mountain Plum Blossom. She came, of course, from Soochow, that city where all the women have a celestial beauty, and where the canal boats seem to sail across the fields whenever the wind is fair."

I stopped, for nothing I was setting down was what I wished to say. I paused, searching for some better combination of ideas, and instead I began thinking of the wind bells on the Soochow Pagoda that rose above an artificial pool. It was not a good pagoda; it was decadent when one compared it with the ruinous classic beauty of the pagoda which stood in the fields near Ting Jo. I had climbed to the top of it once with General Feng and his staff to adjust artillery fire upon the troops of the Christian general.

It had all become so real that a sound behind me made me jump. I had forgotten where I was. The sound only the gentle opening of my door, but it made me turn almost guiltily.

It was Bella, and I had nearly forgotten about Bella Brill.

"Good God," I said, "aren't you asleep?"

She was in her nightdress, which was covered by the ice-blue Chinese robe I had given her, and she was wearing the little embroidered slippers I had bought her in Shanghai. Nothing about them was right, in the Chinese sense, but they were becoming to Bella Brill. Her black hair fell in two braids over her shoulders just as she had worn it when she was a little girl, and the straight, decorous lines of the robe gave her the same sort of childish purity.

"Jim darling," said Bella, "I can't button this damn thing right."

I had never felt that it was wrong for her to be in my room before.

"What's the matter, Belle?" I said. "Can't you go to sleep?"

"Jim," she said, "button it up the right way for me, won't you, darling? Of course I got to sleep and then I woke up and remembered that I hadn't said good night to you at all. Button the damn thing up, please darling."

I walked toward her, not sure that I wanted to button the damn thing up.

"Oh," said Bella, "so that's the way it goes," and I tried not to be disturbed by her being so near me.

"Well," I said, "there you are. Good night, Belle."

"Darling," said Bella, "I thought you'd like to know—I'm so happy. Everything's all right when he's with me."

"Oh," I said, "that's fine. So you love him, do you, Belle?"

"Yes," she said, "I love him when he's with me. I've been so silly, haven't I? I'm not going to be silly any more. If I can just keep thinking this way, that's all there is to it. There's only one thing that frightens me—it's when I don't think this way."

"How do you mean?" I asked.

"He's so darling," Bella said. "Jim, what did his father say?"

"Never mind," I said. "It doesn't matter, Belle."

Bella smiled faintly.

"Well," she said, "*they* can't stop me. I'm going to marry him just as soon as I get back from Italy. No one's going to stop me. Clothilde isn't or Archie or anyone."

"Why should they want to?" I asked.

Bella sat down on the edge of my bed.

"Well, they do," she said. "I just feel it. Everybody's trying to stop me. You're trying to stop me."

"No, I'm not," I said. "Go ahead and marry him. Don't talk so much about it. Go ahead."

"Well," said Bella, "you are trying to stop me, and you can't —so there."

"Why should I?" I asked.

She crossed her bare white ankles and leaned backwards on her hands, looking up at me.

"You are," she repeated, "aren't you, darling? Just as soon as you saw Avery."

"No," I said. "For heaven's sake, stop thinking about yourself. Good night, Belle."

"Darling," said Bella, "please don't be so cross with me. I don't know what I'm saying. I don't mean half of what I say. Aren't you going to kiss me good night?"

I thought of Avery Gifford, who believed that God had meant him to love my second cousin, Bella Brill. She was leaning back, looking up at me, and the smile had left her lips, and somehow I was thinking of other women I had kissed and what she had said to Harry long ago.

"It's just kiss, kiss, kiss," she had said.

I didn't know whether I liked her or not at the moment, because I could see right through her, and I understood why she wanted to marry Avery Gifford as clearly as if she had told me. She desired security, and yet again she did not desire it. I bent over and kissed her forehead close by the part of her soft black hair.

"You want everything, don't you, Belle?" I asked.

I was right about it too. Just as my lips touched her forehead, she threw her arms around me. I saw her eyes half-closed looking into mine, and then I kissed her because she wanted

285

everything, and I forgot to be ashamed of myself, or to be ashamed of her.

"Belle," I said, "you'd better get out of here."

Her arms were still around me and her lips moved softly against my cheek.

"Darling," she said, "you'll stand by me, won't you? That's all I want, no matter what happens."

"Yes," I said. "You God-damned little bitch," I said.

She must have understood the way I meant it because she smiled.

"You're always so sweet," she said. "You're the only one who understands me."

"Belle," I said, "don't marry him till you get back. Think it over, that's all, Belle."

"All right," she said, "but I'm still going to marry him, darling."

XXV | Dreadfully, Dreadfully Happy

I was very busy that autumn and winter, although I cannot recollect much of what I did. With the exception of Cousin Clothilde, everyone I knew was busy through the winter season, always seeing someone, always moving from one place to another, always looking for shirt studs and a clean collar and usually being behind-time. When the record was balanced after those winters were over, I wonder, sometimes, if others were like me, rather bewildered. There were the speakeasies and the rounds of the night clubs and the dinner parties on Park Avenue. There was the awning on the sidewalk and the doorman and his buttons and the reception hall with its Jacobean furniture— or else there was no doorman but instead a bell to push and a flight of stairs to climb, over by Third Avenue or down by Washington Square, but the whole framework was the same. There would be all the cocktails and then everybody would be talking louder and a little louder as more drinks went down. Then there would be the dinner table where you would see how far you could get with the lady on the left or right when you talked about Theodore Dreiser or "What Price Glory?" Then all the men would go somewhere to drink bootleg Scotch and talk about the stock market or about what someone had said who knew Calvin Coolidge; and then they would join the ladies. There were a lot of amusing details besides, but when it was all over, the details were hard to remember.

I was occupied a good deal with writing and I recall more clearly than anything what Mr. Stanhope said about the sing-song story and how I took it apart and put it together again. Down on Twelfth Street they were all mildly amused that I was trying to write, because they had all been thinking of doing the same thing themselves, and Cousin Clothilde went to sleep when I read the story to her.

"It seemed a little confused," she said when she awoke. "I don't like those stories that make me think, and I never did like foreign people. I wouldn't show it to Archie, darling. It would make him very nervous, and I wish you wouldn't worry about it so. You're not attractive when you worry."

I also remember very well the day we saw Bella and Archie off on the boat, a cold afternoon early in December. There were a great many people—Sid and Harry and Mary and Cousin Clothilde, and Avery Gifford, of course, and Bella was wearing the orchids he had sent her. There were a lot of others also whose names I don't remember, who were intimate friends of everybody, and also there were three Communists who were admirers of Archie Wright's. Everybody kept wandering through the social halls and up and down the stairs, and the stewards looked very bored and tired, waiting at their stations, ready to tell where B deck was and that no liquor could be served while the ship was at the pier. On B deck, where Bella and Archie had their rooms, a number of people were already singing "Auld Lang Syne." Avery Gifford was away somewhere with Bella, but everyone else seemed to be in Archie's cabin, sitting on his bed and drinking rye, and there was not much room because Archie weighed nearly three hundred pounds by then and looked a good deal like G. K. Chesterton. Archie was very glad that he was going somewhere. The one thing he wanted everyone to know was how much he loved Cousin Clothilde. She was bourgeois but he loved her just the same, and he wished that Cousin Clothilde would go over too; he wanted her to change her mind right now and go.

"Archie's always so cunning," Cousin Clothilde said, "when he's going away. Look at him, he's just like a little boy, he's going to have such a lovely time."

Archie did not look like a little boy, but I had no doubt that he was going to have a lovely time. Pretty soon he began to sing "Funiculi, Funicula"—and then he could not remember what he had done with his passport and everybody began hunting for it.

"Now wait a minute," Archie shouted. "Jim can find it!"

"Jim," said Cousin Clothilde, "please help him."

"Don't keep beating your pockets," I told Archie. "Look. Look slowly."

"God Almighty," Archie shouted, "that's what everybody says. I tell you I know God-damned well it isn't in my pockets. It's the Government. The Government doesn't want me to leave."

"Now listen," I said, "the Government would be glad to get rid of you. Just get it into your head that everyone wants to get rid of you."

"That isn't so," Archie answered. "Clothilde doesn't want to get rid of me. Do you, Clo?"

"Isn't he cunning?" said Cousin Clothilde. "Archie's always so cunning when he's going away. He's only got one extra pair of trousers. He was so cunning when he was packing."

"Where's the steward?" called Archie. "Which button do I push? I want some more ice and I want to get away from America."

"Never mind the steward," I said. "Did you give your passport to the purser when you came aboard?"

"Absolutely," said Archie, "I gave it to the purser. Now everybody stop looking in my pockets."

Then I found myself next to one of Archie's friends who had been a conscientious objector in the war, and who wore his hair in a black marceled pompadour. He leaned against the cabin wall, looking unsmilingly at the scene.

"All this will be over in a little while," he said.

"The sooner the better," I answered.

"I am afraid," the man said, "that you don't catch my meaning. I'm referring to the capitalistic structure."

"Any change," I said, "will probably be for the better."

I had the wish one always has at such a time, that the parting might be over and done with, and that all inconsequences and incoherencies might cease. They were beginning to beat on gongs for visitors to go ashore.

"Well," said Harry, "I must say good-by to the Percivals. They're on A deck."

"Good-by Archie," I said. "Look up Joe Stowe when you get to Rome."

"Absolutely," said Archie.

Then I walked over to Bella's cabin opposite. The door was half-opened and Bella was in Avery Gifford's arms. I was wondering what had happened to her orchids until I saw them safe on the washstand.

"Excuse me," I said, "I'm sorry."

I was sorry because Avery looked upset and pale.

"She'll come back, Avery," I said. "Good-by, Belle. Be sure to look up Joe Stowe. He can show you a lot of things."

"Who's that, sir?" Avery asked. "Who's Stowe?"

"Don't worry about him," I said. It seemed absurd that anyone should worry about Joe. "Good-by, Belle. Have a good time."

"Keep Avery on ice for me," said Bella, "won't you?" And then she whispered to me: "Be kind to him, darling, please. He's so damn serious."

"All right," I said. "Good-by, Belle."

I saw her when the gangplank was up, standing by the rail, waving, and Avery Gifford was beside me, white-faced and silent.

"It's all right, Avery," I said. "She's coming back."

Cousin Clothilde always hated to have anyone read at Twelfth Street in the afternoon. She was sitting on the sofa when I came in and Sid was putting some wood and lumps of coal on the fire. It was late afternoon, but it was light outside, which showed that winter would eventually be over.

"Jim," said Cousin Clothilde, "please talk to me. Please don't read. Nobody has been in all day. I don't know where Harry is. Have you seen Harry?"

"I saw him at lunch," I said. "He was having lunch with some vice-president."

"That must have been very stupid for him," Cousin Clothilde said. "Harry must be at his club now. Sid is going out to dinner and I don't know where Mary is at all."

"Do you mind if I borrow one of your shirts?" Sid asked.

"There was a letter from Archie this morning," said Cousin Clothilde. "They're sailing next week. Archie never says anything in his letters. He says they're sailing, but he doesn't tell the boat."

"I don't suppose you've heard from Bella," I said.

"No," said Cousin Clothilde, "Bella never writes. Sid, will you see if there are any cigarettes? Harry took them all, and now Mary's started smoking. Jim, please don't read. You and I will be here for dinner alone. I wish everyone wouldn't keep going out. I suppose you've been talking to that Mr. Stanhope again? I don't see what you see in him, I don't think he's attractive. I don't know where Mary is at all. I wish people would let me know where they are going. I don't like to be wondering about them. I don't see why anyone bought that story of yours, Jim. It was such a stupid story."

"The only time you heard it, you went to sleep," I said.

"That's exactly what I mean," said Cousin Clothilde—"It was such a stupid story. . . . Didn't you think it was stupid, Sid?"

"No," said Sid, "it was all well enough. It had form. I've been giving a good deal of thought to form lately. I'm thinking of writing myself."

"Are you?" I said. "That's good." Since I had sold that story everyone else had been thinking more than ever about writing.

"I wonder if I couldn't write," said Cousin Clothilde. "I think about a great many things. Both Mr. Fisher and Mirabel Steiner say I could. I never was good at spelling, but someone could help me. It's just a matter of ideas."

"Not entirely," said Sid. "Jim, did you ever hear of a man named Frizzelhart?"

"Who?" I asked.

"Frizzelhart," said Sid, "Anthony J. Frizzelhart."

"That's a funny name," said Cousin Clothilde. "I wonder if it's Jewish. Jews always do such funny things with their names."

"Just who is Mr. Frizzelhart?" I asked.

"I just thought you might have known him," said Sid. "He's a Consulting Counselor on the Short Story. I've been in to see him and he thinks that I can write. He charges five dollars for every consultation, in advance. He says success is a matter of fluency and form. I'm thinking of going ahead with Mr. Frizzelhart. Last week he placed one of his pupils in the *Saturday Evening Post*. He doesn't believe in formula but he believes in form."

"Well, I wouldn't have anything to do with him," I said. "He's probably a fake."

"Darling," said Cousin Clothilde, "you mustn't be so hard on other people. Sid makes a very careful study of everything and Mr. Frizzelhart must be very intelligent to place someone in the *Saturday Evening Post*. . . . Is that the doorbell ringing? Someone must be coming in to tea. Sid, see who it is." Cousin Clothilde lowered her voice as Sid walked into the hall. "I don't think many people Sid's age would go into things so thoroughly," she said. "I wondered why he wanted five dollars yesterday. It must have been for Mr. Frizzelhart."

Sid came back holding a blue and white envelope.

"It's a cablegram," he said.

Cousin Clothilde had been reclining on the sofa. Now she sat up straight. She always hated telegrams and cables and I did not blame her much. She reached toward me and took my hand.

"Jim," she said, "I know it."

"What?" I asked.

"It's Archie—Archie's dead."

"Now listen," I said. She was frightened and I did not like to see her frightened. "It probably *is* from Archie. Perhaps he's sailing earlier."

Sid still held the cablegram limply in his fingers, and I felt a little of Cousin Clothilde's own dread.

"No," said Cousin Clothilde, "no. Archie wouldn't send a cable. He knows exactly how I feel about them. Something's happened to Archie. Jim, please keep holding my hand."

"You'd better open it," I said.

"No," said Cousin Clothilde, "let Sid open it, and Sid can tell us if it's terrible."

Sid always moved slowly and it seemed to me now that he moved more deliberately than I had ever seen him. He walked over to the lamp on the long table. He was astigmatic and he squinted his eyes as he read.

"Go ahead," I said. "What is it?"

"Is it about Archie?" Cousin Clothilde asked.

"No," said Sid, "not Archie: Bella."

I dropped Cousin Clothilde's hand. I found myself standing up.

"Go ahead. What's the matter? Is she sick?" I said.

"No," said Sid, "not sick. She's dreadfully happy, that's what she says—dreadfully happy. She's engaged."

"You mean she's announcing it about Avery?" I asked.

"No," said Sid, "not that. She's just got engaged to a man named Stowe. He's a friend of yours, isn't he? Joe Stowe?"

I walked over to the table where Sid was standing and snatched the paper from his fingers.

"Dreadfully, dreadfully happy," I read. "Going to marry Joe Stowe. Caracalla's Baths did it."

"Whose baths?" said Cousin Clothilde. Her voice was sharp. "What was she doing in a bath?" I stood looking at the cable.

"It's a ruin," I said. "It isn't a real bath. That's right—she's going to marry Joe Stowe!" And then I found that my voice was different, stronger.

"You remember Joe Stowe. It's the best news I've heard since the Armistice."

Cousin Clothilde was looking at me hard from across the room.

"Sid," she said, "will you get me a glass of water from the pantry? I think it's perfectly dreadful. He'll take her away somewhere."

"You used to like him," I said. "I don't see why you think it's dreadful."

"Did I?" said Cousin Clothilde. "Well, I never thought he was distinguished."

"I don't see why you think it's dreadful," I heard myself saying again. "It's a surprise, but after all—"

I stopped without finishing my sentence. Something was stirring Cousin Clothilde; something was stirring both of us, which perhaps neither of us wished to understand or to acknowledge.

"Sid," she said, "go upstairs and telephone Harry. He must be at his club. Tell him he must give up any engagement he has and come home right away."

When Sid had closed the door, Cousin Clothilde walked over to the fireplace and back to the sofa and that restlessness of hers was disconcerting because she was so seldom restless.

"You don't understand it," she said, "because you're not a woman, dear."

"What's that got to do with it?" I answered. I was experiencing that repressed calm which comes over one after something has been smashed, and now I was piecing it together again, first dully, then more cleverly.

Cousin Clothilde sighed, sat down on the sofa and wrinkled her forehead.

"A woman understands things that a man doesn't, dear," she said. "I'm trying to think and I can't seem to think. Bella has so many possibilities and now to see her throw herself away on someone without her background, without any of her traditions—"

"How can you say that?" I asked. "You haven't seen him for years and years."

294

"I can feel things like that," said Cousin Clothilde. "I know he hasn't the same traditions. He'll take her away from everything she has."

"Suppose he does," I said. "That's exactly why she's marrying him, because she wants to get away from everything she has."

Cousin Clothilde frowned at me a moment before she answered.

"Yes, dear," she said, "perhaps she does. I know what Bella thinks. I used to think myself that I could get away from home simply by marrying. Then when I was married I wanted everything to be like home. Bella wouldn't be anyone without her own traditions."

"But what do you mean," I asked, "by traditions?"

Cousin Clothilde made a hopeless gesture with her delicate ringless hands.

"I wish you wouldn't be so tiresome, dear," she said. "I know what I mean but I can't explain it. Tradition is what we're taught to live for. Bella's tradition is what she's been taught to live for. All of us have tradition."

Although the conversation was growing nebulous and peculiar, she was evidently referring to an attitude toward life, and to the strange, unworldly existence of all the Brills, to a world which she had built up to keep out another world, and the futility of our argument was a part of it.

"Will you please give me a cigarette, dear," Cousin Clothilde said.

We sat there without speaking for a while, and I wondered what it was that Bella had been taught to live for. Whatever it was, Bella Brill didn't want it.

You can tell when people are happy, and I was thinking that in spite of everything Cousin Clothilde was a happy person. She must have been over fifty if she was a day, but she looked agelessly beautiful. Her face, even when it was worn and tired, had a composed sort of sweetness. It had the content and the understanding of someone who has resolved all questions, but as far as I knew she had never resolved anything.

"Well, I wonder what you live for," I said.

Curiously, my remark did not disturb her in the least.

"Now, that's easy to answer," Cousin Clothilde said. "I live for Archie and the children and for other people, dear. I don't do it very well. I'm a very careless manager, because no one could ever teach me to add or subtract in school. Nearly all my teachers were very disagreeable people, but I try all the time to make Archie and the children and other people happy. That's what I live for, dear, and I think that's what every woman wants to live for. You would understand if you were a woman. I suppose it may be different with men."

"No," I said, "I don't believe so. What do you get out of it?"

"How should I know, darling?" Cousin Clothilde asked. "It just makes me happy, that's all. I love to have them ask things of me. I love to have you ask. It makes me feel that there's a reason for me."

She reached out her hand and I bent down and kissed it, a thing I very rarely did.

"Now that," she said, "a thing like that makes me very happy, dear."

But I was still thinking of Bella and Joe Stowe.

"Well, how about Bella?" I said. "Perhaps she wants to do something for someone too, if that's what every woman wants; and she hasn't a chance to do it here. You do too much for everybody, and now they all expect it. You've never weaned one of them. Even Archie isn't weaned. Perhaps that's what she means when she says she wants to get away. Perhaps she wants to do something for Joe Stowe."

A cloud came across Cousin Clothilde's face.

"Well, I'd like to know," she said, "what Mr. Stowe is going to do for her. They haven't the same tradition. He isn't going to fit in. He's going—"

"He's going to what?" I asked.

"Darling," said Cousin Clothilde, "I wish you'd get me an aspirin and another glass of water. He's going to try to take Bella away, and he can't. Don't ask me what I mean."

There was a sitting room upstairs on the second floor where Harry found me after he had seen his mother. Harry closed the door behind him and began pacing up and down, rubbing his hand over the thin spot in his hair. I was surprised that he should be so concerned, because most things did not ruffle him, and after all he had always quarreled with Bella.

"Jim," said Harry, "this is all your fault. I don't suppose it means anything to you, but I happen to be the head of the family."

"Oh, go hoist up your pants," I said.

"I don't suppose it means anything to you," said Harry, "because you always take this sophisticated attitude that nothing means anything. I am the head of the family and I have to think of my sister's reputation."

"Sit down and take the weight off your feet," I said. "What's the matter with her reputation?"

Harry did not sit down; instead he squared his shoulders and looked at me speculatively down the bridge of his long nose.

"It isn't up to you," he said, "to defend my sister's reputation. It just happens that you don't move around with anyone who matters. Now the question is just this." Harry leveled his finger at me and shook it gently. "The question is, what are we going to say? That's what I've been trying to take up with Clothilde, calmly and without emotion, and she hasn't been any help at all. And now you're not being any help. What explanation are we going to give to people? The papers probably know about it already."

"I don't understand a single thing you're saying," I said. "What is it to you? You're not going to marry Joe Stowe."

Harry looked at me and patted the thin spot on his head.

"Gifford," he said, "Gifford, Gifford, Gifford. Does that mean anything to you—Gifford? It just happens that everyone knows that my sister was going to marry Avery Gifford."

"Oh," I said, "you've been telling people, have you?"

Harry's thin and rather handsome face assumed a pinkish glow.

"Leaving that point for the moment," he said, "as having no bearing upon the present situation, there is such a thing as rumor. People talk, and everyone who amounts to anything knows that Bella was to marry Avery Gifford. It's the one decent thing she could have done, the one thing that would get the family anywhere. I took the trouble to point that out to Bella myself, patiently and diagrammatically. And now what happens? She drops him. Why did she drop him? She must be crazy."

"Maybe she likes Stowe better," I said.

"My God," said Harry, "she can't like him better. Try to face the thing with detachment, Jim. *Who* is Stowe? *What* has he ever amounted to?"

"He's a friend of mine," I said.

"Jim," said Harry, "I don't see why you can't face this thing rationally. Does his being a friend of yours recommend him to other people? Now Jim, you know damn well it doesn't. He has no money and he has no position. In all sanity you don't drop someone like Avery Gifford for a man like Stowe. It just happens that I've grown very fond of Avery Gifford."

I knew what Harry meant. He had been telling people one thing confidentially and now he had to tell them something else. He pointed his finger at me again and moved his arm in a gentle, rotary motion.

"Think of it without bias," he said. "Let us try to consider this objectively. It all boils down to a simple and very ugly fact. There's only one reason why a girl like Bella should drop a Gifford and marry a Stowe. It's because she has to, that's why."

"Look here," I said, "you know damned well that Bella hadn't made up her mind."

Harry made a gesture of weary impatience. "Don't raise your voice," he said. "Let's try to view this dispassionately. It just happens that everyone knows that Bella has been petting her head off for the last two years. Didn't you know that?"

"Not particularly," I said.

"Well," said Harry, "if you don't, everybody else does, and that's what everyone will say. She has to marry Stowe."

I got up and walked over to him.

"That's a God-damned lie," I said. "Joe's a friend of mine, and he doesn't have to borrow money from his mother either. You'd better take that back about Joe Stowe."

Harry raised his eyebrows.

"Now wait a minute," he said, "wait a minute."

"And while you're about it," I continued, "you'd better take that back about your sister too."

Harry shrugged his shoulders and waved his hands in a helpless, tolerant gesture.

"That," he said, "is exactly what happens in this family when I try to treat things sanely. Try if you can to make an honest effort at least to reconsider what I've said. Then, if you control your temper, you will perceive that I imputed nothing against Joe Stowe or Bella."

"Then what did you do?" I said.

Harry shrugged his shoulders and waved his hands in another broad and expansive gesture.

"I simply pointed out what people would say, Jim," he said. "I don't like it any better than you, but unfortunately someone has to be constructive about it. Why should you be so upset?"

"I'm not upset," I said. "You are. You're upset because she isn't going to marry Gifford."

"Then why are you upset?" said Harry. "Because she is going to marry Stowe?"

"Suppose we both shut up," I said, "and go downstairs and have a drink."

Harry put his hands on my shoulders. After all, Harry and I had known each other for quite a while, longer in fact than we had known anybody else.

"Why do you suppose it did happen, Jim?" he asked.

I had been asking myself the same thing, but I did not tell him.

"You don't know Joe," I said. "You haven't seen him for years and years. You'll like him when you see him. He's one of the best foreign men in the newspaper business. Joe is quite a boy."

"But what's he going to do?" asked Harry.

"Don't worry," I said. "He'll look out for Bella. He's coming home this spring." But Harry's face wore a bewildered look.

"But listen, Jim," he said, "why the *hell* do you suppose she did it?"

"Perhaps she loves him," I suggested.

Harry shook his head.

"No," he answered, "no. That doesn't sound like Bella."

"Well," I said, "perhaps he loves her."

Harry looked at me for a moment before he answered.

"Well," he said, "God help him if he does."

XXVI | Stowe Proposes
Sid Disposes

"I felt right away that I knew Bella better than anyone else," Joe Stowe wrote me in one of his long, rambling letters. "It's the desperation in her that I'm talking about now, and I'm going to change all that. I knew right away she wasn't happy. Well, I'm going to make her happy. . . . We both have the same sort of tastes. We laugh at the same statues. You know how the Romans are about statuary. She says that Harry and Sid are like Romulus and Remus on the Capitoline, and that Clothilde is like Niobe, and that Archie is like one of the Bernini Tritons, always blowing his horn, and that Gifford's like the Dying Gaul.

"I'm only telling you this to show you that the Gifford thing was never serious and to show you what a good time we're having. When we're alone together everything is fine. I know that Bella's a genius in a way. She has an intuitive sense about everything she sees, and that enthusiasm of hers makes everything wonderful; but I don't like that desperation in her. She's told me a lot—more about the family than you've ever told me—so much that I seem to have known them always. Of course the whole result is that I must give her a new point of view. I'd take her out to the East right now if I had money enough. Well, I'm going to make it for her. A lot of people are going to hear from me before I'm through. I'd marry Bella right now and get it all over with, but I suppose all women are queer that way, even

Bella. For anyone so unconventional she has an unexpected admiration for conventions. She wants to go home and get married at home like other people. Maybe it's just as well because I've got to get back myself. I've been writing to Stanhope. Home's the only place where you can make money. Bella's going on ahead and I'll be washed up here in about two months, and then I'll come right over. I'll bring some short stories and the beginning of a novel, and besides they want some syndicated articles on Europe. We'll get married just as soon as I get back, and then I want to take her away somewhere where I can have a typewriter and where I can be quiet.

"Now what I want you to do is to look after her until I get back. Don't let anybody get her frightened. Keep letting her know that I mean what I say and everything's all right. Everything is always going to be all right. Just let her know I mean it."

I have the letter somewhere still with a good many others of his, hastily scrawled and obviously not intended to go into any posthumous collection. Now and then I have looked them over and my reaction toward them has never changed. I have always recaptured that feeling of his that everything was going to be all right. Perhaps it might have been, if circumstances could have been a little different. There is such a similarity always in the phenomena of the unhappy marriage. I could see the right in him and the wrong in him; I could see what Bella saw and what she did not see; and I could see why the family did not like him, because after all I was in the family.

Even then I was disturbed by that feeling of his that he knew everything about us, and that he knew everything about Bella.

Bella brought a lot of things from Italy—the ring and the green jade necklace that Joe had given her, and in addition all those odds and ends that one always brings back, the white Pliny doves around the yellow marble basin, the marble columns of the temple in the Forum, the leather Florentine boxes, the gold-framed madonnas, the Della Robbia babies, and the little bowls of colored pottery fruits; and also a picture of Joe Stowe in a blue Florentine leather frame. Joe was in his shirt sleeves in very brilliant sunlight, standing on a terrace.

"Darling," Bella called, "come in. Why are you always in a hurry? I never see you any more."

"I'm going uptown," I said.

Bella had been looking at herself in the mirror above her bureau, and that was how she must have seen me passing down the hall.

"Well, you don't have to go right away," she said. "What's the matter, darling?"

"Nothing," I said. "What do you mean?"

"You've been so peculiar," Bella said, "ever since I've come back home."

"I haven't meant to be," I answered, "but then maybe things are different, Belle. After all, you're going to be married next month."

She looked at me and smiled. The smile was in her eyes too, and she knew what I meant.

"But that's what I've been trying to tell you in every way I know," Bella said. "It doesn't change things with you and me, darling. What's the matter with me? What have I done?"

"You haven't done anything," I said.

"But you act as though I had done something," said Bella. "Everyone is so cross with me. No one ever seems to want to talk to me any more. My God, I only want to get married, darling."

"Belle," I said, "are you sure you want to get married?"

Bella gave her shoulders a petulant jerk.

"Absolutely sure," Bella said, "this time. Why should you even ask?"

"I was just wondering," I said.

"Well, you needn't wonder any more," said Bella. "Why should everybody be wondering? Everybody keeps getting me in a corner and asking me if I'm sure. Why shouldn't I be? Why shouldn't I want to get married and get out of this house and go somewhere where—"

"Go ahead," I said.

"Where someone's nice to me," Bella said, "where there's some order about something, where someone's sweet—"

"Well, you haven't been so sweet yourself," I said.

Bella bit her lip.

"If that's all you have to say," she said, "get out."

"All right," I said. "I've always heard there's nothing worse than being engaged."

"Jim," she called after me, "please don't, *please*. Don't be so silly, darling. I was just asking why you seem so strange. I'm so lonely, and nothing's the way it used to be."

She wanted everything to be the same, when common sense should have told her that it could not be. I looked at the picture of Joe on the bureau, grinning at us out of the frame.

"Bella," I said, "if you don't want to marry him, now's the time to say so. Of course it's going to be different. No one can help that."

Bella closed her lips tightly, raised her hands up to her thick black hair, pressed her palms against her ears, and looked at me and let her hands drop back.

"Honestly," she said, "I think I'm going to have a nervous breakdown. I really think I'd better go and see a doctor or something. Why does everybody keep telling me that if I don't want to marry Joe, I don't have to? There isn't anything wrong about me, is there? Joe isn't insane or a pervert, is he? I tell you I want to marry Joe, do you hear me? I don't care if he's a nigger, I want to marry Joe."

"Bella," I said, "there's no use yelling at me."

She lowered her voice a trifle and the strained look left her face.

"I have to yell," she said, "to get it through your damned thick skull that I want to marry Joe. Just because I didn't want to marry Avery Gifford doesn't mean that I d⁻n't want to marry Joe. And everybody seems to act as though there were something really sinister about Joe. Everybody's trying to break it up. That's what it is. Everybody's trying to give me a nervous breakdown.

You'd all like it if I got sick. First Clothilde's nasty about Joe, and then Harry's nasty, and now you're nasty about him— and you say he's your best friend. You wait till I tell Joe about you, just you wait."

"See here," I told her, "I never said anything against Joe."

"Then why do you say I don't have to marry him if I don't want to?" Bella asked. "That's saying something against Joe, isn't it? I just wish Joe were here."

"Well," I said, "he's coming back tomorrow."

It occurred to me that the sooner he came the better it would be for everybody.

"Jim," said Bella, "don't be angry."

"I'm not angry," I said.

"Then don't get disgusted either," Bella said. "I know what you're thinking. You're thinking I'm not right for Joe. Maybe that's true. Maybe I'm not fit to marry anyone."

"What do you mean by that?" I asked.

"Darling," said Bella, "you know what I mean. He's so nice that sometimes I think I'm not, even when I try to be. There's only one thing I'm afraid of."

I had known that she was afraid of something. I had seen it in her all the time.

"I'm just afraid," she said, "that he'll destroy the thing that's my personality, the thing that's me. I want to be me, no matter what I do. And he's so strong. He has such strong ideas. You don't think he'd do that, do you, Jim?"

"Get this into your head," I said. "No one can do that. The only one who can destroy you is you."

"You really think so?" Bella asked.

"Yes," I said, "I know so."

"You always stand by me," she said, "always. You see I don't want Joe to change me, I want to change Joe. That's really why I want to marry him. Now there wasn't anything I could do for Avery Gifford, and I can do so much for Joe. That's why I love him, Jim."

And I knew why he loved her: because he could do so much

305

for her. And something else came over me when I left her, the way a voice appears to speak sometimes in one's dreams. She did not want to change the little things about him, the ties he wore or the way he ate his soup or the way he brushed his hair. She wanted to change the very innate quality in him, the part of him that she did not wish altered in herself. It was not love, it was something else, and it was not her fault either; it was something she could not help at all.

Sid called to me just when I was looking for my hat in the front hall. He was alone in the big room. It was spring outside and the street was bright with sunlight and a man by a wagonload of potted flowers was calling out his wares, just as his father must have called them in the flower market of Naples. The parlor, however, was as dusky as if winter had not left it yet—which was not surprising, for the windows had not been washed for a long while. That big room was always a place to avoid in the daylight. Sid was reclining on the sofa where his mother usually sat.

"What are you doing?" I asked.

"Nothing," said Sid, "except thinking. I've stayed away from my course today because I have rather severe cramps, high-up—here. How is your stomach, Jim?"

"Why don't you go outside in the sun?" I asked.

"Frankly," said Sid, "I don't like the sun except when I can lie on the beach. I've been having these spasms in my stomach and sometimes a touch of nausea before breakfast ever since Bella got back. Have you noticed that the whole psychological aspect of the place has changed since Bella's back?"

"Maybe you're pregnant," I said.

Sid was not amused. He took his fingers from his knees and laced them together and unlaced them.

"Please don't do that with your fingers," I said.

"It's an exercise," said Sid. "If I am to be a scientist, it's very important to have dextrous, supple hands."

"I thought you were going to be a writer," I said. "I thought

306

you were doing some consulting work with Dr. Anthony Frizzelhart."

"Oh yes," said Sid, "yes, that. That was very interesting. Experiences like that are a very real help in finding out what I am finally going to do."

"Well," I said, "I'm in a hurry. I'm going out."

Sid laced his fingers together again and unlaced them with a soft cracking of his knuckle joints.

"I suppose you've been talking with Bella," he said. "She's so intense she gives me nervous indigestion. There's an atmosphere of frustration, everywhere frustration."

I looked at him with a new interest. Usually he was self-effacing, but now and then he said something succinct.

"Everyone here is thwarted," Sid said, "except Clothilde and me. Did you ever think of that? Probably it's all sex. There's too much love, too much thwarted love."

His words sounded suspiciously like the printed page.

"You've been reading a book, have you?" I asked. "Did you get it by clipping a coupon?"

"No," said Sid, "I borrowed it. It's never worth while to buy books. Most people you borrow them from don't really want them back. If you're interested, it's a book called *Love, Life and Sex.*"

"Well," I said, "for God's sake, don't do that to your fingers."

"It's a difficult exercise," said Sid, "and besides it stops me from smoking. Jim, when Joe Stowe comes I think you ought to tell him. Someone ought to tell him."

"Tell him what?" I asked.

Sid looked up at me, squinting.

"I've given it a good deal of thought," he said. "Really someone ought to tell him that he shouldn't marry Bella. Jim, it absolutely isn't going to work."

"You know a hell of a lot about it, don't you?" I said.

"Listen," said Sid, and he passed his hand wearily over his eyes, as though he had been doing too much reading. "They don't like him, Jim. None of us like him. In fact, we all hate him. It's going to be impossible if we all hate him. Clothilde hates him, and you've heard Harry going on about it, and Mary hates him. And I don't like to say it, but so do I." He made me both angry and uneasy.

"You're crazy," I said. "Why don't you get off the seat of your pants and stop your bellyaching? You've hardly ever seen Joe Stowe. None of you know him."

Sid shook his head and twisted his hands together.

"It isn't attractive," he said. "I know it isn't attractive. It isn't anything that any of us can help. Have you ever seen a lot of dogs together?"

The weary detachment of his voice grated on my nerves.

"If anybody starts making trouble," I said, "I'll know who started it. What have dogs got to do with it?"

Sidney was unruffled. When I came to think of it, I had never seen him angry.

"Look at it this way," he said. "We're all a very funny breed of dogs, inbred and overbred. I don't know what we're good for. Probably we're good for nothing."

"Now you're talking sense," I said.

"But then," said Sidney gently, "lots of dogs are good for nothing. I never did like dogs, and I haven't much respect for human beings either."

"Get on with what you're trying to say," I said.

"When a new dog comes," said Sid, "the others hate him, don't they? Particularly when they're abnormal dogs. Well, Stowe's a new dog and we're abnormal. We don't like him and we'll never like him. We won't like him because he's abler than we are. You can't help it, Jim, we're going to hate him."

"All right," I said, "go ahead and hate him. Why should he care? Joe and Bella won't be around here."

Sidney nodded and rubbed his eyes again.

"I don't know why we don't hate you, Jim," he said, "or why you don't hate us either. I've thought about that quite a little. It won't make any difference where he and Bella are."

"You know everything, don't you?" I said. "Why won't it?"

"I'm glad we've had this talk," Sid said. "My stomach really feels a good deal better now. The point is that Bella doesn't really like him either."

I reached forward and grasped Sidney by the coat collar and jerked him to his feet. He made no resistance; he simply looked at me.

"Suppose you get up," I said, "and get your circulation going." But Sidney still spoke mildly.

"I'm right," he said. "She's attracted to him, fascinated by him, if you want, but I'm right. Really, Jim, it isn't going to work."

Sid stood there, quiescent beneath my hands. He had spoken about frustration and I could feel it. There was inertia over everything.

"You listen to me," I said. "It's just the way you get from sitting around. You're going to be nice to him. Do you understand?"

"Of course," Sid answered, "we're going to be nice. We're always nice, and we're tolerant and moderately intelligent. I hope I'm wrong, but I don't think so. I've given it a lot of thought. I think you ought to tell him, Jim, when he comes tomorrow."

By the time four o'clock came next afternoon Cousin Clothilde had grown very nervous, and the contagion of her nervousness communicated itself to Harry and to Sid and to Mary and to me.

"Harry," Cousin Clothilde said, "you know sometimes you don't get things right over the telephone, dear, or perhaps they didn't really know about it. You can't always trust people. I think you'd better call up again."

Harry sighed gustily and his voice was honey-sweet with patience. He pulled out his watch and consulted it. It was a watch that had been presented to him when he went to college, and during his college course it had usually been in a Boston pawnshop.

"Precisely three-and-three-quarters minutes ago," Harry said, "I telephoned. Oddly enough, the man who answered me was in complete possession of his faculties. Why should there be any reason for mendacity? He said the God-damned boat had docked. It costs exactly three-and-a-half cents to have him repeat this information. I suggest that we save that three-and-a-half cents and buy a portable house with it. You say that you want a portable house so that you can get away from people at Wickford Point. Saving is the only way to start. Three-and-a-half cents at compound interest—"

"I'm not asking about compound interest," said Cousin Clothilde, "and I'm not asking about portable houses. I simply want to know if the boat has docked. I don't like to think of Bella standing there waiting in the cold."

Harry pulled out his watch again.

"Four-and-a-quarter minutes ago exactly," Harry said, "it was officially confirmed that the boat had docked thirty-eight-and-three-quarters minutes ago."

"Oh hell! Shut up!" I said.

"Darling," said Cousin Clothilde, "it isn't pretty when you swear. I don't know what there is about me that makes people think that I don't mind swearing, but I do mind it. Are you sure there are enough things to drink? It will be so much better if we all have enough."

Mary turned her face from the window.

"There are four gallons of sacrificial wine," she said. "Half of it is red and half of it is yellow. And then there's Archie's alcohol. He can make it into gin right away."

"Mary," said Sidney softly, "sacramental wine, sacramental wine."

Mary burst into tears.

"I don't see why everybody picks on me," she said. "Whose fault is it, if I haven't got an education?"

"Mary," said Cousin Clothilde, "would you mind going upstairs, dear, and seeing what has happened to Archie? If he's still in the bathroom, tell him to get out of the tub. I want him to be here when Mr. Stowe comes. I don't want to do everything myself." She glanced eloquently after Mary and listened while her

310

feet stamped loudly on the stairs. "I don't know what gets into her," she said.

"She's frustrated," Sidney answered, "that's all."

"Why don't you think of another word?" I suggested.

"Just a moment," said Harry. "It does not mean that you're a purist because you've sold a couple of stories. Sid is saying exactly what he means. Why not admit it candidly? Mary is frustrated."

"What does frustrated mean?" Mary's voice from the hall made her mother start.

"What did Archie say, dear?" Cousin Clothilde asked.

"He says he's seen a lot of Joe Stowe," Mary answered, "and now someone else can see him."

"Well, sit down, dear," said Cousin Clothilde. "Don't just stand there in the door. I don't see why they don't come. Bella will catch cold. I don't think it's very considerate of Mr. Stowe to keep us all here waiting."

"They're coming," said Sid. "Here's a taxi now."

Cousin Clothilde stood up. I had never known her to stand so straight, and I remember wondering if she were feeling ill.

"Sid," she said, "go out to the door. Mary, don't pull away if he tries to kiss you, and for heaven's sake powder your nose. Jim, come here and hold my hand."

"What's the matter?" I asked. Her hand was cold as ice.

"Jim," she said, "why did you ever know him? Poor, darling Bella."

"Don't," I said. "Joe's all right."

Then Bella came into the room with Joe Stowe just behind her, and we all stood observing him. Sometimes when you see a person in a new place he does not look at all the way you think he is going to, or perhaps I was too solicitous, because I wanted him to look his best. As it was, I thought he was overdressed. He was wearing a plum-colored suit, and those Italian tailors always do something unnecessary around the waist. The plum color went very badly with his reddish hair, and the purple silk handkerchief in his breast pocket did not help, and his face had a strained look, even when he smiled. His greenish-yellow eyes met mine for a moment before they darted about the room, seeing everything. Then he walked over to Cousin Clothilde, clicked the heels of his yellow low shoes together and bent over her hand.

"Madame," he said.

It was a trick which he had learned and one which I was able to repeat myself, with the proper person, but I could not help observing, then, that it was a silly gesture. It was impossible to forget that Joe Stowe came from Woburn, Massachusetts. Harry was looking at him in a way I did not like, and I saw Mary's mouth fall slightly open.

"Joe," said Bella, and she gave a meaningless little giggle. "Joe!"

"I'm so glad to see you, Joe," Cousin Clothilde said. "This is Mary. Do you remember Mary?"

"I've always remembered Mary," Joe Stowe said, "and I always will remember Mary."

"Joe," said Bella quickly, "kiss her, don't kiss her hand." Then everyone was talking, and Harry was shaking hands with him.

"Hello Joe," Harry said, "I haven't seen you for a long while."

"No," said Joe, "that's so. You haven't." And then he raised his voice in a shout.

"Jim," he called, "God damn you, Jim." And he threw an arm over my shoulders and punched me in the chest like a boxer in a clinch. I could see Harry looking at us, and I understood his look.

"Harry," I heard Cousin Clothilde say, "I think we had all better have something to drink."

"Joe," I said, "who let you out in that suit?"

"Isn't it terrible?" said Bella. "I told him it was terrible."

"Now listen, sweetness," Joe said to her, "it isn't terrible at all."

Then everyone began talking and Joe looked around the room again the way he always did when he came to a place entirely new to him. I remembered how it had been when I had come into that room not so long ago. I had fitted into it as though there had been no lapse of time, but Joe Stowe could not. He had only seen the Brills at Wickford Point.

312

"I'm awfully sorry we were so late," Joe said. "The boys got hold of me. They wouldn't let me go."

"He means the reporters," Bella said. "They were asking him about everything. And then they wanted our pictures. They wanted a picture of Joe kissing me."

"Oh," said Harry, "you didn't do that, did you?"

"Why not?" said Joe. "It's news. I'm not ashamed of kissing Bella anywhere." And then he looked at Harry and began to laugh. "I remember now," he said. "You don't mean to tell me you're still worrying about what people say."

"It just happens—" began Harry, but Cousin Clothilde interrupted him.

"Harry dear," said Cousin Clothilde, "I think we all would feel better if we had a little more to drink. It must have been a very pretty picture."

"All right," said Joe, "let's have another drink. *Gambei.*"

"What does that mean?" Mary asked.

"It means 'bottoms up' in Chinese," Joe said.

"Bottoms up?" said Mary vaguely.

Bella began to laugh.

"Mary," said Bella, "don't be so silly, Mary."

"In Chinese," Joe Stowe repeated. "Jim knows what it means."

Cousin Clothilde started slightly.

"Something wet struck me on the head," she said.

Joe Stowe looked up quickly.

"It's water," he said. "It's coming through the ceiling."

"Oh dear," said Cousin Clothilde, "it's Archie. He's gone to sleep again and he's left the water running. My husband goes to sleep in the bathtub quite often."

"Oh," said Joe Stowe, "that's it, is it?"

"Sidney," said Cousin Clothilde, "hurry and wake him up."

I thought that someone would laugh, as we should have at any other time, but no one did. Instead everyone seemed embarrassed, and Joe went on talking.

"First the boys got hold of me, and then there were the customs," he said. "They went over the baggage pretty carefully,

313

but they didn't get this off me." He plunged his hand into his vest pocket and pulled out a string of pearls.

"China," said Joe looking at me. "You remember?"

"Yes," I answered, "I remember."

"Well," said Joe, "here you are, Bella."

"Why, Joe," said Bella, "*darling!*"

"I meant to keep them until we got married," Joe said, "but it doesn't matter. When are we going to get married, Bella?"

There was a silence, only momentary but long enough to make Joe's expression change.

"Why," said Cousin Clothilde, "we haven't really thought—"

Then Bella struck an attitude.

"I want to be married at Wickford Point," she said, "when the apple trees are out. I want a big reception on the lawn."

"A big reception?" Joe repeated.

"Yes," said Bella.

I saw Harry rubbing the thin spot on his head.

"All right," said Joe, "all right. Well, I'd better be going now."

"Going?" said Bella. "You can't do that. Why, Joe, you've just come."

"I have to go up to the News Club," said Joe. "Some of the boys are up there—I've told you. It's business, Bella."

"Business?" said Bella. "You want to talk about business? You can't go away and leave me now."

"I thought I'd explained it to you," Joe said. "It won't be long. Isn't there somewhere we can go and talk about it?"

"Yes," said Bella, "we can go upstairs. But Joe—just when you've come?"

"All right," said Joe. "Excuse us just a minute, will you?"

"Why yes," said Cousin Clothilde, "of course. Harry dear, I think I'd like another drink."

Through the silence beyond the half-closed door I heard Bella speaking to Joe as they walked upstairs. Her voice was low and intense, but it carried down to us.

"Not even gracious," she was saying, "not even decently polite."

Then Joe was answering more loudly.

314

"I *told* you, Bella," he said.

"It's you," said Bella, "it's always you. What about me? How do you think I feel?"

"I have friends of my own," Joe said. "If you won't come with me, I'll have to go alone."

"Oh dear," said Cousin Clothilde, "what on earth is the matter with them?"

"He wants her to go with him somewhere," I said. "Someone may want to talk to him about a job. Joe has a lot of friends. I don't see why she shouldn't go."

"Well, he needn't be in such a hurry," Harry said.

"He's always in a hurry," I answered. "That's just the way he is."

Harry shrugged his shoulders with elaborate eloquence and sat down and looked at the floor. Cousin Clothilde looked across the room at Sid, and no one spoke until Mary made a remark. Mary never seemed to know when it was better to be quiet.

"I think he's very conceited," Mary said. "I don't like him."

"That's just too bad, isn't it?" I said. "Well, you don't have to like him."

"I think he's very conceited," Mary repeated, "and he doesn't know how to dress."

"What do you know about it?" I said.

"He doesn't know how to dress," Mary repeated, "and I don't think he's a gentleman."

"He may hear you," said Cousin Clothilde, "if you speak so distinctly, darling. I think he may be very nice in time, if he just gets over hurrying. He's so in love with Bella, that it makes him rather charming. I love it when someone is in love."

Harry glanced upwards toward the wet spot in the ceiling.

"Small-town," he said.

"I love it," Cousin Clothide remarked; "but I wish they wouldn't stay up there so long."

Harry rose and pointed his finger at me.

"Speak to him," he said, "at once about those clothes. Those lapels, that waist—he must not show himself in them. Small-town."

Sid looked up.

"Not small-town," he said; "race-track—pari-mutuel."

"It's exactly what I said," Harry said, and he pointed at me again. "Everyone will say exactly what I said, if they see him in those clothes."

"Darling," said Cousin Clothilde, "it doesn't make any difference."

"Not essentially perhaps," said Harry. "The hair will be there and the face, but clothes will make a superficial difference. He never dressed like that in college, Jim. Small-town."

"That isn't at all what I meant," Cousin Clothilde answered. "I meant that nothing can be done about it really, because they're so much in love. Did you see them even when they were quarreling? They couldn't keep their hands off each other. I thought it was rather cunning."

"I thought it was very disgusting," Mary said.

"No," said Cousin Clothilde, "it's only because you don't understand."

"If you mean that nobody's kissed me, you're wrong," Mary said. "I've been kissed a great many times."

"Perhaps they won't be married," said Cousin Clothilde. "Perhaps they will only have an affair."

Harry stood up straight.

"What are they doing?" he asked. "Why don't they come down?"

"You always fuss about Bella so," said Cousin Clothilde. "Don't worry about her. They're coming down."

They both looked happier when they came into the room again.

"Well," said Bella, "what have you all been doing? We don't have to go out. Joe says it doesn't matter."

"No," said Joe, "it doesn't matter."

Joe looked at me, and then he turned to Cousin Clothilde and smiled. "I've been running around loose for quite a while," he said, "but I hope you'll get to like me, because I love Bella, Mrs. Wright."

316

Cousin Clothilde wrinkled her forehead, and at the same time she laughed.

"Sit down beside me, Joe," she said. "Why doesn't everyone sit down? Everyone loves Bella. But don't love her too much, Joe."

Joe sat down beside her and looked surprised.

"I didn't remember you said things like that," he said. She reached her hand toward him as she would have toward someone who might be hurt, and placed her hand over his where it rested on his knee.

"I know now," Joe said, "you were always kind."

"Yes," said Cousin Clothilde, "I try to be. I just say what I think and I don't always know what I mean. Don't love Bella too much, Joe. It isn't good for anyone to love Bella too much."

He glanced across the room at Bella. It was a strange, puzzled look, and Bella laughed back at him. She evidently thought it was very funny.

"She's warning you, Joe," she said. "She always warns everyone against me."

Joe looked back at Cousin Clothilde. Even then he may have known it was a warning.

"The worst of it is," he said, "I can't help it, Mrs. Wright."

"Don't call me that," said Cousin Clothilde. "You're one of the family now."

"Joe," said Bella, "come over here. Why don't we all do something? What's the use of everyone sitting here?"

But Joe did not move. I had never seen him sit so still, and Cousin Clothilde's hand still rested over his.

"Don't be so active, Bella," said Cousin Clothilde. "It's much better to sit and do nothing almost always, and then something usually happens. Someone will be coming in or something. Just sit here beside me, Joe dear, and try not to love her too much."

XXVII | When You
Call Him
That
—Smile

A nice thing about Pat Leighton was that she did not talk all the time, and that she never became an intellectual effort. There was nothing about her which disturbed me in the least; instead I was being harassed by my own ideas. The coolness on the rooftop, which had been agreeable earlier in the evening, was changing to a sort of humid warmth. The darkness was like a curtain that seemed to stop the lights and city sounds from traveling upward. My thoughts were always influenced by the weather, and I was restless with a sense that something not pleasant was impending.

I began wondering if anyone knew where I was. It was possible that George Stanhope might know, for he had seen Pat Leighton and me together a good deal. It was quite possible that we were being talked about, although I had received no intimation of it. No matter who you are, someone is always curious about your private life; there is always someone who can put the worst construction upon anything. I liked to think that I was not concerned for myself but for Pat Leighton. It seemed to amuse her when I was worried. I realized Bella might have guessed. Not so long ago she was continually asking me questions about whom I was seeing and what I was doing, but lately she had stopped asking.

Everything up on the roof where we were sitting had grown breathless. When I turned my head, there was no hint of breeze.

"We're going to have a thunderstorm," Patricia said.

"Yes," I said, "I wish it would get over with. Thunderstorms always act as though they were so damned important."

"Nature is never right in the city," Patricia said. "There should never be any nature in New York, not even Central Park. Let's stay right where we are until it starts—and keep on telling me some more. It isn't often that you talk so much. What was it you were talking about?"

"Weren't you listening?" I asked.

"Yes," she said, "I was listening, but I was thinking about you, and you weren't talking about yourself."

"I was talking about love," I said.

"Oh," she said, "yes. I remember now."

"I was saying that it was just love, love, love. Did Bella love him? Did he love Bella? And if so, exactly how did they love each other? That's all I was saying."

"You never talk about love to me," Pat said.

"No," I said, "that's true."

"Well," she said, "I'm glad you don't. It means it doesn't bother you at all. It isn't right to fuss about things like that."

"Isn't it?" I asked.

Her voice was near me, but it was so dark that I could hardly see her. It seemed almost as though I were carrying on a conversation with myself out there on the roof alone.

"No," she said, "it isn't. If you *worry*, there's always something wrong. Does anyone know you're here?"

"What makes you ask that?" I asked her.

"Because I knew you were thinking of it," she said. "You always get so proper when you think of things like that. What would Bella Brill do if she knew you were here?"

"She would use it," I said. "She would wait until just the wrong time and bring it up. Or else she would get me to do something for her so she wouldn't mention it."

Pat's voice, tinged with a note of amusement, came to me through the dark again.

"Why do you care?" she asked.

"On account of you," I said. "She's dangerous sometimes."
She laughed, but I could not tell why she was amused.
"Well," she said, "I rather wish she knew."
"That isn't funny," I said.
"I wouldn't mind," she said. "It doesn't matter as long as I don't. I wish you didn't."
"You'd mind," I said, "if you'd ever done anything like this before."
She did not answer and her thoughts must have moved away, for next she mentioned two words pulled out of nowhere.
"Harris Harbor," she said.
"Exactly why," I asked her, "did you think of that?"
I remembered that Joe Stowe had thought that it would be all right when he and Bella moved to Harris Harbor for the summer in 1932. He had thought that it would be all right because she would not be at Wickford Point. There were no Brills at Harris Harbor, at least not until Harry and Sid found that they could commute there quite comfortably from New York, and not until Mary found that it was a good place to go to get over the time she had had with the minister's son. Yes, Joe Stowe had thought, when he rented that place on the Sound, that everything would start going smoothly, and he had borrowed a thousand dollars from the bank to do it.
"Harris Harbor," Pat Leighton repeated through the dark. "I came over with the Hopewells for a drink. Bella was always asking people over, and they had that Japanese who made *canapés* and little baskets out of carrots."
"Igawa," I said; "and he used to have little flags on toothpicks. He went crazy." This did not seem peculiar to me, because everyone went crazy after working for a Brill. "That's true—he was always making little baskets out of vegetables."
"Harris Harbor," she said. "That was where I met you, dear. You and Joe Stowe were drinking whisky."
"Well, everyone has to meet somewhere," I answered.
"And you didn't pay any attention to me at all," she said. "We

might just as well have been on the subway. It's funny, isn't it?"

"Depending on how you look at it," I said.

"And do you know what Bella wanted? She'd been reading that Mrs. Bertrand Russell book, *The Right To Be Happy*, do you remember?"

I doubted if Bella had been reading it, because I knew that Bella was too lazy to read much of anything. She had the desire for erudition, but not the will to work for it. She had an especial gift for taking things from other people's minds and making them appear her own contributions, so that she really seemed very clever. She gave the impression of knowing all about the stock market and all about the National Socialist party in Germany and about ideology and psychoanalysis and about Philip Guedalla. Sometimes she would carry books around from room to room, intending perhaps to read them, but never doing so. Also she was usually talking about writing, really good writing, not the sort of thing you did for money. It was quite a joke to her that she was married to someone who wrote for money.

"Do you know what she wanted?" Patricia asked. "She wanted me to have an affair with Joe."

"What?" I said. "You never told me that." She had been there at Harris Harbor, and I had never noticed her. I could scarcely remember what she looked like at Harris Harbor, and yet now here we were.

"No," she said, "I never told you. It wasn't particularly important because she hoped that almost anyone would have an affair with Joe."

"Why?" I asked.

"Why?" she repeated. "I suppose she wondered how she would feel. Hasn't she always wanted to know how she would feel about things?"

"Perhaps," I answered. "I don't know." But I knew well enough. She always wanted to experience everything without ever being touched herself.

"But she was beautiful," I said, and that seemed to explain

321

everything, for somehow her beauty excused a good deal when I thought of Bella Brill. It had always been something on which she could rely. . . .

Harris Harbor was one of those places which you recognize even if you have never been there—the station with its shrubbery, the open space by the platform, and the row of taxicabs.

"I want to go to Mr. Stowe's house," I said to the driver who took my bag. "He rented it for the summer." The man scratched his chin, evidently reviewing all the personalities he had recently encountered, and then he grinned.

"Oh yes," he said, "I know him, the guy with the sandy hair."

They lived in a brown frame house with a big veranda, set on a square of lawn fronting a road called Seashore Drive, although there was nothing but a distant view of Long Island Sound.

"But there are lots of lovely people here," the driver said.

I walked across the porch, into the hall, without knocking; and then I heard low voices from a room on the left.

"Norman," I heard Bella say, "please don't, Norman."

"Belle," I called, "where are you?"

She was in a long room furnished in the nondescript fashion of houses that rent for the summer. She had been sitting on the sofa beside a blond young man with horn-rimmed glasses, who got up so awkwardly that he nearly tipped over a little table with ice and bottles on it. Bella had on a violet jersey and a violet tweed skirt. Her legs, and somehow one always saw her legs, were bare and beautifully brown, and she was wearing sandals.

"Darling!" said Bella, "Jim! Why didn't you let me know the train you were coming on, and I would have met you? How did you ever find this funny little place?"

"It wasn't hard," I said. "I didn't mean to disturb you, Belle."

"You didn't disturb me at all," said Bella. "Joe always picks out the stuffiest places to live in. This is Mr. Epps, Norman Epps."

"How do you do," I said.

"I think perhaps I'd better be going now," said Mr. Epps.

"No," said Bella, "don't go, Norman. You and Jim will have so much to talk about. Jim writes too, you know."

Mr. Epps and I examined each other critically. There may be a certain amount of brotherhood in other arts, although I doubt it, but certainly not in the writing profession.

"Oh yes," said Mr. Epps, "I know. I think really I'd better be going." And he went.

"Mr. Epps and I are going to collaborate," said Bella.

"Collaborate on what?" I asked.

"Darling," said Bella, "some people think I have brains—not my family, of course. But Mr. Epps happens to think so, funnily enough. I'm helping Mr. Epps with his book. He comes over every afternoon."

"Who is he anyway?" I asked. "I have never heard of Mr. Norman Epps."

Bella smiled at me condescendingly, and there was a constraint between us as if we were strangers, except that the constraint was worse because we were not. We knew each other perfectly well; and even when I told myself with a certain surprise that Bella Brill had changed, something deeper in me contradicted. She was the same person I had always known. It was only that certain tendencies that were latent in her had developed.

"Well," said Bella, "he didn't know you either, darling. And if you don't know Norman Epps, it simply means that you don't keep in touch with book reviews and critical comment, darling. It simply means that you're just like Joe, stewing in your own juice. It just happens that Norman Epps is very worth-while and interesting."

"You mean you're interested in him?" I asked.

Bella shrugged her shoulders.

"Don't be so old-fashioned," she said. "That isn't what I mean at all. I can't sit here all by myself all the time, can I? There's a poky little bathing beach down the road, and I'll watch you go for a swim if you want one."

"No thanks," I said. "Where's Joe?"

Bella pointed toward the ceiling with an elaborate, wearied gesture.

"Upstairs working," she said. "At least he calls it working. Any time I look at him he's usually reading a magazine. The whole house has to be kept quiet. He can't be disturbed about anything, and there he sits reading the *Saturday Evening Post*. Or else he goes down to the beach and sits in the sun, but he can't be disturbed on the beach either, and when he is disturbed, all he talks about is money. He'll be down after a while. Don't you want a drink, darling?"

I bent over the little table and poured myself a drink, and sat down and shook the ice gently back and forth in the glass. I began to think that Bella had grown hard. I did not like the way she was behaving.

"Where have you been?" she said. "You always keep going away, abroad and places for months and years, and we always just sit here. Joe never takes me anywhere. He says he hasn't the money. I tell him he could save all the money he wants if he would only go to Wickford Point."

Bella sat down heavily on the sofa and curled her legs under her.

"Darling," she said, "will you give me a cigarette? Sometimes I think I'm simply going to scream."

"All right," I told her, "go ahead and scream."

She looked very pretty sitting on the sofa, but it was the disturbing beauty of discontent. It was dangerous for anyone to look the way she did.

"Darling," she said, "I always feel better when I see you. I just mean that I wish someone would take me away somewhere when everything is dull."

"Most of life is pretty dull," I told her.

"Well," said Bella, "it shouldn't be."

"You can't help it, Belle," I said.

"Well," said Bella, "then someone ought to help it. Everyone should have a chance to develop."

"Why don't you have a baby, Belle?" I said.

Bella looked at me and laughed.

"You do think of the damnedest things," she answered, "don't you, darling? Of all the obvious damn things! What good would a baby do me? It simply means that you don't think I'm interesting. You used to think so—everybody did, and I was interesting too. I want to see people. I want to do real things."

"Well," I said, "Joe is interesting. Look here, what's happened? What's the matter with you, Belle?"

"Sometimes," Bella answered, "I simply think I'm going to scream."

I asked again, "What's the matter with you, Belle?"

It was a stupid question. I had seen other people like her. She was only demonstrating that marriage is a difficult institution—too difficult for her, at any rate. There was no use asking her, because everything was the matter.

"Oh God," said Bella, "I don't know. Why do you make me sit here and make everything turn around in my mind? Maybe no one is interesting if you see too much of him. Maybe it isn't Joe's fault, darling. It's probably just the way people are. I thought—"

"What did you think?" I asked.

"Oh hell," said Bella, "I don't know what I thought. Let's forget about it. We're having some people over for dinner, lots of people. Joe doesn't know it yet. Here's Joe now."

Joe was in his shirt sleeves and he looked hot and rather tired.

"Jim," he said, "why didn't someone tell me you were here?"

"You said you didn't want to be disturbed, darling," Bella answered. "Don't you remember? You were very emphatic about it at lunch."

"I didn't mean Jim," Joe answered. "Jim doesn't disturb me."

"How did everything go?" Bella asked. "Did the boy meet the girl?"

Joe looked at her and started to speak and checked himself.

"Listen Bella," he said, "please don't do that." It was more of

325

an appeal than a request, but both of us must have understood him.

"All right, dear," Bella said, "but don't complain that I don't speak to you about your work, because when I do speak to you, you don't want to talk about it."

"I know," said Joe, "I guess I'm pretty difficult. Excuse me, Bella."

"And now you'd better go and get on some other clothes," Bella said. "Harry and Sid are coming on the six-fifteen."

"Oh," said Joe, "they are, are they?"

"But I'll drive down to meet them, dear," Bella said, "and then some people are coming over for dinner, and we're all going to eat on the porch."

"Who?" said Joe. "What people? I didn't know that anyone was coming."

"It won't be any trouble, dear," Bella said. "We have to have people over sometimes."

"Sometimes," Joe said. "How often is sometimes? I wanted to see Jim."

"Joe, dear," said Bella, "you'd better take Jim upstairs and show him his room, and I have to go and see Igawa. He's making things for cocktails, and Joe——"

"Yes," Joe said.

"Igawa has a friend helping him, and I have to give him five dollars, and when you're upstairs will you write out a check of fifty-five dollars for Mr. Pitsky? He's coming with some more liquor."

"Now look here——" Joe began, but Bella interrupted him reproachfully.

"Darling," she said, "Jim's here. We have to do something for Jim, don't we?"

"I just hoped we were going to be quiet, that's all," said Joe. "I wanted to have a talk with Jim."

"But Joe," said Bella, "we're always quiet. You'll have plenty of time to talk with Jim. Don't be so cross. You act——"

"I'm not being cross, Bella," Joe said. "Come on, Jim, let's go

326

upstairs. If Bella wants to have a party, Bella's going to have a party."

"Be sure to put on a clean shirt, darling," said Bella, "not the one you wore last night. And you'd better let Jim look at you before you come downstairs."

"What for?" I asked.

"Well," said Bella, "you know the way Joe dresses, dear."

Joe walked ahead of me carrying my bag.

"Jesus," he said, "I didn't know anyone was coming."

"Bella's looking fine," I said.

"Isn't she," said Joe. "Bella's wonderful. Here's your room."

The room was done in faded chintz, with white wicker furniture, and a white iron bed. Joe put my bags on a chair and explained the details of the plumbing, which Harry and Sid would use also.

"You're looking tired," I said.

Joe shook his head and grinned at me.

"I've been working all day," he said. "You know the way it gets you when nothing's coming out just right."

He must have read some expression on my face because he went on more quickly: "The thing I'm doing, I mean. You know the way it is. It's sort of hard on Bella, but she's been wonderful. She doesn't know much about money, that's all."

"If you're hard up, Joe..." I said.

"No," said Joe, "that's all right. I'm going to have them all licked yet. Someday Bella isn't going to have to worry at all."

"Well," I said, "that's fine."

He looked at me, and he did not have to speak. He was telling me quite definitely in that single glance that there were matters which he did not want discussed. He wanted me to feel that it was fine as far as he was concerned.

"Thanks ever so much for having me, Joe," I said.

"It's swell having you," he answered. "I guess we'd better get dressed now, if everybody's coming."

I was left alone faced with the impersonality of their guest room. I had the uncomfortable sensation of listening to things

327

which were not meant for me to hear or see, of spying upon what Joe Stowe wished to hide. And he was a friend of mine. Bella had been hard, but Joe looked worn and defeated.

I had been away a good deal since Bella and Joe were married. Perhaps the length of my absences and my other preoccupations may have added to this sense of uneasiness. Very few individuals of my acquaintance were the same after they married. The matters one had in common with them no longer were of much importance; yet I had not expected that silence from Joe, and Bella's attitude was disconcerting. I had seen marriage make plain girls pretty and cross girls jovial. Indeed marriage was a remedy commonly suggested, by persons who knew no better, for almost any case of anti-sociability.

"What she needs is to get married," they used to say. "She would be perfectly all right if only she were married."

No doubt the same authorities had said that Bella would be all right when she was married; but marriage had not helped Bella Brill. It had made her, in my estimation, selfish and disagreeable. It had brought a lot out in her, but not the right things. . . .

Bella had acquired the power—more common in women than in men—of changing personality under a given stimulus. In fact I heard someone say that night—I don't know who it was, and at any rate you can hear almost anything if you listen long enough:—

"Isn't Mrs. Stowe charming? It did her so much good to get married."

She had changed her mood with her dress—and the dress was remarkably successful—purchased, she explained to me, from an acquaintance, a model at Madame Mumford's, who was having trouble with one of her boy friends so that she simply had to sell something. It had the severity of a very expensive garment; now that Bella was wearing it, she was self-possessed and gay.

"All the women will be interested in Joe," she said, "if Joe will pay any attention to them. I do wish he would look at someone else sometime. Now I want you to meet everyone, darling."

She put her arm through mine and led me around to the men

in dinner coats and women in summer prints. There were men who were drinking too much and girls who were drinking too much, some who were bored and some who were happy.

"Those are the Hopewells over there," said Bella, "and that's a girl staying with them. She went to college with Elsie Hopewell. I don't like college girls, do you?"

"No," I said, "they show off as a rule. What's her name?"

"Leighton," said Bella, "Patricia Leighton. It's a rather common name. This is Jim, Patricia, my cousin Mr. Calder."

That was how I met her, and it meant nothing at all. Igawa's Japanese friend, in a white coat that was too large for him, handed me a cocktail which was warm and which contained too much French vermouth.

"You haven't been around here much, have you?" Miss Leighton said.

"No," I said, "I've been abroad."

"You're related to Bella, aren't you?" she asked. "You don't look like any of the Brills." And that was all I can remember.

Then there were other names and faces. I heard Harry talking very cordially to some people in a corner and I heard Sidney discoursing on art. I saw Joe Stowe mixing a highball and I walked over to him.

"You'd better have some whisky, Jim," he said. "It does better than those cocktails. Did you ever see so many people?"

"They're very nice," I said.

"Yes," said Joe, "they're very nice. I guess they think I'm queer."

"Why should they?" I asked him.

"Why shouldn't they?" said Joe. "Maybe I am queer. Look at Bella. Isn't she beautiful?"

"Bella's all right," I said.

"Did I say she wasn't?" Joe asked me, and then I saw that Joe had finished nearly half the bottle of whisky.

"Now," I said, "take it easy, Joe. You haven't had anything to eat."

"All right," said Joe. "I'm all right. Do you remember things?

Let's remember things. I don't see you any more. I don't get a chance to see anyone any more."

Harry tapped me on the shoulder and looked meaningly at Joe.

"We're all going to eat out on the porch," he said. "We'll have to pass things, Joe." And then he whispered to me: "He's drunk, isn't he?"

"Not noticeably," I said. "Joe can drink a lot without showing it."

"Well, it doesn't look well," said Harry, "standing in the corner drinking whisky."

As a matter of fact the whisky did Joe more good than harm. It did as much for him as the new dress had done for Bella. It polished all the half-concealed facets of his character. Now that he was making an effort, he was head and shoulders above everyone in the room from the point of view of intellect or ability or experience. He had been dull before; but now his face, which had been uncouth and tired, became animated. By the time supper was over nearly everyone was listening to him. There are so many people who can travel and yet return home with almost nothing, but Joe's mind was full of neglected details—the way the straw fires snapped in the mud stoves, the way iron-shod wheels jolted over rocks, the way the camels' bells sounded.

"Jim," he called to me, "do you remember?" And I began to remember, too, all sorts of anecdotes about this and that. We were having a good time.

Quite a long while afterwards, while Joe was still talking, Harry touched me on the shoulder again.

"Come out on the lawn," he said. "It makes my head tired listening to him."

I followed Harry down the creaking steps of the piazza, out to a dark square on the small lawn, and from it we could see the lighted windows and hear that background of voices. I was feeling better, a good deal better then.

"Quite a party," I said.

"Oh," Harry said, "you think so, do you?" He laughed lightly. "You think it's nice for Bella to be here, do you?"

"Yes," I answered. "What do you think?"

Harry gazed at the house and made an eloquent, careless gesture. His tone was elaborately patient. "The neighborhood," he said, "the plumbing."

"It looks all right to me," I said.

"You have taste," said Harry; "why not try without prejudice to use your taste? What do you see? Nothing that isn't second-class. My sister is being dragged down into humdrum second-class."

"I'd like to see you pay the bills to run this place," I said.

"Your remark," said Harry, "has nothing whatever to do with the situation. The point is that my sister, my own sister, is being made to live the life of the second-class. I sit here night after night and see it."

"Well, why don't you go somewhere else?" I said.

"Your question," said Harry, "has nothing to do with the point. We are not second-class people, Jim. Call it background, call it anything you like. We have never been humdrum, we have never been second-class. You don't know what it does to me just to sit here and watch it, and to watch Bella being dragged—" He paused and shrugged his shoulders, still staring at the house.

I was tempted to laugh, but I knew that he was serious according to his lights, and I appreciated the peculiar composition of his mind which had led him so far from reality. I knew him well enough to see that he was deeply moved.

"Perhaps I am not making myself clear," he said. "I simply mean that Bella needs something else. None of this is Bella; none of this is us. It makes us all very worried."

"What are you driving at?" I asked. "You're his guest, aren't you? He's paying for it, isn't he?"

"I supposed that would be coming," said Harry, "some obvious thought like that. What is money? Do you think we care about money? Do you mean money influences an attitude toward life? I'm discussing attitude, not money. I'm discussing background, tradition. I happen to be very broad-minded. I can stand starvation if it isn't second-class, and so can Bella, but not second-class—oh no."

It never did any good to tell him what I thought of him, but I tried again. It was one of the last times that I tried.

"Has it ever occurred to you," I asked, "that you're getting more preposterous, and more ridiculous every year you live?" Harry gave no sign of being angry.

"Hardly that," he answered, "hardly. Not preposterous, not ridiculous, no, no. I am only growing more realistic, while you allow yourself to move away from realism. I know what I live for and I know what Bella lives for, and it isn't for any of this."

"Suppose you talk sense," I suggested. "What do you mean by 'this'?"

"Why not be frank," said Harry, "and admit you understand me? I mean Stowe, of course. Obviously he's not making Bella happy. Suppose one looks at it fearlessly. He is not making Bella happy because he does not give her what she wants or what she is used to or what she must have for any suitable development. He cannot do it because he is second-class."

A sense of futility came over me which was greater than any particular sensation of anger.

"Look at it logically," Harry continued, "and without emotion. Joe is obviously not first-class. He won't get any further. He's trying, I admit he's trying, but Bella can't stay this way always. Face the facts; he'll never make more than ten thousand a year."

"Suppose he doesn't," I said. "Why should he?"

"I'm not supposing," Harry answered, "I know. He's a typical ten-thousand-dollar-a-year man, or less. I'm not speaking of the sum as money."

"Oh, you aren't aren't you?" I asked. "When did you ever make ten thousand dollars?"

"I'm not speaking of the sum," Harry replied patiently. "I'm speaking of the point of view. There is nothing in this country worse than the ten-thousand-dollar point of view—the ten-thousand-dollar attitude. It gets nowhere at all except to mediocrity."

"That's interesting," I said. "If you feel this way, you ought to get out of his house."

332

I was thinking of the basic laws of hospitality, but they did not trouble Harry Brill.

"Has Bella ever spoken to you about a man named Norman Epps?" he asked.

"I saw him," I said. "What of it?"

"He illustrates the point," said Harry. "Norman Epps is first-class. I think that Bella should marry Norman Epps."

I gave an incredulous start.

"Now exactly why," said Harry, "should that remark surprise you? Why not face the obvious? Bella can't go on this way. She ought to marry Norman Epps."

I moved nearer Harry and looked carefully into his face where the lights from the house fell on it. I examined his high nose and his high forehead.

"You God-damned son of a bitch," I said.

Harry's face and his whole body swung toward me. I saw him open his lips and close them.

"Coming here," I said, "to someone else's house, being his guest, sponging off him—"

Harry found his voice before I finished.

"Jim," he said, "try to be a gentleman. Try not to lose your temper. Listen to me carefully while I repeat what I said. Bella should get a divorce, of course. I'm speaking for the whole family. Clothilde thinks she should marry Norman Epps. Everybody thinks so."

I was so intent on my own feelings that I did not know anyone was near us until I saw Harry's expression change.

"Why hello, Joe," he said. "Come on over here." And then I saw Joe Stowe walking toward us across the lawn, not ten feet away.

"Hello boys," Joe said. "Having a little argument?"

"Oh no," said Harry, "not an argument at all. Quite a party, Joe. I've been meaning to ask you something. Bella wanted me to ask you. I told her you wouldn't mind."

"Mind what?" Joe asked.

333

Harry smiled.

"I don't know whether you know the Jaeckels," he said, "some friends of ours living on the shore up beyond Boston? They asked me up for the week end."

"You mean the day after tomorrow?" Joe said. "Well, that couldn't be better. Is Sid going too?"

"Yes," said Harry, "Sid's going too, and Bella was wondering if she couldn't go along, just for the change. She said you wouldn't mind if we all took your car."

"What?" Joe asked. "Does Bella want to go? I thought she was having a good time here."

"Just for a change," Harry's voice sounded casual and smooth. "You know how Bella is. She likes to move about—just a day or two at the Jaeckels and then a day or two at Wickford Point."

"Oh," said Joe, "she wants to go to Wickford Point?"

"Just to see the family," Harry said, "just for a day or two. You wouldn't mind if we used your car, would you, Joe?"

"No," said Joe. "I gave Bella that car. I'll talk to Bella about it later. Maybe I've been rather busy lately. Of course if she wants to go—Are you going too, Jim?"

"Not by a damn sight," I said. "I never heard of this before." Harry put his hands in his pockets and smiled as he did when he had done something clever. He was beyond all reason and beyond all pain, moving in an intellectual sphere which was entirely his property.

"That's awfully nice of you, Joe," he said. "I'll tell Bella. We're awfully much obliged." He turned and strolled back toward the house while Joe and I stood watching him.

"I heard what you called him, Jim," Joe said. "You're mad about something, aren't you?"

"Yes," I said, "I'm pretty mad."

"Well," Joe said, "I've often wanted to call him that myself, but he isn't that, not really. He's really a collector's item."

"Oh," I said, "you think so?"

Joe still stood watching Harry's back as Harry moved languidly away.

"He's what you called him, all right," he said; "but he ought to be in a bottle. It's the way he excuses himself for living. We all have to excuse ourselves some way. Sid does the same thing, but he's better because he doesn't excuse himself so much, and what's more they do something to you simply by existing. They're very, very interesting."

"To hell with the whole lot of them," I said, and I meant it then. I had a feeling of revulsion against the whole *galère* such as I had never felt before. I wanted to say what I thought of them, but I was struggling with repressions and with queer unhappy jealousies which were too much a part of my own life for me to get them straight.

"I wouldn't say that," Joe answered.

"You're too easy on them, Joe," I said. "It doesn't pay." Joe still stood there, and he did not answer for quite a while.

"Not really easy," he said finally. "As a matter of fact I hate their guts, but I wonder—" His voice trailed off into silence, and then he must have caught his mind back from some other thought. "I wonder what's going to happen to them."

I had often wondered the same thing, but I knew the answer. "Nothing," I said, "absolutely nothing."

He simply stood there, and he made no reply.

"You mustn't let her go," I said. "Do you hear me, Joe?" I asked the last question because he was so long in answering that I was not at all sure that he had heard me. That silence of his showed me that I was interfering in something which was entirely his business.

"If she wants to go, she can," he said. "Never mind it, Jim."

Somehow I was absolutely certain that this was an ending, that if she went away she would not come back, ever. I have often wondered if he realized it, too.

"Let her go if she wants to," he repeated. "She's always restless. I'll be waiting for her when she gets back. I'm pretty damn tired."

335

He did look very tired. His love of life was no longer there, and again I had that uncomfortable sensation—I was seeing and listening indecently to things that were not meant for me. I seemed to be prying into all that was private between Joe Stowe and Bella Brill. I seemed to be hearing conversations in their bedroom and to be examining all the furtive thoughts they had covered up.

I started to answer but he put his hand on my arm and stopped me.

"Let's skip it," Joe said. "I don't want to talk about it now."

"All right," I said, "I'm not talking."

His fingers gripped my arm more tightly and perhaps he was glad that I was there. For a moment I thought he was going to say something more, and it might have been better if he had, but perhaps he knew me too well for unconsidered confidences.

"Let's go on back to the house," he said, "they'll be wondering where we are."

Bella saw us when we reached the porch. She came up to me and put her arm through mine and pressed it close to her side.

"Jim," she said, "aren't you going to talk to me?" And then she whispered so that no one else could hear: "I've missed you so much, darling." But I knew that it would do no good to talk. There was nothing for me to say.

XXVIII | Thunder on the Left

It was getting darker, and in the direction of the Hudson River there was a flash of lightning, and a sound like a distant gun.

"We'd better be going in," I said.

"No," Pat Leighton answered. "Let's wait till it begins to rain."

That distant thunder and flash of light reminded me of the way things come out of the past and strike you. You think that everything is over and then it all comes back out of nowhere. I had the same feeling of revulsion and the same dull, hopeless sort of anger, although that night at Harris Harbor was quite a while ago.

"And you didn't look at me at all," Pat said. "I remember when you came up on the porch. I thought you were in love with her. Were you in love with her, Jim?"

It was the first time she had ever asked me that.

"No," I answered, "I don't think so."

"Of course you didn't think so," she said. "You wouldn't because you are so unanalytical about those things."

"Am I?" I asked. "Anyway, it doesn't matter."

"Of course," she said, "it doesn't matter. There was nothing you could have done, nothing anyone could have done."

I sat there silently, still thinking of Harris Harbor. I was thinking that Joe was fortunate to have recovered from that marriage. By the time it had broken up it was almost too late. Patricia

337

Leighton's thoughts must have been moving in the same direction. "What year was it," she asked, "when you were in Harris Harbor?"

For a moment I had difficulty in recollecting. Time has a curious way of contracting or of extending itself, so that years occasionally lose their meaning.

"That was 1932," I said. "I remember because I had come back from abroad." I paused and looked out over the city. It was growing darker all the time.

"Then they had been married for six years," Pat Leighton said. "I hadn't realized it was as long as that."

"There was another year," I answered, "before she finally went to Reno. They should have broken off years before. They must have known it wouldn't work."

"It's hard to stop when you've started," she answered, and then she repeated what she had said before: "There was nothing you could have done, nothing anyone could have done."

"To hell with the whole lot of them," I said again.

"And you called Harry a name," she said. "I think it was rather sensible of you."

"That's a silly remark," I said.

"No," she said, "it isn't silly. . . . Jim," she asked me, "will you really take me to Wickford Point? I'd like to see them there."

"They'll all be there this week end," I said, and then something made me laugh. "They'll all be just the same. I'll meet you on Saturday if you take the midnight to Boston."

"That's fine," she said. "I can leave Friday night."

Everything always seemed to end at Wickford Point. I had just left it and now actually I wanted to return, although I would surely be planning to get away from it as soon as I arrived.

"Cousin Sue's dead," I said, "and Mr. Morrissey is dead. She used to read him Tacitus when he had rheumatism—but everyone else is just the same. Why do you want to go there?"

"I don't exactly know," she said, "but I'd really like to. When did you see Bella last?"

"It's funny," I said, "I've been thinking of it all day. I saw

338

Bella yesterday. She was going to stay with the Jaeckels. Then I saw Joe, and then Avery Gifford was on the train. Just like cards in a poker hand—they might have been dealt out. It's funny how faces keep turning up, just like cards."

Rain fell on my hand, a single, heavy, cool drop out of the dark sky. Its contact was like a period to everything I had been thinking. It brought me back to the present and reminded me that I was living and that all the things I had recalled were much better forgotten.

"It's beginning to rain," I said. Pat's voice came through the dark more clearly.

"No," she said, "it isn't raining yet. When did she get here?"

"Who?" I asked. "I'm sorry..."

"Bella Brill," Pat said, "when did she get here?"

I was as startled as if Bella had suddenly appeared right beside us at that moment.

"Let's talk sense," I said. "I don't see what you mean. Bella isn't here. I left her back there with the Jaeckels."

Pat Leighton began to laugh.

"My dear," she said, "she isn't there, because she's here. I saw her this afternoon on Forty-Second Street with one man, and I saw her this evening out at dinner with another."

"Oh," I said, "you did?"

It was so like Bella that I was not particularly surprised. No matter where she was, she was always trying to go somewhere else. Then I remembered the last thing she had said to me.

"What's the matter, Jim?" Pat asked.

"Nothing," I answered, "nothing much. I just remember—she wanted to know where she could reach me if she needed me."

There was a moment's silence and then her voice was sharper.

"They're always after you, aren't they?" she said.

Neither Pat nor I was happy any longer. There was an awkwardness between us just as though someone else had come in. "And if Bella needed you," she said, slowly, "you'd leave me, wouldn't you?"

I thought for a little while before I answered.

339

"No," I said, "not exactly."

"You would," she asked me again, "wouldn't you?"

Bella Brill would have enjoyed listening to that question. It was just the sort of situation that appealed to her. I wanted to explain exactly how I felt about Bella Brill, but I could not explain even to myself.

"I wouldn't know," I said. And I was right. "I'd help her," I added. "I'd help her out of anything."

"There's one thing about you," she said, "you always tell the truth. I don't care much what happens as long as you tell the truth. I wonder why you'd help her. Do you know?"

"Yes," I said, "that's easy." And I was not uncomfortable any more. No one had ever asked me such questions and I felt better now that I was answering them. "I'd help her because I always have. That's the only reason."

"That's true, of course," Pat said. "Everybody always does things because they always have. You're worried about her, aren't you? Well go ahead, it doesn't make me mad, particularly."

"Something's going on," I said. "Those men she was with, do you remember what they looked like? I just have a feeling that something's happened. I've been thinking about her and then we've been talking about her, and now you say she's here."

"Jim," she said, "don't think so much. I didn't pay much attention to them. The first one was tall and dark, rather handsome, with a hard face, the sort of man you'd see at a night club dancing—shiny hair."

"A snappy dresser?" I inquired.

"Yes," she said, "a very snappy dresser." And I knew who it must have been. It was Mr. Howard Berg, and she had traveled down to New York with him. On the whole I thought it better not to ask myself why.

"Did you ever hear of a Mr. Howard Berg?" I asked, "a big power in Wall Street? That's what Bella says he is."

"No," Pat Leighton said. "Did you?"

"Well," I said, "that was certainly Mr. Howard Berg. What did the other one look like?"

340

"Pleasant," said Patricia. "Blond, rather large. He didn't look like one of Bella's friends at all." I had a suspicion at that instant that made me catch my breath.

"You mean he was respectable," I said, "and not a snappy dresser?"

"Yes," she answered. "He was in a gray flannel suit, a rather baggy suit. He might have been someone from out of town. You know the way they look—not used to things."

I knew who it was then. I was just as sure as if I had seen them both.

"What's the matter, Jim?" she asked.

"Good God," I said, "it's Avery Gifford, Pat. She's got hold of him again. It's starting all over again. Nothing ever stops."

There was another clap of thunder. I started up from where I was sitting because the rain was coming down. It had arrived suddenly as those summer downpours do, and now the whole roof was wet.

"Hurry," I said, "let's go inside. Nothing ever stops."

I slammed the French door behind us, and there we stood side by side in the dimly lighted living room. There were flowers on the piano and chintz covers over the chairs and sofa, and I saw the landscape I had bought for her above the fireplace. We had seen it in a window once when we were walking together and she had said she liked it. We stood there and the wind had risen so that the rain came splashing against the windows as though a hand were throwing it. She looked up at me and smiled.

"You can't get away now," she said.

I had never been so glad to be with her. Everything in the room seemed safe.

"Pat," I said, "I don't want to get away."

It was as though I had arrived at a place where I had always wanted to go; it had something to do with that rain and something to do with Avery Gifford. It was a silly enough thought but it made everything seem all right.

"You'll have to stay here," Pat said. "You can't help it, now it's raining."

The rain had shut out everything—all the Brills and Wickford Point. It was like a mathematical equation that left us only with ourselves. "You're not thinking about anything else?" she asked me.

"No," I answered, "not a thing."

"That's fine," she said. "Forget about all the rest of them."

"You know the answer to everything, don't you?" I said. And she smiled.

"Yes," she answered, "everything, as long as it's just you and me. But please forget about the rest of them."

The air was cleaner after the rain but the streets were growing hot again already. It was as hot that morning as it might be in Singapore. Pat Leighton and I walked part way downtown together. Then we stood on the street corner talking for a while, and I don't believe either of us wanted to say good-by. I knew that when I left her all sorts of uncomfortable odds and ends of life would reappear again.

"Tell me where you'll be today," she said.

"I'll be seeing Stanhope," I answered, "and then I'll take the one o'clock or the three o'clock or the five o'clock to Boston. I'll be back at Wickford Point tonight."

When I said it, I felt that I was going a very long distance away from her.

"I'll think of you there tonight," she said. "But I'll see you on Saturday. It's only a day or two, isn't it?"

"I'll be there," I said. "Be sure you remember to come." I began to be afraid that she might not come. So often when you said good-by to someone, everything was over.

"Don't worry, I'll be there," she said, "and Jim—"

"Yes," I said.

"You're thinking of going away somewhere. You really are, aren't you?"

"I've been considering it," I said. "That's what always happens when I stay up there too long."

342

"All right," she said. "But just remember this—maybe I'll go with you."

"You'd be an awful fool," I told her.

"That's up to me," she answered. "You'd better kiss me now. We can't stay here all morning."

"Not out on the street," I said, and she began to laugh.

"Hurry up," she said, "and get it over with. You're awfully funny sometimes."

XXIX | Nothing Ever Stops

The girl behind the early American pine table at the Stanhope office was twisting her mouth to one side and working on it with a lipstick, but when she saw me she straightened it and smiled.

"Good morning, Mr. Calder," she said. "Mr. Stanhope isn't busy, and someone has been trying to get in touch with you. We said you were expected. That's all right I hope."

"Did they leave a number?" I asked.

"No," she answered, "they didn't leave anything. They said they'd call again."

George Stanhope was speaking over the telephone. He was in his shirt sleeves bending over his table and he waved his hand at me in a gesture which indicated that he wanted me to sit down and be quiet. Then he continued drawing squares and circles on a piece of paper in front of him.

"Definitely," he was saying, "yes, definitely. She will do two more of the Mr. Blumpey stories, but there will have to be a raise in rate if she is going to stay happy. She'd be happy the way it is, but the Midtown people want to put Mr. Blumpey on the radio. Definitely, it's just what they were looking for. We can't give you all rights without a raise in rate. No, definitely, John. All right. Are you buying the Baxter? Yes, Jim's right here in the office now. I'll see you at lunchtime, John."

George Stanhope set down the telephone and pressed a button.

"Just a minute, Jim," he said. "We're cleaning up the Blumpey thing. All right, Ella darling, come in and take this telegram to Mrs. Marietta Fosdick. 'Dear Etta, they are simply nuts about the Blumpey thing and they are raising one hundred dollars. Isn't that perfectly swell? Congratulations.'" George tapped the desk with his pencil.

"What's the Blumpey thing?" I asked. "Is it a series of stories about a lovable character?"

"It really looks as though Marietta had gotten somewhere this time," he said. "It's about an old crossing tender who befriends anyone whose car stops at the crossing. He's just what they wanted down the street."

"And then the car gets stalled right out in the middle of the tracks," I said, "when the Chicago Flyer is going by, and there he has a problem."

"As a matter of fact," George Stanhope said, "the young people are quarreling and the car does get stalled. But those Blumpey stories are going to go. Have you got those revisions?"

"Yes," I said. "I did them yesterday afternoon. The boy misunderstands the girl. They hate each other, but they love each other."

"That's exactly right," said George. "You'd better let me see it. They want it down the street. The Old Man was asking for it this morning. I've got plenty of time to read it. Ella darling, I don't want to be disturbed for fifteen minutes."

George picked up the manuscript I gave him and arranged the papers neatly. He had already forgotten about the lovable crossing tender, and now he would be able to remember everything I had ever written, and I wondered how he could do it.

"Where were you last night?" he asked. "I tried to get hold of you."

"I must have been out," I said.

He picked up his pencil and drew a square on his yellow paper. "You aren't in any trouble, are you?" he asked.

"No," I answered. "Why?"

"It just crossed my mind," said George. "Someone's been

trying to get you on the telephone, a woman. I tried to talk to her myself. She wouldn't give a name."

"Well," I said, "I don't know who it is, definitely, George. Do you see where those revisions go in the manuscript?"

George Stanhope nodded and lighted a cigarette, and he began to read while I sat looking out the window watching a spot where the sun struck on the East River. I was thinking of all the times I had sat there while George Stanhope was reading, and of all the fictitious destinies he had handled.

"Jim," he said, "that's swell."

I knew it was not swell, but I knew it was what they wanted, and I was pleased to hear him say so, for it gave me a sense of pride in my craftsmanship. None of the characters we were dealing with were real, but after all they worked. They were better than human beings in their way because they worked, and came out properly in the end.

"Of course," I said, "in real life the boy and girl don't always misunderstand each other."

George shook his head.

"Definitely," he said, "they have to, Jim. Now all of this is swell. That minute where she hates him, but has to touch him—"

"All right," I said, "all right."

"It is all right," he answered. "What's the matter with you, Jim? Have you got something on your mind?"

"No," I said, "I was just thinking about actuality, where there aren't any lovable crossing tenders and where the boy and girl don't always misunderstand each other."

George Stanhope was distressed.

"Now don't get your tongue in your cheek," he said. "I don't mean that we don't know better, but, even so, everything in life has a pattern. We may be working here on an arbitrary pattern, but everything in life fits together. No matter where it is."

"You're wrong," I said. "Sometimes it doesn't fit at all."

"But just the same," said George, "it's a pattern. Everything you do sets up a force which affects the thread of a plot. You think that all the stuff that goes over this table is unreal because it fits a standard. Now I've read more of it than you have, and I'm not sure that it isn't real. Now just this morning someone wants to get you on the telephone. Even that is part of a pattern."

"Someone's always trying to get me on the telephone," I said.

"You have too much imagination, George. I'd like to try to write something that doesn't have this pattern you speak about. You have it on the brain."

"You couldn't do it," said George, "and if you did, it would be definitely bad. I'm not defending the standard of the popular magazines, but just the same the public that reads them believes what they read. Now why do they?"

"I'll tell you why," I said, "because they have the intellectual equipment of a child of twelve."

"A child of twelve is pretty bright," said George. "Maybe he's brighter than you or me. I know the way you feel. Sometimes I'm that way myself, but when I am, I put it out of my mind."

"You'd better, George," I said, and then his telephone rang. This meant that someone had been watching the time in the outer office and that our fifteen minutes was up. In anther moment he would be coping with a fresh problem, with life in the South Seas or with a college story, or with a wild animal story, but George Stanhope was ready for it because it would have a pattern.

"Excuse me, Jim," he said, and he picked up the telephone. "Hello," he said and paused and looked at me. "Yes, he's here." He beckoned toward me and picked up his pencil.

"It's for you, Jim," he said, "the same call."

I leaned over his table and put the receiver to my ear.

"Hello," I said. "What is it?"

"Hello," a voice answered, and I knew at once who was speaking. It was my second cousin, Bella Brill.

"Jim," she was saying, "Jim."

I could hear her catch her breath as though she had been running.

"What's the matter?" I asked.

"Jim," she said, "you've got to come up here. I'm telephoning from the bedroom. They can't hear me."

"Who can't?" I said. "Tell me what's the matter."

"I can't tell you over the telephone," she said. "You have to come up here right away. Howard Berg is here."

"Where?" I asked.

"Here," she said, "here, here, here."

"Don't yell at me," I said. "Suppose he is. Where are you?"

"I told you," she said, "in the bedroom in my apartment. Where else would I be? Jim, you've got to come. I don't know what they'll do. Do you hear, Jim?"

"All right," I said. "Can't you tell me what's the matter?"

"No," she said, "I can't tell you. Please hurry."

I put down the telephone and picked up my hat. George was standing up.

"Anything wrong?" he asked. "Anything I can do?"

"No," I answered, "I guess not, George."

"Is it something," he asked, "where you'd like to have a friend along?"

"No," I answered, "I guess not, George. That was Bella Brill. She was telephoning from the bedroom in her apartment so no one could hear her, whatever that means."

"Good God," George said, "has it got anything to do with Joe?"

I put my hat on and pulled the brim over my eyes.

"I don't know what she's after," I said. "She's always after everybody. Maybe you'd better get three hundred dollars in cash, George, and have it waiting in the office. I don't know what's the matter."

But I knew from her voice that she was frightened. George Stanhope had been speaking of a pattern. Perhaps for once in her life she was facing some sort of artistic retribution.

"I don't know what's the matter, George," I said, "but it looks as though the boy and girl misunderstand each other."

Being used to the vagaries of writers, a literary agent is disturbed by nothing. In fact there was hardly a day that George Stanhope was not involved in some acute domestic, financial or moral crisis, confronting one of his clients. He was constantly negotiating to get them out of jail or to Reno or in touch with

348

legal talent capable of handling the embarrassments of seduction or breach of promise, and he was broad-minded about these matters. In fact they only annoyed George because they cut into the earning capacity of his clients.

"Keep her away from Stowe," he said. "You know what happened the last time he saw her. It can't help cutting down his production. He'll go and get drunk. He won't be good for anything for a month."

"It's all right, George," I said. "Stowe isn't around here. I told you yesterday he's somewhere up in Vermont."

George Stanhope looked grim and competent.

"You can't ever tell where he is. You know him, Jim. He was talking about her the last time he was in here. I've got to get him here where I can watch him."

"This isn't about Joe," I told him, "it's about a man named Berg."

George pressed a button on his desk.

"Ella darling," he said, "get out the private book and look up Stowe. I want to speak to him right away. First try the Vermont number. Then go over all the places he may be; then call up his friends. Drop everything and work on it till you get him. Never mind about the Max Fargo thing and never mind about the Blumpey thing. Drop everything until you get him."

For several years Bella Brill had found it difficult to live with the family. She used to say, and I imagine she was right, that whatever room she slept in was the very place that Archie needed for his canvases and paints. He generally left them all over her bed and all her dresses usually smelled of linseed oil. Besides Bella wanted some place where she could see her friends quietly; that was why she had an apartment, but she never used it much, because she hated doing housework. Sometimes she would invite another girl to share her quarters with her, but this never turned out well, because she had never been able to find another girl who would do all the housework indefinitely, single-handed, and when it came to paying a maid, Bella had always spent the money

349

for something else. Thus though Bella had her own apartment, she was generally with the family.

Sometimes, though, she gave cocktail parties, and sometimes she would sublet it to Harry or Sidney, so I had seen the place often enough. It was between Third and Second Avenues in a tall yellow building which had been constructed hastily in a period when realtors felt that the whole region of brownstone houses would turn into a veritable garden spot. Perhaps the owners still had some such hope, for there was an awning across the street and a doorman, and even a nose and throat specialist on the ground floor. Because of the doctor I had always associated the place with a cleanly, antiseptic smell, an odor, however, which did not extend beyond the entrance hall. There was a time when Bella thought the doctor was delightful, and he could stop a cold right away if you went to him. She even used to have him up occasionally for a drink until there was some trouble about his bill, and after that the doctor stayed where he belonged, a common, vulgar man who had never attended a proper medical institution, and whom you could not trust once he got you in his office.

There had been the doctor, and there had been lots of others of both sexes around the apartment at odd times, for Bella had developed an amazing faculty for sudden friendships. They made a sprightly little company, which changed whenever there were quarrels. At the small parties which Bella sometimes gave, the faces of the guests on nearly every occasion were different, and yet all those changing faces had a striking similarity. I had once thought, when I was there, that it was as though Bella looked into the restive surface of a wind-rippled pool that gave back her own reflection in a score of different distorted ways. Certainly there is something of one's self in every person whom one knows and likes. Once there had been Winty Hollingshead, who used to make flowers out of wax, and Marcia Titmarsh, who wanted to do book reviews and who spoke with a Southern accent, although she came from Michigan. Marcia had been one of Bella's very dearest friends, and their friendship had reached the point where they used each other's clothes almost indiscriminately. Then one of them said something unpardonable about the other, and Marcia disappeared, not that it made much difference. Just around the corner someone new was waiting who would understand Bella Brill, who would really understand this time, and everything would be all right this next time and everything else had been a hideous mistake. It was not entirely amusing to conjure up the kaleidoscopic friends of Bella Brill. It meant that she was looking for something desperately which she might never find, and yet she had never lost the hope of finding it.

I thought of all the other people, most of them unhappy like herself, who must have stood as I was standing, waiting to be carried up to apartment C on the twelfth floor. I took off my hat and mopped my forehead. The elevator boy did not remember me—Bella Brill had too many friends—and the look he gave me seemed more searching than was necessary; it reminded me that elevator boys know almost everything.

"Is Miss Brill expecting you?" he asked.

"Yes," I told him, "absolutely."

He was a dark, olive-skinned boy, probably of Italian extraction, and he still stood looking at me.

"Call her up if you want to," I said. "Tell her her cousin is waiting downstairs."

"Oh," he said, "that's all right—as long as she's expecting you."

It seemed to me that he wanted to add something more. I wondered if the night man might have told him something, but he volunteered nothing further. The elevator moved upwards in an uneasy sort of silence.

Bella's doorbell made a hollow, buzzing sound, and a dog in an apartment across the way began to bark. I could hear the creature scratching and snuffing at the crack. Then I heard footsteps and Howard Berg opened the green metal door. He was dressed in a tan linen suit and wore a salmon-colored necktie.

"Well," he said, "hello."

I did not like the way he said it.

"Hello, Berg," I said. "What's the matter?"

Mr. Berg shook his head and he ended his headshake with a little upward nod.

"Not a thing," he said. "What makes you think there is?"

I followed him into a narrow hallway where a lamp was burning on a red lacquer table. The hall ran into the living room and there were two doors off it, one to a coat closet and one to the bedroom.

"Bella called me up," I said. "Where is she?"

"In the living room," Mr. Berg said. "So she called you up, did she? So, that's what she was doing. Well, she can get in the whole damned fire department and life-net too..."

His voice trailed off into silence as I followed him down the hall to the living room. The sun was shining through the windows upon that disorderly room, which I had always thought was so much like Bella's mind. There were some rather nice pieces of furniture, which had come from Wickford Point—a small kneehole desk covered with a heap of bills and letters, a claw-and-ball-foot mahogany table littered with magazines and empty glasses, two Chippendale end-chairs and then some comfortable chairs, and a divan sofa with pillows, and a built-in bookcase with volumes still in their wrappers. One of the volumes caught my eye the way such things do now and then; it was called *The Sex Life of the Apes*. Bella was standing by the window in a slate-gray dress, and Avery Gifford was standing near her.

His appearance surprised me more than the fact of his being there. That seaside coloring of his was gone. His forehead glistened with perspiration and his jaw was set.

"Hello, Belle, hello, Avery," I said.

Avery swallowed and cleared his throat. Berg walked over to the table and picked up a magazine. I could hear him turn the pages while I stood waiting for someone to speak.

"How did you get here?" Avery asked. "This is all damn nonsense. We've all got to be reasonable."

352

Bella shook her head as though that simple, physical action could drive something repugnant from her mind.

"For God's sake," she said, "don't talk any more about being reasonable. I called Jim up. Jim darling, in the first place I want you to understand that nothing anyone says is true. It's all preposterous."

She was trying once again to escape from a situation which she did not like by reducing it to an absurdity.

"What have you been doing this time, Belle?" I asked.

Bella glanced across the little living room at Howard Berg and smiled tolerantly.

"It's Howard, darling," she said. "Howard is being perfectly preposterous."

I looked at Berg again. He had set down the magazine and was leaning against the table. I began wishing that he would do something or say something more, but he did nothing. Avery Gifford was the one who spoke.

"Now here," Avery said, "just understand I'm willing to pay for this."

Berg straightened himself up from the table, not quickly but almost wearily.

"You said that before," he said, "and you've said it enough. I'm not interested in money."

Bella glanced at me and shook her head again.

"You see, darling," she said, and she looked very pretty standing there, very patient and very sweet. "They don't know what they're talking about. I can explain everything perfectly easily. It's what I say—it's all perfectly preposterous."

I did not answer her.

"Suppose you try to tell me," I said to Berg.

XXX | Howard Writes the Ticket

Berg hesitated.

"I can handle this myself and I'll settle it with Bella. Your being here won't change anything."

"Go ahead and tell him," said Bella. "That's why Jim's here. You thought I couldn't get anyone to help me, didn't you? You can tell any lies you want. I always knew you had a dirty mind."

Howard Berg looked at her; the corners of his lips twitched but he straightened them.

"Go ahead," I told him.

"All right," he said. "Here's the way it is. I've been good enough to dance with Bella and to take her places, as long as I paid enough; but I wasn't good enough for anything else—not quite nice. Now I find that Gifford was here last night, all night. He was here when I came this morning."

"Avery!" Bella cried.

Until I heard her call to him I had nearly forgotten Avery.

"Get away, Jim," Avery said, "I'll take care of this."

"What are you going to do," I asked him, "knock him down?"

It was the only thing he could do, considering everything, but my question checked him momentarily.

"He isn't going to say any more," Avery said. "I'll take the blame for everything, but he isn't going—Why do you stand there and listen to him, Jim?

354

"Because it looks as though it's time to listen," I said.

I was beginning to fill in the gaps of this disjointed conversation and I realized that Avery was not important; that Berg was the one who mattered.

"Just how did you get in here, Berg?" I asked him. I was surprised that Bella had not been more careful.

He shrugged his shoulders.

"That's easy," he answered, "the superintendent. It cost me fifty dollars."

"Do you think that was scrupulous?" I asked. He stared at me coldly, and I knew that Bella was right to be afraid of him.

"No," he said, "it wasn't. I just wanted to find out who was here."

Then Bella spoke quickly, easily, with a hint of laughter in her voice.

"Darling," she said, "if you will just let me explain. If anyone will please only let me get in a word. It's all so perfectly grotesque. Howard and I had a quarrel. It wasn't anything much, except he kept trying to pin me down. I just thought we were having a good time together, and then last night I met Avery, entirely by accident."

Bella shook her head and laughed.

"It's so preposterous," she said. "I hadn't seen Avery for such a long time, and we had such a lot to talk about, and then it was raining, and it was so late, he—" She paused. "Why, he just stayed and slept on the couch, darling," Bella said. "You can understand that, can't you? And then Howard came in here, and Howard has a dirty mind. He's so vicious about it."

Avery Gifford rubbed the back of his hand across his forehead and his expression was bewildered and incredulous.

"I just didn't think," he said. "I just didn't."

"Avery," said Bella quickly, "won't you please be quiet?" And then they both were quiet while Mr. Berg stood looking at them.

"Suppose Gifford was here," I told him. "I don't quite gather what you think you can do about it, or why it's any of your business, Berg."

His face reddened slightly, but his answer was quiet enough. "I don't mind telling you why," he said. "Because I gave her a lot of my time, and now I find I was just a meal ticket for her."

"A good many people have been," I said. "I still don't see what you're going to do about it."

Mr. Berg studied me carefully.

"She isn't going to get away with that with me," he answered.

"Go ahead," I said, "why isn't she?"

His glance moved to Avery and back to me.

"Because she isn't," said Howard Berg, "for once in her life—unless she and Mr. Gifford want this public."

"Oh," I said, "so that's it."

"Yes," he answered, "that's it. Just as a matter of personal satisfaction, Bella's going with me to Bermuda. The boat leaves at two o'clock. For once in her life she's going to pay for something."

"You know," I said, "that is rather an unusual idea. You'll still be a meal ticket, Berg."

"That's my business," he answered.

"Now, darling," said Bella quickly, "of course I don't want any trouble on Avery's account. Of course I don't want any scandal, but you must make Howard see—"

"Look here," Avery began, "I said I'd do anything, anything—" and then he stopped.

We must have all known what he meant—that he would give all his money, anything, to turn the clock back.

"It won't do any good to get mad, Calder," said Mr. Berg. "I mean it."

"Darling," said Bella, "I really think I'm dreaming. He wants to take me to Bermuda just because Avery was sleeping on the couch. Why, it's almost blackmail or something, darling."

I made no reply. The whole situation was absurd, but Howard Berg was not.

"Darling," Bella said. "Don't you see you'll have to do something about it?"

"Suppose," I said, "you just stop calling me 'darling.' You've got yourself into this mess. Why should I get you out of it?"

356

The worst of it was that she knew I would help her; I would do it out of habit. She had taken it for granted as soon as she had heard my voice, and that assurance made me unexpectedly weary. I looked at my watch and saw that it was half-past eleven.

"Well," I said, "you'd better go to your room and pack your bags."

"Jim," said Bella, "are you crazy? You haven't been drinking, have you, Jim?"

"It's half-past eleven," I said, "and you'll want to look attractive on the boat. Avery had better help you. Now both of you get out of here."

"Look here," Avery began and then he stopped. I walked down the hall and opened the bedroom door.

"Go on," I said, "both of you. Don't you see Mr. Berg means what he says?"

"I won't," Bella began, and then she flounced past me to her room. "Well," she said, "of course if you're crazy—" And I closed the door behind them.

"Be quiet, Avery," I heard her say. "He wants to be alone with him."

It was inconceivable to Bella that anything untoward could happen to her. There had always been some way out of everything. It was inconceivable that she might be an object of scandal, like those unfortunate people who, she used to say, had "made fools of themselves." She was probably thinking already that Berg did not mean it.

Berg had selected a chair and he was waiting—a rather bizarre figure. He did not mind in the least that he was not behaving like a gentleman. I was thinking that there was a great advantage in being able not to mind. Women, at any rate the ones who are termed nice women, were forever expecting you to behave according to an arbitrary and possibly an outmoded standard.

He was leaning forward with his hands clasped, staring at his heavy fingers.

"I know what you think of me," he said. "You needn't bother to tell me."

"Oh, that's all right," I said. "Don't have it on your mind."
I sat down opposite him and reached in my pocket for a cigarette. The only feeling which I seemed to harbor toward him was one of stiff formality, and I wondered if I were getting old. I should have been melodramatic just a year or so ago. I should have told him that he was a cad and a coward. I should have acted according to a code that would have called for physical collision, but now it did not seem to matter.

"She'll go with you if she's sensible," I said. "You can do what you like about it. Frankly, I don't care." I could not get over my astonishment that I did not care.

He looked up at me and down at his hands before he answered.

"I'm rather surprised you take it this way," he said.

"So am I," I answered.

"Well," he said, "it doesn't make much difference. I'm sorry she got you here."

"Why?" I asked.

"Frankly," he said, "the whole thing doesn't give me much satisfaction."

"You're pretty mad, aren't you?" I asked.

"Yes," he said, "I have a right to be. I was under the impression until last night that Bella was going to marry me, and then because I asked her exactly when, she threw me over."

"So you really wanted to marry her?" I asked.

"Yes," he said, "I was that much of a fool."

Everything was clear enough without his telling me. She had been something rare and beautiful to him, and he had reached for her and she had let him reach.

"If I were you I wouldn't fall in love with her again," I said.

He looked at me without answering and scowled.

"She'll try to make you again, some time or other," I said. "You see she just wants everything at once. It isn't worth anyone's trouble, actually."

"Are you trying to give me some good sound advice?" said Mr. Berg.

"No," I said, "I'm just telling you it isn't worth while. It's all a waste of time because you don't get anything back."

"Why not?" he asked.

"Because she hasn't got anything to give," I said. "You think she has, but she hasn't. It isn't her fault."

I had not meant to say anything of the sort when I had started, but now it seemed perfectly natural. Howard Berg straightened his tie and looked at me.

"I wish I could see you on the boat," I said. "She's hit you and naturally you want to hit her back in some way, and you can do it, but it won't pay."

He stood up suddenly and scowled again.

"I suppose you think you've talked me out of it?" he said.

"I told you I didn't care," I replied, "and I don't care. She had it coming to her."

"Well," said Howard Berg, "to hell with it. I'll be going now."

"Where?" I asked.

"Just checking out," he answered, "getting on my way. I guess you're right. It isn't worth my time."

He smoothed out his linen coat and walked to the table to pick up his hat, a handsome Panama.

"You're really going?" I said.

"Yes," said Howard Berg, "absolutely. Let's not analyze it. Let's forget it, shall we?"

"Yes," I answered, "let's forget it." We shook hands and I went down the hall with him.

"Well," he said, "so long."

The door slammed and I mopped my forehead, for the room had grown oppressive. I had the same desire which had overcome him—to get away from there.

"Bella," I called, "you can come out now. Mr. Berg is gone."

XXXI | Good-by, Girls

I had often thought that women did not mind emotional excitement as much as men, and I was sure of it when I saw Bella. She had that resiliency of her sex which could turn in a second from fear and fury back to laughter. I wondered whether she were totally unaware of the consequences she had just escaped, for she had the ability to deceive herself about such things. I wondered, until I examined her more carefully by the unflattering north light of the living-room windows.

Then I saw again what I had noticed on that ride with her from Wickford Point to the Jaeckels', that indefinable look that told me she would not always be young. It was nothing more than a sharpness about her nostrils and a thinness about the molding of her cheeks which was far from unattractive, for it actually added to that patrician sort of beauty, that untouchable, challenging aloofness of hers which so many men admired. In spite of it she had that look, which I remembered, of a little girl waiting for the Christmas tree just before the parlor door was open—a look indicating that the waiting had been hard and disagreeable, but that everything would at last be delightful for always. Christmas trees were gone, but there were substitutes for Christmas trees every day she lived, and now the absence of Mr. Berg was just like that—a gift that had come to her because she had been good, because she was Bella Brill.

It was all over now—in an hour or so she might entirely forget it—and she was turning it efficiently out of her thoughts already. Nevertheless I knew that for the first time in her life she had been frightened, not of something in her thoughts—she was afraid of her thoughts often enough—but of something much more devastating, because it was real and tangible. I remembered when I had been first afraid of something real, and I could still recall my reaction when it was over. I could recall that feeling of relief, mingled with my sense of shame that I had been frightened; and I could recall that time-worn mental promise that I would never, never do anything like that again. Yet one avoided such matters quickly, once they were finished, and one forgot them as one forgot a dangerous illness. I had never seen Bella look any happier or more engaging.

"Darling," she said, "are you sure he's gone?"

"Yes," I said, "I'm sure he's gone."

"Well, you needn't have frightened me so," said Bella, "pushing Avery and me out of the room like that. Did you ever hear of anything so ridiculous? Did you ever really? All this trouble about nothing, absolutely nothing. I never knew that anyone could be so common, so absolutely . . ." She shook her head and wrinkled up her nose. "Tell us what you said to him, darling."

"Never mind about it now," I said.

"Well, don't be so cross, Jim," she said. "It's all over now. I never really did like him. I should have known what he was by the people he's played around with."

"I remember, Belle," I said. "You told me he had lunch with Mr. Galsworthy just last week."

"That's exactly what I mean, darling," Bella answered. "He was always telling lies like that, such preposterous lies, just as though everybody didn't know that Galsworthy was dead. And the idea of his wanting me to go with him to Bermuda after everything. Avery, wasn't it all ridiculous?"

The corners of her eyes narrowed when she smiled at Avery. She seemed to be expecting him to laugh.

"No," he said, "it wasn't ridiculous. I'll take the blame for everything."

"Avery," I said, "the best thing for you to do is to forget it." But I knew that he would never forget as long as he lived.

"Avery," said Bella, "don't take it so seriously, for heaven's sake. You act as though something really had happened."

Avery Gifford did not answer; he did not even look at her. Some men would have passed it all off easily enough, but not Avery. He should have shaken hands with Bella and he should have gone away, but instead he lingered.

"The worst thing is what you must think of me," he said.

"What do you mean, what we'll think of you?" I asked. "Don't have yourself so much on your mind."

"There's Betty," said Avery, "Betty and the children—"

"Why Avery," Bella cried, "you don't mean you're going to tell her. You haven't got anything to tell."

"I've got to tell her," Avery said. "I can't—"

Bella's voice grew sharp.

"You always were a perfect fool," she said. "That's why I never married you. You act as though I'd made you come up here."

"Don't," I said to Bella. "Be quiet, honey bee."

"I won't be quiet," Bella said. "I can guess where you were last night, Jim. And I don't need three guesses either. You were—"

"Be quiet," I told her, "be quiet, honey bee. I'm talking to Avery now."

"You want to change the subject, don't you?" Bella said.

And then she stopped. She glanced at me and smiled, but she stopped.

"Avery," I said, "I wouldn't tell anyone if I were you, because there are some things which you just don't tell."

"Avery," Bella said, "I wish you'd please go away now, if you don't mind. If you keep standing here I think I'm going to scream."

"Jim," said Avery, "you're sure there isn't anything I ought to do?"

"No," I said. "You'd better go. Bella's going to scream."

"Well," Avery said, "good-by. I'm awfully sorry, Bella."

Suddenly Bella began to laugh. She put her hand over her mouth, but she could not stop laughing. I took Avery Gifford by the arm.

"Avery," I said, "it's time you were going home. I haven't seen you here, remember; I haven't seen you for years." As I spoke I pushed him down the hall, and all the way I could hear the peals of Bella's laughter, but she had stopped when I got back. She was sitting on the couch and wiping her eyes.

"Jim," she said, "I'm all right now. It's just when he said that he was sorry."

"Do you want some ammonia?" I asked her.

"No," she said. "I'm all right now. I'm sorry I did that. He was worse than Howard Berg, wasn't he, darling? How could anyone be like that?"

"Because he couldn't help it," I said. "He was trying to do his best."

"Jim," said Bella, "you're laughing at him too, and you're laughing at me. You always laugh at all of us."

"Don't start that again," I said quickly. "Go and wash your face in cold water, honey bee, and powder your nose."

"All right," Bella said. She was meek and gentle. "I don't know what I'd do if you weren't here."

"You'd scream," I said. "Go and wash your face."

"There's some whisky on the kitchen shelf," she said, "and there's some soda in the icebox. I guess you'd like a drink, even if it's early. I wish you'd kiss me, darling."

"Never mind it now," I said.

I felt better when I had the drink. Bella must have seen that she did not look well, because she was gone for quite a while and I sat alone, holding the half-empty glass. Although the business seemed finished, I still could not understand exactly what had brought her there. There had been something about that morning at Wickford Point that made me think that she was being secretive. She had gone to the Jaeckels with her bag packed for the night, and it might have been only an impulse which had brought her to New York with Berg. I should have liked to think of it that way but instead I was uneasy.

She looked better when she came back. She sat down on the couch and curled her legs under her, and then she opened her box with its lipstick and powder and pursed up her lips in front of the little mirror.

"Well," she said, "thank goodness that's over." And she glanced at me sideways, trying to read what I was thinking. "You're not angry with me, are you?"

"No," I answered, "not particularly."

"You won't tell, will you?" she asked.

"No," I said. She patted me on the knee, and I looked down at her nervous, restless hands.

"You didn't come down here to meet Avery Gifford, did you?" I asked.

Bella began to laugh.

"You have such funny ideas," she said. "You're just like all the family. You always think I'm up to something. I don't see why you all keep spying on me. I just saw Avery at the Holland when I went to get my hair set. I told you we had dinner, I told you about everything. Why do we have to keep going over it and over it? I was at the Jaeckels'—"

"And you didn't stay," I said. "I'm just wondering if you meant to stay."

Bella snapped her powder-box shut.

"I do wish that *someone* would understand that I am grown-up," she said. "It just happened that Howard Berg was going to New York yesterday morning in the plane, and I came down with him. Now do you understand? Don't you believe me, darling?"

"That's all right," I said, "it doesn't matter."

She looked at me and pressed her lips together.

"You don't believe me, do you?" she asked.

"No," I said, "I don't, but it doesn't matter, Belle."

Instead of making her angry my remark only brought her to a stage of sweet martyr-like resignation, and she raised her hands

364

in a helpless, gentle gesture and let them fall beside her limply on the couch.

"All right," she sighed. "If you don't believe me, I can't make you, but it does seem the strangest thing that everyone should think that I'm a crook or something. Isn't it perfectly logical that I should want to get away? You keep wanting to get away. I just can't stand it at Wickford Point all the time. It gets me nearly frantic to see them sitting around and talking." Her voice broke and she clenched her fists and beat them on the couch. "I can't stand it and I won't."

"You've said all that before, Belle," I told her. "You can't stand anything."

But there was a pleading note in her voice which caught my sympathy. She was reaching for me again, asking for my help, and it was worse this time than it had ever been before, because I could not help her.

I wonder if she understood that something in our relationship had disappeared without either of us knowing how. Its absence gave me a definite sense of loss, and yet when I tried to recapture that lost sympathy, I could not do it. It had gone into nowhere with something like the irretrievable certainty of death. Mutual liking and sympathy and even love and antipathy are such impermanent matters, resting on a tenuous balance of give and take. There was nothing new about her, her conduct had been characteristic and I was no more surprised or shocked by it than usual. I was just the same and she was just the same, but the truth was that I did not care, I did not care a damn.

It was as if she had been my mistress and I had suddenly turned away from her. I had never thought of her in that capacity, for she had not been my mistress; yet I suddenly saw that there had been something between us that resembled such a tie. Perhaps there always is in every friendship, no matter how platonic, between a man and a woman. The room felt hot and close and I could hear her talking, but I could not listen. It *was* as if she had been my mistress and as though I were getting through. I had

365

given a good deal to her; in fact I had always been giving, and I thought she had given something in return. Whatever it was, it had possessed some sort of value, but now that value was gone. Actually she had not given me as much as a lady of the evening, and the whole thing was suddenly unhealthy and abnormal. It would have been better if I had taken her, but I could not even remember having experienced such a desire. I must have always known her too well for that, and yet there had always been something. . . . There had been her gaiety, for instance, and the sense that she needed me; but now it was gone. Instead I experienced a lonely emptiness combined with a faint revulsion.

I heard her voice calling to me through my thoughts. It was like the desperate voice of someone who was lost.

"Jim," she said, "aren't you feeling well? You aren't listening to me, darling."

"Yes," I said, "I'm listening, Belle."

She put her arm around me and looked hard into my face.

"You're not shocked by anything?" she asked me.

I could feel her waiting for my reply, as though a good deal depended on it.

"No," I said, and I touched her soft black hair. "Of course not, Belle."

She took her arm away and sighed.

"Then it's all right," she said. "I just thought so for a moment because you looked so grim. I was just saying, darling, that life hasn't been fair to me, and it isn't because I haven't tried. But you see it, don't you? Nothing has come back to me. That's what makes me frightened. It's beginning to make me desperate. That's why I did what I did last night, darling. I don't want anyone like Howard Berg. When I understood he thought we were engaged, it really did upset me. It just made me realize that I didn't have anything at all. And then when I saw Avery—Well, I haven't got anything, and Jim, I'm getting old."

I had never heard her speak exactly that way.

"Jim," she said, "you don't think I'm getting old, do you?"

366

"No," I said. "Don't let that worry you. You're the prettiest girl I know."

When I heard her speak again I knew that she had been giving an explanation for everything and that I had not heard a word of it.

"Then it's all right," she said triumphantly. "You see why I came down here, and that all of this doesn't mean a thing? I'd just hate it so, if you didn't believe me. I do lie to myself sometimes, but I never mean to lie to you."

"Yes," I answered, "you do lie to yourself sometimes."

"But then everybody does," said Bella. "It's the only way that you can get along. It's awful when you really see yourself, and I do now and then—just lately."

She smiled and she looked like a little girl who was up to some sort of mischief.

"I seem to be two people, and when that happens I have to lie a little."

Her explanation even had a sort of charm entirely her own. Nevertheless I felt uneasy.

"You know the game," she was saying. "We used to play it at parties." She gave a little laugh and stopped. "What *is* the matter? You're not listening, darling."

"I'm sorry, Belle. What game?" I said.

"You know," she said. "Cousin Sue used to have it when I had birthday parties. Going to Jerusalem. All the chairs were back to back, and the music would play and we would walk around them and then the music would stop and we would all sit down, except one of us would be left. Well, the music's nearly stopped."

Her voice paused as though she expected me to reply, and that little room seemed to me as still as death.

"So it's nearly stopped?" I said.

"Yes," she answered, "you see what I mean." And her eyes were soft and deep. "We used to run around and play and be silly, awfully silly, but if you were too silly you didn't get a chair when the music stopped."

367

"Well, sweetness," I said, "a lot of nice boys have offered you chairs. I remember another game where someone offers you a chair and asks you to sit down and then just when you are starting to he pulls it out from under you and you go down boom. You've never had that happen to you, have you?"

Bella wrinkled her nose and laughed.

"That's fluff," she said. "You know what I mean. I mean I haven't anything, not anything left." She paused and rested her hand on my knee again. I repressed a desire to move away when I felt her touch me, because I must have guessed what was coming.

"Except you," she added. "I'll always have you, darling."

I felt my face reddening with a sense of my own disloyalty. I wondered whether it would be better not to speak, simply to let it go, and I had that same unhealthy conviction that my mistress was speaking. Her voice was gentle, but it was insistent.

"I think I care more about that than anything else in the world," she said. "I mean, really care. We quarrel and we fight, but you tell me what you think of me. I knew it was all I cared about when you came up here. You're always with me. You're still with me, aren't you, Jim?"

No man likes a time like that. It goes against the grain of ordinary chivalry. The palms of my hands felt moist and I wiped them on my coat.

"Belle," I began—but she stopped me.

"Aren't you, Jim?" she asked.

I pulled myself together—it was like something in the war—but when it comes to breaking, it may not matter much how one does it. The result is just the same.

"Belle," I said, "I've always told you the truth. I've never thought of you exactly like this. You've always been a sort of habit up to now."

She smiled, and I don't think she knew what was coming. It was like hitting someone who did not have his hands up.

"That's it," she said, "it's habit, darling."

"Well, sweetness," I said, "I don't know how it's happened. It isn't anything that anyone can help. You'd better get ready

368

because I'm pulling the chair right out from under you."

Bella sat up straighter. She pressed the back of her hand to her lips and took it away again.

"Jim," she said, "don't be silly. There isn't any chair."

"Oh, yes, there is," I said, "and there always is. I'm sorry, but I'm through, absolutely through."

I waited, wondering what she would do, and while I waited I realized that she would probably be like any woman in her place and that she would follow a dreary course of action as old as the Book of Proverbs. Then I saw that she did not believe me any more than if I had told her that the sky was a china plate.

"I knew you were cross, darling," Bella said. "I don't blame your being tired of me. I'm pretty tired of myself."

"I'm sorry, Belle," I answered. "I didn't say that I was tired, I said that I was through."

"Darling," said Bella, and she moved close to me. "Just tell me what I've done."

"There's nothing you've done that you can do anything about," I said. "These things happen."

"But, darling," said Bella, "that's perfectly absurd. I must have done something to hurt you. Just tell me what it is." She laughed incredulously. "It isn't about Avery Gifford, is it? You couldn't be as silly as that."

"It isn't anything definite," I said. "I can't help it and you can't help it."

"Then you must have heard something about me," she said. "Tell me what you've heard. It's only fair." Her eyes grew narrow. "Was it anything about Joe Stowe?"

"No," I said, "it wasn't."

"Then it's Pat Leighton," Bella said. "She's told you something."

"There's no use talking about it, Belle," I said. "I'm through. I don't care what anybody says about you. It isn't important any more."

"I knew it," she said. "It *is* Pat Leighton."

"Give it any explanation you like," I said. "It's a fact."

"You mean you don't like me?" said Bella. "You don't like me at all?"

"It's worse than that," I said. "I feel impersonal. I can see your good points and your bad points. I'm sorry, Belle."

She gave a sharp exasperated sigh.

"For heaven's sake," she said, "don't keep saying you're sorry, and don't look like that and don't be so disagreeable, and don't talk about being impersonal. You're just doing it to be nasty and you know I hate it."

I did not answer.

"Darling," she said more softly, "don't you know I hate it?"

I did not want to make her unhappy, I simply wanted to make her understand.

"You can try anything you like," I said. "It won't make any difference, Belle."

She got up and walked across the room and fingered an empty glass from the table.

"All right," she said, "be nasty if you like. It won't make any difference to me. Jim, what's the matter with you? Aren't you feeling well?"

"I'm feeling fine," I said. "I'm sorry, Belle."

"Then, please," Bella said, "please tell me what's the matter."

The words kept going back and forth monotonously in a repetition like the swinging of a pendulum, first here then there, and then I tried to explain what I had said to Howard Berg.

"I told him it wasn't worth while," I said, "and that's what I mean. It isn't your fault; it's just the way things are. You haven't got anything to give to anyone that anyone wants."

I stopped, because I had not meant to go as far as that. Her white strained face showed me that I had said an unpardonable thing.

"I didn't mean exactly that," I said. "I'm sorry, Belle."

Her hand which held the glass was shaking and her face was white. I stood up watching her, half-ashamed, half-fascinated by what I had done, and then she threw the glass. I swayed sideways when I saw it coming, and it crashed against the wall behind me. Then I grabbed her wrist.

"Don't do that again, Belle," I said. I felt incompetent and clumsy, which was probably the way she wanted me to feel, because she leaned against me and rested her head on my shoulder.

"Jim," she sobbed, "I'm sorry, darling. You just made me so mad. It's all right, darling. You've got me so afraid. Just tell me you didn't mean it. I couldn't get along without you. I'm so damned afraid!"

Her arms were around me and she was sobbing on my shoulder and it might have been kinder to have lied to her. I pushed her away from me gently.

"Let's not fight over it, Belle," I said. "I've always told you the truth. I mean it, Belle."

She put her hand up and wiped the tears from her eyes. I remembered that she never liked to cry.

"I don't see how you can hurt me so," she sobbed, "but you'll be all right tomorrow, dear."

It was curious: her mind had traveled in a complete circle and we were back exactly where we had started.

"Belle," I said, "you can't be polite about things like this. I've seen it tried, but it never works. Just remember that there are a lot of fish in the sea. There'll be someone else tomorrow."

I was holding her by the shoulders, but I had not been conscious of it until she wrenched herself away.

"Then get out!" she cried at me. "Don't let me look at you. Get out!"

A sound came to us both at the same moment, although I knew somehow that I had been hearing it for nearly half a minute without noticing. The telephone on the little bookshelf in the hall was ringing.

XXXII | Definitely He's Crazy

It would be interesting for communication executives to compile statistics with illustrative paragraphs as to how the inadvertent ringing of the telephone has served to alleviate human tension. Surely it has been an agent that has frequently prevented murder and mayhem. The insistent sound of that automatic signal had the effect on both of us which might have been exerted by the sudden appearance of an unsuspecting third party—a meter inspector or the young man who could put himself through college if you subscribed to his magazine. We must have realized almost simultaneously that we were making a vulgar exhibition of ourselves, well enough for the vicious intimacy which existed between us but not fitting for someone else to see or hear. We both stopped short, and as I looked at her I remembered how the telephone had rung at Wickford Point that morning not so many hours ago, and how it had wrought its own amazing change. She was Bella Brill again, that delightful, intelligent Bella Brill, who was able to get all the men around her and to hold them captivated by her ideas of whatever it was that anyone was talking about. She was the Bella Brill whom people wanted on the telephone, not the one I knew; and I was James Calder again, who knew his way about and who had a life of his own. It all was coming back to us because the telephone was ringing.

With a gesture which could hardly have been conscious, Bella raised a hand to tidy her hair and assumed a less abandoned posture. Her voice became silvery with an unconscious expectation. "I'll go," she said. "I wonder who it is." And she walked with that light quick step of hers, half on her toes so that her heels made just the faintest tap, down the little hallway to the bedroom.

"Hello," I heard her say. "Hello. Yes, this is Miss Brill's apartment. This is Miss Brill speaking." She spoke just as if nothing had happened and as if the world were a fascinating place full of delightful surprises when one was a nice girl looking for them. I stood listening to her and looking at the pieces of the broken glass.

"Yes," she was saying, "yes, he's here. It's for you, Jim."

"How the devil can it be for me?" I asked. "No one knows I'm here."

Bella put her hands on her hips.

"Well, why the devil can't it be?" she said. "You must have told someone."

We seemed to be dropping back again into our old friendly relationship.

"Didn't you ask who it was?" I asked her.

"Don't I know enough not to ask who calls you up?" she answered. "It sounds like a switchboard operator."

"Mr. Stanhope wants to speak to you, Mr. Calder," a precise voice said, and then I remembered that of course George Stanhope knew I was there.

"What does he want?" I said. "I'm busy."

"Just a minute please." The tone was inexorable and sweet. "It's important, Mr. Calder." Then the voice that had consoled clients in Hollywood and Honolulu and London was on the wire.

"Is that you, Jim?" said George. "Can you talk?" He spoke with a contagious tenseness. "Is she there?"

"Who?" I asked. "Miss Brill? You just had her on the wire. Do you want her?"

"No." George Stanhope's voice was louder. "No, no, no. Jim, can you get her out of there?"

"What are you talking about, George?" I asked. "Has anyone frustrated you?"

"Say anything you like," George said, "but don't be funny. I located Joe but I couldn't hold him here. He's just left the office. He's definitely crazy."

"What?" I said.

I was trying stupidly to put things together and my mind was working slowly.

"Are you deaf?" I heard George ask. "Joe Stowe has left the office."

"Don't be funny yourself, George," I said. "He was up in Vermont, delivering a lecture to some schoolmarms."

"Listen," George Stanhope called to me, "will you listen, Jim? He's just left here. He wants to try to fix things up with Bella Brill. Do you hear me? She sent him a wire to Boston and they forwarded it to Vermont. He showed it to me. She asked him to come down, so that they could talk about how to fix things up. Are you listening? Are you on the wire?"

My silence must have made him uneasy.

"Yes," I said, "of course I'm listening."

"All right," said George. "He's crazy, definitely. When he got it, he dropped everything. He'll be there any minute. You've got to get her out before he comes."

He began speaking with a frantic sort of patience more irritating than his haste. I had suspected that Bella had been lying. She must have acted on some sudden impulse back there at the Jaeckels'. And then I remembered what she had said about the music having very nearly stopped. George Stanhope was still talking, endeavoring to stave off the inevitable as facilely as he might have constructed a motion-picture plot.

"It's hysteria," he was saying. "He definitely can't go back to her. It's taken him three years to get over it, and now he's back in production. He definitely can't make such a mistake. Will you get that little two-timing hussy out of there before he comes, or won't you?"

"Why, George," I said, "George!"

"Do you want him to ruin himself?" George Stanhope shouted.

"You know what she does to him. He can't get himself ruined now that he's a big name. It's his production, Jim."

He was not thinking entirely of Joe Stowe's production; he was thinking of his career and he was devoted to Joe Stowe. Yet I knew that there are some things you cannot stop any more than you can stop a buzz-saw by putting your finger in it. He was trying to deal with facts as if they were pages of fiction, to be altered by inserts and erasures. He was trying to change the end of actuality, as he might have juggled with the ending of a client's story.

"George," I said, "you can't do that."

If Joe had really answered her appeal, there was nothing that I or anyone else could do. He would never stop until he had found her and given her whatever it was of him she wanted.

"All right," I said. "I'll do what I can. All right."

I agreed only so that I might get rid of his voice in my left ear.

"All right," I said, "but you're not God Almighty, George."

It would have done no good to tell him that I was going to do nothing. I did not feel omnipotent or even potent, but I felt a new resentment against Bella Brill. I had a new revulsion against her meddlings with other people's lives with those delicate un-skilled fingers that could never sew a stitch or tie a knot.

"Jim," she said, "for heaven's sake, what is it?"

She backed away from me when I came near her.

"So you lied to me?" I said. "So you just came down here for fun?"

"Then it was someone talking about me, was it?" Bella answered.

Her thoughts were darting about swiftly in her effort to cope with this unexpected crisis.

"And you sent a wire to Joe Stowe," I told her, "after you said you never wanted to see him again. Well, he's on his way here now."

"Jim," she said, "don't look like that."

"Never mind how I look," I told her. "I said you were a liar.

375

I don't know why God lets you interfere with people who are better than you are, Belle."

"Oh Jim," she cried, "please. I think I'm going crazy. Don't begin it all again."

But my mind was centered on what appeared to me the only important, irrefutable fact; and I clung to it stubbornly.

"Well, you lied," I said.

I thought that she was going to deny it, but her answer was even more naïve.

"He can't be coming here now," she said, "because I told him to come tomorrow. Won't you please let me explain? It's just that I can't get along without anybody. Jim, he's making a hundred and fifty thousand a year."

She stated that last fact as though it excused everything. There was no way to deal with a mind like hers, which darted from prevarication to revealing, unadulterated truth.

"Go ahead, sweetness," I said, and I picked up my hat from the chair. I had had enough of her and a good deal more than enough, but she ran to me and held tight to my arm.

"Now really," she said, "what do you want me to do?"

I wrenched my arm away from her.

"I don't want anything," I said.

"Jim," she said, "don't act like a child of twelve."

There was no use talking about intelligence measurements then, but it was a subject to which she often referred in times of stress.

"Do anything you like, I'm going, Belle," I said.

"Jim," she cried, "you can't, you *can't* do that to me." And then she began to cry again. She began to cry the way Mary did, without bothering to hide her face.

"I haven't got anybody, Jim," she sobbed, and the whole thing began again just as if it had never stopped. Then I heard the buzzer on her apartment door. It was too late for me to go.

"Please give me your handkerchief," she said. And I tossed it to her.

"Won't you please let him in?"

"Let him in yourself," I said, and I stood there with my hat on.

Suddenly, in the erratic way ideas sometimes come out of no-where, I remembered a man I had met in Persia once, who had eaten so much caviar that he could not stand the sight of it. I was thinking that no matter what you have of anything, whether it is sturgeon eggs or human interest, when you have had too much you do not want any more; and I had had too much of that re-lationship between Joe Stowe and Bella Brill. I had been plagued by it, I had made efforts about it too often. As I considered the hours in which I had discussed Joe with her and the weeks when I had discussed her with him, it occurred to me that all that time and energy, when it was added in a single column, represented a very appreciable fraction of my life. Neither of those two had a right to demand so much. They had used me for their own pur-poses exactly as if they thought I liked it. I might have done a good deal better with all that wasted time. It stretched before me in its futility, now that I had begun to understand the truth that nearly everyone learns when it is too late—that you actually can do almost nothing about other people. I had wasted my time with both of them, unless I admitted that they had made a doubtful and unsolicited contribution to my own store of human knowledge.

"Hello Joe," I heard her saying. She had been able to put every-thing behind her once more in that short walk to the apartment door. I remembered how often she had said that she wanted to be rid of him. It made it the more amusing when I heard her say "Hello."

"Here I am, Bella," Joe said, "I came right away."

"You're looking well," I heard Bella answer. She said it with a sort of hurt surprise.

"So are you," said Joe, "very well. How did you know where I was, Bella? You know I always said—"

He stopped when he saw me, and he scowled. He was wearing the same tropical suit that he had worn the night when we had dined, but now its knees were baggy and soiled, the sleeves and trousers were all wrinkled, and his shirt was so wilted that some of the color of his necktie had run upon the collar.

"Hello Jim," he said, but his greenish-yellow eyes were watching me suspiciously. He resented my being there, because it made him look foolish.

"Bella sent me a wire," he said.

"Yes," I answered, "so I heard. I thought you were in Vermont."

Joe gave his narrow shoulders an impatient, upward jerk. It reminded me of those times long ago when I went with difficulty out to Brookline or somewhere to call on some girl I liked, only to find that someone else was there ahead of me. His sunburned, freckled face had the same disconcerted look that mine must have worn in that distant past.

"I *was* in Vermont," he said.

"You must have come mighty quick," I said.

"Airplane," he said. "I hired one."

"Oh," I said.

"How did you hear about that wire?" he asked, and then before I could answer his face cleared and he grinned.

"Stanhope's been after you, has he?" he asked. "He's the damnedest person for putting his finger in other people's pies. George thinks he's God Almighty."

"That's what I told him," I said.

Joe grinned at me and put his hand on my shoulder.

"Listen, boy," he said, "it couldn't be that you're getting that complex too?"

"No," I said, "I'm not."

"Because it doesn't do any good," said Joe. "No one can make himself or anyone else behave. I never thought I'd do anything like this at my age, but here I am." He gave my shoulder a gentle slap. "Let's forget it. Now you run along. Bella and I have something particular to say to each other."

"I wouldn't stop for anything," I said. "It's all too beautiful."

"Oh, shut up," Joe said, and he grinned at me. "You can talk yourself blue in the face but it won't help."

"So all she had to do was whistle?" I said.

He looked at Bella again and nodded, and he had a singular expression, puzzled and yet triumphant, triumphant and yet grim; but at the same time he gave the impression of being very nearly happy. He must have believed that this was something he had hoped for, in some way a victory which had finished all the struggles and antagonisms between them. Conceivably he thought that at last Bella Brill had appealed to him in womanly surrender. It was curious to see him so wrong about her, when he knew so much about everybody else.

"Yes," he said, "she only had to whistle. Run along now, Jim."

"You act as though I wanted to stay," I said. "Go ahead and make a fool of yourself. Go ahead, if you want to get mixed up again with a ——"

I left the last word in a silence not unlike the dashes and asterisks to which we had been accustomed in the early days of our profession, before Messrs. Hemingway and Faulkner had turned plain words into art; but it was unnecessary to tell him what I thought of her or what I thought of him, because he knew.

"That's about enough from you," Joe said. "I don't want to get mad at you, Jim."

Sex, it seemed to me, was very odd. Joe and I had been friends for years and now that friendship was breaking, simply because I had cast an aspersion upon a woman of whom he happened to be fond, although he knew that my opinion of Bella was entirely correct.

"I'm sorry," I said. "You're getting just what's coming to you. Well, go ahead and get it. Go ahead and live it all over again. Personally, I don't care."

"That suits me," Joe said. "If we do it all over, we can do it without you this time."

"You're going to, Joe," I said.

I had often prided myself on my composure, but now I felt that my hands and my voice were shaking.

"Well, to hell with you," I said.

It was an expression that I had been using very freely and its meaning was worn thin. Nevertheless I wished it to be absolute.

Joe frowned at me for a second; then his face became expressionless, and we both turned away from each other because Bella was speaking.

"Jim," she said, "no, no!"

I had nearly forgotten her, and I think that he had too, until her voice came to us, cutting between our voices. She was speaking with that exasperating ability of hers to impress herself on everybody.

"I want you to stay," she said, "really, Jim. This is all so dreadfully silly."

Her words were familiar. There was the old lightness in her voice, giving the customary impression that she could manage everything if you would only let her explain; but now there was something else, a trancelike unworldly note.

"I'm such an awful fool, you know," she was saying. "I never can do things right. You're both of you so patient."

"Never mind it, Belle," I said, but she could not have heard my interruption. She was speaking more quickly, almost breathlessly in her anxiety to make us listen.

"Please," she said, "oh, please listen. Joe, you've been so darling, coming when I wanted you, but it won't do any good."

"Now wait a minute, Bella," Joe said. "Don't get so upset, Bella."

"Darling," said Bella, "I'm so ashamed. I—Jim, where's your handkerchief?"

"You have it in your hand," I said. She had a look of blank surprise when she saw my handkerchief still dangling from her fingers.

"Don't you see what I'm saying, Joe?" she asked. "Can't either of you help me, please?"

Joe Stowe had always been incompetent to manage those moods of hers. He reached toward her, hesitatingly and clumsily, but Bella backed away.

"Don't talk," he said, "until you think. Wait just a minute, Bella." But Bella did not wait.

"Don't you see?" she said. "Joe, it won't do any good."

"Wait a minute," Joe repeated, "wait a minute, Bella."

It was clear enough, just then, why they had never got on together. There was something that did not mix, some lack of sympathy, which made them like two individuals speaking in different tongues.

"I'm so ashamed," Bella said. "It all seemed so easy, Joe. I thought that we could just go back. When I wrote that telegram I was so sorry for everything. Do you remember Rome when we were in the Borghese, and the way the ducks were swimming in that pond? I thought it would be like that, darling. I forgot that there was so much else."

"There doesn't have to be," Joe answered. "You and I can make it just the way it was, if both of us really try."

She was twisting the ends of my handkerchief into hard knots. She shook her head.

"That's what you always kept hoping, wasn't it, dear?" she said. "We can't. It wouldn't be fair to try, because I don't want you enough, Joe. I thought I did, but I don't."

Those moods of hers had always hurt him and what was worse, he could never take her seriously when it was necessary.

"Bella," he said, "you don't know what you want right now. Let's talk about it later."

Bella rolled the handkerchief into a ball and threw it on the floor.

"Don't talk like that," she said. "You always talk like that. I do know what I want, and I don't want you, Joe. That's what's making it so dreadful. I don't want you, Joe, because—"

Then the compulsion, or whatever it was, that had made her speak must have weakened, for she looked at us both almost timidly.

"What do you make me say it for?" she cried. "Why do you just look at me and make me? I don't want you, Joe, because I want Jim. I only want Jim—and he says he doesn't want me."

She stopped and looked at me and drew her breath in sharply and bit her lower lip to check herself from saying any more. She put her hand over her mouth and ran into her bedroom and slammed the door.

Joe and I stared at her closed door, and he must have felt as foolish as I did, because Bella had managed the scene very well.

In such matters she had always possessed an abandon and a consummate sort of art.

After a moment he turned to me with a bewildered expression implying that anything that had occurred could now be entirely discounted, that there was no further use in quarreling over Bella.

"Jesus!" Joe Stowe said.

I shrugged my shoulders without answering, and he still looked blank.

"What do you suppose she does want, Jim?" he asked.

"Cosmos," I said.

Joe opened his mouth and closed it.

"Jesus," he said again. "And I hired an airplane." Suddenly he grinned at me. "And I was sick in one of those paper bags."

"Hire another, Joe," I said. "It's the first break you've had in quite a while."

He did not answer, but he looked back again at the closed door, and I spoke to him softly.

"You're out of it, Joe," I said, "for good." And I might have been congratulating him on a brilliant achievement. "Get that into your head, Joe. It's the first generous thing I've ever seen her do."

His mind moved swiftly to another aspect of it, and his eyes grew narrow.

"I guess," he said, "it's been you, Jim, all the time."

"Joe, if you think—" I began, but he put his hand on my shoulder.

"I don't think you two-timed me," he said. "It's just that way."

"You needn't wish her off on me," I said.

"Jim," he said, "that's pretty hard on her."

The amazing thing was that he felt no resentment toward her; instead in another minute he would be defending her again.

"Maybe it's time that something was hard on her," I said.

Joe sighed and looked back at the door.

"Jim," he said, "couldn't you—?"

"No," I said, "definitely not."

"That's pretty hard on Bella," he repeated. "Do you think she's all right in there?"

"Yes," I said. "Don't worry. I'll look out for her." We were speaking in the tones one uses when there is illness in the house.

"Jim," Joe said, "let's go away somewhere."

"Where?" I asked.

"Anywhere," he said. "There's Spain."

"I never did like Spain," I said.

"All right," said Joe. "I don't care. There's the Chinese war. If we were just to get to Shanghai . . ." He stopped and stared at me. "What's the matter? Are you getting soft? Don't you want to go?"

"I don't know," I said.

"Is there something you haven't told me?" he asked.

"Yes," I said, "but not about Bella, Joe."

"I knew there was something," he began. "That's a hell of a way—not to tell your friends."

"Listen," I said, "I'll tell you about it later. Just keep your mind on one thing at a time. You're out of this for good, and I'm staying here to take care of Belle. Don't ask if she's all right again, and don't worry about her. She isn't any different from what she ever was, and what's more she never will be."

"You'll be kind to her," he said, "won't you?"

I nodded without speaking.

"Well," said Joe, "I'm going somewhere if you're not. If you change your mind you know where to get me, Jim."

"Yes," I said, "I know." Our conversation did not mean much, but everything was all right again.

"It's a hell of a mess, isn't it?" he said.

"Yes," I said; "but it's no worse than it's ever been."

He held out his hand and I took it.

"Well," he said, "I'll see you later."

"So long, Joe," I said. "Good luck."

XXXIII | Even the Weariest River

I knocked on Bella's door.

"Bella," I said. There was no answer. I knocked again and listened, but I could not hear anything, and then I opened the door and went in. She was lying face down, on the bed. Her gray dress was rumpled above her knees and she was gripping one of the pillows hard.

"Belle," I said, but she did not move or answer, and I bent over her and put my hand on her shoulder, and I felt her body shake.

"Snap out of it, sweetness," I said. Then she turned her head and looked up at me, trying to read in my face what she wished to see there.

"Jim," she said, "I sent him away, didn't I?"

"Yes," I said, "you did." She had spoken in a gentle, stunned way, as though she could not understand why she had done it.

"Jim," she said, "I didn't have to."

"No," I said, "that's true." I had never thought of its being deliberate until just then, when I saw her looking up at me.

"Darling," she said, "it was what you wanted, wasn't it?"

"Belle," I said, "I didn't ask you."

"But it was what you wanted, wasn't it?" she said. "That's why I did it, darling."

"Belle," I said, "I'm very much obliged. Maybe it makes you feel better."

She turned around and sat up, facing me.

"Why?" she asked.

"Because you've done something decent," I said.

She smiled at me, but there was no humor in her eyes.

"You like me better, don't you?"

"Yes, honey bee," I said, "I like you a good deal better. You've been very generous." I wondered what she would have been like if she had always been generous.

"You didn't mean those things you said? You take them back now, don't you, darling?" she asked.

Although I felt no response to her, I still could feel the compliment. It was a transient moment, but for just a little while she must have cared more about me than she had ever been able to care for anyone. As surely as I was looking down at her, she had thrown away Joe Stowe for me. She had thrown him over with the calculation of a card player who deliberately loses a trick to win another. Once it would have moved me, but it did not move me then; it only made me feel sorry for her because she was so sure again that everything would be all right.

"Let's forget about it, Belle," I said. "It's only that we've both been fighting." But she must have understood.

"So it didn't do any good?" she said. She must have been sure at last that everything was over.

"You're wrong," I answered, "it's done a lot of good. You're nicer than you've ever been right now."

She got up and smoothed her gray dress.

"Darling," she said, "it's like an operation. I feel so weak. My head keeps going around. You'll be kind to me anyway, won't you? Anyway?"

"Yes, of course," I said.

Bella gave her head a little shake.

"I feel so damned unattractive," she said. "Let's go somewhere and have lunch and have some champagne."

"All right," I said, "but now you'd better pack."

"Why?" she asked.

"Because you've done enough for one day, sweetness," I said. "I'm going to take you back to Wickford Point."

Bella shook her head again.

"That's all that ever happens," she said. "No matter what we do, we always go back to Wickford Point."

I had thought of the same thing often enough before.

"Well, what of it?" I said. "Even the weariest river flows somewhere safe to sea."

"It's discouraging, isn't it?" Bella said. "I try to get away and I always end up right there. Sometimes it doesn't seem to do any good to try—but you like me better, don't you?"

"Yes," I said, "I like you better, Belle."

For a good many years there had been a dispute with the town about the condition of the side road which led to Wickford Point. Once the entire road had been sandy, and I can remember looking down from the buggy seat to watch the fine sand carried along the thin rims of the wheels by centrifugal force until it dropped back perpendicularly into the dust again. I can remember the whispering sound which it made against the wheels, and I can remember the sweat and the dimples in the hide over the horses' rumps as they struggled against its insistent pull. Cousin Sue used to say that she always felt better when the carryall turned from the gray macadam main road onto that sandy surface. She often said that it rested her head not to hear any more bang and clatter from the horses or the wagon. The sand, she said, was like a feather bed; but then most of Cousin Sue's similes were inaccurate. She was very much upset when they finally surfaced the Wickford road back in the early twenties. She always contended that it was much rougher than before, and for a long while she closed her window at night because, she said, the smell of the road oil made her ill.

That was quite a while ago, and the town must have felt that it had relieved itself of all responsibility by that single effort. At any rate, beginning with the Jeffries farm and continuing down to our place, the road was never repaired, and finally it became full of caverns and pot-holes. The local authorities invariably expressed surprise when anyone objected. They always said the road could not be as bad as that, because it had just been surfaced; and they kept on saying it. Once, a good many years back, when a cook named Heloise—Cousin Clothilde had brought her up from the city for the summer because Josie was about to have a baby—began having queer spells and throwing things, it looked as if something might be done in the way of repairs. Cousin Clothilde had called for the police the night that Heloise was really violent, and the car which was to take her to the state hospital broke three springs and twisted an axle. The police chief, whose name was Mr. Finnegan, was definitely annoyed about it, since it was his own car; but finally the only thing that happened was that the county bought Mr. Finnegan a new automobile, and after that he too was averse to having the Wickford road repaired, in fact he kept wanting to drive down it again on business.

As a result of this anyone driving to Wickford Point had to be on the alert, and as Cousin Sue used to say, it was probably just as well, since people only came there who really wished to come —no insurance agents, or lightning-rod salesmen, or Armenians selling laces.

"For heaven's sake," said Bella, "look out where you're going, darling."

I had forgotten about the road and without thinking I struck the bad place at the corner just beyond the Jeffries farm. Bella bounced upward so that her head collided with the top of the car. Not only had the pain made her angry but she had crushed the bunch of grapes on the straw hat which she had borrowed from a friend of hers on a houseparty at Easthampton.

"All right," I said, "all right. Why can't you hold on?"

"You'd better let me drive," Bella said, "if you can't manage."

"Hold on and shut up, honey bee," I said.

I had forgotten about the road, but now it all came back like something one has memorized from a book at school. I could remember the road without watching it. There would be a series of bumps and then some gravel, and then a big hole in the middle where one must pass to the left, and then a bad gulley on the right near the big rock, and then the piece bordered by the oak trees which my great-aunt Sarah had planted when she was already an old lady, thirty years ago. Aunt Sarah was always getting baskets of acorns from the great oak near the river and carrying them up the hill and poking them into the soil on either side of the road. When she used to get lost, in the days her mind was leaving her, she almost certainly could be found somewhere up the hill, making little holes in the ground with her ivory-headed walking stick. She used to refer to the trees as her babies, and they were big babies now. Then a little farther on it was necessary to go into second gear, for here the entire surface of the road was washed out, and after this came the first view of Wickford Point with the roofs of the hay barns and the chimneys of the house, and the stand of white pine and the elm trees near the river.

No matter how often I came to Wickford Point there was an indefinable excitement about the first sight of it, a sense of relief that it was still there waiting. It did not matter whether I had been away for years or for just a day or two, the expectation was the same. There was nothing like it anywhere, and all the people who had lived there and all the things that had happened were waiting for my return. There was the same close musty smell in the air, from the river and from the trees. I had not been away from it for many hours, but it seemed like a long while. It always required a certain readjustment when I was coming down the road. The unseen things that were in the air might be peculiar, but all of them were friendly. Nevertheless there would be a moment of uncertainty when I first saw the place, a moment when all I had learned from the outside world still gathered about me. All the buildings that had seemed so large when I was very young, and were now small and meager and unimportant, made me wonder what I was expecting and what it was all about. Now I was seeing it through the gathering dusk, which blurred all the outlines so that the plumes of the elms, black against the faint light in the sky, tossed clouds of darkness upon the house and lawn. I had turned on the headlights some time before and now they picked objects out of the darkness—the trumpet vines on the garden fence, the glowing eyes of one of the barn cats, the broken little wagon which Josie's Herman played with. I heard Bella sigh.

"Well," she said, "we're back. My God, he always leaves that wagon in the road."

I did not answer because both of the remarks were trite.

"Harry's come," she said. "He must have brought someone with him."

Her deduction was not clever. She had seen, as I had, that there were more lights than usual. The windows of the dining room and the little parlor were glowing oblongs and there were lights upstairs.

"If Harry's here, Mirabel Steiner's here," Bella said. "He must have come in Mirabel's car. I don't know why it is, I feel dreadfully tired."

"Perhaps you didn't have much sleep last night," I said.

"Jim," said Bella sharply, "won't you please shut up. Jim—"

"What?" I said.

"Don't say anything about it, please."

"You don't have to ask me that," I said.

She leaned her shoulder against mine. In a way she was saying good-by to the last few days. It was what always happened when one came to Wickford Point, for nothing anyone did outside made the slightest difference.

"Thank you for everything, dear," she said. The remark was surprising because she very seldom thanked me. We were at the side door by then and I blew the horn, but it really was not necessary because they must have heard the car and the door was already open. It was the same as always. When anyone arrived at Wickford Point, it was like a ship arriving at an island. Sid, wearing a pair of white flannel trousers which belonged to me and which must have just returned from the cleaners, came out first and leaned against the wall of the house, and Cousin Clothilde followed in a brown, billowy dress which belonged to Mary. Then the

laundry door opened and Earle and Frieda came out, and the house
cat and the setter followed them, and then Josie came carrying
Herman. When the headlights struck Herman I saw that he was
eating a hard-boiled egg, the yolk of which was smeared on his
cheeks. He had also obviously been eating a good many other
things.

Bella made a gagging unladylike sound.

"Josie," Bella called, "can't you take him in and wash his face?"

"Why, Miss Bella," said Josie, "I just washed his dear little face
half an hour ago. He got into something at the sink, and I was
just going to wash it again as soon as Frieda and I had finished
with the dishes, but he wanted to give Mr. Calder a kiss."

Then everyone was speaking at once. It was just as if we had
been downtown and not away at all.

"Did you have a happy time?" Cousin Clothilde was saying.
"It's so nice you're back. I get so restless when people are away.
Jim, if you've remembered the gin and the cigarettes, Frieda had
better take them. Everyone in the parlor is drinking gin."

Frieda moved forward, swaying slightly at the hips, but her new
high heels made her imitation of Bella's walk entirely incorrect.

"Did you think," she asked in a languid voice, "to stop at the
drugstore, Mr. Calder?"

"Get out my bag, Earle," I said, "and take it to my room. Everything's in my bag."

"Darling," said Cousin Clothilde, "Mirabel Steiner's dressing in
your room."

"What?"

"There just didn't seem to be any place to fit Mirabel Steiner,"
Cousin Clothilde went on. "You don't mind Mirabel in your
room, do you, darling? She's dusted it all out for you. So many
things have been happening. I thought that if you came back you
wouldn't mind sleeping with Sid."

"Well, I do mind," I said. "Let Mirabel sleep with Sid. Let her
sleep anywhere. I want my room."

Bella began to giggle.

"Darling," said Cousin Clothilde, "you don't know how hard

it's been, getting everyone in here without getting them mixed up. You see there's Harry, and then of course there's Mr. Northby— he has to have a room to himself. And the roof has been leaking through the attic into it. I'm so thankful that you've come, darling, because nobody understands about leaks."

I still sat in the car leaning on the wheel, watching them.

"Who did you say was here? Northby?"

Cousin Clothilde frowned thoughtfully.

"That nice friend of yours. Why didn't you tell me he was so charming? You never have brought down any of your interesting friends. Mr. Allen Northby—he is writing such a delightful book. He has to have a place to himself where he can write it."

I remembered something that seemed to have happened years ago. "Do you mean to say that Southby is here right now?"

"He was so charming about it," said Cousin Clothilde. "He said you asked him for the week end and he simply couldn't wait. He came down yesterday."

I had completely forgotten about Allen Southby.

"He's got a nerve," I said. "It isn't the week end yet."

Days and time and space were moving erratically through the fading light, but Cousin Clothilde was dealing with them calmly.

"Isn't it the week end yet?" she said.

"No," I said. "It's only Thursday night."

Cousin Clothilde sighed.

"I don't see why everyone worries so about time," she said. "It doesn't really make any difference, and he's been such a help. A man always is. He was so nice about the leak. There was a thunderstorm and it came right down on his head and he thought of things to put under it."

"What sort of things?" I asked.

"All those things that used to be in bedrooms, dear," Cousin Clothilde said. "He found them in the attic."

But my real worry still centered on Mirabel Steiner, who was dressing in my room.

"Look here," I said, "Steiner is going to get out of my room. She can sleep with Mary."

"Darling," Cousin Clothilde sighed again, "you don't understand everything that's happened. Mary has been very difficult all day. Mr. Northby has been so charming with her, but it seems to make her difficult."

"Well, let Steiner sleep with her," I said.

There was a sound above my head. The back bathroom window had opened and Mary was leaning out. She had been doing something to her hair. Its yellow waves and her straight nose and the slight twist of her upper lip made her look aristocratic and commanding, although she was holding a towel in her hand.

"I don't care what anybody says," she called, "I don't see why I should make any more sacrifices when no one makes any for me. I won't have Mirabel in my room. She smells of musk."

Mary slammed the bathroom window shut and Cousin Clothilde looked at me meaningly.

"You see, " she said. "She's been that way all day." But I was still thinking of the immediate question and Mary did not worry me.

"What about the north room?" I said, for the north room had not been mentioned. Cousin Clothilde looked at Sid before she answered.

"It hasn't been swept out," she said. "Sid uses it, you know. Sid has to go somewhere."

Bella got out of the car and gave her shoulders an impatient shrug.

"My goodness," she said, "can't anyone do anything? Of course she can't stay in Jim's room. Put Harry in Sid's room and put her there."

"Darling," said Cousin Clothilde, "Harry seems so worn out."

"Well, I'm worn out too," said Bella. "Frieda, move the things around, and for heaven's sake let's stop talking."

"And the north room will have to be ready by Saturday," I said. "I've asked someone else down."

As I got out of the car I noticed that Bella and Cousin Clothilde were staring at me, and I remembered that I had told Bella nothing about it.

"I've always hoped you'd ask people down, dear," said Cousin Clothilde. "I only hope he's as nice as Mr. Northby."

"Southby," I said, not that it made any difference. But they all kept looking at me. "It's a girl, as a matter of fact. Bella knows her. Her name is Patricia Leighton." I tried to say it casually, but I knew that I had been unnecessarily emphatic, and everyone seemed to be hanging on my words, waiting for me to continue. Bella had said she was tired; and now she looked it, even in that favorable half-light. Her face, when it was turned to me, was white and strained; Sid had pushed himself away from the wall, and Cousin Clothilde had a curious, apprehensive expression.

"Well," I said, "what's so queer about it? Everyone else is asked down here."

"Why, Jim," said Cousin Clothilde, and her voice sounded faint, "it's only—it's only that you've never asked anyone before. It's the only girl— But I think it's perfectly lovely. It's—it's just that it's so unlike you, darling."

"Well," I said, "she's coming Saturday morning."

Bella spoke suddenly and her voice was unfamiliar.

"I'm tired," she said, "I'm going up to bed."

"Why, Bella," said Cousin Clothilde, "aren't you feeling well, dear? Don't you want some supper?"

Bella shook her head.

"No," she said. "I don't want any supper." She walked into the house, and I could hear her running very quickly up the entry stairs.

"Now I don't understand," said Cousin Clothilde, "why something should always be the matter."

"Mr. Calder," Josie said, "there's some corn and there's some chicken, and I can just heat over some after-dinner coffee in just a minute, Mr. Calder. And Frieda can give it to you in the dining room when she finishes moving that lady's things."

"Don't bother," I said. "I'll have it in the kitchen." Then Sid spoke to me.

"Did you remember that eyecup and the boric acid?" he said.

"The pollination has been very heavy. It seems to affect my eyes in the morning and the evening, but not otherwise."

"How's your digestion?" I asked.

"It troubles me a little," Sidney said. "I keep having a sharp and burning pain right here in the pit of the stomach, not in the duodenum. I always have it when all the family's here. They're all so—" He paused and blinked his eyes.

"So what?" I asked.

"So much as usual," Sidney said. "You know very well that I am the only properly adjusted person here, except Clothilde."

We were standing in the side entry where the coats were hanging. I could hear the dishes clattering in the kitchen and voices coming from the parlor. The sound swept above my head like water. I was like a swimmer in a tide-rip now that I was back at Wickford Point. It occurred to me that we all were characters, and our sportive attributes were developing. Everyone had always been a character at Wickford Point, obeying impulse without the proper repressions; and all the talk was natural once one heard it there. I wondered if I were becoming a little eccentric myself.

"How did you get adjusted?" I asked. Sidney smiled faintly.

"Just by not trying," he said. "The trouble with everyone here is that they try, except Clothilde. It's always struggle, misdirected effort; and frankly, I've given up."

"Oh," I said. "When did you give up?"

"A year or two ago," said Sidney, "and I've been much better ever since. I just let things go. I sit and watch it all move. It's very, very interesting."

"Where's it moving to?" I asked. Sometimes I had a respect for Sidney because he had a way of seeing things.

"No one gets anywhere," he said, "except Clothilde. She's the only one who matters. She's very wonderful."

I thought of her standing on the doorstep, half-frowning and half-smiling, and glancing here and there to watch the effect of words, and then I remembered her look when I said that Pat Leighton was coming.

394

"Suppose . . . she dies," I said.

For the first time in a long while I saw Sidney Brill look concerned.

"What's wrong with her?" he asked. "Don't you think she's
looking well?"

"Why yes, of course," I said.

"Then don't talk about her dying," Sidney said. "She mustn't
ever die."

The kitchen sink was full of dishes and glasses, and Herman and
the setter and the cat were under the table.

"The dear little thing," Josie said, "Herman's been asleep there
all evening. He just woke up when he heard you, Mr. Calder. It's
been such a day, and dear Mrs. Wright just doesn't understand.
Everyone keeps asking for everything, and poor dear Frieda, she
keeps wanting to go to the movies with Earle, but he can't ever
take her. There's a movie tomorrow night called 'Up and Down
Broadway.'"

I tilted my wooden chair back comfortably and looked at the
murky ceiling. I was thinking of all the times that I had sat in that
low-studded kitchen, and, as I thought, a pleasant languor came
over me. There was even a reassuring sort of reason in its disorder.
There was the same pine dresser and the same stove with its kettle
of boiling dishwater. I thought of the early mornings when I had
gone there while it was still dark, to get bread and meat before
I had started for ducks on the river, and of how my dog had been
waiting under the table, just where Herman slept. I remembered
the evenings when Mr. Morrissey and I had sat there drinking
hard cider, when he told me of ghosts in Ireland, and I remembered how the whole place had smelled of vinegar and spice when
my great-aunt Sarah was making watermelon pickle. All those
thoughts drifted aimlessly and dreamily through my mind. I gathered that the young people wanted to go to the movies but could
not because Earle's wages were still in arrears.

"Poor dear Mrs. Wright!" Josie said. "Ever since you went

everyone has been in her pocketbook. First Mr. Sidney had to get sun glasses, and that fish man wouldn't leave anything unless we paid him, and then Mr. Harry needed gin, and then there wasn't any food in the house. I don't know what we should have done if Mr. Sidney hadn't looked in Miss Mary's pocketbook, and there she had eight dollars and seventy-five cents. I don't know where Miss Mary got it."

"He took it, did he?" I asked.

"Yes," Josie said; "but Miss Mary didn't mind, because that man was here."

"What man?" I asked.

"That man who came from Harvard University," Josie said. "Dear Miss Mary has been so happy. They went right downtown in that nice car of his—he has a lovely green car that Earle put in the barn tonight—and that man spent some of his own money for gin and vermouth and cigarettes; but they're all gone now; and then we made out with the corn in the garden and some wax beans. Earle has been working so hard on that little patch of corn. That poor boy, he feels so badly because he hasn't been paid for a long time. He's only had that dollar you gave him, Mr. Calder, but I've told him not to talk to dear Mrs. Wright about it any more. It only gets her so upset. I've told him that I haven't been paid for three weeks either, Mr. Calder, and nearly all the soap is gone and there isn't any Bunzo for the dishes."

"What's Bunzo?" I asked.

"That kind of powder you put on the dishes," Josie said. "I asked that man if he could get me some this afternoon, but he forgot."

I took a ten-dollar bill from my pocket.

"Give a little of it to Earle," I said. "Mrs. Wright has overdrawn her bank account. I'll give you a check tomorrow."

Josie wiped her hands on her apron.

"I just told Earle to wait," she said. "I told him you would fix up everything, Mr. Calder, as soon as you came back. It's just that everyone is after dear Mrs. Wright for money. And then there was the roof. I always said that carpenter didn't lay the valleys right, and it leaked so in that little bedroom where that man was sleeping. It leaked right on his pillow. Poor dear Miss Mary felt so badly. She's been so happy since that man came, Mr. Calder."

"You mean Mr. Southby?" I asked.

"Yes, Mr. Southby," Josie said. "He looks so young, although he has gray hair. He looks so cute."

"That's because he's never done anything," I said, "except be at Harvard University."

"Yes," Josie said, "I suppose it does keep them young to be at Harvard University. Why, he's been acting just like a boy, Mr. Calder, carrying on so with Miss Mary, and he's been so jolly out here in the kitchen. He had his coffee here just the way you do, Mr. Calder, and he's asked so many questions, all about the family. He wanted to know where that Negro man and all the dogs were buried."

"Well," I said, "that's fine. I guess I'd better go and see him now. How's Mr. Harry, Josie?"

"He's just been joking all the time," Josie said. "I think he's got some position in some office in New York. Frieda heard him talking about it when she was waiting on table, but I told Frieda that of course it couldn't amount to much because Mr. Harry's always getting new positions; but he's been so jolly with that dark young woman. I knew it wasn't right to put her in your room. I told Frieda that you wouldn't like it, Mr. Calder."

"Well, I'd better go and see them now," I said. "Tell Frieda to open all the windows in my room, and dust out the north room tomorrow, will you Josie?"

I pushed my chair back from the table, but it was never easy to leave when Josie had started talking.

"Poor dear Miss Bella," she said. "She looked so tired. I suppose she was kept up all hours of the night at the shore with those Jaeckels."

"She'll be all right in the morning," I said.

"Poor dear Miss Bella," Josie said, "after all she's been through. I was telling Frieda just this afternoon—she still looks just as pretty as a picture, after all she's been through."

XXXIV | Wickford Lights

Whenever anyone died at Wickford Point an easy, expansive year would follow, because some frozen assets would be released from Mr. Caldicott's office in Boston. When Cousin Sue died it was, moreover, revealed to the family that she had made extensive collections of all the things one buys at the post office in order to help an impoverished Federal Government. At the time of the war she must have felt very strongly that if she did not "come across the Germans would," and in subsequent years she had wanted to help the Administration in every way. The result was that Cousin Clothilde found in Cousin Sue's upper bureau drawer, beneath some half-finished moth-eaten knitted articles and some Indian basketwork, a great many books of thrift stamps and Baby Bonds. I have often thought that Cousin Sue believed that these books of stamps and documents represented a grateful nation's receipt for donations, and that as such they possessed no intrinsic value; for Cousin Sue never could understand finance. When Cousin Clothilde came upon them she did not understand them either, and she would have thrown them all away if Sidney had not stopped her. Actually they were cashed at the post office for three hundred and eighty-seven dollars, and the whole thing was so unexpected that before anyone had time to get the money Cousin Clothilde had started to wire the house for electricity.

That is, she wired the lower floor, but before the workers could get upstairs Harry needed a new dinner coat and Mary lost her wrist watch and Sidney began to suffer from an impacted wisdom tooth.

As it was, it did not make much difference in the general appearance of the house, because all the old lamps were wired also, but it is hard to get away from habit. When I came into the back parlor with Josie's voice still ringing through my head, I was as usual not adjusted to that new bright light, and I thought momentarily that all the lamps had been turned up too high and that the chimneys would be cracking if the wicks were not turned down. The night was warm outside and the windows were open, and all the assorted shapes of the nocturnal insect world were beating against the screens. Even though Earle and I had patched the screens earlier in the summer some moths had found their way inside, with that contortionist ability peculiar to their species; and now they were fluttering and blundering against the lamps, dropping their dusty scales and their weary bodies upon the table.

The brightness of the light bulbs made everything stand out unnaturally, I thought. First I saw the crack in the parlor ceiling and next I saw my great-grandfather's books with the yellowed enlarged photograph of the bearded Wickford Sage above them, and I noticed that his flowing white beard was growing yellow, which was not unnatural since portions of it had been yellow enough in life. Then there was the picture of the brig *Alert* upon which my great-grandfather had sailed around Cape Horn. It had been painted by an unknown Chinese artist in the roadstead at Wampoa. Then there were the sofas and all the old chairs, and the table in front of the empty fireplace with its ashtrays and bottles and glasses. Everyone was there except Bella. Sidney was sitting in a corner, moving one thumb clockwise and the other counterclockwise. Cousin Clothilde was reclining on one sofa, and Mirabel Steiner was lying upon the other, looking at the ceiling and smoking a cigarette, with her hands clasped behind her head and her knees bent upward. Mirabel was dressed in a polo shirt and abbreviated shorts, and when I saw her legs I was glad that she had remembered the shorts at any rate. Mary was dressed in an embroidered peasant's gown which she had won in a raffle at a fair, and she was wearing a pair of red bathing sandals. She was sitting stiffly in a Jacobean chair. Her blond hair, her blue eyes and her red cheeks gave her a vivid intensity as she watched Allen Southby.

"Suppose," Harry was saying, "we endeavor to be impersonal. What is indicated is a concentration camp for nonproducers."

"But they have to eat, sweetheart," Mirabel called across the room.

"Harry," said Cousin Clothilde, "I don't see why you won't listen to Mirabel. Mirabel has a Ph.D."

"This is priceless," Allen Southby said, "all so priceless!" and I knew that they were talking about nothing as usual.

Then they all saw me and everyone got up except Cousin Clothilde and Mirabel.

Mary was nearest to me and she kissed me with an enthusiasm I did not expect.

"Jim," she said, "I'm so glad you're back. Everyone has missed you so."

They all looked pleased to see me, and I remembered that they always had been pleased. Now that Mary had spoken to me everything was the same as it always had been. Even Mirabel Steiner upon the sofa and Allen Southby rising from his chair were not discordant notes, because Cousin Clothilde was always gathering extraneous and ill-assorted faces.

"Hello, boy," Harry said. "Would you like a drink perhaps?"

"Well, Jim," said Allen in a melodious, hearty voice, "well, well, well."

He was welcoming me and putting me at my ease in a house which was not his but partially mine, but it did not bother me particularly. He looked just as he had the other night in his study at Martin House. His graying hair was just sufficiently rumpled; he had on gray slacks and a silk shirt open at the neck, and he was smoking a straight-grained pipe. His tanned face was distinguished, and as Josie had said, he did look surprisingly young. He appeared exactly the figure that he wanted to appear, a literary man.

"Look," said Allen, and pointed playfully at the table. "Hebe yonder in the shape of Mary Brill has furnished me with a pewter mug and beer."

"Well," I said, "that was thoughtful of her."

"Jim," said Cousin Clothilde, "have you a cigarette, dear? They're all arguing about all those things that I don't understand —about Mr. Roosevelt and about Mr. Harry Hopkins, and then Hitler's name keeps coming into it, and then they talk about Russia and Mr. Southby has been telling us about how self-contained the American farm used to be and about the American Dream. You'll argue with them, won't you dear? I like to hear about the American Dream, but I've always hated Germans. The backs of the men's necks are always fat."

Allen Southby smiled at her gravely.

"There are no fat necks in the American Dream," he said. "The American Dream is thin and hard-bitten. It is born from the rocky soil. In a way this room is the American Dream."

"Phooey," said Mirabel Steiner from the sofa, and for a moment my heart warmed toward her.

"Jim," said Cousin Clothilde, "won't you argue with them? I don't understand about the American Dream." She wrinkled her forehead and smiled at me at the same time, and looked sideways at Allen Southby. She was reclining on the sofa in a dream world of her own that nothing could disturb, not even Allen's speech. I thought he was a fantastic ass, but she evidently did not. I was thinking that now he was at Wickford Point he was worse than I had ever imagined him, that nothing about him was exactly right; but Cousin Clothilde was impregnable in her peace.

"Not tonight," I said. "I'm going out to see the river."

"That's splendid," Southby said. "I'll go with you."

"Don't bother, Allen," I said.

"No trouble at all," said Allen, "I need a breath of air."

I walked across the lawn away from the lights of the house with Allen Southby striding beside me, breathing the air lustily ʳ¹ ₜrough his nostrils.

"Jim," said Allen, and his voice was playfully reproachful, "why did you keep this from me?"

The breeze was moving faintly through the pine trees. The trees were never silent out there on the point, and now they were whispering through the night air.

"Jim's back," they were saying. "Jim's back, but he's going away. He's always going away."

I wanted to forget that Allen Southby was beside me. In all my life I had never desired so much to be alone.

"Why," I heard him ask again, "why did you keep it from me?"

"Keep what?" I asked.

Though I could not see the gesture I knew that Allen was raising his arms embracingly.

"All this," he said, "everything—but then I don't suppose it can mean to you what it does to me."

"Probably not," I said.

"No," he said, "of course not," and there was no stopping him now that he had started. "It's all so utterly priceless. It's what I've always wanted and what I've known must exist somewhere. It's like returning to a spiritual home."

"Oh," I said, "it is, is it?" Allen laughed softly.

"Don't be so literal, Jim," he said. "I have never faced such an experience. I was so worried about that novel. There was something which seemed to me wrong about it. You know how one gets, that feeling of creative insecurity, actually a sort of checkmate. I simply could not tell whether or not my conception of the picture was correct, and then I came down here on a sort of pilgrimage of desperation, just to look; and then I knew that the book was right, absolutely right."

While I listened to him, I wanted to laugh; and I wished that Joe Stowe might be there to hear him . . . but then, Allen was no more singular than anyone else at Wickford Point.

"That must be a big consolation," I said. "How do you know it's right?"

"Jim," said Allen, "I felt it as soon as I came here. I don't see how I can ever tear myself away. All the little nuances are so perfect, things that you have probably never noticed." And he waved his arm again. "That priceless little graveyard for the dogs, and the fugitive slave in the orchard, and the books, and the Brilliana."

"What's the Brilliana?" I asked.

"Those letters," Allen Southby said, "and the presentation copies, and the Brill mementoes. Mary showed them to me this afternoon."

"Oh," I said, "she did, did she?"

"Of course, Jim," he said, "you're so damnably literal that you don't see them as I do and how they fit together in a priceless picture."

He went on talking and there was no way to stop him, but somehow it was annoyingly grotesque because everything he said was off-key. He was making the whole place into a museum. His mind was filling it with curios as he had filled his study with pewter and pine at Martin House.

"Don't you think you're running away with yourself?" I said.

Allen laughed again in his most delightful, friendly way.

"You would say that," he said. "You've always lacked enthusiasms. That's your trouble, Jim. Excuse me, old man, I haven't hurt your feelings, have I?"

"No," I said, "but just don't talk about it, Allen."

His voice sounded hurt, but he was very bland.

"I must talk," he said. "I'm at my best when I have creative enthusiasm, and this has been so real, a great discovery. Why, all this place is like a novel, and all the people in it."

"Maybe you're right," I said, "but don't talk about it, Allen. I know all about it. I've lived here."

"Lived here. . . ." Allen Southby repeated, and his tone was amusingly ironical. "But you don't know it as I do, Jim, who have been here for only a day. I'm trying to paint the characters in my mind already, and Mary is running through it like a glowing thread."

"Mary?" I repeated. "When Mary has a chance, she's fine."

"Yes," Allen said. "I suppose you've never seen it—her loneliness, her prim, quiet beauty, her shyness, and her desire to escape. Jim, she's like Hester Prynne."

"I don't think she's ever committed adultery," I said.

"Always the same," said Allen Southby; "always bitter, always the same old Jim."

"Well," I said, "I guess I'd better go to bed, and you too, Allen. You'll feel better in the morning."

"You don't mind my going on this way, do you, Jim," said Allen, "just giving myself my head? There's so much I want to see, so much I want to think about."

"That's all right, Allen," I said. "I'm glad you like it here, but I'm going to bed. Good night."

"Good night, old man," he said.

I left him standing in the shadows, breathing the night air deeply, and I walked back toward the house. His complacency had always disturbed me, but this new enthusiasm was worse.

"Ass," I muttered, although I told myself that there was no use in taking Allen so hard. It was simply that every word of his was discordant and every word hurt me because he was talking of something that I loved. I had never known until I heard him that I loved Wickford Point so much. I wanted to throw everyone out of it; I wanted it to be as it had been when Cousin Sue and Aunt Sarah were there.

I met Mary when I was halfway to the house. I knew it was she by the way she walked and by the light color of her dress.

"Oh," she said, and stopped in front of me. "Where's Allen Southby, Jim?"

"He's out near the point, thinking," I said.

"Oh," she said. "Jim, isn't he wonderful?" I tried to look at her, but it was too dark to see her face.

"Well, if you don't think he's wonderful," Mary said, "don't

404

say it. I'll tell you what I think. He's the only friend of yours I've ever liked. Don't say he isn't wonderful."

"All right," I said, "but don't be so excited, Mary." She laughed and threw her arms around me and hugged me tight.

"Don't be such a thing," she said, "such an old disagreeable thing. Jim, I'm so happy, so happy. I've had him to myself all day and Bella isn't going to get him away from me either."

"All right," I said, "I hear you, Mary."

"Well, she isn't," Mary said, "and I'm going to find him now. Don't be such a stick. Don't you see I'm happy?"

"Yes," I said, "I see."

"And Mirabel Steiner isn't going to get him either," she said. "He says he doesn't like Mirabel Steiner. Isn't that wonderful? And what do you think, I'm going to take him to the Brill house tomorrow. It's so lucky that I'm a Brill. And I'm going to find him now and you can't stop me, or Clothilde or Sid or Harry, no matter if you try. Nobody can stop me."

This was a new side of Mary Brill. She must have been thinking always, ever since she was little, that all of us would stop her.

"Mary," I said, "wait a minute. I want to tell you something. You're pretty, Mary, and you're quite a number, when you aren't angry. Listen Mary—you're more attractive than Bella, and everyone likes you better. If you really want him, there's no reason to be too anxious about him. Just don't run after him too hard. Men don't like it, and you don't need to." Mary laughed, a high, delighted laugh.

"Don't be so silly, dear," she said. "I'm not running after him, he's running after me." And she ran off through the shadows and the dark after Allen Southby.

Cousin Clothilde always had trouble with her coffee. No matter what else might happen at Wickford Point, the coffee was never right, and it often made her feel that everyone connected with its sale and preparation had been deliberately unkind. I was not surprised that she dealt with her coffee first when I saw her next morning, but I knew she had asked me up to her room for other reasons. She wanted me because there had been something unspoken between us which had disturbed her the night before.

I had felt a tenseness in the air all that morning. It had awakened me early and it had followed me when I walked alone through the familiar rooms downstairs. Always before, I had been able to drive other preoccupations out of my mind, and Wickford Point and all its details would rise up about me restfully. Now, though I was there among familiar things, I might as well have been a thousand miles away, just thinking about Wickford Point. I was a thousand miles away, even when I was standing on the lawn watching the sun dance on the muddy blue river as its surface stirred under the southwest breeze. I was thinking of Pat Leighton. She had been in my mind all night. The simple fact that she did not allow me time to concentrate my attention on Wickford Point gave me a sense of disloyalty, and there was nothing in my previous experience to tell me what to do.

Cousin Clothilde was sitting up in bed in her purple kimono, looking at the half-empty cup on the candle-stand beside her pillow.

"When I do everything for everyone else," she said, "I don't see why someone can't get me a good cup of coffee." She looked at me and frowned. "Jim, do you think it's that man downtown?"

"What man downtown?" I asked her.

"The man who sells the coffee," Cousin Clothilde said, "the fat one in the dirty white apron with brown eyes, who has the cat. I think he's doing something to the coffee on purpose. He might because we haven't paid his bill. Don't you think he might?"

"No, I don't," I said.

"Well," said Cousin Clothilde, "there's something the matter with it. It's bitter. I wish you'd taste it, and I wish you'd give me a cigarette and then sit down. Everyone's so restless. I don't know what's the matter."

I did not answer and she leaned back on her pillow.

406

"Besides," she said, "I have a queer feeling in my foot, an aching feeling. Perhaps I'm getting old."

"No, you're not," I said. She looked surprisingly young.

"Nothing was restful last night," she said. "Everyone was moving about so. I don't know why Mary couldn't be still. Jim, do you think Mary's in love?"

"I don't know," I said. Cousin Clothilde sighed.

"Mary always makes such a fuss about it when she's in love," she said, "and she runs after every man until he is frightened. I can't remember that I ever behaved that way, and I used to be in love quite often. I was never restless when I was in love with Archie. I wonder where Archie is. I haven't heard from him for three days. It always makes me nervous when I don't hear."

"Perhaps it's the coffee," I said.

"No, it's something else," she answered. "I feel nervous in different ways. I feel nervous when I can't do things for people. Now Mary's upset and Bella is upset. Has Bella seen Mr. Northby yet?"

"Southby," I said. "He and Mary have gone away somewhere in his car. No, Bella hasn't seen him."

"He's so charming," Cousin Clothilde said, "so delightful."

"Personally, I think he's terrible," I said.

"Darling," said Cousin Clothilde, "you mustn't be so hard on people. He must have some money to have such a nice tweed coat."

Her point of view was always young and it made me laugh and she laughed back at me.

"I'm so glad you're back, dear," she said. "You always think things I say are funny when I don't mean them to be funny. You're glad you're back, aren't you?"

I must have been asking the same question of myself without knowing it.

"I don't exactly know," I said.

"Of course you know," she answered. "You always have been glad when you come back to us. You're glad because you know

407

that everyone depends on you. It's the nicest thing there is. I know it is. If everyone didn't depend on me I wouldn't be happy."

"Are you happy?" I asked.

"Yes," she answered, "always, when I'm helping other people. It's the only thing that's worth while, helping other people."

"But perhaps it's hard," I suggested, "on other people."

"That strikes me as a very silly thing to say," she answered. "It can't hurt anyone when you do something kind. I wouldn't feel comfortable if it did."

"It stops him doing it for himself," I said. Cousin Clothilde looked thoughtfully out of the window.

"Now that isn't fair," she said. "You only say it because you're able to do so much. There are so many others who aren't able."

I thought of telling her that a good deal of the world was not fair, but she would not have understood it.

"Well, it doesn't help people to be perpetually kind to them," I said, and then I realized that it was better to let it go, because I knew that there was no way to change her, and perhaps I did not want her changed.

"You know," she said, "they are really such good children." She was thinking of them as children still, and that was what she wanted them to be.

"They're so fond of you," she said. "You love them, don't you?"

"Yes," I said, "perhaps I do, but don't you ever get tired of them?"

"What a funny thing to ask!" she answered. "No, I always like to watch them. They always come to me. They're such good children. Jim, I wonder what's the matter with Bella."

"The matter with all of them," I said, "is that you look after them too much."

"But Jim dear," she said, "I have to. Someone does. Now I don't know what Bella will do when she sees Mr. Northby. Mr. Northby is so charming, and he won't look at Mary again when he sees Bella, and then I don't know what Mary will do. And

408

then there's Sid. I wish you'd talk to him about his stomach."

"I've talked to him," I said.

"He always has been so delicate," Cousin Clothilde said; "and then there's Harry."

I sat and listened. Everything moved on nowhere.

"I've always wondered what Harry would do," Cousin Clothilde said, "and now I really think he's going to do something. He's been given a very satisfactory job. There's only one thing that bothers him; he has to have a car."

"Why?" I asked.

"Well, you know the way those things are sometimes," Cousin Clothilde said. "Harry is now in some very important position. I've forgotten what he said it was about. I never can remember those things. I think it's a Colony. Yes, it is about a Colony."

"What sort of a Colony?" I asked.

"It's somewhere in the woods," Cousin Clothilde said. "Some people have bought lots of woods around a lake and they're building a big clubhouse, and then they're building bungalows for people so that it will make a Colony, and Harry is going to see his friends about it. That's why he needs a car."

"Oh, he's selling real estate, is he?" I asked.

Cousin Clothilde looked puzzled and shook her head.

"No," she answered, "he distinctly said it isn't real estate. It's just getting people, really important people, to go and live in those little houses around the club, and it's just the thing for Harry, because he knows so many important people; but the trouble is he has to have a car. It has to be a car that looks well, because he will have to keep taking those people out there."

"Where?" I asked.

"Why, out to those little bungalows in the woods," said Cousin Clothilde. "And then he has to direct something, something to do with a carnival. He was talking to Mirabel Steiner about it. He has to buy five hundred lanterns and a lot of those things that they have at tables sometimes that make noises, but the main thing is the car. Did he speak to you about it, Jim?"

"Not yet," I said.

"Well," said Cousin Clothilde, "he was going to speak to you about your car."

"He hasn't got up his nerve yet," I answered.

Cousin Clothilde's mind had wandered from the subject.

"I don't understand what has happened to those people at the bank. They're being very disagreeable. They wrote me an impertinent letter yesterday. They've been very impertinent since dear old Mr. Dolhard died. They want me to put in some more money, and I can't because there isn't any more money until the first of the month. Do you see why they don't understand it?"

"If you'll give me the letter, I'll answer it," I said.

"I always throw their letters away, dear," Cousin Clothilde answered. "If you throw them away, they always write again. And then there's the roof. If the roof keeps on leaking we ought to have more basins to catch the water. Darling, I'm so glad you're back."

When I did not answer she asked me that same question.

"Aren't you glad you're back?" she asked.

I shrugged my shoulders.

"Why, darling," said Cousin Clothilde, "aren't you feeling well?"

"Sometimes," I said, "I remember that I have a life of my own, that's all."

Cousin Clothilde dropped her cigarette into her half-empty coffee cup.

"Why, of course," she answered, "everybody has."

"It's hard to remember sometimes," I said. Cousin Clothilde looked at me hard.

"Darling," she said, "I was afraid of that last night. It's made me so unhappy. That woman who is coming down—"

I was growing angry with her for the first time in my life. I pushed myself out of the rocking chair and stood up, but even as I did so my action seemed absurd.

"I'm sorry," Cousin Clothilde said quickly. "I didn't mean that, dear. I didn't mean to say it in that way. I only hope she's

410

nice. I know just what you mean. Don't say it, dear. It makes everything so different that I don't like to think about it. Are you sure it's going to make you happy, dear?"

"Now wait a minute," I began, "I haven't said anything."

"No," she said. "You never do say anything, but everybody knows about it. Even Josie was talking about it when she brought up the coffee; and Harry has been in to see me about it. He says she works in a department store."

"Well, suppose he minds his own business," I said.

"It's only that we want you to be happy, dear," Cousin Clothilde said, "and I don't see if she works in a department store—"

"Well, never mind," I said. "I didn't say anything."

"But everybody knows, dear," Cousin Clothilde said. "It isn't that we're selfish. We all love you so because you belong to us. Do you think she'd like to live here?"

"No," I said, "I don't."

"Well," said Cousin Clothilde, "I should think she'd like it better here than in a department store."

"Let's leave the department store out of it," I said.

"Bella doesn't like her nose," said Cousin Clothilde. "She told me long ago."

"I don't know what you're talking about. I like her nose," I said.

"But she isn't good enough for you, dear," said Cousin Clothilde. "She couldn't be, and no one thinks she's good enough. Is she the sort of person who would understand us?"

"Frankly," I answered, "I don't know."

"I knew it," said Cousin Clothilde. "I knew it. She's going to take you away. You don't have to tell me. We won't ever see each other any more."

"I don't know why you take everything for granted," I said. Cousin Clothilde sighed.

"I don't see how you ever met her, dear, if she works in a department store. Department stores have always made you nervous."

"Do you mean to say that everyone is talking about this already?" I asked.

411

"You're so dreadfully stupid sometimes, dear," Cousin Clothilde said. "Don't you see we talk about it because we love you? We only want you to be happy. But then, perhaps she might fit in with everybody and be good to the children. You could have the top floor or you could fix up one of the barns."

"Let's not talk about it now," I said.

"I want her to like us," she said. "I don't see why you did it just now, dear. It might have been some time later, when Bella wasn't upset and Mirabel Steiner and Mr. Northby weren't here. It makes it so confusing to have this on top of everything, because I really want her to like us, and I know she won't. I'm perfectly sure she won't."

"Never mind," I said. "You haven't seen her yet."

There was nothing else for me to say. There was no use telling her that Patricia Leighton would like them because I knew she would not.

"Will you give me another cigarette, dear," said Cousin Clothilde, "and if you see Harry downstairs, won't you talk to him about those bungalows? And if you see Bella, don't be cross with her, because she's so upset. I don't know what we're going to do. I just can't seem to think, now that you've been so frank about it and told me everything."

I had told her nothing, but I had confirmed a rumor, and in a measure I was relieved, for now it was in the open and not a part of the perennial gossip of the place.

The sun was up high by then and another hot day was beginning. I could hear the humming song of locusts in the trees and the occasional somnolent chirp of a robin, but otherwise everything was motionless and drowsy. The heat was beginning to find its way into the shadows of the back parlor which was usually cool in the early part of a hot day, and Bella and Sid and Harry were there talking in earnest, low voices. Harry was dressed in a tennis shirt and white ducks and sneakers as if he were about to give an exhibition on some nonexistent court. I was surprised by his costume until I remembered about the Colony. Harry was

412

already rehearsing his part in the Colony, becoming a vigorous athlete and a lover of the out-of-doors. Bella was in violet beach-pajamas with a bandanna tied about her neck, and Sid was still in my white trousers.

"Hello," said Sid, "we were talking about Allen Southby."

I accepted the statement without for a moment believing it was true. Harry patted the thin spot on the back of his head.

"They don't believe," he said, "that Southby has any money."

"What does he look like?" Bella asked. "Is he attractive, darling?"

"As a matter of fact," Harry said, "he doesn't dress so badly. Do you think so, Sid? In a way, considering that he came from Minnesota, he's almost *soigné*, always within limitations. If one understands these things it is clear that Southby dresses conservatively within his income, and I should say his income is in the neighborhood of ten thousand a year. He has that ten-thousand-a-year look. It's unmistakable."

"What look have you got?" I asked. Harry stroked the thin spot on his head again. I could see that they were ready for a round of conversation which would last until they took naps after lunch, and then they would talk again till midnight. Bella looked at Harry and made a face at me behind his back. I was forgetting about New York already and so was she. We were there listening to another morning's talk at Wickford Point, listening to Harry deliver another academic lecture, and there was a sympathy between us derived from our having heard him so often.

"There is one thing about all of us, thank God," Harry said, "we have no financial look. No one can tell from our appearance whether we are worth five million dollars or five cents, and that is an achievement. We belong in no financial category."

They were all busy building themselves up again. It was a perpetual consolation to them that we were interesting people.

"Now," said Harry, "let us put that aside for the moment. We belong in no category, but most men even more than women dress according to their incomes. I have given this a good deal of

413

thought. It helps me to size up people. You can tell the fifty-thousand or the hundred-thousand-a-year man as easily as the ten-thousand. Yes, Southby is ten-thousand. Those tweeds were made by some second-string London tailor. He left his measurements three years ago when he was in London. They haven't got the best fit, and the pipe goes with them, expensive but not expensive enough."

Bella crossed her knees and laced her hands behind her head and looked thoughtfully at Harry's back.

"Where is this Southby now?" she asked.

"Mary's taken him to the Brill house," I said. "They're going somewhere for lunch."

"He has a medium-price car," Sidney said. "It's green."

"That's significant," said Harry, "very significant. Green to go with his tweed coat, do you see? Only a ten-thousand-a-year man would think of that. It's a ten-thousand-dollar mind."

"Oh," said Bella, "for heaven's sake, shut up."

"Exactly why," Harry asked, "should I shut up?"

"Because I don't want to hear you talk," Bella said. "It gives me a headache."

"Then go somewhere else," said Harry. "I'm talking for a definite purpose. I'm thinking out loud. Southby is exactly the sort we want for one of the inshore bungalows at Lake Poomow —not on the frontage—inshore. The ten-thousand-dollar class should be the very lowest there. You haven't heard about Lake Poomow, have you, Jim?"

Bella stood up and stretched herself and yawned rudely.

"It's just another of those damn things you'll make a mess of," Bella said. "Jim doesn't want to hear about it, and I don't either." And she left the room.

"Bitch," said Sidney softly.

"No," said Harry. "She's troubled about something. You wouldn't like to go up to Lake Poomow, would you, Jim? Oh, I forgot, you'll be tied up."

It seemed selfish not to listen, but I did not want to hear about Lake Poomow. I was not thinking of Harry's troubles or

414

of Sid's or Bella's. Instead I was thinking of something that George Stanhope had said just a day or two before. Stanhope had been in his shirt sleeves by the table with the picture of the police dog on it.

"The trouble," he was saying, "is with the ending. That's why they didn't buy it down the street, because the ending was definitely wrong. No one got anything in the end. They misunderstood each other and there was definite conflict, but no one got anything. And what's the use of characters and conflict if they don't get something out of it, something definite? That's what everybody wants, and there's no use arguing. The boy has got to get the girl and he's got to get the money, and he must have a happy future. There is no excuse for all the loose ends. You have to tie them up."

Harry Brill was speaking, but I did not hear him because my mind was still on George Stanhope's voice. Everyone at Wickford Point was struggling fitfully for something without getting it. Harry was talking about Lake Poomow now, and for the moment Mary was pursuing some visionary goal in Allen Southby's green car, and in a little while Bella also would be storming a new Valhalla, but none of it would last. The trouble was with the ending. There was nothing in the end.

"Well," I said, "so long. I'll see you later, boys."

Harry looked hurt.

"Jim," he said, "you haven't been listening?"

"I'll listen some other time," I said.

Neither of them answered but I could feel them staring after me.

There was the smell of fresh-cut grass on the lawn outside and Earle was oiling the lawn mower.

"Say, Mr. Calder—" Earle began.

"Never mind it now," I said.

Then Josie was calling to me out of the kitchen window.

"Mr. Calder," Josie called, "if you're going downtown could you get me those bobby pins? You forgot them, Mr. Calder."

"Never mind it now. I'm not going downtown," I said.

415

The canoe was by the old boat landing and the paddles were under it. I had already turned it over and pushed it into the water when I heard Bella calling to me. She must have watched me from somewhere and she must have run after me for she was out of breath.

"Jim," she said, "where are you going?"

"I don't know," I said.

"Well, aren't you going to take me with you?" she asked.

"No, not this time," I said, and I remembered when I had taken her with me once, long ago.

"Jim," she said, "you're not angry with me, are you? Can't we just forget about everything?" And her words came so quickly that I had no time to answer. "Darling," she cried, "don't—"

"Don't what?" I asked. "What are you talking about, Belle?"

There was a pause and I could hear the locusts in the trees and a breeze was stirring through the pines. I tossed a paddle into the canoe and it gave that strange dull clatter which one can only hear when a small boat is in the water.

"Darling," said Bella, "it's so ridiculous. I don't know why I feel it, but it's as though you were going away and leaving us. Please don't leave us, Jim."

I stepped into the canoe carefully and pushed it away from the bank. I wanted to speak to her, but I found it difficult. It was a simple act to take the canoe out, so simple that her pleading was not natural, and yet it was true what she said. It was exactly as if I were going away.

"Jim," she called again, "please don't."

XXXV | It Can't Go on Like This

When I was out in the center of the stream I could still see her watching me from the bank. The tide in the channel was taking me downstream, away from Wickford Point, and the heat waves were shimmering over it, giving to the trees and the barn roofs an unstable mirage-like quality. As the distance increased it all moved uncertainly in that haze of summer heat. I kept thinking that if I looked away, and then looked back, it really might be gone; and then it was gone, as far as I was concerned, once I was far enough downriver.

When I got back the sun was low and the breeze was dropping as it often did at the end of the day. The heat had gone out of the sun and a coolness rose from the surface of the water. Quiet sounds were carried over from the houses across the river—a voice, the sound of a hammer, and the bark of a dog—all distinct in spite of the distance, as sounds are at that time of day. First there came the sharp bend in the channel near the woods in front of the Jeffries farm, and then came Wickford Point. I had a sharp sensation of relief when I saw it. I walked up the bank and through the pines and across the hayfield to the lawn. The shadows from the trees were lengthening and I could hear no sound of voices from the house. There was no one in the dining room and no one in the little parlor. There were no sounds upstairs either, and I pushed open the door of the back parlor noisily. Then I stood

417

without moving. Pat Leighton was sitting entirely alone in one of the chairs by the fireplace.

Often before when the house was still I had felt that other people were in the room with me, but the impression had never been as clear as this. For just the fraction of a second I had an idea that she was there because I had been thinking of her all day long, and it took me an appreciable space of time to realize that she was actually there.

"Don't look so astonished," she said. "Didn't you expect me?"

"No," I said. I stood in the doorway and it was still too unexpected for me to get it straight.

"Didn't you get my wire?" she asked. "I sent you one yesterday. I said I was motoring up."

"You sent a wire?" I said. "Well, that's just the way things happen here. They're so careless about things like that."

She smiled at me. "Well," she said, "aren't you glad to see me?"

"Yes," I answered, "very glad. I'm just surprised. It's just as though I had been thinking about you and then you were here."

"Well, that's why I am," she said. "Have you really been thinking about me?"

"Yes," I answered, "all the time."

"Then don't look so embarrassed," she said. "I sometimes wonder. . . . Once you get away you seem to disappear. Well, I've come to get you." And then she laughed and added: "It's awfully funny here, isn't it?"

Taken all together I must have spoken to Pat Leighton for a good many hours about Wickford Point. She was always glad to listen, but she had come of a methodical family which had never behaved like mine. Of course, she must have formed some preconceived idea of it, which, like all impressions one gains at second hand, was not correct.

"I suppose it's different from what you thought," I said.

"Yes," she said, "but you're not, and that's all I care about. I rather dreaded that."

It pleased me to hear her say it. The half-careless, half-laughing

418

way she spoke made me forget my first astonishment at seeing her there at all.

"You aren't any different either," I said.

She stretched out her hand toward me and smiled.

"It's because we're honest people," she said. "Honest people never change. I'm glad we're both like that."

Now that she was there, it seemed to me that the room was just as it was meant to be when it had first been built.

She looked away toward the yellowing, enlarged photograph of Mr. Brill, and then at the painting of the brig *Alert* anchored off Wampoa.

"Pat," I said, "you're quite a girl. You have good ideas."

"It isn't hard," she said. "You're quite a mental exercise, but I like you the way you are. . . . It's awfully funny here."

Then I remembered that she might not have seen her room, and that no one had brought her bags upstairs.

"Did anything happen?" I asked. "Have you seen anyone? I wonder where they've gone."

She laughed again, not at me but at something she had seen.

"I sent you that telegram," she said. "I fixed things so that I could leave a day earlier. There's a new girl who's good at handling routine, and I thought it would be fun to motor up. I'll tell you about that later. Out on the main road there was a gas station with a man who said he went to school with you. We had quite a talk about you and he pointed out the road. You've told me so much about the place, that of course I recognized it, and then when I came into the yard here I saw a queer thing."

"What?" I asked.

"There was a boy in overalls with a bucket," she said, "over by the barn, and a man in white trousers had a rubber tube. He was sucking the gasoline out of your automobile."

"Oh," I said, "that's Sid. They never have any gasoline."

"And just then the door opened and everyone came out. There was Bella all dressed up. She was talking to a man who turned out to be your friend, Mr. Southby, and then Harry came and introduced me to everyone. I recognized your Cousin Clothilde right away. She was very pleasant; and then there was a lady in shorts."

"That's Mirabel Steiner," I said.

"And then there was another cousin of yours," Pat Leighton went on, "who had an orange ribbon in her hair and looked put out about something. She didn't want to go and everyone said she'd better."

I knew it was Mary. Pat was smiling as though she still saw the scene.

"They were awfully pleasant," she said. "Your Cousin Clothilde wanted me to come with them. She said they were going downtown. Nobody seemed to know where you were. They just said you were out on the river, and I said I'd just stay and wait, if they didn't mind, and then they all got into two cars. Mr. Southby and Bella got in one. Mr. Southby was quoting poetry."

"What sort of poetry?" I asked.

"Tennyson," she said, "'Locksley Hall.' Then he said that everything was so priceless, and everyone else got into an older car. They called the car 'Cousin Sue.'"

"Yes," I said. "They inherited it."

"Well," said Pat, "they all got into Cousin Sue, and then they asked me again if I was sure I didn't want to come along. They were just as nice as they could be, and your Cousin Clothilde said they were going downtown to get some whisky and ice cream."

"Ice cream?" I repeated.

"Your Cousin Clothilde said she had been thinking about ice cream all day and that she couldn't stand it any longer unless she had some. And then a kitchen door opened and a woman came out holding a little boy who was eating something. She called after them to buy her something."

"She wanted bobby pins," I said.

Pat looked at me.

"You know everything about them, don't you?" she inquired.

"Yes, I remember now, she wanted bobby pins; and then they all went away and I came in here. They asked me to wait here because someone was sweeping out my room. Then a little girl covered with lipstick came in to talk to me. She said that she had heard that I worked in a department store and she wanted to know about foundations. She wanted to show me one."

"That's Frieda," I said, "Josie's girl. I didn't know she wore anything like that."

"And then the little boy who was eating something," Patricia said, "came in and began turning somersaults, and then there were some kittens, and then they all went away. It was like everything you'd ever told me."

"Yes, I suppose it was," I said, but I was thinking about Bella in Allen Southby's car.

"Jim," Patricia said.

"Yes," I answered.

She was looking at me and only part of her smile lingered at the corner of her lips.

"They haven't got you yet."

She could take me away from all sorts of things. I only had to ask her, and I had no fear of consequences. I was sure that I could be what I had always wanted to be if I were with her. It was only necessary to ask her.

"Pat," I said, "you're the only thing that's worth a damn."

"That's why I love you, dear," she said, "because you say things like that."

I was amazed that she could make me feel as I did, because no one else ever had, and there was one thing that I wished made absolutely clear.

"I love you, Pat," I said. "I wish I didn't sometimes."

"Jim," she said, "you'll have to make a break. You see it, don't you?"

"Yes," I said, "I see."

"Well," she said, "I'm leaving tomorrow." She put her arm through mine. "That's what comes of not getting telegrams. I told you I could only stay for a day."

"But I thought you were going to stay over the week end," I said.

"No," she answered, "a day is long enough just now."

"How do you mean a day is long enough?" I asked.

She pressed my arm against her and put her hand over mine. "You're generally so clever," she said. "It's silly for you and me to say obvious things, but I suppose everyone does sometimes. Nothing is right when it stays the same. Dear, we can't go on like this."

I must have known that last definite sentence would come sometime. I had heard it before from other women, and often enough it had filled me with a sense of relief, but now it did not.

"No," I said, "I don't see how we can."

She smiled at me and there was a pause while she waited for me to say something more.

"It sounds so trite, doesn't it?" she said. "And what I'm going to say won't be much better. So many women have said it so often. Women are always stupid after a certain point."

"Perhaps," I told her, "but you're not stupid, Pat."

"It's stupid to be grasping," she said, "but I don't know any other way to put it."

Her fingers touched mine softly.

"You see," she said, "this has to stop. We ought to be married, Jim. My suggestion is that we go away tomorrow, and I really don't think it would be so bad, not as such things go."

I heard the wheels of an automobile in the yard, and then I heard voices and the screen door slammed.

"Here they come," I said, "with the whisky and ice cream."

"You're not put out, are you, Jim?" she said.

"No," I said. "I love you, Pat."

"Then don't be so grim about it," she said. "Kiss me before they come."

I was not annoyed that they were back, because it gave me time to think. She had said that we both were honest people, and I wanted to be as honest with her as she had been with me.

They were coming into the parlor and all of them were talking.

"Hello," said Mirabel Steiner. "Oh? I hope I'm not intruding."

"Not any more than usual," I said.

Cousin Clothilde came next. "Darling," she said, "where have

422

you been all day? You never told me that Miss Laughlin had sent a telegram."

"Her name is Leighton," I said. "No one told me about a telegram."

"I don't know why it is," said Cousin Clothilde, "that I always can recall faces but not names. I remember now. The telegram was left right on the table in your room. Mirabel must have taken everything off it when she was dressing. I'm dreadfully sorry, Miss Leighton."

Pat smiled and they both looked at each other curiously.

"Jim has spoken of you so often," Pat said, and Cousin Clothilde answered:

"I don't know what we'd do without him, dear."

Then Mary walked into the room alone and her face was white and set. Sidney and Harry followed, talking about clothes.

"At the Racquet Club," Harry was saying, "and at the Field Club—How do you do, Miss Leighton."

Allen Southby and Bella appeared next, and Bella had that starry look, as though the doors might open at any moment for the Christmas tree.

"Hello, old man," Allen Southby said. "Where have you been? It's been such a priceless day. I'm just going to pop upstairs and change."

"Never mind it, Allen," Bella said. "Allen is taking me out to dinner."

"But Allen—" Mary began, and then she stopped because Southby had gone, and Harry and Sidney had gone with him.

"Is there anything for dinner?" Cousin Clothilde asked, and Bella began to laugh.

"Not much," she said. "That's why I'm going out."

Then Mary spoke so loudly that everyone looked at her.

"No," said Mary, "that isn't why you're going."

"Why, Mary," said Bella, "darling!"

"You're going out to dinner," Mary said, "because you want to take Allen away from me."

"Why, Mary," said Bella gently, "what under the sun is the

matter? You've had him for a whole day. You can't monopolize him all the time."

"Well, I did before you came," Mary cried; "and now you make him take you out to dinner. You always do that to me."

"Mary dear," said Cousin Clothilde, "I do wish you wouldn't raise your voice, and I think you'd better go upstairs and do your hair, and don't slouch your shoulders so. No one will like you unless you stand up straight."

She stopped because Mary had run away and slammed the door.

"I don't know what has got into Mary," said Cousin Clothilde. "I don't see why she should be jealous just because Bella is nice to Mr. Northby."

"I want everyone to understand," said Bella, "that I asked Mr. Southby again and again if he didn't want to sit next to Mary or have Mary in the car, and he didn't. I can't help it if he didn't, can I?"

"No, honey bee," I said, "you can't help anything. You can't help taking a crack at Mary, because you know she's too decent to hit you back."

"Jim," said Cousin Clothilde, "I do wish you'd try to do something about Mary. There ought to be some man somewhere. Don't you really think that you could telephone and find some man, just anyone, just for tonight, Jim? There might be some boy on the float at the Yacht Club if only you and Miss Laughlin would go down there and look. See if you can't find someone."

Bella opened her compact and got out her lipstick.

"Yes," she said, "go out and find one, Jim. Anyone in pants will do."

"That's about enough from you, honey bee," I said.

"But Jim," said Cousin Clothilde, "can't you think of anybody? If you were just to take your car and go down to the Club."

"There isn't any gas in my car," I said, "unless Sidney puts it back."

"But darling," said Cousin Clothilde, "Miss Laughlin has a car. I'm sure Miss Laughlin wouldn't mind."

"You see," I said to Pat, "we're all unworldly here."

"Yes," said Pat, "I see. Do you always find them on the Yacht Club float?"

"No," said Cousin Clothilde, "I just thought of it. I don't suppose it's sensible; but I don't know what's got into Mary, and besides there *might* be someone on the Yacht Club float. They always look so young there, and so brown. I've often thought of speaking to one of them and asking him to dinner—but then it might be too obvious."

Bella had opened her compact again, and now she dabbed her lipstick across her lips and looked down at the little mirror and then up at Pat.

"All the women here are trying to catch the men," she said. She spoke casually but the room was quiet after she finished. She put some more red on her lips, but her eyes never left Pat's face.

"Yes," Pat answered, "that's true. I hadn't thought of that."

"I don't see why people don't understand," Bella said, "that men don't like to be pursued. It's biologically wrong and it never does any good, and besides it's frightfully inartistic. Don't you think so?"

"Yes," Pat answered, "I suppose it is."

Bella closed her compact again and shrugged her shoulders.

"You can't get them off the Yacht Club float," Bella said, "if they want to stay there, any more than you can get them if you follow them to their houses. No man with the guts of a guinea pig likes it. If you have to run after a man it simply means that he's getting tired of you—and it's so damned silly not to see it. There's something about Jim that makes all the girls run after him. Isn't that true, Pat?"

I have never seen Pat Leighton lose her temper, and she did not lose it then.

"Have you ever tried?" she asked.

Bella gave a light, amused laugh.

"Why, darling," she said, "I've never had to try. I do hope you're not taking anything I've said personally."

"No," said Pat, "I'm not taking it at all."

425

"Because I never meant such a thing, of course," Bella said.

"Of course you didn't," Pat answered. "It would look so like personal pique, wouldn't it? And you're always so nice about such things, Bella."

"Well, darling," said Bella, "I'm so glad you didn't misunderstand me. You're always such a determined person—so executive."

"Yes," Pat answered, "I suppose I am."

"I know you are, dear," said Bella. "Everybody says so. Well, I must be running upstairs. Jim, there's something I want to tell you, if you're not busy, darling."

"Never mind it now," I said.

"Well," said Bella, "I'll see you later, darling."

"Not if I see you first, honey bee," I said.

Cousin Clothilde sighed. "I don't see what's got into Bella," she said. "But she is sweet, isn't she, and I think she's looking better."

"She's the way she always is," Pat Leighton answered, "so natural."

Cousin Clothilde sighed again. "But I don't see what's got into her," she said. "I wish that everyone could be happy, like Mr. Northby."

"Southby," I said.

"I wish you wouldn't be so cross, dear," Cousin Clothilde answered. "You know exactly what I mean."

"Yes," I told her, "I know what everybody means."

XXXVI | The Wickford Sage

A breeze moved through the dining room making the candles drip. The last of the blue Canton china, very badly chipped around the edges—for Josie was never careful of the dishes— was on the bare mahogany table. It was not one of our happier meals. Mary sat looking stonily at her plate, eating nothing. I heard Sidney expounding to Patricia some idea he had, and I knew that he was being bright and entertaining, but Harry was maintaining the burden of the conversation.

I was thinking of that statement of Pat Leighton's that we could not go on like this. It kept repeating itself in my consciousness, spoken sometimes slowly, sometimes hastily, or then loudly and finally softly. I heard it while everyone else was speaking.

"I was selected," Harry was saying, "because of my connections. My object has always been to know as many people as possible, and now it's beginning to pay—not at the moment, of course, because no one yet is drawing a salary except Mr. Fruitgate."

"Darling," said Cousin Clothilde, "who is Mr. Fruitgate? It sounds like one of those foreign names translated into English."

"It was probably Mr. Apfel-something," Mirabel Steiner said.

Harry set down his knife and fork gently.

"On the contrary," he said, "enlightening as your deduction may appear, Mirabel, Mr. Fruitgate comes of an old Huguenot family which settled here shortly after the revocation of the Edict of Nantes."

"You're sure he wasn't killed at the Massacre of St. Bartholomew?" I said.

"Mr. Fruitgate," said Harry more loudly, "comes of Norman French Huguenot extraction. Mr. Fruitgate, by ability and not by accident of birth, has been connected with some very important promotions. Tim Fruitgate and I hit it off right at the start."

"Oh," said Cousin Clothilde, "is his first name Tim? I knew a man once named Tim, who played a mandolin. I didn't mean to interrupt you, dear." And she looked at all of us meaningly, signaling to us not to interrupt.

"Tim Fruitgate," said Harry, "is the one who thought of a colony of Distinguished People, not just this one and that one, but people who have achieved something. He wants them all to be together so that they can exchange ideas. Every applicant for a bungalow must be passed by a board of governors, after Tim Fruitgate investigates his credit. Well, I'm a member of that board of governors."

"Oh," said Cousin Clothilde, "I think that's lovely, dear. It must mean so much to you, but I wish you wouldn't squint that way, Harry. It makes such dreadful wrinkles between your eyes."

"Perhaps his eyes are out of focus," Sidney said. "He might do exercises looking at a pencil."

"What sort of exercises?" Cousin Clothilde asked.

"You hold a pencil in front of you and move it toward your nose," said Sidney, "until you see it double."

"But I'm sure no one wants to exercise with a pencil," said Cousin Clothilde. "I never did like pencils, and when I want one it's never there, and when I find one it's always broken or Mary has been chewing at it."

Mary pushed her chair back and rose.

"I should think I might be allowed to chew on a pencil," she said. "If everyone's going to pick on me I'm going upstairs."

"But dear," said Cousin Clothilde, "no one's picking on you."

She had no time to finish because Mary had left the room. "Oh dear," said Cousin Clothilde, "I really don't understand Mary."

She never did and she never would, but I could not consider it then. Those words of Pat's kept passing through my mind, obscuring all the talk—*We can't go on like this.* There was no reason why they should have surprised me. I should have realized that nothing remained unchanged indefinitely. Now here at Wickford Point everyone had said several times a day that they could not go on like this, and yet they always had. I had always thought that Pat Leighton and I could continue for a long while, indefinitely perhaps, and now she meant what she was saying. It could not go on as it had.

They were all pushing back their chairs and rising. I had not realized that the meal was over. I had not tasted what I ate. I could not remember what they had been saying. I only knew that we could not go on.

"Pat," I said, "let's go outside before the light is gone. It all looks better in the dusk."

It was quiet enough outside except for the sound of the crickets in the grass. We were walking through the old flower garden toward the hay barn near the south orchard, and then through the gap in the fence where the first rows of apple trees, too old to bear much any longer, shut us from the house. We were alone out there with the crickets and the waning light. I wished sometimes that the darkness would come down suddenly, like the tropic dark, and that the light would not keep lingering in the sky the way it did at Wickford Point. Pat's hand rested on my arm and though she did not speak I could tell that she was happy.

"Do they always talk like that," she asked, "just on and on?"

"Yes," I said, "just on and on."

"Well," she said, "I see what you meant about your Cousin Clothilde. She's beautiful, and everything she says is kind—but it's not for you, Jim, is it?"

"No," I said, "it shouldn't be."

"What are all those little stones?" she asked. It was nearly dark, but the stones were white against the grass.

"Those are the dogs' graves," I told her.

"Oh yes," she said, "I remember. I wish you'd light a match, I'd like to see one."

We were standing near a stone where one of my Llewellyn setters lay, the one I had used for woodcock years ago, and I was wondering if there were woodcock in the coverts nowadays. I knelt beside it and lighted a match and she bent over to read.

" 'Nauna, a good bitch,' " she read.

"She was mine," I said, "and that's exactly what she was."

Pat's voice told me that she was smiling. Her hand was resting on my shoulder.

"Well," she said, "I rather like it. There are so few of them, aren't there?"

"Yes," I said, "not many."

"If I died," she said, "I wouldn't mind it if you put that on my stone, but I don't suppose the grounds committee would allow it, would they?"

She was silent for a while.

"You know she was absolutely right," she said.

"Who?" I asked.

"Your cousin Bella Brill," Pat answered. "It made me rather angry when she said I was running after you, because I hadn't thought of it that way at all, and it isn't very attractive, is it? Perhaps I *am* doing it because you're getting tired of me."

"No, I'm not," I told her.

"Well," said Pat, "perhaps you ought to be. But I didn't always run after you, did I? Do you remember—"

"Yes," I told her, "I remember."

"Well," Pat said, "that's the way things happen. It has to be settled one way or the other, doesn't it? I don't mind what Bella said really, but that's another reason why I'm leaving here tomorrow. I might lose my temper if I talked to her again. Are you coming with me, Jim?"

430

I waited for a moment because I wanted my voice to be steady. "I'd go twice around the world with you tomorrow, Pat," I said. "There's nothing I'd like better."

"And farther than that?" she asked.

"Farther than that," I said. "The sky's the limit. I could go anywhere you say and as long as you like, up to the moon if you wanted or down in a diving bell, but finally, dear, I'd always come back here, and you couldn't stop me and I couldn't stop myself, and you wouldn't have any more of me than you've ever had. Part of me would always be here, perhaps most of me that matters; and you wouldn't like that at all. It isn't anything I can help. It isn't any one person; it's everything. You're not going to be mixed up in all this, Pat.

"No," I went on, "you wouldn't like it, because there's nothing for you here. You saw the way it was tonight. I'd have asked you to marry me long ago, if it weren't for everything here. You wouldn't like it, Pat."

She did not answer immediately and instead of speech there came the notes of all the crickets in the grass rising in an ageless stringlike surge of music which promised to continue long after human beings had vanished from the earth. The sound reminded me again of that naïve remark of Bella Brill's that the music had nearly stopped for her, and now I knew exactly what she had meant. Pat was still silent and I wished that she would speak and be done with it.

"I'm glad you told me that," she said then, "but of course you would have. Do you mind if I ask you something else?"

"Anything you like," I said.

"You're not saying this," she asked me, "on account of Bella Brill? You'll be frank about that, won't you? I don't mind if it hurts."

It was foolish to have thought that she would not notice my preoccupation with Bella Brill. I only hoped that she would never misunderstand the fragile inhibitions of the relationship.

"No," I said, "not now. It's something else."

"Well," she said, "I'm glad it isn't that. I don't think that I should have liked it—not at all." There was a soft sort of surprise in her voice as though something incredible had happened. "Jim," she said, "I wish you'd put your arm around me. I feel a little dizzy. I thought it was all over. Women all have different ways of being jealous. I don't mind anything as long as it isn't Bella Brill."

"Do you really mean that you can put up with all the rest of it?" I asked.

"It's funny," she answered, "but that is just what I mean. As long as it isn't Bella I don't mind how often you come back. I don't mind anything. Jim, let's go away tonight. You can take my bags down for me and put them in the car."

"You heard what I said," I told her, "that I'd always be coming back."

"And I told you I didn't mind," she answered. "And, Jim—"

"What?" I said.

"You'll make me a nice tombstone, won't you?"

I was thinking that they would all be in the back parlor talking, and that it would not be hard to get her car. Even if they heard us they would only think that we were going somewhere for a little while.

"We can stop along the way at a stonecutter's," I said. "Where do you want to go?"

"You can work that out," she answered; "anywhere at all."

I stood in my room with a suitcase opened on my bed. It didn't matter how I left things as long as it was certain that I would be back, as long as it was certain that I would see the cracks on the ceiling that looked like a map again. I had been leaving that room for almost as long as I could remember. The upper bureau drawer stuck, but I knew exactly how to get it open. The only thing I wanted was not to see any of the family, because any explanation would grow complicated. I began moving about softly, opening the bureau drawers and opening the closet door, trying to select a few of the things I really wanted. I had only a few minutes to pack, and I was so absorbed in the process that I heard no footsteps. The only sound that interrupted me was a loud decisive knock. I shut the suitcase hastily and put it in a corner.

"What is it?" I asked, and I heard Allen Southby's voice. "May I come in, old man," he asked, "just for a moment?" I could think of nothing more superfluous than a call from Allen Southby. He was smiling; he was dressed in his slacks and his green tweed coat.

"I didn't think you and Bella would be back so soon," I said. "I'm just putting things to rights here."

Then I saw he was not interested in what I was doing. He had not even noticed that I was packing.

"It isn't like Bella to get home early," I said. "You haven't had a row with Bella, have you?"

Allen Southby raised his eyebrows incredulously.

"You're joking, aren't you, Jim?" he asked. "I can't imagine anyone ever having a row with Bella Brill. I've never known a sunnier disposition. I've never known . . ." He stopped as though he thought it might be just as well not to tell me what he knew.

"Then why did you come back so early?" I asked him.

Allen Southby smiled as if his own thoughts pleased him.

"She wanted me to read to her," he said. "We've discovered a common love—poetry, Jim. You haven't a copy of the *Canterbury Tales* up here, have you?"

"You mean you and Bella came back here," I asked him, "because she wanted you to read her the *Canterbury Tales?*"

"Why, of course," Allen answered. "What's so odd about that?"

"Nothing at all," I said. "You'll find a volume of Chaucer downstairs with the books. You're sure she wouldn't rather hear 'Beowulf'?"

I thought he would go then, but instead he took his pipe and his tobacco pouch out of his tweed coat pocket.

"Have you a match, old man?" he asked. "Thanks. There's nothing like a pipe, is there? Actually it wasn't only the poetry

433

which brought us back, although old Geoffrey can lead his devotees for long distances. No, it wasn't only the knights and the friars and the prioresses—no, it wasn't only that—"

"It must have been uncomfortable in your car then," I said. "Bella isn't usually uncomfortable in cars."

"No," said Allen, but it seemed to me that my last remark embarrassed him. "No, it wasn't that. We have another love in common, Jim."

"What?" I asked. "Biology?"

Allen's tanned face reddened slightly, but he smiled.

"The same old Jim," he said. "You can't ever be serious for long, can you? Our other love is Wickford Point. We both confessed that we could not stay away from it for long. She loves it, not as you do, but as I do, Jim. She sees the sadness of its neglect. It hurts her as it hurts me that so few love it. Something should be done about the place here, Jim."

"What would you suggest?" I asked.

"Frankly," he answered, "I could not say exactly. But there should be someone here who could cherish it, someone who could carry on its tradition. Bella understands what I mean."

"Bella's always understanding," I said.

"That's fine of you," Allen answered. "Fine of you under the circumstances, Jim."

"Under what circumstances?" I asked.

Allen Southby looked embarrassed. He puffed at his pipe and coughed.

"I hope you won't mind my saying this, old man," he said, "but Bella and I were rather frank this evening. We told each other a good deal about ourselves, the way two people will who discover themselves utterly congenial. She said that you and she never have been able to get along, old man—not that she said it unkindly, I don't mean that for a moment. I don't believe there's a single unkind thought in Bella Brill. She's so shy, so hesitant, so unlike Mary, isn't she?"

"I thought you said that Mary was shy," I told him.

"Oh no," Allen said, "I could never have said exactly that . . .

434

but Bella, even you must admit she's very rare—like a shepherdess watching her white thoughts."

"Yes," I said, "she's a shepherdess."

"And she's so alone," Allen said. "Has it ever occurred to you that she seems to be afraid of being alone?"

"You may be right about that," I answered.

"There's a desperation about her," said Allen, "a strange, gay, gallant desperation."

"You know," I told him, "Joe Stowe said that, once."

Allen nodded.

"She told me a great deal about their misunderstanding," he said. "I think we are both a little bit astonished at how much we told each other tonight. It was a moment of self-illumination. It was as though we had known each other always, like a brother and sister, but not exactly like that either."

"No," I said, "of course it wouldn't be . . . exactly."

Allen looked at me almost sharply.

"You aren't laughing at me, are you, Jim?" he inquired. "It's just that I wanted to talk to someone about Bella, and you know a good deal about her, don't you?"

"Yes," I answered, "quite a lot. I'm not laughing at you, Allen."

He was so intent on his own thoughts that he did not notice when I continued with my packing.

"She's very rare," Allen said again, "very rare and withdrawn. I'm going to make a confession to you, old man. I seem to be in a revealing mood tonight. This place makes me see everything so clearly. I really think that all my life I've been a little bit afraid of women. I understand them, of course, but I'm not what you'd call susceptible. There has always been my work—and yet you know it's curious, I'm not afraid of Bella Brill."

"She wouldn't want to frighten you," I said.

Again Allen looked at me suspiciously.

"That's what she said about you," he said, "that you have a bitter, disillusioned mind . . . but you do know enough about her to understand what I mean. It isn't often that one finds someone with one's own point of view, with one's own sense of appreciation, with one's own humor. She's told me so much about everything that I can understand her better than you do, Jim. Of course Stowe couldn't understand her. He treated her very badly, don't you think?"

"It's hard to tell," I answered, "about anything like that."

"He never helped her," Allen said. "He never gave her a feeling of security, and that's what she needs: the same sense of security that I feel here. She says for instance that you are never secure, that you are always going away. If all this were mine, I should never go away."

"Well," I said, "you don't have to necessarily."

"I wonder," said Allen Southby, "yes, I really wonder . . ." He paused and hesitated, but there was something else on his mind which made him continue. "May I ask you a question, old man?" he went on. "Mrs. Wright is so charming, but sometimes I don't seem to know where I am with her. Could you tell me—does she like me—I mean really like me?"

That question of his first filled me with incredulity—and then with an unexpected sense of freedom; and when I thought of Bella Brill waiting for him to read from Chaucer, I felt grateful to her in some strange, perverted way.

"Of course she likes you," I answered. "She's always a little vague, Allen, but she'll always like you, if you make her feel—"

I paused, wondering exactly how to put it, and again I realized that I had not felt so free for a long while.

"Yes," said Allen, "you said—make her feel . . . ?"

"That you'll look out for her," I told him.

Allen nodded gravely.

"I see what you mean," he said. "That's true. She's so like Bella . . . with no one to look after her. Well, I mustn't stay here running on in this vein. You say the Chaucer is down there with the old books? I wonder if it could have been John Brill's copy. Well, I mustn't keep her waiting."

"Don't," I said, "she doesn't like to be kept waiting." And I snapped my suitcase shut.

"Then you'll excuse me," he said, "won't you, old man? Do you remember that bit from Sir Thopas—just a snatch, but suitable?"

"Go ahead," I said. "What is it?"

Allen smiled mischievously, and his voice became throaty and very Saxon.

"Just a snatch from Sir Thopas," he said, "but a mirror to my mood:

> Alle othere wommen I forsake,
> And to an elf-queene I me take
> By dale and eek by downe!"

Library of Congress Cataloging in Publication Data

Marquand, John Phillips, 1893-1960.
Wickford Point.
(Time Reading Program)
Originally published in 1939 by Little, Brown, Boston.
I. Title.
PZ3.M34466Wi 1980   [PS3525.A6695]   813'.52 80-19424
ISBN 0-8094-3578-0 (pbk.)
ISBN 0-8094-3577-2 (deluxe)